FUTURELAND

ALSO BY WALTER MOSLEY

Fearless Jones

Walkin' the Dog

Blue Light

Devil in a Blue Dress

A Red Death

White Butterfly

Black Betty

R. L.'s Dream

A Little Yellow Dog

Always Outnumbered, Always Outgunned

Workin' on the Chain Gang

Gone Fishin'

ε

Returning to science fiction for the first time since his acclaimed, visionary *Blue Light*, Walter Mosley mixes cyberpunk with biting social commentary and masterful literary skill.

FUTURELAND

"Brims with an acute awareness of history and social unrest. . . . FUTURELAND is populated by assassins and revolutionaries . . . working stiffs and scrappy fighters. Against a bleak landscape, their resilient spirits feel like rays of hope."

—New York Times Book Review

"Mosley uses stylish characters and technobabble to navigate an intricate, grimy, technologically baroque urban landscape. . . . A vivid, exciting, and well-executed take on cyberpunk that measures up."

—Kirkus Reviews

"[Mosley] breaks rules and transcends the familiar confines of genre . . . to set pulses racing, even as he engages the intellect and explores the nature of the soul."

—Locus

"Well-executed storylines . . . rich in ideas."

—Bookreporter.com

. . . AND GREAT ACCLAIM FOR *BLUE LIGHT*

"A writer whose work transcends category and qualifies as serious literature."

—TIME

"A mind-bending trip into the brave new world . . . good writing, regardless of genre."

—USA Today

more . . .

"Plenty of thrills, both visceral and ideational . . . skill and vision."

—San Francisco Chronicle

"Part utopian fantasy, part nightmare . . . a page-turning thriller . . . believable and sympathetic."

—Denver Rocky Mountain News

"Mr. Mosley is a kind of jazz musician, a Wynton Marsalis of the printed page, his themes subtly, obliquely, quietly stated, almost imperceptibly bubbling up from the rhythms of ordinary life."

—New York Times

"A writer of great acuity and style . . . prose of such deceptive simplicity and fine-hewn poetry that it sings."

—San Francisco Chronicle

"A beautifully written, deeply spiritual novel. Recommended."

—Library Journal

"*Blue Light* provides the social history, character studies, humanity, and vivid violence for which Mosley is justly praised. . . . Well-drawn characters as well . . . ordinary people made extraordinary, and Mosley knows how to make them believable and sympathetic. . . . A success."

—Denver Rocky Mountain News

"More evidence that Mosley is the Gogol of the African-American working class—the chronicler par excellence of the tragic and the absurd."

—Vibe

FUTURELAND

WALTER MOSLEY

WARNER BOOKS

An AOL Time Warner Company

This book is work of fiction. Names, characters, places, and incidents are the product of the author's imagination or are used fictitiously. Any resemblance to actual events, locales, or persons, living or dead, is coincidental.

WARNER BOOKS EDITION

Cover design by Rob Santora/Don Puckey
Cover illustration by Rob Santora

Aspect® name and logo are registered trademarks of Warner Books, Inc.

Warner Books, Inc.
1271 Avenue of the Americas
New York, NY 10020

Visit our Web site at
www.twbookmark.com.

An AOL Time Warner Company

Printed in the United States of America
Originally published in hardcover by Warner Books
First Paperback Printing: November 2002

10 9 8 7 6 5 4 3 2 1

For Danny Glover: Futureman

Contents

FUTURELAND

Whispers in the Dark

1 "Yeth he did too. Popo called me on the vid hithelf an' he wath on'y two year ole," Misty Bent said to her wide-eyed niece, Hazel Bernard. They were sitting out on the screened porch above the Tickle River. Misty's drooping left eyelid and gnarled, half-paralyzed hands did not mask her excitement.

"You kiddin'?" Hazel exclaimed.

"Tole me hith mama wath thick on the flo', that he called the hothpital but he wanted me to know too." Misty shook her head, remembering Melba's death. "I beat the ambulanth but Death got there quicker thtill. Doctor Maynard called it a acthidental overdoth tho we could put her in the ground with a prietht and thome prayer beadth, but you know Melba had had all thee could take. You know it hurt me tho bad that the blood vethel broke in my head."

"Her life wasn't no harder than what we all have to go through," Hazel Bernard said. She shifted her girth looking for a comfortable perch in the cheap plastic chair, but there was none.

"But you cain't compare her an' uth, or you'n me for that matter. Ith all diff'rent."

"What's that crazy talk s'posed to mean?" the big woman challenged. Hazel said she dropped by to see how Misty was coming along after the stroke but really she was there to see if Chill Bent, Misty's ex-convict son, had come back to live with her as she had heard.

"Ith juth what you thinkin'," Misty replied.

"What you know 'bout what I'm thinkin'?" Hazel asked. She was thirty years younger than Misty, but she was also the eldest of thirteen. Hazel had been the ruler of the roost since the age of nine, and no old woman's pretending was going to trick her.

"You thinkin' that the tht'oke done methed wit' my mind, that I'm feeble in the head 'cuth my left thide ith parali'ed. You think I cain't take care'a Popo but you wrong."

"I do not think any such thing."

"Oh yeth you do too," Misty said. "That'th why you heah. I know. And you wrong but you done anthered your own queth'ton in bein' wrong."

Hazel shifted again and grunted. This was a day taken away from her housework and her children.

She swallowed her anger and asked, "Are you tired, Auntie?"

Little Popo wandered onto the deck then. He was small for thirty months but his movements seemed more like those of an old man lost in memories than those of a child discovering the world.

"Hi, Popo," Hazel said. "Come here."

"Huth," Misty hissed. "He thinkin'. He'll talk when he want to."

"What? You don't call him to come sit on your lap?"

Popo went up to the edge of the deck and pressed his face against the loose screen.

"Don't fall, baby," Misty whispered.

The boy rocked back on his heels, his tiny black hands replacing his face upon the screen. He wore a white T-shirt and denim blue jeans with no shoes. His thick hair stood out long and wild but it wasn't matted.

"Rain's comin'," Popo said.

"That's right," Hazel said. "Weatherman said that a storm's gonna come outta the Gulf tonight. You're right, Aunt Misty. He is smart to hear that on ITV and remember it like that."

"No Internet in thith home," Misty proclaimed. "Not even no old TV or radio that work. Thill thay it would meth Popo up."

"Chill? No ITV?" Hazel didn't know which road to hell was worse. Both together tied her tongue.

"I smell it," Popo said, looking at the big visitor in the purple dress. "It smell like the knife an' fo'k when they wet."

The boy climbed up onto Hazel's big thigh and sat like a tiny Buddha staring into her eyes. Beyond him Misty wheezed and doddered, grinning madly.

"He been readin' though," Misty said. "Thometime he read in the paper an' then he try an' fool uth, actin' like he got the thight."

"No uh-uh Gramma no. Not Popo. I smelt it. I did."

Hazel was a little disconcerted by the steady stare of the toddler. She was used to children his age having wandering, slightly amazed eyes. She shifted him to the crook of her left arm and bent over to snag the edge of the newspaper from the dinner tray between her and Misty. Popo giggled at the sudden movement. When Hazel sat back he hugged her big breast.

"Read to me from this," she commanded, handing him the *Thaliaville Sparrow.*

Popo took the paper from his aunt and looked at it as if it were some sort of foreign document that he had to study before he could even tell which way it was meant to be read.

"Hm," Hazel grunted.

Misty grinned and drooled just a bit.

Popo shifted the paper around and finally held it sideways.

"'Jacksonville, Mississippi,'" he said, pronouncing each syllable as if it were its own word, "'was rewarded yesterday by one of its native sons, Lyle Crandal. Today that son of a carpenter performed a miracle by breaking the four zero second bar-I-er on the four zero zero met-er at the two zero two four Oil-Im-pics.'"

"No," Hazel said on an intake of air.

"Uh-huh," Popo squeaked indignantly.

"This is amazin'," Hazel said to Misty.

"You thee," Misty replied. "You cain't compare yo'thelf to Melba'th mind or mine or hith. I got a blood clot and Melba had the blueth tho bad that thee couldn't breathe right half the time. Popo got thomethin' in hith head that thmell thunderthtormth an' read before he potty trained. Tho Melba could die if thee want to and that don't make her leth than you. Ith on'y God can make a judgment. On'y God can thave uth or no."

"On'y God," Popo said, staring deeply into Hazel's eyes.

"You got to get him tested," Hazel said over the child's

head. "You got to get him registered and trained by the Elite Education Group in Houston or San Francisco."

"No." At the sound of the masculine voice Popo's head jerked around.

"Chilly!" the boy shouted excitedly.

Popo jumped out of Hazel's lap, tumbled down her shins and hit the floor. His tiny lips trembled near tears from the fall but his eyes stayed focused on the powerful man in the denim overalls.

"Hey, baby boy," Chill said. He bent over and scooped Popo off the floor with one hand. In his other arm he cradled a colorful box and a big red book. "You got to stay up off'a the flo'. It's dirty down there."

"Sorry," the boy said as he snatched the book from the crook in his uncle's arm.

"My first shimistree set," the boy read out loud.

"It's got all kinds'a experiments you could do with chemicals," Chill said. "They got ones for electricity and computers too."

Popo giggled and bounced on Chill's arm to indicate that he wanted to be put down. Chill leaned over again, allowing Popo to sit in an empty plastic chair. The clear-eyed child was already deep into the words of the book.

"What you mean no?" Hazel said.

"I mean we not sendin' Popo away to some white man's idea of what smart and good is. All they do is wanna turn him against hisself. He's my nephew an' he belongs with his family."

"But you can't help him, Chill," Hazel argued. "He needs computers and tests and teachers smart enough so he cain't fool 'em."

"He ain't gonna fool me," Chill said dismissively. The

pale and jagged scar along his black jawline spoke of the violence and rage in the young man's life. "An' the books all say that he just needs to keep his mind busy learnin'. First books and things to keep his hands and mind busy, and then later he can be taught by teaching computers. That's what the experts say."

Chill put the bag down next to his nephew, who was already halfway through the children's chemistry primer.

"Look," Hazel said, pointing. "He almost finished with that book already."

"Naw. He just read the words. He have to go through it five or six times 'fore he be through with it. It'a be more than a week 'fore he gets through all those experiments."

"And you gonna buy him a chemistry set or whatever every week? Where you gonna get money like that? Do you even have a job?"

"I'm workin' for the catfish farms and doin' some work around here and there."

"That's gonna pay for a boy like Popo's education?"

"I got other plans."

"Like the plans put you on Angola Farm?"

"Prison," Popo said even as he turned a page.

Chill stared at Hazel. He clenched his fists hard enough to make his sinewy forearms tremble.

"Thtop!" Misty Bent commanded.

Popo sat up in his Buddha position and Hazel flinched. Misty had pulled herself to her feet by holding on to her plastic walker.

"Aunt Misty, sit down," Hazel said.

"You go," the elder woman replied. "You go and don't meth with uth. Thilly want to do right. Popo jutht lotht hith mama an' he never knew hith daddy. That Johnny Delight wath juth a hit'n run with hith mama. We ain't thendin' him nowhere."

2 "M Bill Bent?" the white man asked. He was standing at the front door, tam in hand.

Chill had been doing push-ups and wore only a pair of sweatpants. His muscular chest was heaving and sweat poured down his face.

"No," Chill said.

"Oh." The white man hesitated. "Then is M Misty Bent here?"

"She in the bed."

"Oh, I see," the small white man said. There was a hint of Mississippi in his voice but in spite of that he spoke like a Northerner. "Well, you see, I'm Andrew Russell from the state board of education. I've come to speak to someone about Ptolemy Bent."

In the background Chill could hear the radio receiver that Popo was experimenting with in his grandmother's room. The high-pitched wavering reminded Chill of the sound effects from the old science fiction movies that they showed on Saturdays at the juvenile delinquent detention center.

"What you want wit' Popo?"

"Popo. Is that what you call Ptolemy? We have been informed by various interested parties that the child is exceptional, bright. There's a state law that we must test exceptionally bright children to make sure that they're getting the proper education. You know IQ is our greatest resource." Andrew Russell smiled and nodded a little. He wore the popular andro-suit—green jacket and pants with a loose tan blouse and a brown tam.

"State law is you can't touch 'im till he sixty-one mont's," Chill said.

"But with his guardian's approval we can test as early as twenty-foah," Russell said in what was probably his friendliest tone.

Chill closed the door slowly, controlling his rage. He knew that he couldn't lose his temper, not while Popo was his responsibility.

"Popo," Chill called.

"Wit' Gramma," the child shouted.

She was surrounded by colored lights that Ptolemy had wired around the room. Yellow and blue and green and pink paper shades that had been colored with food dyes, lit by forty-watt bulbs. Four-year-old Ptolemy sat at his grandmother's vanity working on six disemboweled antique radios that he had dismantled and rewired. He turned the various knobs, roaming the electronic sighs, momentarily chancing upon talking or music now and then. Six bright green wires connected the radios to an archaic laptop computer on the floor. Waves of color crossed the old-fashioned backlit screen. Now and then an image would rise out of the haze of pixels.

His hair had never been cut but Popo brushed it out as well as he could every morning. In the afternoon Kai Lin would come over and comb out the tangles that Popo missed at the back of his neck.

Misty had cranked her Craftmatic bed to the full seated

position. She smiled at her little mad scientist while he searched for something, a secret that he wanted to surprise her with.

"Popo," Chill said.

The boy glanced over at the screen and giggled.

". . . former Soviet Union today gave up its last vestige of sovereignty, much less socialism, when it entered into a partnership with MacroCode Management International in a joint venture to return order to Russian society . . ."

A long pure note wailed between stations.

". . . born to be wi-i-i-ld . . ."

Static came after the song, but the volume rose.

"Popo!" Chill called again, but the static drowned out his words.

An almost imperceptible clicking blended in with the white noise. The volume dropped. The clicking became clearer. Popo brought his hands to the sides of his head and pulled both ears.

"Popo," Misty Bent said as loud as she could.

"Yea, Gramma?"

"Thill ith talkin' to you."

The boy turned around and stood on the white satin vanity chair. He was naked and smiling.

"Chilly."

"They wanna take you to get tested an' sen' you to Houston, Po," Chill said.

Ptolemy automatically put his hands in the air when the man came near. The child loved the feel of his skin against the muscular man's bare chest.

"No," Popo said. "I don' wanna go."

"I don't want you to go neither. But we got to figger sumpin' out."

"We could run," the boy suggested. "We could go in the swamps like them slave men you said about."

Almost every night Chill told Popo stories of runaway slaves on the Underground Railroad. He said that it was because he wanted Popo to know African-American history, "like them white kids know their history. From stories at home." But escape was the real story he wanted to tell. He had been obsessed with escape ever since the day he was convicted of armed robbery. The only way he could fall asleep in his cell at night was by imagining himself a slave who had slipped his chains, pried open the bars, and outrun the dogs. Even after his release Chill needed this fantasy to drop off most nights.

For a moment he considered his nephew's innocent suggestion.

The desire for flight burned perpetually in his chest. He owned an illegal ember gun. With that he never needed a reload, one LX battery could last a year.

But then his eyes fell upon his mother, Misty. She only walked for exercise now—fifteen minutes in the morning and five at night. Ptolemy loved his grandmother more than anything.

"No, baby boy," Chill said. "No."

"Then, what?"

"If we had money we could prove to the state that we could afford to get you hooked up to the EEG's Prime Com Link. If they could give you tests and we could get you into that Jesse Jackson Gymnasium that they got for city kids, then maybe you could stay."

"I could get money," Ptolemy said.

"It's gonna take more than your dollar allowance, honey."

"How much, then?"

"Just to pay for the computer link is a hundred fi'ty thousand a year. And then there's forty thousand for the JJ Gym, 'cause you not in the city limits. Three million prob'ly do it with costs goin' up like they do."

"I could get that," Ptolemy said.

"Where at?"

"On the computer."

"Naw, man," Chill said. "Computer's all linked up. They got identity cards along with your PBC on every computer."

"Nuh-uh," Ptolemy said, shaking his head and grinning. "My Personal Bar Code ain't on my computer."

"That thing? That's just a toy. It ain't connected up."

"I can wit' my radios. I can too."

"Show me."

The child jumped around in the chair and started turning dials. The computer's gaseous-looking screen went black. Letters and numbers appeared and reappeared in rapid succession on a line in the center of the screen.

Ptolemy hummed and sang while the computer spoke French and Chinese through the various radio speakers. Chill sat down on his mother's bed and watched.

"Don't let my boy get in trouble, Thill," Misty said.

"He was born in trouble, Mama. Born in trouble."

"But that don't make him no thief."

"If we cain't get in the money then the government gonna take him. I'ma just get 'im to show me, Mama. Ain't nobody gonna steal nuthin', but even if they do it's gonna be me. I'll push the button. But don't worry, I'm just lookin'."

As they spoke, words appeared and remained on the screen:

WORLD BANK INTERNATIONAL
B of A, Citicorp, AMEX, HITO-SAN

welcome to our entry screen

****UNAUTHORIZED ACCESS IS PUNISHABLE****
BY NATIONAL AND INTERNATIONAL LAW

Below the words were a series of codes and blank lines.

"See," Popo exclaimed. "They gots lotsa money."

"An' they don't know your bar code?" Chill asked.

"They get the bar code from your eyes," Ptolemy said. "When you buy your computer they make you give 'em a eyescan. But they didn't do that way back when they made these laptops. I just borrow somebody else's bar-c from one'a the Jacker DBs and then I put it back when I'm through."

While Ptolemy spoke the blanks were being filled in one at a time by an automatic code-breaking program that the boy had adapted from the illegal Jacker Database. After all of the blanks had been filled in, a flurry of screens passed in quick succession, ending finally on a screen whose header read

PROJECT MAINTENANCE FUNDS.

"This ain't nobody's money," the child said. "It's what they got for extra."

There were sixteen place numbers on each coded entry of the file.

Chill's upper lip began to sweat.

"Turn it off, Popo."

"But—"

"Turn it off!"

3 "Ow!" Ptolemy Bent yelled.

"You'll need a haircut soon," Kai Lin told him as she dragged the large brush up from the back of the child's neck. "There's more hair than there is little boy."

Misty hissed her paralytic laugh and held a gnarled hand up to shoulder level. She was sitting straight, thanks to her mechanical bed, watching the squat Vietnamese woman torture the poor boy's head.

"He don't wan' it cut," Misty said.

"He'll look like a girl, then," Kai said, giving a hard tug.

"Ow! I don't care," Popo said. "I want my hair like the Jewish man who made relatively. Bushy and big."

"By the time you're his age all we'll be able to see will be your feet." Kai tickled Ptolemy's skinny ribs and the boy doubled over in her lap.

Misty rocked back and forth in sympathy with the boy's glee. Even Kai's impassive face broke into a smile.

Popo grabbed Kai's brush hand, trying to wrest away the implement of torture. But Kai laid him flat on her lap and bent over to blow a loud kiss against his belly.

"I give! I give! You can brush, you can brush." All of the air rushed out of the boy's lungs, making him too weak even to sit up.

"No," Kai said. "All done."

The boy cheered and jumped down, hurrying over to

the radio corner, as Misty called it. By then he had deconstructed fifteen old radios, putting their parts together again on every available space. The wires and transistor chips resembled some new form of technologic life growing like fungus down the sides of the vanity onto the floor. There were three old-time laptop computers connected here and there. One of these cast indecipherable images of color and light. The forms sometimes seemed to have an alien sense about them, but mostly they were abstract events appearing for a nanosecond or an hour, changing almost imperceptibly or faster than the eye could follow. Another screen flashed strange characters at various intervals and in differing colors. These characters were being printed horizontally across paper, slowly unfurling from a two-hundred-foot roll on an antique dot matrix printer that Chill had brought home from a yard sale in Jackson, he said.

The final screen was connected to a HondaDrive AE storage system. The three-foot-high canister, encased in crystalline green plastic, was one of the two new pieces of equipment that Popo owned. The HondaDrive was a micro-level storage system that held trillions of bytes of information. It also had an I-crunch that could encode data, making it possible to exponentially expand its capacity. Three years ago a HondaDrive AE would have cost a million dollars. But within the past year, General Electric had stunned the scientific world—and the stock market—with the GE-AI-Drive and its virtually unlimited storage capacity. The GE-AI was big, the size of a refrigerator, but it answered the memory problems of even the most demanding user.

Now a HondaDrive AE cost only ten thousand dollars.

No one wanted them, so security had dropped to the point where Chill had been able to steal one from a Radio Shack in Memphis. Along with the drive, Chill stole a LIBCHIP library box, a series of two hundred library chips containing over ten million volumes.

"Let's see you read your way outta that," Chill dared his nephew.

"I will," the boy replied.

The computer connected to the HondaDrive was taking information from the radio receivers, translating it to mathematical codes, and storing the equations. Ptolemy sat naked in lotus position between the screens, watching them and making adjustments to the radio dials now and then.

Kai sat behind the boy and pulled him into her lap. He didn't resist. She usually came to the Bent's house last on her rounds as visiting nurse for the state. She told her supervisor that it was because Misty needed to take her walk late in the day, but really it was to be able to spend more time with the child.

"What is all this?"

"Computers," the boy said. "Computers and radios and electricity and, and, that's all."

"But what are they doing?" Kai asked the same question every day. And every day Ptolemy said that it was a secret.

"It's readin' what the radio says and then it's puttin' it into numbers and then it's puttin' the numbers on the HondaDrive."

"But how do you know how to do all that?"

"I don't," Ptolemy said as he leaned over to turn a dial. The clicking from the speakers changed tempo, and the boy nodded his head as if he were listening to a piece of music.

"But how can you do something and not know how to do it?" Kai asked.

"You use words that you don't know what they mean sometimes. You drive a 'lectric car but you cain't make one." Ptolemy was talking but his attention was on the screens. The image screen showed an eerie landscape of pastel greens and metallic blacks interwoven and slipping away into a distant red maw. "I just count the numbers in the radio waves and then use a equation that I got from the math lib'ary on the net. It makes up the numbers and then I look at 'em later."

"What are you looking for?" Kai asked almost timidly.

Ptolemy turned to the visiting nurse. His deep brown eyes were like polished stones.

"It's God, I think," he said. "It's God sangin' through radio waves."

"What do you mean? How could that be? I mean why hasn't anybody else heard it before?" An instant hysteria bloomed in Kai's chest.

"Maybe they did," Ptolemy said in a matter-of-fact tone. He had turned back to his screens. He wasn't really thinking about his nurse. "Maybe they did and then when they talked to him they lefted."

"Left where?"

"To God, I guess. Maybe not, though. Maybe they went to heaben."

"Isn't that where God is?"

"No," Ptolemy said, turning again to the squat, mask-faced woman. "Heaben is somewhere else."

"But, Popo," she said. "Why hasn't anybody else heard these messages?"

" 'Cause they don't play with the radio like I do. They all wanna make things but they don't listen too much, you know?"

"No. I don't know."

"When I listen to the radio waves I can hear little pieces of him talkin'. And then, when I turn the knob I hear a little more. His words comin' through in pieces all over. They think it's static. They made the digit-thingy to block it out. Nobody wanna hear it in they music, so they miss it."

"What does God say?" As Kai heard the words coming from her mouth she realized that she meant them.

"Hi," answered Ptolemy. "How are you and can you hear me."

"Could it be some alien race and not God at all?"

"I guess. But I don't think so."

"We should tell somebody about this," Kai said. Behind her Misty Bent had fallen asleep.

"I did."

"Who? Who did you tell?"

"Chilly."

4

"I have to talk wit' you, Kai," Chill Bent said three weeks after the social worker/nurse was forced to reconsider the existence of God.

It was a cool autumn day. The Tickle River was

swollen with waters from recent rains, and fish could be seen darting around in schools numbering in the hundreds.

"Yes, Mr. Bent?"

"I'm gonna have to go away for a few weeks."

"Where?"

"Outta the country."

"Oh." The nurse frowned.

"I gotta get some money or they gonna take Popo away. My cousin Hazel been talkin' to child welfare and the EEG. They wanna take Popo to Houston but I won't let 'em."

"But maybe it would be better," Kai suggested hesitantly. "M-maybe if he was in Houston you could visit and he'd have all the best guidance and education."

"Boy needs a family and a home," Chill said. "I been in the state institution before. It ain't no good."

"But that was a detention center," the short nurse argued.

"No different. He gonna be detained in the school too. He cain't come home when he want to. You know his grandmama'll die a week after he's gone."

Kai Lin didn't argue that point. She watched the large man's dark face. He had aged in the two years since Kai had met him. Deep furrows had appeared in his cheeks, and something was wrong with his knees. He was still very handsome, though Kai would have never said so out loud.

"Where are you going?" she asked.

"I can't say. But I want you to take care'a Popo. I want you to make sure that Hazel or M Russell don't get him."

"They won't."

" 'Cause I know you love that chile," Chill said. "I seen

how you are wit 'im. How come you over on your days off. And you know I'm right too. He learnin' all he can right here, right here in this house."

Tears sprouted from the ex-con's eyes. They rolled down his face.

"I love that boy more than I love anything," he said. "I will not let them take him. I will not let them white people and them people wanna be white turn him into some cash cow or bomb builder or prison maker. He will find his own way an' make up his own mind, god dammit."

Kai reached out to touch Chill's arm. He pulled her close, holding her forearms in a powerful grip. Kai winced but didn't fight him.

"Maybe that's what they're afraid of," she said. "Maybe they don't want these children to make up their own minds. Maybe if they did that, the world would change."

"I know you know," Chill said. "They afraid Ptolemy would be their king if they didn't brainwash 'im."

"Maybe you're right," Kai said. "Sometimes I'm afraid when he talks. Sometimes I'm afraid of what he can see."

"When I come back you an' me gotta talk," Chill said.

Kai did not ask about what.

Chill was gone for six weeks. The first ten days he called every evening. Ptolemy traced the call on his illegal Internet connection and told Kai and Misty that he was in Panama City. After the third week, they received only one faxgram.

Dear Mama, Ptolemy, and Kai,

I'm out in the backcountry down here and so I can't call. I'm fine and I will be home as soon as I can. Just a little more work and I'll have enough money to pay for Ptolemy's home education and we don't have to worry about what anybody else wants to say. Take care of your grandmother and Kai, Ptolemy. I'll be home soon.

Chill

"Thill din't write nuthin' like that," Misty Bent said after Kai had read it out loud to both her and Ptolemy.

"Sure didn't," Popo agreed. "Chilly never say no Ptolemy when he talkin' t' me."

"He must have had somebody write it for him. Maybe he dictated it over some kind of radio system," Kai said to allay the family's fears. She wasn't worried whether the faxgram came from Chill. What bothered her was how the ex-convict intended to make so much money in Panama.

The Vietnamese nurse had found a home in southern Mississippi. She loved the land and the people more than her native Hanoi, and more than Princeton, where she'd spent so many years going to school. The people reminded her of the stories that her grandmother told. The great jungles and the wild forests. By 2010 Vietnam was divided into twelve highly developed corporate microstates that produced technical and biological hardware for various Euro-corps. Gone were the farms and rice paddies. The back roads were paved with Duraplas, and the giant cobra was extinct. Kai reveled in the Mississippi heavy air and the meandering back roads, the thick drawl on the English words and the life that sprang from every tree and rock and stream.

And then there was the child who listened to God. Kai had only lived in Hazel's house since Chill had been gone, sleeping on the Bents' couch, but she had felt that that house was her home since the day she'd crossed the threshold.

Six weeks after Chill had gone a private ambulance drove up the Bents' dirt driveway. The attendants were from New Orleans, as was the van. The two white men rolled Chill into the house on the wheeled stretcher.

Chill was there under a thin sheet. His head was shaven and his eyes were covered with bandaged gauze. The form his legs made under the sheet was straight and motionless.

"Where should we bring 'im, ma'am?" one of the attendants asked Kai Lin.

"What's happened to him?"

"Uncle Chilly!" Ptolemy screamed in dismay.

"Don't know nuthin' 'bout that, ma'am," the second paramedic said. "We just picked him up from the airport with instructions to brang 'im here."

"Am I in the livin' room?" Chill asked.

"Yeah," the paramedic replied.

"Chilly!" Ptolemy yelled again. He hid behind Kai Lin's red silk dress, afraid of the white men, the chrome stretcher, and Chill's decimated form.

"Then leave me here. Kai?"

"Yes?"

"Give these men fifty dollars each. I'll pay you back later on."

The white men were surprised at the generosity of the black paraplegic. They both thanked him, gave their apologies to Kai Lin, and left.

"There's a clinic in the hills," Chill was saying. They had wheeled him into his mother's room and cranked his cot until he could sit up too.

"What have they done to my baby?" Misty cried. But when Chill smiled in a way that Misty hadn't seen since he was a child, her tears subsided.

". . . up there they cain't be bothered and so they can operate with no problem. They wanted my eyes—"

"And you give 'em up?" Misty said, louder than she had spoken in years.

"That was one million seven hundred an' fi'ty thousand," Chill said. "My eyes were a perfect fit for a Swiss banker's son who lost his in a ski accident. But when I was there they had a emergency. It was a Russian general needed the nerve in the spine where he could use his legs. They offered two million for that. I figgered that if I cain't see then I really don't need to walk. One thing led to another and I got outta there wit' six million. They transferred the whole thing into my name 'fore I went under the knife."

"Why you do that, Uncle Chilly?" Ptolemy asked.

Chill put his hands up in front of him and found his nephew's face.

"I was worried that I couldn't keep on payin' for the house, baby boy. You know mama's social security an' disability been payin' for me, so now my disability be payin' for her."

"Thill, no," Misty cried.

"It's okay, Mama. You know I been lost outside'a the house anyway. Anytime I ain't here I just wanna come back an' hear you laughin' or Popo readin' an' playin' his radio. Don't worry, Mama. Everything's fine now."

5

That night, when Misty and Ptolemy were asleep in their beds, Kai and Chill had their talk.

"I want you to marry me," Chill said, his empty eye sockets staring at the ceiling.

"What?"

"I cain't see. I cain't walk. I got the money to p'otect Popo but I cain't move to block a thing if they wanna come in here and take him away from us. But if you marry me, and move wit' us to Jackson, we could get a big house and a Prime Com Link for Popo's education. You could have boyfriends and free time, just look after Mama and Popo like you been doin'. Just do that an' we can share the money in style."

Chill could have told no more about what she was thinking even if he still had eyes. Kai's face was impassive, even hard.

She blinked once and fifteen seconds passed.

She blinked again.

"Okay," she whispered. "I accept."

"You do?"

"Of course. It's a trust. It's holy."

"There's one thing I gotta tell ya," Chill said.

"What's that?"

"I sold my manhood too. With no legs I knew I wouldn't be able to function no way. So you wouldn't be marryin' a man at all."

"Oh yes I will be," she said. She took his hand in hers and hummed a song she'd once heard on the radio and thought that she'd forgotten.

6 No one believed the lie about a fall at work that left Chill Bent paralyzed, blind, and rich from the insurance he got. They all knew that poor men and women often sold pieces of themselves to the rich in order to give their children a chance. Hazel Bernard tried to get the marriage between Chill and Kai annulled but failed. At the age of nine, in 2030, Ptolemy Bent joined the Jesse Jackson Gymnasium for Advanced Learners so he would have a social life among other children. But his education came from tutors and texts provided by the Prime Com Link. He worked hard on his radio receiver, which he never discussed outside of home, and one day he convinced Kai to buy him a $300,000 transmitter, the state of the art in amateur radio communications.

"Chilly, you awake?"

"Is that you, Popo?" The ex-convict put out a hand to gently caress his nephew's face.

"Uh-huh."

"You got peach fuzz on your chin."

"You always say that. When you gonna call it a beard?"

"Peach fuzz," Chill said behind a chuckle.

"I made contact, Chilly."

"You did?"

"Uh-huh. An' I told 'im 'bout you."

"You think the big man'd have somethin' better t' do than worry 'bout a blind an' crippled thief."

"You the best man in the world, Uncle Chilly. He said he wanna meet you, you'n Gramma Misty."

"Really? He said that? Damn. Well I guess it won't be too much longer anyways. Kai said that the doctor said that my kidneys wouldn't get a nickel down in Panama."

"You don't have to die, Chilly," Ptolemy said, his voice wavering between high and low adolescent tones. "I'm'a just put some wires on your head. You and Grandma."

"You there, Mama?" Chill called out.

"Yeth, baby. Popo gonna make uth out a ethperiment. He thure look fine." Misty's ancient voice was weaker. Chill knew that time was short for both of them.

"I bet he do, Mama."

After what seemed like hours of preparation, Ptolemy said, "Ready?" Then came a white-hot flash at Chill's temples and then the feeling of electric fingers going up under his skull and into the brain.

Suddenly he could see again. Ptolemy was sitting there looking at another Chill lying on the bed. The boy, almost a man, wearing a lavender andro-suit with no shirt, had hair that made him look like the king of lions. He was still skinny, and darker than he had been. *From brown to black,* Chill thought, and then he was gone forever from the Earth. First his thoughts were elsewhere, and then slowly, electron by electron, the matter of his soul was transported. Somewhere there were bursts of stars and lines of reality that connected uncounted voices.

God, Chill thought. But there was no answer to his assertion. A halo of winking lights radiated next to him, mingled with him, and he knew in some new language that this was his mother. The word *freedom* occurred to Chill, but the meaning faded with the clarity of his light. So much he knew that he was unaware of. So much beyond him even then.

It's like I'm a breath, he wanted to say.

Yes, Misty's new form replied.

Ptolemy Bent was arrested and tried for the euthanasia killing of his uncle and grandmother. He was sentenced to twelve years to life in a private prison run by the Randac Corporation of Madagascar.

At the trial God was ruled an improbability.

"He is aware that he disintegrated their brain tissues," claimed Morton Tremble, the prosecution's expert psychiatrist, "by using feedback from a powerful radio transmitter. Maybe he thought, consciously, that he was sending their souls to God or whatever. But in truth he only did this because both were so close to death already, as he himself has testified. He admitted that he knew their bodies, including their nervous systems, would die. This is a classic case of mercy killing. And Ptolemy Bent was completely aware that euthanasia is against the law."

Kai Lin, who was by Ptolemy's side every day of the trial, stored his radio equipment in her basement. She never visited her husband's grave.

The Greatest

1 "Ladies and gentlemen!" veteran ring announcer L.Z. Scappelli proclaimed. "Now you're in for a treat. For the first time anywhere the Universal Boxing Authority has sanctioned a pro heavyweight bout between the sexes."

A whole tier of seats taken up by women rose in loud acclaim in the vast underground complex of Manhattan's Madison Stadium. So boisterous was their cheering that the boos and hisses from elsewhere around the arena were drowned out. Women hooted and screamed; they rose to their feet and pounded the plastic backs of their chairs.

"It's quite a scene tonight, isn't it, Billy?" said audiovid announcer Chet Atkinson. The fight was blacked out in the Twelve Fiefs of New York City because the main event—Brigham versus Zeletski—hadn't sold out the 120,000-stadium seats by fight time.

"You better believe it," Billy "the Eclipse" Bonner, onetime UBA lightweight champion, replied. Each word seemed to roll around on a bed of marbles before leaving his mouth. "The ladies want to see blood."

"What do you think about Fera Jones stepping into the ring against a man, Champ?"

"Well, Chet, I'm old-fashioned. I don't like to see ladies with the gloves on. I mean, even the WUBA is too much for me to watch sometimes. But there's no denying that women have been becoming more competitive. They hit harder and move faster every year."

"So do you think she has a chance tonight?"

"I don't think she'll get hurt too bad," Bonner replied. "Jellyroll is more of an act than he is a fighter. They set him up with opponents that have no chance against him. I mean, the crowd loves it, I do too, but Jellyroll tipped the scale at almost three-eighty at weigh-in, and he doesn't have a knockout punch."

"Three-eighty," Chet agreed. "And six seven. But Fera Jones weighs an impressive two-sixty and stands six foot nine. She has the reach, age, and height advantage over Jellyroll. And she looks like she was molded from iron. I mean, just look at the muscle definition on those legs."

"Nice legs, I'll agree with that, Chet. But this is a brutal sport. Man is the warrior. I don't care how much the Radical Feminist Separatist movement wants to play with genetics, a man will always come out on top in one of these wars."

It was never proven that Fera Jones was the product of SepFem-G, an outlawed genetics program that came out of the feminist studies department at Smith College. Actually, there was evidence to the contrary. Fera lived with, and was managed and trained by, her father, Leon Jones, a onetime history professor at U. Mass. Not that there weren't lots of questions about them.

Leon was Negro, medium brown with thick, kinky hair, generous lips, and a broad nose. Fera was a natural, if dirty, blond, with skin too dark to be Caucasian but not exactly the right coloring for Negro, either. Her mother was unknown to the public. Fera claimed that she didn't know anything about her mother.

"Your father must have known who she was," a woman's magazine journalist once suggested in an interview.

"If I bring it up I can see the hurt in him," Fera replied. It was the most she ever said about her mother publicly.

There were plenty of questions about Fera Jones. She was tall enough to play men's basketball and strong enough to compete in a strongman contest. She'd run through the Women's Universal Boxing Association's list of contenders in one year—all wins by knockout. In twenty-four fights she'd gone to the second round only once. That was against Slippery WandaJoe Williams. WandaJoe managed to avoid Fera's haymakers for the first three minutes, but ninety-one seconds into round two she caught a fist that was what Fera called her tooth decay preventative.

"If the tooth is out it can't get decay," she joked with Billy Bonner after the bout.

Fera was so proficient that many said she was actually a man trying to make it by pretending to be a woman. The WUBA had performed DNA tests proving Fera's gender (also disproving the theory that she was the product of a separatist test tube). But the public was not convinced by computer graphs and petri dishes. So Fera went on the X-rated people's access vid show *Behind Sammy Rosen's Blue Door.*

Sammy's usual guests were porn performers who had special talents and fan clubs, marital aids to hawk, or a performance schedule that needed advertising. Fera had only one thing to prove on Sammy's show. When he tried to kiss her she pushed him to the floor and held him down with her bare foot. Then she pulled off her dress and told the vidder to get close-ups of her breasts and genitals.

"You wish I was a man," she said into the camera. " 'Cause if I was, somebody might have a chance to beat me."

That one live airing moved Sammy's show to new heights, but he never forgave Fera for his humiliation. From then on, each of his shows began with a replay of him smashing her glass image with a hammer. Of course, this only served to make her more popular.

The referee was going over the rules in the middle of the ring when a fight broke out between a man and woman on the floor of the stadium. Women poured down from their exclusive tier and security guards closed in to stop the melee.

When the ref said, "Go to your corners and come out fighting," there were already blows being thrown and blood being spilled.

"This is exciting isn't it, Champ?"

"I don't know, Chet. All I can say is that I'm glad the

viewers here in New York can't see this. Even though Jellyroll is shorter, he looks much bigger than Fera."

"I agree, Champ. She looks frightened, fragile compared to him. And you know Jellyroll says that he's not going to go easy on her."

The next voice heard was not one of the announcers but the gravelly deep voice of the exhibition fighter Jellyroll Greg-ory. "I'm gonna beat her to the floor just like she did to my friend Sammy Rosen. I'm gonna beat her down in the first round. I like to get these fights over quick, 'cause they don't let me eat till after it's over."

The bell rang.

"Looks like the security forces have stopped the brawl just in time for the real fight to begin," Chet Atkinson reported. "Fera Jones comes to the middle of the ring. Jellyroll seems cautious . . . No! He's leaping right at her, both fists flailing. Fera barely avoids getting hit. She falls back. He's jumping again! He's run right into her. Almost four hundred pounds of man and muscle. She's going down!"

"They're both going down, Chet," Bonner corrected. "The referee, Xian Luke, is calling it a fall. He's rubbing both boxers' gloves off on his shirt."

"We should say that Luke is one of the best refs in the game today," Chet said. "He asked for this job tonight because he said that he didn't want to see anyone get hurt."

"I don't think he was worried about Jellyroll, Chet."

"Me nei—Oh no! Jellyroll throws a roundhouse right that connects with Fera's jaw. She's falling back. She's on the ropes. I think she might have gone all the way down if the ropes hadn't been there to stop her. Jellyroll is on her again. He's throwing everything he's got. Jones is covering up."

"Jellyroll wants to get her out of here quick. He doesn't want to be out there carrying around three hundred and eighty pounds in the later rounds."

"Another fight has broken out in the seats!"

"Forget that, Chet! Fera's coming back! She's jabbing in the center of the ring. Look at the speed of that jab! One, two, . . . six jabs before Jellyroll could get his defense up. His eye, yes, there's a cut open over his left eye! Jellyroll is bleeding. Jellyroll is bleeding!"

Chet Atkinson jumped in to say, "It's like old times. Like back when they fought bare-knuckled. They're swinging in and out of the ring. Fera Jones is going for Jellyroll's spare tire. We can hear the blows here at ringside. He's trying to mount a counterattack. Fera better watch it. She's leaving herself open swinging away like that. Oh! Jellyroll connected to her jaw again."

"That was right on the money," Billy Bonner cried. "Jones is backing up, but she's not going down. Oh! He connected again. What's holding this woman up?"

"I don't know, Champ. But she's not falling back on the ropes this time. Fera Jones is going to the body. These blows are vicious. It doesn't matter if it's a man or a woman when you get hit like that. Oh shit!" Chet Atkinson never complained about the $10,000 he was fined for cursing on a show with only a V rating. "She connected with an uppercut! Jellyroll is lifted from the canvas! He's down! He's down! Jellyroll Gregory is down!"

"And I don't believe that he's getting up," Billy added. "No. Luke is waving Fera away. He's calling the fight over. The parmeds are jumping into the ring. Six of them."

"They'll need that many if they have to carry him out of here."

"Look, Chet. The women are tearing up the stands! They're throwing the chairs into a group of taunting men. Fights are breaking out everywhere."

"You better get in there and talk to the winner, Champ. Before they tear the house down."

"So, M Jones," the Eclipse asked amid the hubbub of the crowded ring, "how did it feel in there against a man?"

"I've had harder fights, Billy," Fera said. "But first I want to give thanks to the goddess Diana, and I want to thank my daddy for making me the greatest fighter in the world."

"He hit you pretty hard a couple of times. We thought you were going down once."

"He never hurt me. The first time he hit me I moved back in case he was throwing a combination, but I stumbled and fell into the ropes. He never hurt me."

"Well, you sure hurt him."

"Bring on Zeletski," Fera said. "Bring on your champion."

"What do you think, Professor Jones?" Bonner asked Fera's father/trainer/manager. "Do you want to see her jump up in competition to Zeletski's level this quickly?"

"Fera could beat Zeletski any day. She has the power and she knows how to get it to him. You saw how Jellyroll hit her. I tell you Fera would make Sonny Liston quiver in his boots."

"Thank you, Professor, Fera . . ." An uproar rose. "Someone has just thrown a chair into the ring. There are fights breaking out everywhere. The police are trying to restore order, but I don't even know if the main event will go on. Back to you, Chet."

"There you have it. Fera Jones has an impressive win tonight and her trainer says that she's ready for a championship shot. There would be a lot of money in that fight. But not if a brawl breaks out like this one. I'm being told that we will go off the air while the police regain some semblance of order. This is Chet Atkinson, with the Champ, Billy 'the Eclipse' Bonner, saying—"

2

"But, Daddy, I *am* ready. I can take him. I can. You said so yourself after the fight with Jelly Belly."

"You got the power, Fifi. You got the heart. But you need more experience."

"Nobody's ever beat me, Daddy."

"What about the last fight you had, with Bobo Black?"

"I told you. I was off. I had trouble getting it to him."

"You had trouble because you couldn't get to him, and you couldn't get to him because he was outthinking you in there. If he hadn't'a got tired you would have had your first UBA loss."

They were in Fera's permanent suite on the three hundredth floor of the Fifth Business, *the* Broadway hotel. Fera had had eight UBA fights by then. All with men. All ending by KO.

"Zeletski can box better than Black, and he doesn't get

tired. He hits hard enough to put you down. We need a little more time. You need a better class of fight. Like this Black. You have to go through a couple of wars. And there's something else."

"What, Daddy?"

"Money, baby. Lotsa money. It's been chump change up till now. We got this suite, but that's just 'cause this hotel wants to brag on you. You lose one fight and we're outta here."

"We've been broke before."

"Yeah, but," he hesitated. "You know with the Pulse I can't take chances. Ever since Congress legalized Pulse you got to have money. You got to have money or you're dead."

The Pulse was a drug dealer's dream. Cooked up at CalTech in the late hours when the professors were in bed. The gene drug altered the structure of the pleasure centers of the brain, temporarily allowing consciousness some measure of control over dreams. With just the right amount, a pulsar, as the users called themselves, could create a complex fantasy, build a whole world and live in it for what seemed like days, weeks. The original intention of the students was to create a time warp in the brain where they could do months of complex research in an evening.

"But the drug gave entrée to the id," Dr. Samboka of NYU explained in the *EastCoast DataTimes* after it was far too late. "And the id has a powerful inclination for sensuality and instinct."

Pulsars' minds drifted into passionate love affairs and musical performances that lasted for days. Many lost interest in the world around them, making better worlds in their unconscious minds. And to make matters worse, or better from a profit point of view, it turned out that after four or five uses, the brain collapsed in on itself without regular ingestion of the drug. It was an addiction from which death was the only withdrawal.

The Pulse, named after the heartbeat many addicts reported hearing before slipping into fantasy, was legalized in 2031. Pulse party parlors appeared everywhere. The cost was fixed by the government, but there was no coverage on state medical insurance and no emergency fund for the poor pulsar who went broke. And because the user had to have the drug every three days, there were few job cycles that a pulsar could hold.

Pulsedeath was an everyday event. Almost every user died horribly from a collapsed brain. Only the rich could be sure of long-term supply. And even they died ultimately, their brains like overstretched rubber bands snapping finally from overwork.

"I know it's going to kill me," Rickert Londonne, Pulse proponent and user, proclaimed on prime vid. "But last night I was the emperor Hadrian. I controlled the Roman empire. I strode the city streets and lived among the people, common and extraordinary. I battled the Vandals, the Goths, and the Persians. I built a world. What did you do last night?"

Pulse had another unexpected impact on the economy. In the days between use, Pulsars read many books of fiction and history to seed their minds with the possibility of dreams. Electronic publishing industry stocks soared.

"We could make a billion-dollar fight if you get the women of the world on your side, Fifi. Get that and I can live a few more years."

"I will, Daddy. And I'll pay to have the MacroCode GenTeam find you a cure."

"I know you will, baby. I know you will."

3

The night before the Mathias Konkon fight, Pell Lightner came up to the three hundredth floor of the Fifth Business. He whispered his name into the key-mike and the door slid open. He hesitated a moment before entering, took a deep breath, and then walked in confidently, standing to his full five foot nine and a half inches.

"Fifi?"

There was no answer. He went through the entrance area into the living room.

The sight of Leon Jones sitting on the long, overstuffed sofa gave Pell a scare, but then he realized that his girlfriend's father was far beyond worrying about him. The elder Jones's eyes were open, and he seemed to be looking right at Pell, but really he was gazing far away into faded Pulsedreams. After years of use the dreams had dwindled into a kind of bleached-out euphoria. The loss of specific dream content was the first sign that a user's brain was near final collapse.

"Hey, baby." Fera was standing at the door to her bedroom, naked.

Pell liked it that the musculature of Fera's chest hadn't erased her womanly figure. Her breasts were real breasts, and except for that one evening on the Sammy Rosen show, Pell was the only man to see under her dress nowadays.

All of his young life, Pell had lived in Common Ground, the place for all unemployed citizens. He had learned to appreciate a good thing. He was only nineteen, permanently unemployed and without benefits except for an octangular sleep tube underground and regular rations of rice and beans.

"Take down your pants," Fera said.

Automatically Pell took a step forward. At the same time he pulled down his pants. He leapt toward her and she held him up in her arms. Fera grinned broadly when Pell grabbed her hair to keep his balance.

She carried him from the room while her father mused.

Fera had met Pell at a Soul Shack on Middle Broadway. He was strutting around among the Backgrounder girls, acting like the cock of the walkway. She got a hot ribs and yam dinner in a plasbox and then walked up to the group of young Backgrounders. Pell was arrogant and snide, but when she asked him if he wanted to go with her he was in the car as quickly as he could move.

"You remember when we first met?" Fera asked her lover. She was on top of him, grinding her hips.

"Yeah," he coughed.

"Did you love me for my body or my money?" Her coarse blond hair raked his eyes.

A look of confusion came over his face. For a moment it seemed as if he had found an answer, but instead he had a powerful orgasm.

"I can't, I can't," he cried meaninglessly.

—

"Baby, do you love me?" Fera asked Pell in her dark bedroom. Through the open window the spires of upper Manhattan stretched toward the sky.

"We don't use that word underground."

"What do you say, then?"

"I look for you, I see you, I won't turn away."

"That's a lotta words just to say the same thing."

"It's not the same thing. Not at all. 'I love you,' means, 'I need you.' The way I say it means that you can count on me. The way I say it is strong."

"You turned away from your friends to come with me."

"I never told 'em I wouldn't."

Fera laid her big palm on his chest.

"I wish I was like you, Pipi," she said.

"What you mean? Here you up above, butter and cream—and I'm down below, bread and water."

"But you know what you think."

"Huh?"

"If I say something or ask something, you have an answer. Even if you just don't know you sound so sure. All I know is that I love my daddy. That and boxing is all I have. Everything else is a mess. That's why I like fighting, because I get so mad not bein' sure, and hittin' somebody makes me feel better. Even gettin' hit feels good."

"Then that's good enough. It keeps you upover."

"But I want more."

"What?"

"Like you. To look and not turn away."

4

The Konkon fight was the turning point in Fera Jones's career. The night before was the first time Leon experienced a Pulse Reflux episode. It left him bedridden and unable to be in his daughter's corner. She asked Pell to stand in for her father, and the diminutive Backgrounder agreed. He had been sitting ringside for over six months and had some notion of what was expected of a corner man. The only thing he didn't know how to do was stop the bleeding in case of a cut, but Leon had been smart enough to bring in Doc Blevins, the premier cut man of boxing, as a permanent member of Ferocious Fera Jones's corner.

Mathias Konkon was a wily boxer. He avoided the brunt of Fera's initial onslaught. He rolled with some blows and picked others off with deflecting gloves. He had a solid chin, too, and so whenever Fera was accurate enough to land a hard punch, she was surprised with a series of left hooks and right uppercuts in answer.

Over six rounds she had lost all but one.

In between rounds Pell begged his boxer to box.

"Stick and run, Fifi," he pleaded. "Let him come after you. Let him come after."

"I can get him," Fera declared. "All I need is one shot and he'll cave in."

Each round she went out streaming sweat and oozing confidence, but at the bell she came back another point down on the scorecards.

In the seventh Konkon let loose. It was toward the end of the round and Fera was breathing hard. She'd thrown her full artillery at the slippery Fijian. If she had connected with anything, the announcers were certain that

Mathias would have wound up in the hospital. But the shorter boxer had figured out just the right crouch to avoid a haymaker. When he saw that his opponent was temporarily winded, he threw a full-fledged attack at her head.

"Jones is in trouble!" Atkinson exclaimed at ringside.

"He'd do better to attack the body," Bonner added conservatively. "Kill the body and the head will fall."

At that moment, Mathias connected to Fera's jaw with a jolting right cross. Fera Jones sprawled out on her back, unconscious from every indication. But while the referee was waving the exultant Konkon back to his corner, Fera Jones opened her eyes and willed herself to her feet.

"She's cut!" Bonner yelled. "She's cut over her right eye!"

The blood was cascading down the right side of her face. But Fera Jones didn't even dab at it with her glove.

The referee asked her did she want to go on.

She nodded.

He asked her another question.

She answered to his satisfaction.

He waved for the fight to continue, but the bell rang before another blow could be thrown. Doc Blevins was in the corner with his steel compressor and cotton sticks, ready for his charge. His bald head was painted black and red for the colors of Jones's trunks. There was a bright green stripe painted across his forehead for his Irish mother.

The ring doctor stood at the side, watching the procedure closely. Pell stood over his fighter, his fists clenched as if he wanted to hit her himself.

Instead he pinched the flesh at the tip of her chin, hard. Her eyes, vacant until then, cleared.

"He's gonna beat you, you stupid cow. He's gonna beat you 'cause you out there fightin' like a girl. Like a fuckin' girl." Every word was broadcast around the globe on VIN, Video International Network. "You're the best fighter that ever lived and you're throwin' it away 'cause you don't want to do what you're supposed to do."

"I can get him," she said.

"Not if you don't jab. He's got you so girly out there that you forgot how to box. He's made a fool outta you, and look at you. All blooded up and ugly. It's over. I'm throwin' in the towel."

Pell reached for the towel. He picked it up.

"No, don't," Fera said, more like a child than a machine of destruction. "I can do it. I can do it."

Pell paused, towel in midair there between him and his fighter. Over a hundred million people around the globe watched.

"One round, Fera. One round to prove that you can do what's necessary."

The bleeding had been stemmed. Certainty returned to Fera's eyes. She nodded and fifty million women around the world felt their hearts thrum and galvanize. Groucho T, the Internet philosopher, later said, "The whole world changed between the seventh and eighth rounds."

Konkon never had a chance after the seventh. In rounds eight and nine Fera's left jab turned his face into hamburger. In round ten she knocked him to the canvas six times before the referee gave her the win.

"I want to thank Diana for my victory," Fera said to

the Eclipse, "with a nod to Legba for sending me his trickster friend, Pell Lightner."

The Radical Feminist Separatist Party of Massachusetts declared that the next day would be a floating holiday, called Fierce Woman Day, and closed down the state. Women around the world bought T-shirts with the images of Fera and Pell on them. The president came to visit Fera in her suite at the Fifth Business, and *Time* magazine named her Woman of the Century.

Leon Jones had been hospitalized, and was undergoing deep neuronal therapy for severe reaction to Pulse. But he left his bed to come to the victory party thrown in Madison Stadium in honor of the tremendous victory over Konkon.

"I always knew you had it, baby," he told his daughter.

"It was Pell, Daddy. He brings out something in me, something more than boxing."

"What do you mean, Fifi?"

"I don't know, Daddy. I don't even know that it's something I can know."

5

The celebrations that followed the Konkon fight were spontaneous. It wasn't a championship fight. The Fijian was only ranked eighth in the world. But there was something about Fera's heart and about her man, Pell. Everyone watching the fight knew how much he loved her. They saw how deeply his passions went.

THE MAN BEHIND THE WOMAN, the cover of *Sports Illustrated* announced, displaying the photograph of Pell's contorted face between rounds at the Konkon fight. *Sixty Minutes* did a fifteen-minute piece on the vulnerability and valor of her drug addict father and Backgrounder friend, Pell. Fera was being asked to speak at political fund-raisers and feminist luncheons around the world.

"But what do I have to say to these women?" Fera asked Selma Ho, publicist for the Green Party and SepFem sympathizer.

"You don't have to say anything, dear."

"Why invite me if they don't want me to say anything?"

"People talk to explain things, to prove a point. You are the proof, M Jones."

Lana Lordess, governor of Massachusetts, head of the vote-strong FemLeague, came to visit Fera at the Fifth Business three days before the Zeletski fight.

"It would be better if we talked alone," Governor Lordess said as she sat on the overstuffed couch. Pell sat on the edge of the stone fireplace. Leon reclined in his portable electric chair, shocks jolting his thin frame every forty-three seconds. It was one of many therapies he was to try in order to stave off the collapse of his brain.

"This is my family," Fera said.

Lana Lordess was only five foot four, but her presence was large. Even if Fera had not seen pictures of Lordess on the news every night, even if the FemLeague wasn't the third largest party in the Congress, even if Lana had not personally led a march of ten million women in Washington, D.C., even if Fera had never heard of this small, overall-wearing woman, she would have still felt the power of those eyes.

Leon's shoulders jerked.

Pell stared at the floor.

"I don't discuss woman-business in the presence of men without having my lawyers present," Lana said.

"Then get the fuck out," Fera replied.

Lordess's security guards both stiffened. They were big women with chemically enhanced muscles. Fera knew the black one from the ring.

"Watch yourself," the black guard said.

"While I do I suggest that you count your teeth."

Pell snorted out a laugh.

A shock went through Leon. His head twisted and shook.

"I don't want to fight," Lordess said, reaching out with both hands.

"No, you don't," Fera assured her.

"Can we have a word?" Lana asked.

"My father always taught me to make my presence known from the first second I'm in the ring," Fera Jones said. "If you lose the first few seconds, he always says, then the fight is lost until you make up ground."

"I come here as a friend."

"You came here 'cause I won fights against men."

"That makes us allies."

"I never saw you out there with me. I never saw you when me an' Daddy were poor and down."

"But I'm here now."

"I'll tell you what," Fera offered. "You send the girl guards out in the hall, and I'll ask Daddy and Pell if they'll wait in the kitchen."

"As leader of the FemLeague I am bound to defend myself from harm. I cannot be left unprotected."

"Then there's no more to say," Fera said firmly.

Lana Lordess rapped her knuckles upon a denim knee, her dark eyes staring straight into those of the boxer. But Fera Jones was not worried. She'd stared down men who had threatened to beat her to death in the ring. They had tried and failed.

"The FemLeague wants you for our pinup girl." Lordess fell right into the discussion when she realized that she could not expel the men. "Women all over the world adore you. Your heart and spirit and strength are examples for all of us. Millions of women on the line between their false male consciousness and their true self-interests will flock to you. Join our party and you join a real fight, the fight for true equality and for sanity. We will stem the corporations, we will end the senseless starvation, we will stop the insane militias. Your help, just yours, Fera, will make the difference for the future of womanhood."

Fera had heard the same words, except for her name, on the vid three weeks before. They were even more moving in person. She believed in woman power. She wanted the world to be different.

"Will men have a political voice in your new world?" Fera asked.

"All qualified citizens will have their say over the condition of the nation," Lordess answered. "Honest, hard-working citizens will be our guiding members."

"I'll think about it," Fera said.

"We must strike now, sister. Now, just before your greatest trial. Join us and then defeat Zeletski, your words will be diamond."

"I said I'll think about it."

"Can I call on you tomorrow, then?"

"I'm in training, M Lordess. Talking distracts me. I need to concentrate on the fight."

"But we need an answer. Is there nothing I can say?"

"No." Fera had a dim notion of what she should do. But the idea was still totally submerged, rising only slowly, like a slumbering whale from the darkness of the deep.

"What if I could tell you the truth about your mother?"

"Ungh!" Leon Jones grunted. His head flailed back and a foot lashed out.

Fera and Pell ran to his side.

"We'll have to talk later," she said to the governor. "My father is going through deep neuronal therapy."

"Hear me out," Lana said.

"Leave," said Fera, a threat and a command.

6

"... I never told you about her because it hurt me too much," Leon was saying. "She was just about seventeen when she came into my adult school intro to history class. She looked all crazy. Eyes different-color browns, skin just a touch'a green under eggshell tan. Little and weakly, sharp as a pin. She came to every class like she was burnin' to know something, who knew what?" A shock went through Leon, and he bit his lip. "Whenever I tried to talk to her, to get to know what she was about, she'd shy away. If she hadn't had to sign up I wouldn't have known that her name was Nosa an Letona."

"Nosa an Letona," Fera mouthed.

"I told the class on the first day that each and every one had to come to my office to defend their final paper. I told them that without that they couldn't get credit." Fera dabbed her father's bloody lip with a fiber napkin. The next shock made his hands jump. "I didn't think I'd see her even for a passing grade, but she showed up. Her paper was full'a FemLib stuff. How women were the first citizens and how men tricked them over and over again. She talked about genetic plots and the purpose of gender. When I asked her how old she was she said she didn't know."

"She must'a known near about," Pell said. "Even White Noise kids know near about." White Noise kids, the children of unemployable Backgrounders, lived under the city, in Common Ground. Without taxpaying parents they could get no education and lived by their wits.

"She said that she didn't remember being a child. All she knew was an all-girl orphanage. When I asked her did she run away she said that she was there to talk about the paper. I told her that it was very well written and that I liked how clear her ideas were and how strong the language was. She asked did I agree with her ideas and I told her that nobody knows history—"

"—because history doesn't really exist except in the leaky jars of our heads," Fera said, finishing the words that she had heard from childhood.

Leon grinned at her memory and then grimaced from an electric shock.

"When I said that, she blinked, blinked like she had just seen something that she had never suspected was there. After a minute she crawled into my lap and put her arms around my neck. That's when I realized that she was hot. Not sex, but her body temperature was way up there. I thought she was sick but she said that that was normal for her. I'm ashamed for what I felt for that child but I refuse to be sorry. I asked her where she lived and she said in a hole that she dug under a bridge just outside of the town. A hole in the dirt. I took her to my house. What else could I do? I didn't mean to do anything. She was a child. She needed to be held, wanted it. I held her and held myself back at the same time. We never stopped touching for the next few days. If I let her go she got nervous and shaky. We ate side by side and even went to the bathroom together. It wasn't like sex. It wasn't sex at all. It was more like puppies or kittens all on top of each other all of the time.

"I missed my classes. We ate outta plastic cans. Finally I told her that she needed more clothes and that I would buy her some, but she told me that she had another dress in a shelter she had built just outside town. I drove her out there. I remember it so well because I was miserable in that car. That young thing reached out to my heart and I was helpless.

"I was wrong. I crossed the line into unemployment and lawlessness and I didn't even remember making a decision.

"The hole had been torn up pretty bad but only one thing was gone."

"Maybe it was an animal," Pell argued.

"But there wasn't an animal mess, and the only thing missing was her record book from the orphanage. Someone who didn't want her records to be public had gone in there. If she hadn't been at my house they might have taken her too."

"RadFems?" Fera asked.

"I never knew and neither did Nosa." The hunching of his shoulders was deepened by a therapeutic shock. "All she knew were the sisters and a book full of charts and graphs that she was supposed to keep with her at all times.

"She was so scared that it infected me. She said that some of the other girls had disappeared. Nosa said that when her friend Titania had gone missing she decided to go out in the world and look for her. The teachers had taught them that the world was an evil place and that if a girlchild was lost out there the man-demons would destroy them. Men would break them open and bleed poisons into their guts. Then they would torture them with slavery, brutality, and brainwashing. The sisters told them that a girl tainted by the world would have to be put to sleep in order for another girl to come alive. She said that a few girls had disappeared and that they were always replaced by somebody new."

"What did you do?" asked Fera.

"Well that was twenty-one years ago, but even then the government of Massachusetts, especially out in the west, was dominated by the FemLeague. I didn't know what to think and so I drove us to New York City. I cashed all my accounts and drove away from every bit of security I had ever known. I was forty then and it was the dumbest thing by far I had ever done. I had an ex-wife. I had a family. But I left all that behind. We were married. Nosa had you and then she died."

"What did she die of?"

"The doctors thought it was natural causes. You see,

Nosa was the product of genetic tinkering. She was grown in a laboratory."

"But the doctors who tested me said that I was normal," Fera protested.

"You are. One generation down and being coupled with natural DNA and you're fine. Better than fine. You're the most perfect woman in the world. You're my girl." A long thrumming shock went through Leon then, but he never lost his smile or his eye contact with the strongest woman in the world.

7

"My sources tell me that you are due to get ten billion dollars from tomorrow night's fight," Allison Laurie told Fera Jones.

Fera heard the words and understood them but there were too many other things on her mind.

"You know that I represent Randac Corporation. We aren't the largest company in the world, but on the island of Madagascar we're the big dog. We have five seats in the parliament and a place on the prime minister's advisory cabinet."

"So? Good for you."

Pell sat nervously at Fera's side. He had begged her to take this meeting even though she was due to fight Zeletski in less than six hours.

"Of course you've heard of our theme park."

"Uh-huh. Luna Land. Pipi and I wanna go one day."

"If I can get you to say that to the cameras after you

win the fight tonight, we will give you another ten billion dollars."

Even the haunted images of her mother from the three small photographs that Leon had kept dimmed slightly at the mention of so much money.

"Ten billion?"

"Paid in Madagascar, where there are no personal income taxes."

"Why? I mean how can you? I mean . . ."

"It's advertising, Fera," Pell said. "Millions of people will plan their vacation hoping to see you or to be where you were. You'll make it look like something really important if you just say the word."

"That's right," Allison added. "Women and men all over the world look up to you. You're an example for everybody."

It wasn't until after the Luna Land rep left that Fera remembered.

"That's almost exactly what Lordess said."

"What, Fifi?"

"That stuff about people lookin' up to me. It's almost exactly what Lordess said."

"Only," Pell pointed out, "Randac will pay ten billion on the nail."

"You want me to do this, Pipi?"

"It's not for me, baby," the Backgrounder said. "I ain't nobody in this. It's you. You got the professor father, the strength, skills. I just figured if you made enough money you wouldn't have to fight and get brain damage, you wouldn't have to end up in a chair like your old man. You could be somebody."

"Who?"

"I don't know. Anybody you wanted to be. Somebody powerful. Somebody with clout."

"You really think that?"

Pell kissed her on the lips. It wasn't so much a passionate osculation as a careless acclaim, a declaration of something that had already come to pass.

8

"Well, we're finally here," Billy "the Eclipse" Bonner said to UBA boxing fans around the world.

There was no blackout that night. Every seat in the stadium sold for a thousand dollars or more. Movie stars, political leaders, gangsters, Backgrounders, and thieves were present. More women than men filled the 120,000 seats; 750,000,000 people around the world had paid the one hundred dollar pay-per-view price.

"You better believe it, Champ," Chet Atkinson replied. "This is the most important night in the history of boxing. This is it. The battle of the sexes, the War of the Roses. Lady Macbeth and Don Corleone. D Day. Tonight Fera Jones goes after Travis Zeletski's undisputed heavyweight crown in a fight they said could never happen."

"All the regulars are here tonight, Chet, but there are some who never come to these matches. Lana Lordess, governor of Massachusetts and head of the FemLeague, is in attendance, as is the secretary of state. Prince Peter of Great Britain and Premier Hernandez of Cuba are also in the audience. They might do better to have political analysts than two barkers like us."

"That may be, Champ, but we can worry about the

world tomorrow. Tonight there's a fight we have to get through. What are the main strengths and weaknesses we should be looking for?"

"Well, the main thing is the body. Both of these boxers bang pretty hard to the ribs and liver. They're both good on the inside. Jones is the taller of the two but only by a quarter of an inch. Zeletski measures six eight and three-quarters. He's got a slight reach advantage at eighty-five inches and he's the heavier of the two by ten pounds. Moscow-born Zeletski has been fighting since he was ten. He has a good solid jab, a shuddering right cross, and a left hook that we haven't seen since the days of Joe Frazier. He's lean and fast and knows how to cut off the ring.

"Fera Jones is the boxer's boxer when she keeps her cool. She can dance and she can sting. Both gloves have knockout power. Her weaknesses are her tendency to cut and her temper. When Fera gets mad she throws caution to the wind, and that's a dangerous attitude when you're facing a wily opponent with knockout power."

"What are Zeletski's weaknesses?" Chet Atkinson asked.

"He's pretty good all around, but the one thing he has to watch out for is the mistake of treating Jones like a woman. She's a female, but so is the lady tiger. If he lets up at all it will be his downfall."

"How do you see the fight unfolding, Champ?"

The close-up of the boxer/announcer's face revealed the scars under his makeup, small mementos of his eighty-seven fights. There were blemishes on the whites of his eyes and one cheekbone appeared flatter than the other. He seemed to chew on each word before letting it go.

"This is going to be a tough fight for both boxers. Jones's new trainer, Pell Lightner, has no real experience in the game. He's a newcomer but he gives good advice. As you know, Fera's father is hovering between life and death at this moment at Staten Island's Neurological Institute, going through the preparations to receive a tissue transplant to reverse the effects of a decade of Pulse use."

"Will she be able to put it out of her mind and concentrate on the fight?"

"Only time will tell. But even if she can, it will still be a grueling twelve rounds."

The announcers talked for another forty minutes before the fighters were in the ring, and fifteen minutes more while a fight that broke out on the floor was being stopped. It was a full hour before the first bell rang.

In the years since, the first minute of that round has been discussed, watched over, and compared to other great fights in pugilism history. The only way to see it is in slow motion.

Zeletski came out quickly with his hands up and his jab pumping. He hit Fera's nose seven times in less than five seconds. Each blow jolted her dirty blond hair. Each blow landed because Fera kept her hands down, not protecting herself. Zeletski gained confidence and threw a left hook into Jones's side. The blow could be heard at ringside.

Fera smiled and waved her hands for him to do it again.

He did.

Fera flinched and buckled some but her smile remained.

The referee was worried. The announcers were too.

Zeletski grinned and nailed Jones with a straight right hand. While she fell back he sent a roundhouse left.

That was his mistake.

Or maybe the mistake was getting into the ring that evening. Maybe there was no beating Jones that night.

Fera moved gracefully under the looping left hand and then rose delivering a textbook right uppercut. Most analysts say that that was the end of the fight. The impact threw Zeletski back so violently that his left fist boomeranged, making his own glove the source of the second blow of the combination. The third, fourth, and fifth blows were left jabs, and even though Jones missed the following right cross, she followed with a left hook that Zeletski himself says caused the blindness in his right eye and the loss of hearing in that side's ear.

By that time the referee was jumping to save the Russian's life. Fera Jones's punches were so hard and fast that they kept the now unconscious Zeletski from falling. The referee had to wrestle Fera to the floor to stop her. Pell ran to his aid by sitting hard on his fighter's chest.

She threw them off, but by that time her bloodlust was waning. Zeletski lay on the canvas, surrounded by parmeds and bleeding from his ear and mouth. While he was carried from the ring on a stretcher, Fera's hand was being raised in victory.

And when the camera crews came to get her statement, to hear what was next for the invincible Fera Jones, millions around the world and some in the front row froze to hear her answer.

Sweat was pouring down the twenty-one-year-old's face. She was breathing hard and smiling.

"First I want to thank Diana for my strength and Legba for my man . . ."

Lana Lordess rose to leave.

". . . but this win is for my daddy," Fera said.

"I'll be the first to admit that I never thought I'd see this day," Billy Bonner said during the postfight interview. "Zeletski is the best we men have to offer, and you finished him in under a minute."

"It was meant to be," Fera said. She was looking into Pell Lightner's eyes.

"I know that your father is being operated on at this moment. You must be worried about him."

"I'm not worried. I'm a fighter. He is too."

"What's next for you, Fera Jones?"

"Luna Land. I'm going to Luna Land."

9

At three the next morning Fera and her boyfriend were the only ones in the waiting room outside the operating theater where Leon Jones was having brain tissue transplanted into his cortex. Pell had crawled under a row of chairs where he seemed to be sleeping.

"Pipi," Fera whispered.

The young man opened his eyes. "Yeah?"

Fera went to sit on the floor next to him. "I been thinkin'."

" 'Bout what?"

"About my mom and all those things Lordess said. About you."

"Me?"

"Daddy's always sayin' that boxing is just a metaphor."

"What's that?"

"It's when you call something one thing but really it's something else."

"Huh?"

"Like if I called somebody a worm or a germ or a dog. He's not really, but then again he is."

"I get ya."

"Me boxing is like that. They put me out there to stand for the poor girl who can't fight for herself, guy too."

"So I see you fighting and I feel like it's me out there?" Pell pulled out from under the chairs to sit by his lover.

"Yeah. And as soon as they see that the everyday prod and Backgrounder looks to me they start offerin' me money and power. Lordess did it, Randac too. They make it seem like they're the ones helpin' me, makin' me rich. But really it's me that did it, me and the people who wanted me to beat Zeletski."

"But you took the money, babe," Pell said. "You said you were goin' to Luna Land."

" 'Cause I'm through with boxing. I figure the money they paid me to fight'll pay Daddy's med bills and the Randac money'll pay for our new fight."

"What's that?"

"People look at me to fight and win because I'm a woman and men think they're better. People wanna see the underdog win. Everything and everybody in my life is that. You—"

"Me?"

"Yeah. When you saw the chance to get outta Common Ground you made it strong. Daddy's fightin' right now against the Pulse. The government wants to make money off his addiction and let him die, but he won't.

"But most of all I think about my mother. All she ever was was a prisoner. Trapped with those other girls. Made in some laboratory. But she still got away and made a life for herself even though the whole world was against it."

Tears sprouted from Fera's eyes. Pell squatted down next to her and hugged her head to his chest.

"That's what I been thinkin', honey. When people see me fight they feel good, but it doesn't help 'em. I keep thinkin' that I should get out there and fight for real, like you and Daddy and my mom. I could use Randac's money and the FemLeague lovin' me so much to run for some office, to go against the people usin' me to keep people sufferin'."

"Be easier livin' on Madagascar," Pell said.

"You could go there, baby," Fera said. "I'd understand if you wanted to take it easy."

"No, Fera," Pell said, kissing the knuckles of her right hand. "I'm with you down to the nub, down to our last dollar and dime."

She was the first woman to make a man bow down for sure, Groucho T, the Internet philosopher, said. *He never got back up again.*

Doctor Kismet

1 "Welcome, M Akwande," the monocled man said with a bow. He stood atop an enormous ornately carved dais made from a single block of pure green jade.

"Thank you, Doctor," Akwande said, nodding graciously.

"It's so good of you to come to my humble Home." There was a momentary flash of light behind the darkened monocle lens. Kismet's robe was deep green like his throne, its hem reaching his bare feet.

"Home is beautiful beyond compare, Doctor. But no place which serves as both residence and sovereign nation could be called humble."

Kismet descended the six stairs from the dais down to Fayez Akwande's level. Two naked young men rushed to assist but he dismissed them with an almost imperceptible gesture. Immediately the sexually enhanced Nordic teenagers genuflected and moved backward in the same fluid motion.

The monarch spoke.

"Less than fifteen miles in any direction, Home is smaller than many cities in size. Add that to the puny population and you have the smallest, weakest nation in the world."

M Akwande noticed that Kismet did not claim poverty for the large island off the western coast of Mexico. It was rumored that the eccentric CEO of MacroCode International paid a trillion international credits for the island, created in the great earthquake of 2006, and its claim of nationhood.

"Between the saltwater crocodiles and the patrols by land and air I'd venture to say that Home is the most secure nation in the world today." On his part Akwande was all in black—his loose cotton pants and shirt, his skin. The only flashes of white on the guest were his teeth, his eyes, and an uncarved bone pendant, about three inches long, that depended from a silver chain around his neck. The day before in New Jersey, his wife Aja had placed the pendant on him, a queen knighting her people's savior.

"Are you hungry, sir?" Kismet asked, his visible eye losing interest in speculation about his domain. "Maybe a drink?"

"A drink would be nice."

"Then, come."

Akwande was a tall man, six foot five by the old measuring. But Kismet was a head above that, maybe more. He took Akwande by the elbow and led him toward a wide corridor enclosed by forty-foot crystal walls. The semitropical sun blazed around them but the air was cool and exhilarating. Two naked women followed noiselessly. To the left and right were magnificent elevated views of Kismet's heaven on earth. Imported oak and eucalyptus forests, miles-long abstract mosaics achieved by flowers and multicolored leaves. The reproduction of an ancient Phoenician fishing fleet docked in the world renowned Harbor of Gold. There was even a small desert. To the right lay Atlantis, his capital, one of three cities on the island. The red and ochre construction of stone, iron, and glass was home to thirty thousand of his subjects. The buildings had underlying structures of Synthsteel and could withstand winds of three hundred fifty miles an hour. It was said that they could withstand a nuclear attack.

To the left was a clearing that contained drab green domes and long brown barracks. This, Akwande knew, was Sparta, the soldier city. Not far beyond was a circle of blue, a mile in diameter. There was nothing that Akwande could say for certain about the makeup of the Blue Zone, as it was called. Somehow Kismet had designed a camouflage for his research center that defied visual or electronic investigation. One could make out shapes and movement but it was like looking into a blue prism through mist. No one entered or exited the Blue Zone without permission from Kismet or the ranking head of operations, who held the sinister title of Dominar.

Wild birds and strange animals could be seen in the clearing directly below, through the transparent floor. Kismet and Akwande walked in silence for ten minutes before reaching an iron door. The young women ran ahead of them to push the doors open. They exerted strength that Akwande would not have attributed to ones so small and soft-looking.

His surprise must have shown because the doctor said, "Surprise is the joy of life and the secret to survival."

"Is that one of your scriptures, Doctor?"

Kismet smiled and motioned with his head for Akwande to precede him onto a large outside landing. He was met with an almost aerial view of the Pacific Ocean.

"It's beautiful." The words escaped Akwande's lips before he could stop himself.

"The view has that effect," Kismet agreed. "High above the world, looking at the mother of all life, feeling her power and her indifference. Here we stand as near as possible to understanding the truth of our mortal predicament."

As he spoke the women rolled in a table and chairs hewn from the sinewy, twining trunks of banyan trees.

"I've always believed that truth was a conviction tempered by humanity and the mind, Doctor," Akwande said, regaining a sort of emotional balance. "Not a thing."

Kismet smiled and the light flashed behind his monocle again.

"What is your pleasure, Professor?" the absolute ruler asked.

"Come again?"

"How shall I entertain you? There's a wonderful tenor residing in Atlantis at the moment. Also a portrait artist who may be the greatest talent in the history of the art. A painting for Aja?"

Hearing his wife's name issue from this monster's lips disconcerted Akwande. But then he realized that this was Kismet's intention.

"My wealth is all in my work, Doctor," Akwande said. "And, anyway, if I found myself on an unemployment cycle I couldn't bring a painting to Common Ground."

Common Ground, a section of every city in the world; the place where unemployed workers have to go when there is no other refuge. Beans and rice to eat and a doorless sleep cubicle were the bare essentials of those consigned there.

"There is no Common Ground in Atlantis or anywhere else on Home, Doctor," Kismet said. "Here is the home of leadership, art, and science."

"The leader being you."

The shadow that passed over Kismet's face brought both exhilaration and fear into the heart of the co-leader of the Sixth Radical Congress.

"Iced tea?" Kismet asked.

"I could use it."

Kismet turned toward his paradise. Akwande looked also, but his thoughts were not on Eden. Instead his mind's eye conjured up another garden, a garden of dried dirt labored over by skeletal bodies, cried upon by millions of dying Malians. Behind the ocean's roar he heard the hiss of a billion flies feasting on the open sores of human suffering. In his repose he thought of those he'd met who would never rise again.

The iced tea arrived carried on a silver platter by a nude and completely hairless black woman. Her breasts were full and firm.

Well fed, Akwande thought.

His eyes met hers but found nothing.

"Maybe sex," Kismet suggested.

"Excuse me?"

"Maybe you would like to see a live sex show. We could set the stage right here. I can supply any number of performers. You could join in if you wanted. All of my performers are tested and guaranteed for perfect health."

The woman still stood before the guest. Akwande realized that she was waiting for him to choose his glass. He did so.

"I haven't come for fun, Doctor."

"No? That's really too bad. Because you know fun is all that makes life worthwhile. If you can't enjoy life, why live it?"

"I prefer to leave that question unanswered, sir," Akwande replied. The tea was the best he'd ever had. He tasted pomegranate, citrus, and mint amid a floral bouquet. He wanted another glass before the one he drank from was empty.

Kismet smiled. His one eye seemed to notice everything.

"Maybe you would like a different kind of sex show," Kismet offered in response.

"I told you—"

"A white woman, maybe," Kismet stuck out his lower lip and moved his hands in circles indicating that he was throwing out possibilities. "A hardworking secretary, plucked freshly from her secure everyday existence, brought here and raped—for you. Ravished and humiliated—for you."

Akwande wouldn't have been able to suppress the laugh even if he wanted to. It was a deep and musical laugh that sounded more like master than guest.

"You laugh?"

"No offense, Doctor. It's just a sign of relief."

"Relief?"

"You are the great Doctor Ivan Kismet. Your corporations control the greater portion of the planet. Your Infochurch rivals Catholicism in membership. It is said that you can master any intellectual system in days, at most.

"And yet I see that even you are capable of misreading the human heart, that even you can misjudge a man's motives. As I said, I do not mean this as an insult. It's just that I had been told that I would be in the presence of a god. It's a relief to know that you are a man."

Kismet's monocled eye flashed twice. He studied Akwande, or maybe the images transmitted electronically to his brain. His body jerked from a small spasm and then he smiled.

"What do you want, Fayez?"

"Justice," the co-chair of the Sixth Radical Congress said, beginning a long practiced speech. RadCon6 had made a great investment of time and money to bring him there. Two men had died while on investigating missions. Fayez himself spent six months in a bug-ridden hotel waiting to be allowed a one-hour interview with Ptolemy Bent at Randac Corporation's maximum security research facility in Madagascar.

All of that and he had less than a whisper of a hope that he might be successful.

Fayez Akwande felt as if he had been working toward this moment his entire life. He'd always worked to free the minds and bodies of black people around the world. As an archaeologist he pressed to prove superior intellectual and scientific advances in ancient and prehistoric Africa. As the congressman from Newark he fought to increase awareness of the widening gap between rich and poor. And now, as the co-chair of RadCon6, he meant to engage the most powerful man in the world, to force him to bend his will for the good of Africa, Africans, and the African diaspora around the world. He felt that if he could turn Ivan Kismet toward his own goals, the rest of the world must surely follow.

"Justice," he repeated, "and the offer of our friendship."

Kismet nodded. A loud bird screeched somewhere nearby.

"You offer me friendship?" Kismet ridiculed.

"And the opportunity to use your power for history," Fayez said. He had more to say, but his advisors had suggested a slower approach.

"I do what I want," the absolute ruler said. "You would see that if you let me entertain you. The ancients struggled to make gold out of lead. I can make a dog out of a cat, a Hindu god with six arms, an advertisement for Flapjack computers lighting up on the dark moon. I don't need friends."

Akwande had seen the ad. Maybe the rest was also real.

"It's not love we offer, Doctor, but respect for you. Millions are starving—"

"I command more of the love and support among the people that you profess to represent than you could ever imagine." Kismet's tone was derisive. "The black masses have taken to Infochurch like bears to honey. My message that God is a riddle and the world of science filled with His clues has captured more imaginations than any King or X or radical assassin." He eyed Akwande maliciously at the last word.

"We do not assassinate," Akwande said simply.

"Three of your slayers were stopped on this island." Kismet clasped his hands together and squeezed.

"Not mine, Doctor. That was RadCon5. They believed in overthrow. I believe in change."

"For change, my friend, you need power. I am power—but I am not yours."

"Then why am I here, Ivan?"

"You're the one who asked for the audience."

"And you accepted. I find it hard to believe that you would waste time on someone you didn't have an interest in."

Again Kismet smiled. Again the flashes behind his monocle.

"He wears a monocle that's electronic, it has a light that sometimes flashes," Akwande said to the twenty-six-year-old convicted killer, Ptolemy Bent.

"When does it flash?" the lion-haired youth asked. Ptolemy's intelligence was accepted as the greatest in recorded history.

"At odd times. But almost always when he is posed with a difficult problem."

"And you say his weight changed after 2031?"

"Yes. He went from 195 to 202. I only mention it because he had maintained 195 for a dozen years."

"And when did he start wearing the monocle?"

"A year before the weight change."

RadCon5 had studied Kismet for years in order to plan his assassination. Later, RadCon6 continued the study, for more complex reasons.

Kismet also had a change in gait in 2031. RadCon's

doctors said that this was due to the weight gain, but Ptolemy was not sure. He told Akwande that he didn't know which leg, but one of them held the computer that informed the eye.

"It's the future of intelligence," the young man explained. "Chromo-circuitry custom designed for the receiver, and a highly advanced computer built into his body. A computer this size, five or six pounds, could retain nearly all of the information in any particular field with a faster-than-thought delivery system."

"So he's virtually omniscient?"

"The monocle receives information from either the computer or a remote source. That way he can also be in constant communication with his network. No one could outthink him, all other things being equal."

"What does that mean?"

"He might receive information that he doesn't understand. He might receive false information. But considering advances in AI systems that isn't very likely."

"Which leg would the computer be in?"

"I don't know. But you could tell by the way he lands on it in vigorous exercise. A little more of a jolt on the heavier side."

"You want me to ask him to do jumping jacks?"

"I'm just telling you what I know, M," the youth replied. "There's only so much I can do locked up in a cage."

"I know. I'm sorry. Keep strong, brother."

"I am a collector, sir," Dr. Kismet was saying.

"And what is it that you collect?"

"The fruit of human advancement, the best of the best of mankind." Kismet's use of the old term referring to humanity was a serious breach of good manners, further proof of his megalomania. "The finest art and relics of the pinnacles of history grace my lower halls. Atlantis is populated with the greatest scientists, artists, and artisans of our times."

"You claim to own people?"

"Not own, collect. We are very civilized about it. We supply a domicile and a stipend, all stipulated in a mutually agreed upon contract. They are free to travel and seek profit through personal endeavors. All I ask is to be able to request their labor at various times."

"And what does that have to do with me?"

"I want you in my collection, M Akwande."

"Me?"

"Don't be modest. You were a great coup for the Sixth Radical Congress. Without you they would have spiraled into anarchic disaster. It was you who redefined their political agenda. This after an impressive career in archaeology. And, if I am not wrong, you were ranked twelfth in the world as a Go master at the age of twenty-one."

"You are well informed, Doctor. But why settle for twelfth when you could seek out the prime Go master?"

"Ton Li. He lives on the island, of course," Kismet said, waving a spurious hand. "Boring fellow, really. He knows little beyond strategy. And precious little of that outside the confines of his illegal ivory board."

Ton Li had defeated Akwande in just six hours of play.

"I am not for sale," Akwande said.

"What if I told you that the scientists in the Blue Zone had discovered a certain combination of oils, rendered from three distinct legumes, which replicate, almost exactly from a combustion standpoint, the attributes of petroleum?"

"I would buy your stocks for RadCon and forget my quest for financial support."

Kismet smiled again. "If only I were going public. But alas, dear M, MacroCode has evolved past the primitive whims of the stock market. Our roots are deeper than any econsystem."

"Then," Akwande postulated, "I have no interest in your magic beans."

This response brought laughter to the would-be Tsar's lips. Never in any vidclip, photograph, or written report had Akwande seen anything intimating that the madman was capable of laughter.

"You see?" Kismet said. "Your appreciation resonates with mine. You surprise me with your acuity and challenge me with your observations. And you understand people. Why spend all your time on the plight of those most of whom do not even know that you exist? Help me to organize off-planet colonization. Make a difference in history."

The offer filtered past the radical leader's resolve. Unbidden, the notion of power came to him. Rather than fight for ideals he could create millions of real jobs with the flash of an eyescan. Akwande never felt at home among the fanatics and madmen of the Radical Congress. He did not enjoy a research of conspiracies and the poverty pressed upon him. He wanted a comfortable life for his wife and children, good schools and a woody lane. But his desires could not eclipse the fact that the Malians died, and others too, by the thousands each day.

"I haven't seen your famous tennis courts, Doctor."

"What?"

"Your tennis courts. The *DataTimes* says that you still play from time to time, between national buyouts."

"Do you understand what I'm offering you?" It was more a threat than a question. "I'm willing to run my faux-petrol project out of any nation you elect. I haven't paid that much for even an American president."

"I understand you, Doctor. The problem is that you don't understand me."

The monocle flashed on and stayed that way for ten seconds or more. M Akwande was pleased to think how many resources he was tying up. He imagined that somewhere in the mysterious Blue Zone, databases of language and slang were studying his question about tennis courts. Maybe specialists were being consulted. His own personal history was being scrutinized.

Finally, "Do you play tennis?" Kismet asked.

"As a young man I did. I was very impressed with the Williams sisters and how they stormed the tennis world."

"As was I. But I was more interested in their father. There was a man of vision. He created champions. Creation comes before all else."

"I wasn't very good at it," Akwande continued. "Tennis, that is." He was thinking about the nine months of training that began a week after he left Ptolemy's cell. Six hours a day of play, another three of special exercises, and endless hours of concentration meditations. Specialized strength-enhancing and flexibility-increasing injections, electronic acupuncture treatments—all paid for in cash or in kind. There were no electronic trails, no one knew who didn't need to. Even Aja was unaware of his scheme. The only evidence was a trace of body-enhancing chemicals in his bloodstream. And to cover even that, all of the leaders of RadCon6 had entered a quasi-secret training program where body enhancing drugs were requisite. They were preparing for another period of violence, it was leaked, and the leaders were expected to fight side by side with the rank and file.

"Yes," Kismet said. "You played when you went to Howard. Not a bad record, really. You could have gone pro."

"I couldn't sell you my freedom, Doctor. Such a betrayal by any RadCon leader would set us back a century or more."

Kismet did not answer. Maybe this silence was meant as some kind of threat, Akwande wasn't sure. But he decided to act as if it were.

"But maybe we could make a wager," the radical leader offered.

The ruler's one eye searched for the trick. "A wager?"

He's a half-assed gambler, XX Y, co-chair of the Sixth Radical Congress, had said. *He's always entering into contests of skill and knowledge but never games of chance. He'll bet a billion dollars against a blow job. One time he poisoned a dude and then bet him the antidote in a contest of memory.*

Who won? Akwande asked. He was breathing hard after an hour of returning serves from a state-of-the-art servo-master.

Guy fell on his knees and begged Kismet to ask what

he wanted. The MacroCode/Infotel merger was signed that day.

"A bet," Akwande said.

"What kind of bet?"

"The bean farms set up in Mali against my servitude on this plantation." Before he had come there Akwande was unaware of the petroleum substitute. But he had known that there would be some way that the CEO of MacroCode could save the starving millions of Mali.

"Go?" Kismet suggested.

"No. Ton Li defeated me once. Maybe he's given you lessons."

"How about a contest of knowledge about the topic of your choice?"

Akwande appeared to hesitate.

"African-American history, shall we say?" Kismet teased. "You did teach that subject for a while, I understand."

A moment's more hesitation, then, "No. I'd better not. My people tell me that you have the second highest IQ in the history of such things. Anything that has to do with the intellect might give you an unfair advantage."

Kismet's frown came at the claim of his second place standing.

"Intelligence is highly overrated," the leader cooed.

"How old are you, Doctor?"

"Forty-nine last Thursday."

"I'm thirty-nine," Akwande said. "That gives me a physical advantage, theoretically."

"You want to fight for your freedom?" The humor in Kismet's voice was chilling.

"In a way. I was thinking of tennis."

2 There didn't seem to be walls in the room they'd brought him to. It was called the Serengeti room. A woven grass mat was laid on real soil among plants that grew naturally. The sounds of wildlife, Akwande assumed, were recordings or computer generated. But the air—it was real savannah air. How could he create that? Akwande wondered if there was some kind of machine that excited past memories, brought them forward by the use of familiar surroundings.

They had separated after the terms of the wager had been settled. Tournament rules. The first to take three sets was the winner. If Kismet was victorious Akwande would move his family to Atlantis and agree to have at least twelve dinners and twelve lunches a year with the king, whom he would refer to as *sire.* Additionally, he would agree to work for the off-planet colonization project, which he had never heard of before that day. It would be his job to recruit colonists to sign away their lives on Earth in order to assure the future of the race.

"The *human* race," Kismet said with heavy emphasis.

Akwande wondered for the ninth time whether he should simply take Kismet up on his original offer. Generations of political struggle hadn't been enough to fully liberate his people. The weight of poverty, the failure of justice, came down on the heads of dark people around the globe. Capitalism along with technology had assured a perpetual white upper class. Maybe by infiltrating the MacroCode infrastructure he could bring about change. If he took the job he could ensure the safety and future of his children. Maybe he could create an off-planet black colony. Maybe he could build a support station in the Sahara.

For the ninth time Akwande rejected Kismet's offer. XX Y, the radical co-chair of RadCon6, had spoken the truth when he declared that "the purpose of our war is victory, not peace, not compromise."

For his part, if Kismet lost he would give complete rights to his faux-petro project to the sovereign nation of Mali. He would not attempt a hostile takeover and he would protect that nation against other corporate aggressors.

"And if I lose, Doctor—"

"You will."

"—what if I refuse to uphold my part of the bargain?"

"Do you know of Bjornn Svengaard?" asked Kismet.

Akwande did know of the Swedish explorer. His daughter, it was said, had been taken to the land of Home after Kismet proved to have a greater knowledge of ancient Egyptian hieroglyphs than her father.

Some months later, Svengaard had been found dead in a hotel room in Jakarta. The death seemed natural, except that the baby finger of his left hand had been surgically removed.

"No," Akwande said. "Who is he?"

Kismet smiled. "If you don't know of him my point would be lost."

When a lion roared Akwande jumped up from his grass mat. His heart was thumping. He could feel his muscles straining across bone.

He's trying to waste me before the game, Akwande

thought. With this realization came a smile. He allowed himself to fall into the deep patterns of his concentration meditation. The image of a man thrown from a ship in the middle of the ocean came to mind. He was swimming minute by minute, year after year. Swimming toward an alien shore or home, he knew not which. He swam over a deep slumber—exhausted, relaxed, and reprieved all in one.

The next morning, the hairless and naked black woman from the day before came to his room and informed him that they would be driving to the Blue Zone. She waited for him to dress and then drove him in an electric cart down a paved road through a palm forest.

"What's your name?"

"Eye."

"The pronoun?"

"The organ."

"Why do you humiliate yourself for this rich white man?" Akwande asked, certain that his question would disconcert and embarrass the woman.

"It is you who feel humiliation," she said, eyes on the road, more calm, Akwande thought, than stone.

"It's not me," he said, "stripped naked, all my hair shaved off. What am I supposed to think when a woman sits next to me like that? Out here?"

"If you want there's time before the game."

"You offer me your body just like that and you say you haven't debased yourself."

Eye stopped the cart and turned her perfect body toward Akwande.

"In the beginning, there was nothing but cosmic dust," she recited from Beginnings, the first book in the Infochurch bible. "This dust led unerringly to the multiplicity of God."

"I know his party line, sister."

"But do you know the sister?" she asked. "Did you know the Ugandan child whose parents survived the chemical baths rained down in the U.S.–Sudan wars? The child who was born eyeless and legless, with no hair and only stumps for hands? The child set out on a tiny wheeled wagon and made to beg from wealthy black American tourists? The child who prayed every night into the fiber line that goes to the great Idaho transmitter that sends our pleas to Infinity, God's fifth child?"

This was Kismet's genius. A direct link to God. A telephone to eternity. Actually, RadCon agents had learned, every prayer and confession was recorded and logged into what was called the Database of Hope.

"He did this for you?" Akwande asked, looking into her passionate and empty eyes.

"Yes."

"Then drive on."

"When do we get to the Blue Zone?" Akwande asked Eye after some minutes.

"We are there."

"But the color—"

"Is an illusion," she said, finishing his sentence.

They came to a stop at a stand of bamboo.

A man in a scarlet robe was waiting for them. He was short, white, and rather stocky. He had also been trans-capped. The top of his skull had been removed and replaced with a transparent Synthsteel dome. His brain was visible. Even small vessels pumping blood were discernible. Transcaps contained electrodes and transistors that could deliver impulses to the nervous system. They could also read electronic emanations. Transcappers could actually send and receive messages in a manner that could only be called telepathy.

"I am Tristan the First," the robed man said in a mild tone. "Dominar of the Blue Zone."

"Don't you think that title sounds kinda ridiculous? I mean, my nine-year-old would say something like that after reading a comic vid."

"Follow me."

Akwande followed Tristan and was followed by Eye down a slender path of crushed white stone through the thick bamboo forest. The radical leader regretted his bravado, but it was an unavoidable side effect of his mental preparations to play. A silent mantra of rage and restraint sang at the back of each thought.

A few minutes more and they came to a large clearing that contained two professional-size tennis courts, one grass and the other clay. Behind the courts stood a large wall that seemed to be made from solid gold. But this, too, Akwande realized, was an illusion. Mayan hieroglyphs appeared in dark brown relief at various places upon the screen. These hieroglyphs came to life and took on the characteristics of their totems. They traveled the screen fighting, fornicating, or simply passing through one another.

"Good morning, citizen," Dr. Kismet said, rising from a chair at the foot of the giant screen. "Grass or clay?"

"It's up to you, Doctor," Akwande said, suppressing the urge to add, *you motherfucking bastard.*

"But you are my guest."

"But you are my elder."

Akwande did have a preference, but he wanted to give his opponent a sense of control.

You could never beat him under normal circumstances, John Robinson, his coach, told him. *But if you play to his weakness . . .*

"Clay, then," Kismet said. "Last night I sent a representative to your home and asked your wife for this."

Eye came up with Akwande's college tennis racket.

"I had it restrung," Kismet said. "Test it to see if it is to your liking."

Eye proffered a basket of bright orange tennis balls.

Akwande hit a few balls and nodded his satisfaction.

"What did Aja say, Eye?" Kismet asked.

"Tell Fayez that I hope he wins," Eye reported.

Akwande wondered if the hairless beauty had gone to his home.

"Are you ready to lose, citizen?" Kismet smiled.

"Never, Ivan." The chemically enhanced glands of Akwande's body were beginning their strength cycle. It was all he could do to restrain himself from attacking Kismet physically.

"Scores will appear on the board," the Dominar announced loudly as if there were an audience. "Top and bottom of the screen will reflect the players' positions. When the game is over the winner's name will appear on top."

After winning the toss of a coin Kismet took the first four games on the strength of his serve. Another man might have lost heart, but Fayez Akwande, in the depths of his walking meditation, was aware only of the ball and of Kismet's legs. He managed to return a serve for the first time in the fifth game. A volley ensued and the radical leader fell into the hours of training he had gone through. He returned the ball to the opposite end and watched Kismet's easy gait on the returns. The absolute monarch was playing with him, but he didn't mind.

Akwande lost the first set in straight games. He lost the second set winning only one. But one game into the third set Kismet stumbled. He was moving for an easy return toward the front of the court when his right leg seemed to jam or stiffen.

Akwande put the next ball to Kismet's right side. Again he had trouble with the leg. Like a boxer going for a cut eye, Akwande made Kismet work his right side. Through the third set he won his serve. Kismet came back strong, compensating for a slight limp. The doctor lost that set seven to nine.

Kismet took the first three games of the fourth set, but that was his last hurrah. Akwande kept the ball a step away on the dictator's right side. The stiff leg turned into a slight limp; the limp soon became a stumble.

Akwande took every game of the fifth and final set. He tired badly in the last two, but by then Kismet was all but lame. Eye and the Dominar witnessed their master's humiliation. Akwande wondered if there was some sharpshooter in the woods who might kill him before the last point could be registered.

Kismet was trembling when they shook hands.

"You've beaten me," he said with equal parts of surprise and malice.

"Surprise," Akwande said, "is the secret to survival."

3 In less than thirty-six hours the electronic media around the world were reporting on FauxPetro, the new fuel oil developed by Blue Zone Enterprises, a division of MacroCode International. The most surprising development was the fact that MacroCode allowed Mali exclusive rights to production of the new fuel oil without any conditions.

"He could have bought into the British Parliament with a cash cow like this," Letter Philips said on that evening's *Last Words.*

One morning, a week later, Fayez Akwande bought his daily carrot/apple/ginger juice at the Good Grocer chain store near RadCon's Jersey City office. By noon he felt ill. Not sick, but utterly exhausted. It was only on the second day that he had returned to work at the headquarters of RadCon6.

"You look like hell," Rhonda Joll, his executive aide, said.

"Is that a way to talk to the man who saved western Africa, M Joll?"

"We still got north, south, and east to go," the unrepentant grandmother replied. "I'll get Malik to drive you home."

"Maybe you'd better. It must be the letdown from all that work getting ready."

"Is Aja there?"

"No. She was called away on that new job for Ocean Farms."

"Then maybe I should go—"

"No, Rhonda. No. I'd rather sleep alone."

"I wasn't saying . . ." the woman sputtered.

"Don't you get my jokes yet?" Fayez said. He found it difficult to sit up straight in his chair.

By the time he was standing naked next to his bed, Fayez Akwande feared that he was dying.

"Vid on," he said.

The small monitor next to the bed winked on and a man's voice said, "Vid ready."

But by that time Fayez was unconscious on the bed. A short while later the vid said, "Three minutes has elapsed. Vid off."

When Fayez Akwande awoke it was nighttime. He was lying on his back, dressed in a full-length silk Ghanaian burial gown, his hands folded over his chest. The air smelled like the savannah. He stood up feeling both refreshed and afraid. There was a lit candle on his writing desk. Next to that was a handwritten letter.

There was an electric tingle when Fayez first picked up the note, but that faded.

> Dear Fayez,
>
> You have defeated me. This is a rare thing. "As rare as dinosaurs," I usually say, because I frequently terminate those who thwart me in personal or business matters. I suppose that you think me a monster. I suppose I am. But be that as it may, you have given me one of the rarest gifts for my collection—the memory of a terrific con game. You beat me on my own ground, turning my greatest strength against me. For this lesson I will let you live. In the right-hand pocket of your burial gown you will find a relic of another one who challenged me. He did not fare as well.
>
> K.

Immediately that he finished the note, as if it could somehow detect that he was done reading, the paper crumbled into ash.

In his right-hand pocket Akwande found an ochre-colored envelope. Its contents were three small bones that once made up a human finger.

4 "But why, man?" XX Y, the burly madman from Alabama, said in an atypically high whine. "Why?"

"I thought you'd be happy to hear that I'm leaving. Now you can make the Seventh Congress the war council," M Akwande replied.

"I'm the one they want out," XX Y opined. "Everybody wants you, the man who saved Africa."

The RadCon6 co-chair ran his powerful fingers

through a full mane of coarse blue-gray hair, hair that was combed straight back and down to shoulder length. XX Y, chairman of the board, radical separatist, would rather have seen the world burn than give one inch to compromise. His eyes were holocausts of four hundred years of black suffering; their only promise was vengeance.

"Why?" he asked again.

"This world was set when they dragged the first African into a slave ship," Akwande intoned. "Like the child who sees his mother and father slain by devils wearing white faces. Like the girl raped by her imbecile brother in the playhouse next to her dolls. The heart," he said and paused, "the heart is rotten."

"Is it the bones?" XX Y asked. He had never liked Akwande and his diplomacy. He never followed the Go master, he never would.

"No, I'm not afraid. That was a crash I walked away from. No, I'm not afraid. But after I woke up and found those bones I went to the Infochurch that they put up in Newark. You ever been there?"

"No," the Lion sneered. "Never."

"There's five hundred workstations and service twenty-four hours a day. The hologram minister, Dominar of the Blue Zone, blesses and instructs the people on the usage of the terminals in deciphering God's secrets."

"That's a bunch'a shit and you know it."

Fayez ignored the quip. "Almost all of the parishioners are black," he said. "Those who aren't are Dominicans, Puerto Ricans, and poor whites. A couple'a people recognized me but they didn't speak. They just stared at their monitors. They spoke and the computer remembered them and started the lesson where it left off. Lessons in science."

"What lessons?"

"The force of gravity. The bending of light. The path of the living cell through evolution. Infinity and black holes—"

"If it's black then that must be the devil," XX Y interrupted.

"Yes, yes. Black for them is evil or random or unknown. Black robs the mind of sight. It is the collapse of the whole universe."

"And you don't want to fight against that? You don't get so mad that you wanna get a gun and let loose?"

"Oh absolutely I do, Brother X. I felt your arguments in there. I wanted to short out those lessons. I wanted to go back to Home and gut that Dominar. All of those black people kneeling in front of computer screens. Confessing their secrets, robbed of their greatest commodities, their minds."

"Then why leave?"

"Because . . . because I can't change it." Akwande was thinking of Eye. Her genetically crafted body, her soulless orbs. Her life for his, Kismet's. "And so I'm taking my family to Mars."

"Says which?"

"I've been to the master's home. I've been to the master's church. I live on his plantation. I begged him to feed Mali, to give them freedom. They took his money but it didn't buy their freedom. They just joined the International Economic Congress and put mercenaries at their borders."

"But you ended the famine," XX Y said. "You gave them the strength to make their own way."

"They will refuse our embassy," Akwande said.

"You don't know that."

"NGOs are banned by the IEC from any official capacity. You know that, brother."

"But even if it's true, even if they turn their backs on us, what the hell do you accomplish by flying off to Mars?"

"On Mars there will be fewer people. There will be a new world. Maybe we can have something there. Maybe."

"You just runnin' away."

"But I'm leaving the guns with you, brother," Akwande said, laying his hand on the revolutionary's shoulder. "And I leave you my blessings, too."

Angel's Island

1 Six naked men walked into the weak circle of light in a corner of the great chamber. They weren't manacled or restrained in any way but their hands hung down at their sides and there was no escape or rebellion in their eyes. Each man had a bulky sack of iridescent blue-green material wrapped around his upper right biceps. The sacks writhed sluggishly, resembling serpents slowly digesting their prey. There was something hard and particular in each sack.

"This is the new meat," Lieutenant L. Johnson said to the assembly of men. They gave no response. They might have all been deaf as far as Bits knew.

"Vortex 'Bits' Arnold," the lieutenant continued. "He will be number seven in your cell from now on."

"No more Logan?" a young black man with highly defined muscles spoke up.

"Vortex," the lieutenant replied harshly.

The young convict, who was completely hairless and who had no scars that Bits could see, lowered his eyes.

"And as long as you can't keep quiet, Jerry, maybe you won't mind taking him to the center for a fitting," the guard said as he punched something into the palm screen attached to his gloved hand.

"Yes, Lieutenant," the specimen of perfection said meekly.

L. Johnson was not large or strong, and as far as Bits could see, he wasn't armed either. None of the guards he had seen was armed. Bits didn't understand why six full-grown men were docile beside this paunchy and arrogant sublife of a white man. The only reason Bits didn't jump on him was because he was bound hand and foot and floating in a gravity chair.

"Get him to ChemSys," Johnson said to Jerry. "The rest of you get up to the plantation. We need the whole upper tier harvested before the typhoon hits." Again Johnson punched information into his palm screen.

Of the prisoners, four were Negro, one was brown and Asian—a Pacific Islander, Bits thought—and one was white. The oldest of the group, a lanky black man somewhere in his forties, showed distaste when Johnson ordered the harvest. The light of anger shone in his eyes. But fast on the heels of that anger came the jab of sudden pain, and then there was nothing—no anger or will of any kind, just resignation as he joined the herd of five moving back across the huge darkened chamber.

Trussed up as he was in the floating chair, Bits watched the men cross into the room. Before them, on the floor, ran a bright green line which they followed until they finally faded into darkness.

Bits was reminded that he hadn't seen the sun since his conviction for antisocial behavior. It was only his second conviction but the court nevertheless used its prerogative to have him sentenced to a licensing facility that would hold him until it was *scientifically proven* that he was no longer a threat to society.

They tried him in a Manhattan subbasement, had him transferred at night to the tube train that sped through its mile-deep Synthsteel tunnel at over six hundred miles an hour from New York to the East Indian Ocean. He arrived at night also and was delivered in bonds to the tender mercies of L. Johnson, orientation officer of Angel's Island, the first and most feared nonnational private prison.

Bits twisted around to see what the orientation officer was doing but he too was gone. It was only Bits and Jerry there in the weak light.

"Got a cig, Jerry?"

The big man grabbed hold of the handle at the back of the chair, which resembled an oversized fancy plastic scoop, and began pushing Bits ahead of him.

"Jerry, did you hear me?"

"No talk in the halls. Follow the pathway given and speak only when spoken to by authority." Jerry's words weren't the soulless mouthings of the zombie he resembled but soft warnings that chilled Bits into hushed tones.

"They got mikes on us?" Bits asked.

Jerry did not respond. He walked along just behind Bits's left side. The gravity chair, a product of PAPPSI—Polar/Anti-Polar Power Systems Inc.—floated silently down the gloomy hall. The strangeness of the interiors that Bits had seen so far had been due to a trick the architects had come up with. Only things that were meant to be seen received lighting. Doorways, signs, and long baseboard directional lights indicated where you might go and when you got somewhere. Everything else was black as space. The walls and ceiling, even the floors, were coated with a completely nonreflective material that made the inside of the prison seem like the deep of starless space. Every step taken was a step of faith. You'd never see a hole or wall that wasn't marked. Your feet fell on nothingness. People shone in the darkness as did any object not treated with the nonreflective material.

Also, there was very little, if any, sound to be discerned. Jerry's bare feet on the floor might well have been feathers falling on a cloud. There were no machine sounds or human voices or even the far-off echo of the possibility of life.

Jerry walked along for nearly a quarter of an hour as Bits figured. He'd asked the naked black Adonis all sorts of questions but the young man just repeated his admonition about silence.

"Who's this Logan?" Bits asked, remembering the odd altercation between L. Johnson and the kid.

At first Bits thought he was going to get the warning speech again but it didn't come. There was only silence and space.

"Com'on, guy," Bits insisted. "Tell me about Logan."

Silence again.

Bits was getting ready to ask something else when Jerry said, "Logan's my friend. We carried choke leaves from the upper to the lower terraces after harvesting time. There's always work for somebody who wants to move choke leaves."

Choke was the tobacco industry's answer to cancer-causing tobacco leaves. It was a golden aromatic leaf that made you feel mellow with no effect on motor skills and no cancer in the lungs. Jewel Juarez of the People's Health Watch had claimed that choke caused the equivalent of psychosis in lab animals after prolonged use but everyone on the net thought that Jewel was just a nut-broad who saw conspiracy in everything.

"He an' me'd make little soldiers outta the choke twigs and bring 'em down to Loki, Needles, and Darwin. Yeah." Jerry spoke softly but with feeling. "He was a puzzlemaster, a high planes resister. He proved that even the snake could get bit. Oh shit! Oh no!" The PAPPSI chair stopped moving forward, it wavered a little and was still. Jerry moaned. From the angle of the cry Bits thought that the young man had gone down on his knees.

Jerry's cries ceased and there was silence and stillness in the boundless hall.

"Jerry? Jerry, you okay, man?"

Abruptly the PAPPSI chair started moving again.

"Are you okay, Jerry?"

Jerry did not answer.

After another few minutes they came to a sign of luminescent green letters that read CHEM/BEHAV-SYS CENTER.

They entered the doorway and were flooded by light.

The brilliant yellow ceilings and floors illuminated by Sun Master light grids nearly blinded Bits.

A bulky black man in a pale yellow smock came up to him.

"Name and crime," the man demanded.

Bits thought that he was being asked and was considering a variety of smart-ass answers. But before he decided on one an electronic voice reported, "Vortex, aka Bits, Arnold. Member of the outlawed TransAnarchist Trade Union. Hihacking, first degree antisocial code number sixteen point seven."

"Violence?" the bulky black man asked.

"Not reported. Personal commission unlikely. Mass destruction possibility, antisocial, lethal dose pack recommended."

Bits was trying to understand where the voice came from. He thought that it might be a file that the man in the smock had accessed before they'd entered. But it was also possible that a microchip with all this data was stored on his PAPPSI chair.

"Take him to the prep area, convict," the bulky man said.

Again they were going down a featureless hallway. But this hall was the bright yellow of the sun. Bright and shiny and noisy too. Bits could hear the bulky black man's hard shoes stomping the floor. There were also mechanical sounds and music playing softly in the background.

They came to a broad area that was set up as an infirmary of some sort. There was a waist-high bank of cabinets and an operating table made from shiny metal fitted with manacles for hand, head, and foot. A square-faced black woman, also in a yellow smock, came close to Bits and peered at him dispassionately.

"Boo!" Bits shouted while doing his best to lunge at her.

He got the effect he was after. The woman jumped back, startled momentarily. Then she smiled.

"We'll fix that soon enough," she said.

"The justice department wants maximum on this one, Sella," the man said.

"They want it on all of them, M Lamont," she replied. Sella wasn't a pretty woman but she had a figure under the smock and she wasn't yet forty. Bits wondered how many women there were on Angel's Island.

"Put him on the table, convict," M Lamont said to Jerry.

Jerry plucked Bits out of his chair as if he were weightless, slapped him down on the cold metal table and shackled him there. The woman, Sella, pressed a button and the table moved until it held Bits at a vertical angle facing her and M Lamont.

"You may return to your cell, convict," M Lamont said as he punched something into his glove screen.

Jerry left on silent bare feet.

The woman called Sella and M Lamont went about with electric shears cutting off the andro-suit that Bits had worn for the past three weeks—since his arrest, speedy trial, conviction, sentence, and deportation.

"Why do they call you Bits?" Sella asked while M Lamont prepared a needle.

"What's that needle for?"

"Don't you mind about that," Lamont said as he jabbed the needle into a vein in Bits's right arm. "You just stay a good boy and this will be the last time you feel any pain at all on the island."

"Well?" Sella asked.

"Well what?" Bits said while watching Lamont. "Hey, man, what's that?"

"It's another needle."

Sella walked away from them.

"How many'a those things you gonna stick inta me?"

"Four," M Lamont said. "But don't worry, you got good veins."

"Why do they call you Bits?" Sella asked again from somewhere behind.

"Are you a qualified doctor?" Bits asked M Lamont.

"Qualified enough for anything you'll need, convict."

Sella approached them with a white enamel cylinder. As Lamont inserted the last needle she unscrewed the canister, taking out a shimmering blue-green sack. Bits could hear glass tinkling inside the bag. Four tubes, each of a different color, sprouted from a single hole in the shimmering skin. M Lamont attached the tubes to the needles and then wrapped the cloth loosely about Bits's right biceps. The cloth seemed to come alive then as it coiled into a snug grip.

"Ow," Bits complained.

"That's the electronic extenders. They go into the nerve system to read your reactions to stimuli," M Lamont said casually. "The pain should stop almost immediately."

And it was true. As Lamont spoke the pain subsided.

"What is that thing?" Bits asked.

"It's a snake pack," Sella said through sensually pursed lips.

"What's it for?"

Lamont and Sella smiled to one another.

"Should I show him, M?" Sella asked her co-worker.

Lamont cocked his head in a noncommittal gesture.

"Leave us alone for a few minutes," she said to Lamont.

He walked away from the table and out of sight. Bits heard a door closing.

Sella took a white metal stool from nearby and set it

before Bits. She sat so that her head was at the level of his knees.

"You have a very nice cock, convict," she said in a matter-of-fact tone.

Bits swallowed hard. He was only twenty-three and easily excited.

Sella pursed her lips again and blew against his genitals.

Bits thought that M Lamont was probably watching from somewhere but he didn't care. He hadn't been with a woman since before he went into isolation for his hi-hacking caper.

"Oh," Sella said, "I see a little motion there." She blew again. "I bet I could get it rock hard by just blowing, huh?" She kept blowing and at the same time she put on a pair of prophylactic gloves. "These gloves have a powder on them that's almost like oil." She circled the head of his penis with her right thumb and forefinger. He was fully erect just that quickly. She began moving her hand back and forth, lightly caressing the erection.

"Come for me, convict," she purred. Bits moaned as he felt the unavoidable ecstasy begin. But then there was a sting in his right arm and suddenly his erection went limp. He felt pain in his groin and up his arm into his head. The pain was like an orgasm itself, rising to a fast crescendo and exploding behind his eyes.

Bits screamed and strained against his bonds. The pain rose and exploded again. This time Bits went limp and quivered, thinking that he was on the brink of death.

Sella stood up and said, "Any more questions, convict?"

"What, what happened?"

Sella's face was like stone when she said, "You are the property of Angel's Island now, convict. No sex or violence or insubordination will be tolerated. The ChemSys snake pack on your arm can identify almost any antisocial behavior that you might exhibit. It also has an onboard computer that knows where you should be going and what you should be doing. It knows when you should be asleep, when you should be awake, and when you need to go to the toilet. If a question is asked of you and the truth monitor has been activated you will be punished for lying. If you have an erection in your sleep it will be inhibited. If you have an erection when you're awake it will be inhibited and two or more pain doses will be administered. If you attempt to escape you will be put into a coma."

"What about my rights, M?" Bits asked, attempting and failing to get irony into his voice.

"You're thousands of miles from the borders of the U.S.," she said. "And you have been forsaken. Until you prove that you are rehabilitated your citizenship has been suspended."

The supreme court had validated the constitutionality of citizenship suspension in 2022.

M Lamont returned then. He went about loosening Bits's bonds. The young man fell to the floor when he was freed.

"Anything else, convict?" asked Sella, who was obviously the senior of the two.

"Yes," Bits said as he rose on shaky feet. "I have two questions."

"What?"

"As fast as these snakes'a yours might be I'm sure

they can't read minds. What keeps me from giving you a death claw to the throat at my fastest speed?"

"From this moment on," Sella said as she poked at her palm screen, "you will receive a near lethal electric shock if any part of your body comes within eighteen inches of any nonconvict."

Lamont grinned, undulating his three chins, and reached out a hand toward Bits, who leapt backward.

"You had another question, convict?" Sella asked.

"Yeah," Bits said, standing straight and trying not to show how shaken he was. "How can black people be like this to other black people? How could you treat me like this?"

Bulky M Lamont chuckled to himself. Sella lifted one eyebrow and smiled.

She said, "You don't have that to fall back on anymore, convict. Nobody made you break the laws. You're not black or white, American, or even human, really. You are nothing and that's how we see you. That's how we all see you. Now go down this hall and out of the door you entered. You will see a bright blue line. Follow it. It will bring you to your next appointment. If you stray from the line you will receive a pain dosage. If you try to remove the snake pack you will be reduced to a coma. The third time you get a coma-dose you will not be revived."

He went down the jet-black corridor, following a thin but bright blue line that ran along with red and lavender and green neonlike strings of light. Bits crossed paths with one other naked prisoner along the way. He was a bearded and tattooed white man with a large belly and big muscles. He was following the lavender and orange line that veered off down a different hallway. When they passed close to each other the white man made a silent salute. Bits returned the gesture but maintained the silence. He well remembered what had happened to Jerry and the pain that he felt after Sella's treacherous embrace.

The blue line stopped at a doorway edged in blue light. The only indication that it was a doorway was the rectangular outline and the fact that the blue line stopped there.

Through the doorway Bits found himself in a bright, pure white expanse that seemed to go on, in all directions, forever. In the center of this expanse was a black desk. Behind the desk stood an elegant white man in a black andro-suit.

Bits looked from the man down to his feet. The illusion was that he stood on a clear glass floor that looked down upon an infinitely distant whiteness. He wasn't sure how the illusion was maintained, but it was very disconcerting.

"M Arnold," the tall man said in an official but not unfriendly tone. "Welcome to Angel's Island."

Bits felt dizzy. He was afraid to advance the twenty feet or so to the man in black, the spot in an infinite sky.

"Hey," the convict said.

"I'm the warden here," the white man said. "But you can call me Roger."

"Okay."

"I meet every prisoner when he arrives. I tell them the rules, answer any questions they might have, and then send them on their way. It's all very civilized here. The guards are unarmed, there's very little interaction between the staff and the convict population. Weeks might go by and you won't see one of us."

"What if I get sick or get mail or something?"

Roger walked around to the front of his desk. He was exceptionally thin but in no way brittle or fragile. He was clean-shaven, with patches of darkness under his eyes.

"There will be no communication with your old life, Vortex. That was forfeit with the suspension of your citizenship. There is no vid input here. No outside. There's you and your cell mates. There's me and my staff. There's work if you want it, and nothing if you prefer. No books or writing pads or church or time. You have been sentenced to limbo and the only hope you have is if we can scientifically certify that you are no longer a threat to your country."

"H-how do you do that?" Bits asked.

"I don't do it, you do."

"Yeah? How's that?"

"It's very simple," Roger said, waving his left hand in the air. "I take it that Sella and M Lamont have explained the rudiments of the snake pack to you."

In the far-off distance, to the right of Warden Roger, Bits saw something like a passing cloud. It was mostly white but there were pale blue fringes and shadows here and there to define it. He thought that this anomaly was the architect's idea of art.

"Yeah," Bits said. "It's a high-tech shackle. Like my own personal guard."

"Exactly," Roger said. "Every time the snake has to discipline you there is a mark registered. If you have to be awakened or if you have to be put to sleep, if you break the sexual codes or talk while on duty. If you approach too close to a guard or stray from an assigned task. Each offense is a mark on the main computer file."

"One mark no matter what you do?"

"Mostly." Roger smiled.

"Why's that?"

"Your freedom," Roger said, "is a matter of you accruing no points in a span of three years. Follow the rather simple rules we have and you will not be here long."

"Wake up on time and don't jack off and I'm outta here in three?" Bits said.

Roger smiled. He tapped his glove screen a few times. "Why do they call you Bits?"

Bits felt the snake tighten almost imperceptibly when Roger made his entry. He knew that the needles were probing him for the truth.

"Computers are run on an eight-bit symbol system. I developed a virus that would force the operating system to reconfigure itself in RAM allowing an external OS to control it. That way, with the slightest window, I could take over almost any computer system by translating it into a code that no one else could read or decipher. I used a simple two-bit differential to offset the resident system. Because I added two bits my friends gave me Bits as a nickname."

"But then all one had to do was pull the plug and reboot the system to get rid of your smart-virus," the warden said.

"Yes. If they got to the program within one thousandth of a second. After that algorithms would have been placed in thousands of memory devices attached to the computer. The only way to get rid of it would be to purge all data in all files associated with the system." Bits smiled. "It would cost trillions of dollars to abort me. No one was willing to pay that price."

"So you destroyed the intercorporate council's database of economic affairs because they wouldn't pay you to ransom their computer?"

"No," Bits said proudly. "I destroyed it because it was evil. Through that database they were systematically dismantling private property rights around the world."

"I suppose you know my next question?"

Bits stared at the white emptiness behind the warden.

"I expect you to respond to my questions or else a pain dosage will be applied," the warden said.

"I don't know exactly what question you have, Roger. It probably has something to do with how you can obtain my virus or maybe who else knows anything about it."

"I'd like the answer to both if you please, M Arnold," Roger said politely.

"I don't know." Bits ground his teeth, expecting an explosive jolt of pain. But it did not come.

The warden seemed surprised.

"How can that be?"

"Hammerstein, the memory man."

"No," the warden was incredulous. "A scientist like you? The Ripper?"

"My blood for you," Bits said looking directly into the warden's eyes. "The process isn't complete. I remember shreds and I've forgotten some things that had nothing to do with the virus. I forgot a whole episode with a girlfriend and many other minor details. But everything I just told you I read in *Worldweek*. Their science writer understands the system better than I do now."

"Could you rebuild the system?"

"Given years and a lab, maybe. But I'm twenty-three now. Math is a young man's game."

"The Ripper," the warden said shaking his head.

Karl Hammerstein was the Jack Kevorkian of the twenty-first century. He had developed a process that could erase whole sections of memory. Using radioactive dyes and a chemical targeting system much like the magic bullets developed in cancer cures, Hammerstein claimed that he could locate and erase entire episodes from memory. The process wasn't exact, and other memories—even facets of a personality—could be lost. The Hammerstein Process had been outlawed in most of the world. Only his hometown, Berlin, allowed the neurosurgeon to ply his trade.

Bits Arnold smiled a sad smile. "My blood for you," he said again, mouthing the anarchist slogan that he and his fellow revolutionaries had followed.

"Outside of this chamber," Roger said, "you will find a purple-dotted yellow line. From now on that is your color scheme. It will lead you to your cell."

"You didn't answer one of my questions, Roger."

"What was that?"

"How do I communicate with the prison staff if I never see them?"

"You," the warden said and then paused for a moment, "don't see us, but we see and hear everything that you do and say. Just whisper and we will know it."

2 The choke plantation was in a large valley between two mountains on Angel's Island in the East Indian Sea. For many miles the twenty-foot choke plants grew in rows, broad-leaved stalks that spread out from a huge silver and scarlet flower. This flower smelled like a sewer and shed a soft white pollen that was the base for cosmetics used by half the Orient.

All over the valley naked men armed with machetes hacked off the leaves, bound them with the tendrils that spread the root systems of the choke, and carried the bundles to robot-operated flatbed trucks that drove off automatically when their optimum load had been reached.

The sun hovered above the valley, red in the mist of morning. Bits followed his cell mates with an aluminum bucket gathering the silvery pollen bound for production lines in Tokyo, Seoul, and Hanoi. Even through the mask that he was allowed to wear Bits coughed mightily from irritant dust. Choke was named for its pollen's effect on the respiratory system.

Gnats, black flies, mosquitoes, and fire ants infested the island, but after one bite the snake pack developed a serum based on the convict's DNA that would make his skin anathema to that species' bloodlust.

Loki and Moomja worked carrying the bales to the truck. They were young and powerful, enjoying the exertions of their muscles. Loki was an American born in Sweden to a white mother from a black soldier dad. He was thin, with the mischief of his namesake in his eyes, when the snake did not drug him for insubordinance. Moomja was a broad Samoan with murder in his gaze even when he was being drugged for some institutional slight. Jerry, the boy-Adonis, spotted the men with their loads while Needles, Darwin, and Stiles chopped down the five-foot-broad leaves and wrapped them with root.

Stiles was the sole white man. He kept to himself and spoke little. Darwin was the eldest, at forty-seven; he had killed his own mother and never shown remorse. Needles was a drug addict. He stayed up past curfew every night just to get the snake juice that put him in a stupor and sometimes to sleep.

"They can't exceed the dosage," Needles told Bits on his first night with the cell. "They changed my prescription six times already. I figure they got pure H in there now and I still got my eyes open till about a hour 'fore wake time."

They crossed paths with workers from other cells at the robot trucks loading up and sometimes on the paths. This was one of the few times outside of eating periods that Bits had any contact with men from other cells.

The cells were isolated units on broad floors in the bowels of the island. There were twenty-five of these floors and on each one there were over a hundred cells.

A cell was a group of seven men who slept in close proximity and worked together. There were no bars to restrain them, as the snake pack and a circle of light proscribed their mobility. To set foot across the line of the sleep area resulted in a dosage of pain. To cross that line completely put you in a coma. After three comas you were not revived.

"Pretty day, eh?" Darwin said to Bits on the food break after four long hours of work.

"If I could breathe maybe it would be."

"Yeah," the elder convict said. "That powder'll be

comin' up for days. But don't worry, you'll switch off with somebody after a week. They can't let you work longer'n that. That shit'll kill if you breathe in too much."

"How long you been here, Darwin?"

"I don't know."

"Say what?"

"I don't even know what day it is, man. Most the time I don't know if it's day or night less it's harvest. Last time I was on the outside they just put a robot space station on the moon."

"That was over twenty years ago," Bits said. "You were my age when they put you in here."

"I guess so," Darwin said with a sigh. "Don't matter. I'ma be here till the day I die. They ain't never gonna let me be free again."

"What if you go markless?"

"That's not my sentence, brother. My mama had a red monkey on her shoulder an' he kept tellin' her to kill me so I took a shot at 'im. But Mama got in the way'a that monkey and she took the bullet meant for his green eyes."

"But that's crazy, man," Bits said. He felt free to say anything because of the snake pack. The device was so accurate in reading the body's chemistry that its quick response time made an act of violence almost impossible.

"They say it's psychotic," Darwin said with a nod. "That's why they're holdin' me for so long."

"Because you're too dangerous to live in society?"

"Naw. 'Cause they testin' me with the snake. It give me my dosage and I cain't get it off. If it keep me from doin' wrong, even thinkin' wrong, then one day they'll make it that all people who's sick will have to wear a snake to be free."

"Then one day we'll all wear them," Bits said with no irony.

"One day," Darwin agreed.

On the ninth day of the harvest Jerry was stung by a giant tiger scorpion. The venom, faster even than the snake pack, drove the young man crazy with pain. He yelled at the top of his lungs and ran out of the perimeter that defined their harvesting activities. He jumped and hollered, rolled through the ferny underbrush to escape the pain.

Three prison guards appeared, from nowhere it seemed to Bits. When they approached Jerry he leapt at them, socking one in the jaw and pushing another to the ground. He raised a large rock against the third guard but by that time he'd gotten sluggish. Either the scorpion sting was killing him or the snake pack was slowing him down. He fell into the brush and the guards hurried to pick him up and carry him off. It was all over in less than a minute.

"Just like ants," Bits said to himself.

"Say what?" Stiles, the white man, spoke up.

"The chemical stimulation," Bits said, still thinking. "Its immediate programmed response. I bet they got those guards wearin' snake packs under their clothes too."

"Why you say that?"

"To wake 'em up if they're sleeping. To make them strong or alert in case of emergency. It's the technology of production. One day everyone will wear them."

"Maybe the nigs'll be puttin 'em on. Maybe them but not the white race. We'll be pushin' the buttons and you'll be liftin' the weight."

Bits felt a mild chemical shock in his right hand. The thirty-second warning before punishment for slacking off.

"Why didn't Jerry go into a coma when he ran past the markers?" Bits asked Darwin as they rode in the back of a robot truck down the tunnel ramp into the prison.

"I don't know exactly," the madman said. "But when there's a medical emergency in a man the snake pack knows and turns off for a while."

"How long?"

"Maybe two minutes. But it ain't no help for escape. You got to be on the verge of death to stun a snake."

Every evening after choke harvesting the men were given a serving of dried soya protein and a square of chocolate-like carob candy. The men of color squatted together, while Stiles moved to his corner composing lines to a poem that he'd been working on for months.

"Who's this Logan?" Bits asked on one such evening.

The men looked away from him. He was still new and not yet received with full trust.

"This harvest be over soon," Loki said. "That means another six weeks underground."

"Maybe," Darwin said.

"What you mean maybe?" Loki challenged. "It's always the same number of days. Forty-two and then we're back upside."

"Forty-two times wakin' up," Darwin lectured. "Forty-two times goin' t' sleep. But who knows how much time has passed? They can drug you in your sleep, you already know that. They could add a day or even a week to your nap. They could take a year away from you and you'd never know it. Uh . . ." The moan escaped Darwin's lips and his head dipped. "They could, they could . . ."

Darwin lay back on the mat floor and fell instantly into sleep. Jerry lifted the sleeping figure and carried him to his cot.

Needles chuckled.

"They didn't hear him," Needles said to Bits. "His blood just got worked up. Snake pack felt his excitement and put 'im under. But that set off the alarm an' so a guard'll be watchin' us pretty soon.

"Yeah they got our number for the most part. You get too excited, feel the wrong thing, an' the sand man's fairy dust just fall down on your eyes."

"You say for the most part," Bits prodded. "Is there a hole to hide in?"

"Naw, man," Needles sighed. "Ain't no hidin' from these bastards. No hidin', no. But every once in a while you have a dude like Logan—"

"Watch it, junkie," Moomja warned.

But Needles just waved his hand to dismiss the threat.

"Yeah," Needles said. "Logan was a good dude, good guy, but he could be the coldest muthafuckah you could imagine. He was blood in RadCon5: assassin. One day, upside, he saw a guard twenty feet off. You know that screw's wife was a widow the second Logan's stone hit his head."

"Why didn't the snake pack juice him?" Bits asked.

"Because he didn't have no feelin's. For all the snake knew he was just takin' a stretch. Uh—" Needles held up a finger. "They puttin' the H in early tonight." Then he spoke to the unseen roof, "You need more'n that, Roger. You need a lot more'n that."

But Needles was flagging. His eyes were going in and out of focus.

"After that Logan took sick. Finally one day he was just gone. Poof!" Needles gestured with his hands to express the magic of it all and then he slumped over into unconsciousness.

Bits wanted to think about what he had heard but he too felt tired as the drug flowed into his veins.

In the middle of the night Bits came suddenly awake. He realized that he had to urinate. He sat up and saw a purple dotted yellow line leading away through a gap in the circle of light. The line led to a yellow outlined urinal.

On the way back he spied two guards on the tier just below. They were carrying a stretcher between them which held the nude body of a white prisoner.

Bits didn't slow down or allow his heart to race. He just walked back to his cell.

As soon as he put his head down he was fast asleep again.

—

After the harvest, time was the enemy. As much as eighteen hours of every day was spent in the cell. There were three forty-five minute eating periods when the men were herded into a great cafeteria walled in black. There the men from Level 18 could mingle with prisoners from other cells. Stiles always ate with the Itsies, International Socialists—Nazis on a world scale.

Moomja had a friend named Thomas whom he always ate with. Jerry knew a few young men. They played a gambling game with a foreign coin that one of them had found during harvest. The winner could keep the coin until the next meal, when the game would start over.

"How do you play?" Bits asked Jerry during one of the long idle spells in their cell.

"You bet on a number, either one or two," Jerry said. He had won the coveted dinner game and had the coin clutched in his hand for the night. "Then somebody flips. We take turns flippin'. If you bet one and it comes up heads, you get a point. If you bet two and it come up tails, you get a point—"

"How you know the difference between a head and a tail on the crazy coin?" Loki asked. "I seen it. You cain't tell what it is."

"We just decided on what was what," Jerry said. "The side got the star on it's the head. An' ain't nobody talkin' to you anyway."

"Anyway," Jerry said, turning back to Bits. "At the end of twenty-five flips the one with the most points keep the coin."

"What if there's a tie?" Bits asked.

"Then we have a play-off," Jerry said, grinning.

"More flipping?"
"Yes sir."

The cell was round, seven meters in diameter as closely as Bits could figure. There were seven cots spaced evenly around the perimeter. Most of the time Bits stayed in his bed. It was an unspoken rule that no one talked to you if you were on your cot.

The men, with the exception of Stiles, often congregated in the central space. They sang songs, told riddles, and made up long and intricate stories that they had committed to memory.

Time, in between harvests, nearly stopped. The days had no names, the hours had no numbers. There were no seconds or minutes, only spaces spent waiting for the next meal and the next two-week harvest. The only light was the green circle that defined the cell and a weak luminescence that allowed the men to see each other.

There was no physical contact beyond brief handshakes, because any prolonged physical interaction caused a dose of pain.

At first Bits wondered why they hadn't all gone insane. Why hadn't the men decided to cross over that green line three times and go comatose forever? Then he began to see.

The snake pack was an amazing and subtle device. It could read sexual excitation and violence in nerve endings; it could perceive biological needs in the blood. But there was more. The snake could also identify anxiety, depression, and even more complex psychological manifestations. It could keep a man from feeling claustrophobia even if he was buried alive, Bits thought.

Slowly, over time, Bits began to feel hatred. It was a new emotion for him. *Maybe,* he thought, *before the mem-job I hated.* But he didn't remember. All he knew was the spite he felt for the snake and its master—Roger.

The snake didn't keep prisoners from hating. Hate, Bits thought, was good therapy for a man who was buried alive.

He began having dreams about a long, green, luminescent serpent. It would be after him, intent on devouring him. When Bits saw the snake his heart began to race, and then—it was always the same—he would feel a tingling in his arm and the snake's flesh would evaporate, leaving only an empty skin draped over a grinning skeleton.

Every morning Bits awoke exhausted from the drugs and the unrequited hunger of the snake.

The only things that a convict could look forward to were meals, harvests, free days, and jog time.

Jog time was alotted to every prisoner. It was the optional daily regimen for aerobic exercise, mainly running. There were long black corridors with padded floors where the prisoner could run as long as he kept his heart rate within the range prescribed by his snake pack. The first few times Bits couldn't run more than ten minutes before he had to stop. When his heart rate fell below the appropriate cardiovascular level the purple dotted line flashed, indicating that it was time to return to the cell.

At the end of three months Bits could run for two

hours at a time. These were his best moments, the only times he felt free.

Three weeks after the second harvest a Free Day was granted.

The Free Day, Bits learned, was a random holiday that happened anywhere from seven to twenty times a year. On that fortuitous day there were movies and reading lamps with books and censored magazines; there was a music center for loud Jacker tunes and bedrooms set aside for health-cleared and consenting couples or triples or quads to have nonviolent sex together without black marks or inhibitor injections. Prisoners were free to move about, though only after reserving the time, down the many avenues of colored lights in blackness or up on the plantation grounds. There were basketball games and Ping-Pong and porno shows in 3D vid chambers that played all day long.

One of the most exciting events was the gladiatorial arena—the Circus, as Roger called it—where men fought nearly to the death. Regardless of all the control exerted by the snake packs and the monitoring systems, convicts still developed grudges that taxed their bio-limits and the more expensive drugs dispensed by the snakes. This problem was alleviated by these grudges being settled on Free Day.

The period lasted for twenty-four hours and was followed by a rest period of twenty-four hours more. Bits was first made aware of the holiday when he awoke to a flashing strobe of red light that woke all of his cell mates.

"Free Day," Jerry said, leaping up from his mat. He

was still limping a bit from the scorpion's sting but the snake pack had saved him.

Soon all the men were up and talking. It wasn't long before they were voicing their preferences to the void and were off following varied colored lights to their desires.

In less than five minutes everyone was gone except Bits and the white man Stiles.

"You gonna choose or what?" Stiles asked angrily.

"What's your problem, white boy?" Bits retorted.

"I do what I do without a nig peanut gallery if you don't mind."

"Why don't they put you with the white boys if you're so unhappy with us, Stiles?"

"Nuthin' I'd like better," Stiles said. "But they don't want all of any in one pot. You got cells up to six white men but there's still a nig or spic in the cream. That way they got a backup spy if somethin' goes down."

"And you're mad at me?" Bits said with as much sarcasm as he could.

Stiles gave Bits a hard stare and then said, "I could never trust you people. You were born to stab us in the back. It's you who took our good white world and made it into a mess. Raped our women, stole our jobs."

Bits paused a moment as if he were digesting the white man's words. But he wasn't thinking about what Stiles had said. Bits was a worldwide revolutionary. He defined himself as a class warrior, and though he suffered the pain of racism he did not exclude other races from his side. He knew that over 80 percent of American-backed prisons were non-white. He knew that crime by blacks against whites was negligible compared to the crimes committed by universities and corporations. But he also knew that he could never convince Stiles of their common cause.

"You and me, Stiles," he said slowly. "It's you'n me."

"You wanna fight me in the Circus?"

Bits pointed at Stiles and then at himself, then curled both of his hands into fists at his waist level. He knew that there were computers recording and deciphering every word and gesture, that the computers were linked with vid monitors. At the first sign of rebellion Roger would be warned and either he or Stiles would be transferred.

"Fuck you," Stiles said, which was his privilege on a Free Day.

"I want to go to a library if you have one," Bits announced to the powers that be.

Over the next few weeks Bits began to have a different sort of disturbing dream. He would find himself sitting at Roger's desk, in the faux open sky, doing math problems on a reusable paper-screen. At first everything was going fine, but then the numbers began to wriggle on the screen, becoming three-dimensional, growing red fangs and claws as they did so. They'd jump off of the paper-screen and chase Bits into the blackness of the prison's interior.

The numbers mutated into serpentine equations that breathed fire and crackled with electricity. Soon after the monsters appeared Bits would be injected with a sedative. But later in the sleep period the monster equations would rise again, and be squashed again. Each time the dream would unfurl a little further.

He was sure that this was no ordinary dream, that it was a message. But he had no idea what the significance was.

After many nights the dragons assumed names like Master Slasher, Ten-Foot Stamper, and Gutter Gutter. Bits began a nightly meditation to empower himself, allowing him to make friends with the demons. As he overcame his fears the snake pack's medications decreased.

After six months of meditation Bits managed to attain a dream state in which he could exist side by side with his monstrous nemeses. Like different species at a watering hole, the calculate-demons and Bits lived a wary truce during his sleep.

Both Moomja and Needles were taken from the cell in that time. Moomja lost over fifty pounds and spent half the time in the infirmary. He became lethargic, unable to rise at the waking hour even with the pep injections from his snake pack. Finally he was led off by a blue and green line which never returned.

Some weeks later Needles started singing an improvised song. It was a blues song with many repeated lines. He insulted Roger and the guards and called Angel's Island a concentration camp for freedom fighters. Needles sang until the sleep hour and beyond. In the morning he was gone.

Bits hardly noticed these departures. His time was spent studying the lifelike equations. Whenever he thought that he was unobserved he'd make fists at Stiles.

After sixteen Free Days, what Bits figured to be two years and some months, he was ordered by a bodiless voice to follow a red line until he came to his destination.

While he walked he wondered what life was like on the outside. He thought about his mother and brothers, revolutionaries all, and his father the cop. He wondered what Stiles had meant at the last harvest when he came close to Bits's left side, with the wind blowing in his face, and mouthed, *I'm with you.*

Had he understood Bits's offer after all this time?

Bits had tried again and again to beat the snake pack. He awoke at the right time and forced himself to sleep. He followed every order and never spoke when he shouldn't. He worked hard and slept in silence. In the blackness of the cell at night he spoke softly with Loki and Darwin and Jerry, and the new guys, Everett and Charles. He spoke to everybody but Stiles, whom nobody liked and who liked no one.

But try as he might some infraction always brought him down. Crossing a perimeter, breaking for too long at work. Once he veered too close to a guard and received a shock and a nova demerit which meant he wasn't allowed to accrue markless days for eighteen months.

After all that time Bits realized that he would never earn his freedom, that he was nothing and no one forevermore. His crime had been too successful, his threat ended his existence in the world.

"Cancer of the lung and colon," Sella said as Bits lay under bright yellow light on the silvery operating table.

"The snake identified it a month before it would have been irreversible."

There was the sound of success in her voice. Bits wondered, not for the first time, if carcinogens were entered into the prison food and air, if the study of the snake packs was the first step in a much larger plan.

"He'll need three weeks in solitary for the treatments to work."

"I thought the magic bullet took only two days?" Bits asked.

Neither of the meds answered his question.

He was treated in a big white room that seemed to go on forever like Roger's. There was a bed in the room and a console computer in a transparent plasteel casing. Bits received an aerosol treatment from gasses released out of four canisters controlled by the computer system.

When he was attended by guards or the meds, they appeared from thirty feet or more away, approaching like nomadic angels wandering a forever white sky.

Now and again Bits glanced at the computer, never for too long and not at regular intervals either. The vids might be set to watch for his interest in the computer system.

After three weeks of daily treatments he was taken to the infirmary.

"Colon is fit," M Lamont said. "But the lungs have not progressed far enough. Looks like a subbac cancer. A new regimen is indicated."

Sella nodded.

"Can I go back to my cell?" Bits asked.

"Yes," Sella said without looking at him. "You can even work. We will allow the cancer to grow again, so that we can tell exactly what it is. If it's subbac it won't take long. The snake will tell us when you are optimum for the next procedure."

"Another three weeks breathing gas?" Bits complained.

Sella smiled. "No. The next treatment is one shot and then three hours of observation. You may return to your cell now, convict."

3 "Catch a what?"

"You heard me," Bits said as he helped Stiles retrieve a fallen bundle of choke.

"What for?"

"With it I can break a hole in the monitoring system."

"How?"

"That's my worry, white boy. All you need to do is do it. But remember, nuthin' over three inches long. And you got to get me a fresh one every other day."

They were on the hillside and the day was beautiful. Bits had trouble walking because of a pain in his pelvic area. He hadn't been able to jog since being released from the infirmary.

He'd found a scrap of wrapping plastic from some guard's lunch on the truck four weeks earlier. He risked another eighteen markless months hiding the plastic under his tongue. He didn't care if they caught him though. He had never met a prisoner who knew of anyone being released. Some had been transferred to other levels, some had died, many disappeared in the middle of the sleep cycle and never returned. But no one was freed from Angel's Island because there were no real people there. Without nationality they had nowhere to go.

Three days after his talk with Stiles, Bits was ordered to report to the infirmary. He was so weak however that M Lamont was dispatched to meet him with a PAPPSI chair.

"You shouldn't be this weak, convict," Lamont said. "You're just being a hypochondriac."

Bits lolled backward and leaned over, hiding his left hand. He was happy to see his old white room, the trim little bed and the console computer, an XL-2500 Decadon.

"Get up and get in that bed on your own, convict," M Lamont ordered.

Bits did as he was told as best as he could manage. It took him a moment to build up the strength to stand, turn, and fall onto the bed.

"This won't hurt, convict," Sella said as she used a laser injector the size of a rifle to deliver the serum to his veins. "But I must tell you, the snake pack has diagnosed you with a strain of subbac cancer."

"What's that mean?"

"There's no bullet for subbacs. They're a new form of infection. All we can do now is try whatever experimental drug the IDA has approved for testing on prisoners."

"How do you get this subbuk?" Bits asked, but his mind was elsewhere.

"Lots of soldiers from the Mideast Conflagration of

'25 got it," Sella said. "It's made the rounds of permanent residents of Common Ground."

"How did I get it?"

Sella looked away and said, "How would I know?"

Ninety seconds, Bits thought. *When the time comes that's all I got.*

For the next hour M Lamont and Sella read the data transferred to the computer system from Bits's snake. The triple-chinned shapeless Lamont grunted now and then. Finally the grotesque med got bored, walked away into the distance, and disappeared.

Bits waited for what felt like an hour more before injecting the stinger sack into his left buttock. The pain was exquisite and instantaneous.

"Doctor," Bits said through gritted teeth. "I seem to be developing a hard lump on my left buttock."

"What?" Immediately she turned to the screen.

"Please look at it, Doctor," Bits said with the urgency of pain in his voice.

When she turned to look from the prescribed eighteen-inch distance Bits lunged and grabbed Sella's hand, squeezing so hard that he could feel bones snapping.

Before she had time to yell he said, "Tell me your access code. You have twelve seconds or I kill you."

"Sella-118," the woman gasped.

The count going off in the back of his mind had reached twenty-seven.

A red strobe flashed.

"WARNING IN OP-ROOM," boomed a mechanical voice.

Bits dragged Sella to the console and saw that she was already signed on.

"Tell it manual," he threatened.

"Manual," the woman whimpered, and a typing console with an audiophone unit appeared from the bowels of the machine.

Bits socked Sella in the jaw and began punching numbers furiously. The fire in his buttock was almost unbearable. Words began to appear on the screen: Vid access, Sydney, electronic transfer line . . .

"WARNING IN OP-ROOM."

The red light flashed faster.

Bits punched in 14-76T-1187-222.

An image of a green circle appeared on the screen. It broke into eleven equal sections. Twenty seconds went by, thirty.

"Bits displacement system active," a feminine computer voice announced. "Voice pattern Vortex invoked."

"End alert status of current system," Bits said.

The flashing light stopped.

Bits tore off sheets and bound Med Sella to the bed. Then he collapsed on top of her and breathed slowly while the automatic medicine from the snake pack worked to stem the pain and damage from the baby tiger scorpion's sting.

Later Bits located a tranquilizer pistol in Sella's bag. He made sure the gun was loaded and then ordered his virus program to summon M Lamont.

Stiles's eyes lit with amazement when he found that the orange and brown line he'd been ordered to follow brought him to a vast white room where Meds Sella and Lamont were seemingly unconscious and tied to the foot of a bed while Bits sat above them ordering images on a computer like he was a king.

"What the f?" Stiles said.

"We did it, white boy," Bits said.

"The fuck you say, nig."

Bits smiled, thinking that a statement like that would have driven him wild with rage in the world outside.

"Truce?" Bits suggested.

"What is this shit?" Stiles replied.

"The alacrity of justice," Bits said dramatically, "has turned wise men into fools."

"Say what?"

"I went to Hammerstein the memory man and everybody thought I was going to get my memory erased. But I knew that in his earlier experiments with mem-erasure the good Doctor Hammerstein only succeeded in temporary removal. I got that service. So when they asked me what I knew I could say I knew nothing because that was the truth. I got most of the memories back now. They came as monsters in a dream."

"So?" Stiles said.

"The scorpion sting froze up the snake pack and gave me time to grab Sella's computer access. I called a number, downloaded my master virus, and took over the system."

"That had to set off an alarm somewhere," Stiles said, looking over both shoulders as he did so.

"Only temporarily. My virus is sophisticated. It translates the current system to its own code and then makes me the master."

Stiles's eyes hardened.

"You know why I declined to meet you in the gladiator's circle, Stiles?" Bits asked.

"Why?"

" 'Cause I've always known that you could kick my ass."

"Then maybe you made a mistake callin' on me now," Stiles suggested, taking a step forward.

"Before acting on that will you let me explain something about this system?"

Stiles held up his left wrist and tapped it with a smile.

"Max screen three up," Bits ordered.

The infinite white wall behind Bits turned bright blue with thousands of small orange boxes broken into various sections.

"Population reports for Angel's Island," Bits said. His voice was greatly amplified and seemed to come from all around. Fear crept into Stiles's eyes. **"To the left are the majority of the inhabitants—convicts. Bring up Jerry Tierny."**

Immediately a large overlay appeared in the middle of the convict area. It was titled with the convict's picture and name hovering about a series of file tabs with the labels *criminal history, incarceration history, experimental studies, current status . . .*

"I can tell you where he is, what he's doing, his physioemotional state, and whether or not he has to go to the toilet. I can also activate any function on his snake pack, including the death option."

"Who's in those boxes on the right side?" Stiles asked meekly.

"Everybody here is wearing a snake pack, Stiles," Bits replied, though his godlike voice did not seem to come from his mouth. **"The guards, the chaplain, meds, and even Roger."**

"What chaplain?"

"We have a chaplain who prays for us regularly. He comes into our cells when we're unconscious in our beds. The board of directors of Angel's Island Inc. are Christians and they ordered a chaplain to be present at all times.

"He has a snake pack too; they all do. It's why you can't attack a guard without being shocked silly. The snakes talk to each other."

"And you're in control?"

"Do we work together, white boy? Or do you try to jump me and get put in a coma till I say you can open your eyes?"

4

Bits called a general inquisition with twelve convicts, chosen by the qualifications of their files, from all over the prison. He chose those prisoners not deemed homicidal or violently antisocial. He had six Negroes, three Hispanics, two of other races, and Stiles, the international Nazi, to represent the white race.

"We should kill M Lamont and that bitch," Lines Retain, a credit counterfeiter from the Twin Cities proclaimed. "They killed at least four people I know of. And if you let us see the files, Bits, I bet there's a lot more."

There were some grumbles of agreement.

Bits knew that almost five hundred research-related deaths—murders—had been committed by prison officials. That data from these medical experimentation deaths had been sold to research facilities around the world. But he said nothing.

"Escape is our only priority," argued Nin el Tarniq, the Eros-Haus pimp from Miami. "Killing them will just make the law look harder."

Bits stifled a cough and said, "The files are mine and I respect their security. I will not let anyone commit murder here."

"Who made you king?" Edward Fines, a fellow hacker from Cincinnati, wanted to know.

"I did!" Bits replied in an amplified voice that was loud enough to instill terror into the panel of twelve.

"When will the guards start worrying about us?" Stiles asked. "We can't stay in here forever."

"Not that long," Bits said in his normal voice. "But pretty long. Lamont and Sella sometimes have up to thirty prisoners under study. And as long as the staff doesn't know about us we can make our plans in leisure."

"If the guards all have snake packs why don't we just put them to sleep?" Jerry asked.

"Because they have families and friends all over the world. If they stop communicating that'll set off an alarm. I can control what's inside the prison, but if they send in soldiers we're up shit's creek."

After many hours the panel came up with a plan. The great cargo planes that picked up the choke every day of the harvest would be hijacked and flown to various ports. There, all seventeen thousand prisoners would have prepaid transportation to the destination of their choice.

Angel's Island had a large bank account from its choke crop and Bits was now in sole control of that wealth. It was decided that everyone would be freed regardless of his crime or disposition toward violence.

"If America won't claim 'em," Lines Retain said, "then America cain't blame 'em."

Bits would transmit over one hundred thousand C-mails set to a delay of thirty-six hours before being delivered to news organs and families and friends of the Angel's Island population. Bits also planned to send his displacement virus to every revolutionary organization he could think of, including the Seventh Radical Congress and White World Order.

"Who stays to make sure the prison is secure while we leave?" asked King Theodore, the cult leader who had tried to claim Delaware as a free state.

"I'll stay," Bits replied, rubbing a painful spasm in his back. "I figure that they'll have to take me back for a new trial when so many people get the news."

In the infinite white room, sitting in front of the computer, Bits imagined the guards and staff, even Roger himself, slumped into unconsciousness. The naked forms of Sella and M Lamont were there at his feet. He thought about the robot-piloted cargo jets carrying over seventeen thousand prisoners to major hubs around the globe. They had clothes, fake credit accounts, and fake passports based on their eyescans. Some, he believed, would make it to freedom. The rest would have a solid defense—they were no longer members of the American union and therefore not answerable to the justice system there.

"What are you doing there?" M Lamont said as he rose on wobbly legs. He reached out toward Bits but recoiled at the electrical shock from his snake pack.

"What?" Sella said. "What's happened?"

"We're the only ones awake in the whole of this island," Bits said. "And we all have cancer."

M Lamont's eyes went dull.

"What are you talking about?" Sella asked. "Why did Lamont get a shock when he approached you?"

Bits explained everything in a slow painful voice, ending with, "I had the med system duplicate the causes for the cancer you caused in me. The lab is open to you. If there's a cure we will all live. If not . . ." He smiled sadly.

United Nations forces entered Angel's Island on the third day after the escape. They found three hundred seventy-five guards and staff unconscious and unwakeable—victims of the ChemSys snake pack.

Everyone had fallen while going about their duties. The warden was unconscious next to his desk, men slept on toilets or in the long gloomy halls. Two men on guard duty had died from exposure up on the choke plantation.

Everyone else was asleep, except for Sella Lans and Vortex "Bits" Arnold, who were also dead, and Med M Packard Lamont, who was dying in the infirmary.

"What is it?" the doctor who ministered to Lamont asked.

"Subbac cancer," Lamont moaned. "We were studying it. The convict Bits infected us with it."

"Subbac . . . But that's incurable. Who infected him?" asked the doctor, an elderly Swede.

Lamont did not answer the question. Instead he said, "Bits said that he put a timer on the system. His virus will wake the staff and then erase itself. He said that by then I should be dead."

The fat under the big man's skin had dissipated. He was slowly being eaten away by the fast-acting incurable disease.

"He said to tell you that he had the system monitor our deaths because that's what we liked to do." And then Lamont himself was dead.

5 Three years later Fidor Esterman and Meena Tokit, employees for the Manatee Tobacco company, were sifting through the Angel's Island computer records. After an international outcry about the medical practices on Angel's Island, the Manatee corporation had closed the prison and remade the facility into a robot plantation. Fidor and Meena, both computer programmers, were two of fifteen people responsible for the plantation operating system, which included four state-of-the-art GE-AI computer systems, sowing, harvesting, and bundling machines, and various robot vehicles.

"Look at this, Meena," Fidor said. He was seated at the main screen of the central computing system.

On the screen a green circle appeared. It broke into eleven equal sections.

"What's that?" Meena asked.

"I don't know."

"Bits displacement system active," a robotic female voice announced.

"Oh shit," Fidor said. "That's the Bits virus, isn't it?"

"Downloading document Last File," the lady robot declared. "Download complete."

The green segments began sparkling and changing colors. The segments of the green pie swirled together, adding colors and definitions, until they formed the face of a young black man, made old by the ravages of disease.

"Hey," the man said. "I am very close to death and so I hope you will excuse me if I get right into what I have to say. I don't know who you are and you might not know me so I'll start from the beginning. My name is Vortex Arnold. I have no other designation because the United States government has nullified my citizenship and sentenced me here, to the Angel's Island private prison authority. You may already know all of this. I was able to send out a hundred and fourteen thousand C-mails detailing the practices here and the particulars of our escape." Bits stopped a moment to rub his left eye. A large, yellowish tear pressed out of his sagging lid. Bits took a deep breath and then another before attempting to speak again. "I think it was probably the largest prison break in the history of the world. Maybe . . . As I said, I sent out thousands of detailed explanations of this prison and its inhuman practices, with special emphasis on the snake packs that they used on prisoners and guards alike. If this is many years later, which I doubt, and you haven't seen my report, which is more likely, then there will be a copy available to you at the end of this transmission.

"I tried to send out a C-transmission a few moments

ago but I suppose the authorities have received my earlier communication by now and have isolated my signals . . ."

"Should we be listening to this?" Fidor asked Meena.

"I don't know," she said. "I guess we'd better. If anyone is monitoring our system they will believe that we've heard the whole thing anyway. If they ask us what it said we should probably be able to answer."

Fidor touched his large nose and nodded uncomfortably.

". . . my earlier messages had information that wouldn't have been surprising for most people. Maybe many of them would agree with the practices here. After all, there are no beatings, rapes, or dangers to the guards or the guarded. If you follow the rules then you are treated well, well enough for a social deviant. Even if we are political prisoners, what of it? The ruling system, one might say, has the right to protect its constituents." Bits allowed his eyes to close. He nodded, leaned forward, almost fell from his chair. But then he righted himself. "Protect . . . But I have done further study. The ChemSys Corporation has signed contracts with the federal government to supply over three million snake packs to the military and mental services by the year 2053. Snake packs used to make soldiers into drones, our mental divergents into brainwashed zombies. Read these reports and ask yourselves how long will it be before schoolchildren will be snaked. The reports are all here, at the end of this file. All here . . ."

Bits began to fall forward and the screen went to blank green. After a moment two gray option lines appeared. The first was called THE ORIGINAL REPORT ON THE PRAC-

TICES OF ANGEL'S ISLAND. The second option was THE CHEMSYS PROJECTED GROWTH IN THE BEHAVIOR MOD SECTION REPORTS.

Meena and Fidor sat motionless and quiet before the bright green screen.

"Can we delete it?" Fidor asked after a while.

"I don't know. The controls are frozen."

"How about severing the power?"

"The emergency systems will override," the chubby, brown-skinned young woman replied.

"What can we do?" the young man asked.

"Did you excite the virus with an entry?"

"No. I wasn't doing anything."

"Neither did I. It must have been the interaction of programs in the system, or maybe a timer that caused this action."

"So?"

"So no one knows that we were here. We could just leave. Come back later and report a systems glitch. Maybe even somebody else will find it in the meantime."

They stood together and backed away from the console. They turned as one and walked from the room.

The Electric Eye

1 Folio Johnson was sitting at his usual table at Hallwell's China Diner on Lower Thirty-third Street reading the *Daily Dump* on a tiny pocket screen. The high-res zircon imager was eight centimeters square and could display a maximum of five hundred lines of data at one time. Where most people decreased the display mode to eight or twelve lines per screen, Folio, with the help of his blue synthetic eye, read at maximum density. First he read the general International News Agency (INA) stories that the *Dump* supplied. There had been a 14 percent decrease in murders topside—above Common Ground—in the past ten-day span. The Mars colonization program was continuing even though the voters had made it clear in the monthly Internet poll that they did not want their tax money used in that way.

The *Dump* was an unauthorized news agency run by Pacific Rim anarchists and so a back story was supplied for each INA release. The murder rate in Common Ground had increased over 97 percent in the last three spans due to political unrest. This unrest had been caused, the anarchists claimed, by outside agitators paid by

MacroCode America. The increase in crime was used to convince the White House that an interplanetary colonization plan would ease the burden on the labor cycles and reduce the cost of policing.

"What do you think, D'or?" Folio asked the small woman who stood behind the counter.

"About what?"

"You think Kismet wants to make Mars his new home?"

"You readin' that *Dump* again? One day they're gonna put you in the ground over that shit."

"Haven't you ever heard of freedom of the press?"

"They got prisons offshore that link you up to a chemical bag can make you into jelly if you sneeze outta turn," D'or said. "That's what I heard."

D'or Hallwell's blond-gray hair went straight out from her head, making her look quite mad. She wore a black T-shirt and a long, dark brown skirt every day while serving Chinese-American food to anyone who stopped by her eight-seat hole-in-the-wall.

"You scared, D'or?"

"Fear is the tenth intelligence quotient," she said. "All the scientists say so. The more you're scared of what can hurt you, the smarter you are."

"Then I must be a la-la fool and you my face in the mirror."

The small restaurateur shook her head and smiled. Johnson mimicked her movements and expression. She moved her head to the right and Folio matched it with a leftward nod. When she put her hands to her head he followed suit. Then they both laughed.

"Excuse me," a man said.

Folio and D'or both turned to the door.

A slender young man stood there in a black and yellow checkered andro-suit with no blouse or tam. His skin was pale and his blond hair so fine that it set Folio's teeth on edge.

"Bok choy, tofu, and oyster sauce is all I got today, M," D'or said without apology. "Chicken and frog strike'll last at least another twenty-four."

"Are you M Johnson?" the blond man asked. "The investigator?"

D'or turned away and walked through a door that led to the kitchen.

"Who's askin'?" was Folio's reply.

The man approached the detective's table and sat down, uninvited.

"A man named Lorenzo gave me your name for fifty general credits. I need someone to do something for me. He said that you were my man."

Folio's blue eye had already searched the man for eavesdropping devices. Now he was probing for anything else: the influence of drugs, rapid heartbeats, or synthetic implants. All he perceived was synthol and lime flavoring, a lot of it. It was surprising this man could stand up or compose a coherent sentence.

"Well?" asked the drunk. "Are you M Johnson?"

"What's your name?"

"Spellman. Charles Spellman. I live on Upper Park, at a Hundred and Third."

"So, M Spellman, what did you tell this Lorenzo?"

"Are you Folio Johnson?"

"I, M Spellman, am an unaffiliated citizen. Not from Common Ground and not off the employment cycle. This is my office and the woman who owns this restaurant is my friend. It's one of only five independently owned restaurants in all the Twelve Fiefs of New York."

"I don't understand you."

"I'm not really here. Neither is this bistro. If you have something to say then say it"—Folio Johnson fluttered his fingers—"to the air. But don't ask any questions. Save them for the upper avenues."

"I don't . . ." Charles Spellman said and then he stopped. "I mean, I understand what you're saying. I mean, I am on the employment cycle, though I've been lucky enough to avoid Common Ground. But I belong to a club. We call ourselves the Seekers. It's ten guys, only guys, who get together now and then to exercise our minds."

Johnson's blue eye was busy searching the public databanks for Charles Spellman and his men's club.

"Um," Spellman said when he realized that the private detective wasn't going to ask anything, "we get together, like I said, and talk about ideas. We come from all kinds of different business backgrounds. I lease and insure ancient Greek artifacts. Coins, busts, earthenware. Regular kinda stuff. Mostly I deal with interior decorators for corporations but I also have a few private clients . . ." Again Charles Spellman paused, expecting some kind of question.

Johnson silently went through the e-docs that described Spellman's service, Alexander's Bounty. He had customers around the world and offices on Middle West Broadway, Lefrak Avenue, and Rodeo Drive. He was an employee but his cousin Mylo Spellman owned the business.

"The others do different things. Leonard Li is an accountant for Mobil Fuels and Brenton Thyme makes lenses for space exploration. Do you need to know more?"

"I don't need to know anything, M," Johnson said. "And nothing so far has been important enough to say."

"The Seekers ask questions, like I said," Spellman continued. "Sometimes we ask theoretical questions about physics or genetics. Sometimes there are social questions, like for instance Does labor define citizenship?" The antique dealer seemed to think that this last question might get a rise out of Johnson, but when Folio didn't respond he continued, "There is a theory that the right combination of bright minds can yield genius if the group maintains both rigor and sociable relations. It's like playing the lottery, only with the contents of our minds, you see?"

"Uh-huh. Somebody lost his mind and you need someone to go find it?"

"Somebody's been killing us, one by one."

"Who?" Unconsciously Johnson leaned forward, blue gleaming from his black and angular face.

"I don't know. First it was Laddie McCoy, two months ago while he was taking a midnight job on the arch above Central Park."

"They said it was White Noise thugs who wanted his pocket med-computer," Folio read from a report downloaded into his eye.

"How do you know that?" Spellman asked.

"I read the paper every day." While he spoke his eye searched for the identities of the unemployed muggers but there was no record of an arrest.

"Bill Heinz was killed eight days later," Spellman said. "They dropped a chunk of Upper Broadway on his head."

"I remember that one too. Four people got killed. They were working on the new DanceDome."

"Derrick James was killed by a freaked-out prostitute that he had been seeing for the last nine years. The guy picked up Derry and threw him out of the three hundred twenty-seventh floor of the IBC building."

"Was the tramp usin' drugs?"

"He was a divinity student," Spellman said. "He only had three clients and wouldn't even drink synth."

Johnson was reading about James and Heinz in the back of his eye. The images of the dead, published by INA, superimposed themselves on his pale would-be client.

"My cousin Mylo died from an infection he picked up at the hospital they put him in after getting an AIDS booster. He got the virus from his mother, at birth you know, but everything was fine, he just needed to keep up the treatments. But something about the serum reacted with the hive and he got weak. They kept him overnight and suddenly he came down with a blood infection. That was okay too, they said, only the doctor prescribed the wrong ABs and before they knew what was going on his fever shot up to one oh nine and he died."

"You said there's ten of you?"

Spellman nodded.

Johnson asked his blue eye what were the chances of four out of ten members of one club dying separately, and unexpectedly, in such a short span of time. The odds would have bought him a condo on Dr. Kismet's island Home.

"Okay," he said. "You got a story there. Four more or less healthy young men out of fifty-seven million in Greater New York, who know each other, die in a few days. That's not natural, that there's man-made, I agree. So what do you want from me?"

"I want to know why and who, hopefully before they kill me, too." Spellman's words were tough but, Folio thought, bolstered by the synth.

"It's a tight fit, Charles. A conspiracy of some sort. What were you guys inventing that would scare somebody into this?"

"We aren't inventors. I mean, we don't work with electrics or chemicals or anything like that. We thought that that kind of work would slow down the process of pure thought. It's all just ideas, notions. Like at our last meeting, Brenton asked if we made a pole maybe ten million miles long and then push it from one end so that ten million miles away a glass was knocked over, would that act exceed the speed of light? You see, if the pole moved as one unit, the glass would be knocked over almost simultaneously, in less than a second." The young blond man lifted his head with pride.

"That's the kinda stuff you expect to get you rich?" Johnson asked.

"Well, maybe it's not so smart, but that's the process of invention. You use your mind."

Johnson's blue eye was covering all available data through a wireless transmitting station embedded in the prosthetic baby finger of his left hand.

"Is this club of yours registered under the name Seekers?"

"No. We're not registered."

"Why not? It is the law that all intellectual property be catalogued with the feds."

"We were worried that the government would sequester our ideas."

"They only do that if the ideas are dangerous. Were any of your ideas threats?"

"No. No. Just things like that pole and some political questions. But most of them were pretty conservative. I mean, nine of us are International Socialists."

Johnson put his fingers together, making a tent under his blue and brown eyes. D'or came in with two steaming plates of bok choy and tofu under gleaming sheaths of oyster sauce. Spellman put up a hand to wave away the food but D'or ignored him. Folio accepted his serving and bided his time using his blue eye to map molecular patterns in the steam. He considered the young man in front of him.

"What brought you guys together?" he asked at last.

"What do you mean?"

"How did you meet? How did you get together?"

"About half of us knew each other from school. Trent State. Lenny Li and Brenton both went there, and me and Mylo. Laddie did too. Mylo knew Billy from boarding school and Laddie was my friend from the gym. He was a lawyer for IBC. I think Derrick was a friend of Mingus."

"Who is Mingus?"

"Mingus Black, he worked with Derry for a while. A real success story. You know, black, Backgrounder parents—but he worked his way topside and made it as a lawyer. Now he's into buying up leases for Red Raven Enterprises mainly, he really works it. He was one of the four guys who bought up the Tokyo leases and moved those half million Kenyans to Japan."

"Who else?"

"Fonti Timmerman and Azuma Sherman."

"They from Trent?"

"Azuma went there one year and then transferred to Harvard. He did a leverage with Laddie at Macso. It was a real beauty too—"

"What about Fonti?"

"Him and Brenton were friends. He's just a programmer but he's real smart and he knows how to read crystal code. He went to City College."

As the pale antique dealer gave names, Folio recorded them off the Ether with his blue eye and baby finger. He didn't read the whole files into his mind because he was concentrating on what the kid had to say.

"No Jews," Johnson said.

"What?"

"No Jews among your group."

"Is that a problem?"

"Just an observation."

"There are no Jews in International Socialism. Zionism is incompatible with social evolution."

"You got a black kid in there," the detective suggested.

"We're not racist, we're modernists in the modern world."

"Then why not go all the way and accept Jews who agree with your beliefs?"

"A Jew can never fully accept International Socialism," certainty worked its way into the wan kid's words, "because of the deep symbolic knowledge his people have hoarded over the last six thousand years. They can never give up their primitive notions of how the world should be organized."

"No place for them?" Johnson asked.

"Not in our group."

For a moment the detective considered refusing to help the kid. *Why bother saving this fool?* he thought. But then he remembered that he'd been sleeping behind D'or's counter for the past eight days and that his store of general credits was almost depleted.

"Five thousand credits and you'll have to move out of your apartment."

"What?" Charles Spellman half rose from his chair.

". . . down into Common Ground, that's right."

"Are you crazy?"

"Listen, kid. You're in the middle of a full-fledged murder spree here. The cops are obviously coverin' it up because they never caught those muggers—and the cops catch everybody they want to catch. It takes a lotta money to rig an accident like that cave-in on Upper Broadway and more than that to make it look like an architectural flaw. The only reason you're not dead is 'cause they haven't gotten to your name yet. If they did you all at once somebody like the *Daily Dump* might pick up on it. I know a guy can make you a fake ID that'll put you under and safe until I can get a handle on who's doin' what and why."

"There's no fake ID in the world that can beat the Molecular Tester Device," Spellman said. Johnson noticed that he was looking even paler than when he'd walked in.

"You think they suspect people of sneakin' *into* Common Ground? They don't care. They don't check. Anybody off of the cycle is welcome into hell."

"I can't just vacate my place. I have responsibilities."

"You call in sick. I'll stay in your hole. Maybe someone'll try and check you out. That's my best bet for a clue."

"When?"

"Right now. We go to the bank and then to my friend.

After that you take the Develator to Common Ground and stay there until you hear from me."

The fear in the kid's eyes delighted Johnson. He stood to his full six foot seven height, towering over the frightened fascist. He was happy to cause the young man pain, but he was happier to have a bed to sleep in and five thousand creds on his wild card.

2 "You wanna take some more vig and do me again, baby?" Tana Lynn whispered in Folio Johnson's ear.

"Again?" he moaned. "Honey, thatta be seven times. I'ma start comin' red if I do that shit again."

"It'd only be six," the ecstasy girl said, pouting. "And I love it when you make that little noise like you were crying."

"Next time I'll put on the rec-chip and you can listen to that while I heal."

"Can we get somethin' to eat, then?" Tana asked.

"Order whatever you want," Folio said, crawling out of the great round bed. "But charge it to the apartment. I don't want to spend my cash."

She had fine features and dark skin, blond hair, and green eyes. When Folio had met her at the West Side DanceDome a few days earlier, he thought she was an Egyptian heretic. But when he took her out that night she'd told him that she was Ethiopian.

"They kept us in a field outside Addis Ababa," she'd told him, "but then a Peace Corps guy named Lampton put me in a bag and brought me here. By the time I turned eleven he wasn't attracted to me anymore and gave me to this guy named Jim. Jim put me to work cleaning his sister's house and his. It wasn't so bad, really. They let me study and I learned commodities trading. It was kinda weird, 'cause the day I moved out to my new place Jim told me that Lampton had paid him to kill me."

After Tana ate she went to sleep. Johnson sat out on the deck of Charles Spellman's two-hundred-first-floor apartment. He stared at the red-tinged night sky and studied the information provided by his excellent eye.

He had downloaded the information of all ten Seekers while talking to Spellman, but absorbing that information into his brain took time. It was especially hard because the men had lived such boring lives. Everyone but Mingus, the black Backgrounder, was completely unremarkable.

After an hour he went back into the apartment. The entertainment room's lasers were on. A 3D image of a shifting moonscape was being projected. The usual noise dampeners that this image used to simulate the silence of space weren't engaged, or Folio wouldn't have heard her from the bedroom. At first he thought that she'd gotten tired of waiting and was masturbating to take the edge off the vig she'd taken.

He peeked around the corner of the door to see if she wanted him to join in.

The man in the skin-tight glossy emerald one-piece had his hands around her throat. Tana was struggling but weakly. The detective had his knife out in a heartbeat. The targeting system of the eye was instantaneous, and so the hurtling blade severed the assassin's spine in less than a second after Folio had seen him.

The Ethiopian's eyes were bloodred but she was breathing and semiconscious. The dead man was white, with long, micro-braided eyebrows. Folio quickly stripped off the assassin's suit, leaving the corpse nude. The man was bald, with no tattoos, ID jewelry, marks, scars, or defects. Other than his exceptionally well-conditioned physique there was nothing to distinguish him except for his hands—they had six fingers each.

"Assassin synthy," Tana wheezed over Folio's shoulder.

"German issue," he agreed.

"I thought they weren't allowed in the U.S."

"I guess they are—sometimes."

New York's last private detective turned his attention to the blond Ethiopian's neck.

"You okay?" he asked.

"Yeah, yeah. I had rougher make-out sessions when I was fifteen."

"You don't look much older'n that now."

"I'm twenty-four and I been on my own since I was sixteen," the woman said. "And this ain't the first dead man I've seen."

"You weren't his first either," Johnson said.

"There's nobody who hates me that bad," Tana said. "And even if there was he wouldn't have the millions it'd take to buy a test-tube assassin."

"No. They were after the dude lives here."

"I thought this was your place."

"It's time for you to go home, girl," he said.

"The fuck I am," she replied. "I have to know why that man tried to kill me before I can sleep."

"Okay. We'll talk for a minute, but not here."

Folio went to the bathroom and got a fiber swab. He dipped the swab in the assassin's wound and then wrapped it up in tissues.

Then he looked up at the ecstasy girl and said, "Let's go."

Tana Lynn lived in a commune deep in Harlem. It was called the Mau-Mau and proclaimed the ethics of the Third and Fourth Black Radical Congresses. On the way there, Folio stopped at a communications booth and notified the police that there was a dead man in Charles Spellman's apartment.

"Why you wanna do that?" Tana asked.

"Just chummin' the water a little. Later on I might wanna catch me a fish."

Tana's apartment was on the fifth floor of the huge building, midway between Lower and Middle Adam Clayton Powell Drive. The view out of her picture window was eternally night and limited to the featureless walls of the Harlem jail just across the street. Her apartment was a single large room with a thirteen-foot ceiling. She had a bed in one corner and a tiled shower with no curtain or door in the other.

"Pretty spare," Folio said.

"Good for the soul," she said.

She kissed him hard then and he leaned away from her, a little perplexed.

"What's that?"

"You killed that man the second you saw him," she said with a smile. Her eyes got large, as if she was looking at something transform before her. "You didn't hesitate, or I'd be dead now."

"Li'l somethin' I picked up in the Ukraine. You got a desk?"

Tana Lynn went to a door at the midpoint of one wall and opened it. An oak board a meter square fell out, landing against a prop that held it parallel to the floor. From under her bed she drew a metal folding chair.

"This is my chair," she said proudly. "My own property. Not leased or rented or anything. Axel Alpha made it for me in his shop downstairs."

Folio seated himself at the desk and took out the swab of blood. He held the sample five centimeters from his electric eye. It took a full three minutes to map the DNA patterns and another six to find and access the database that held the pod number to which the chromes were related.

"What is that?" Tana asked when he looked up.

"What?"

"That eye."

"It was a gift from a grateful client."

"What's it do?"

"Watches out for trouble and then dives right in."

Folio could see the thrill that went through the young ex–sex slave. Her pulse quickened, and his did too.

"No, baby," he said.

"No, what?"

"I got to get to work on this job I got."

"What job?"

"I'm looking for a reason and maybe looking for a man that has that reason."

"Can I come?"

Folio's eye counted nine hundred forty-two stairs from the eternal night of the lower avenues to the sunlit streets of the upper levels. The buildings that loomed over the busy business streets were clean and gleaming, while the lower and middle avenue walls were filled with graffiti and garish electric signs. Manhattan had been trisected into separate strata thirty years earlier with the architectural masterpiece of the middle, upper, and lower streets. The reason for this separation was to achieve an aboveground approximation of Common Ground. There were many New Yorkers riding the labor cycles who could not afford the high prices of Manhattan's rents and leases but who were still necessary for commerce. It was the brainchild of Brandon Brown, a City College graduate, to extend the city even further into the sky, leaving the lower levels for those who could not afford the sunlight but who still worked for a living.

"I love it up here," Tana said to her new friend. "When I was a kid I used to come up and run around until the Social Police would grab me and try to say I was White Noise. But Jim'd always come to the station and get me. He never got mad or nuthin'. Just tell me to come on and we'd go out for Macsands and maybe a vid."

"Sounds like a good guy, this Jim."

"Unless you was under his sights," Tana said. "Where we goin'?"

"Grand Central Develator."

"Cops?" For the first time Tana looked worried.

Folio nodded and smiled. "You scared?"

"I've been to Police Central before. They thought I was

moving Pulse illegally. I seen what they did to the real dealer." The look in her eyes made the detective want to laugh, but he held it in.

"I won't let 'em hurt you, little girl."

The last stop of Grand Central's Develator, like all Develators around the world, was Common Ground. But this particular mass conveyance device made an intermediate stop one thousand feet belowground at Police Central, the hub of all law enforcement for the Twelve Fiefs of New York. This one massive center was connected, through underground trams, to all police stations in the city. This allowed for speedy deployment of officers on a military scale.

Folio and Tana rode the great flatbed with hundreds of others. At Police Central they debarked into a long hallway filled with people seeking entrée to the Law.

Tana stayed close to Folio's side, holding on to his sinewy forearm. The mob moved slowly, funneling down from a mob to a single-file line.

"Yeah?" a woman said from behind a three-inch-thick, bulletproof pane.

"Detective Thorpe," Folio said with studied nonchalance.

"Name?"

"Folio Johnson and Tana Lynn."

"Reason for visit."

"Folio's follies."

"Come again?"

"I'd rather not."

Tana snickered.

"This is no joke, citizen."

"Listen, lady," he said. "You got a job and so do I. You ask the questions and I give the best answers I can. Type in the words I gave you and that door there will pop open in thirty seconds. So let's get on with it, all right?"

Tana and Folio walked down a long hall that was over a hundred feet in width. The walls were lined with official booths where citizens could file claims, make reports, or show up for warrants. The detective stopped at a door guarded by an armed and armored sentry.

"Folio's follies," the detective said.

The guard waited a moment, listening to an electronic feed in his helmet, then moved to the side. The pair entered a small elevator that began to descend.

"You're quivering," he said.

"I like to have an exit."

"You the one asked to come along."

"I know."

The doors to the elevator slid open. A man stood before them dressed all in red except for a black collar ring that, Folio knew, was made from shatterproof glass. The policeman was white and not quite six feet. But what he lacked in height he more than made up for in width. Detective Aldo Thorpe was heavy with the natural muscle mass of a mesomorph.

"Got your black ring, eh?" Folio asked.

"What do you want?"

"Prussian six-finger, clutch forty-two," Folio said.

"Come on in," Thorpe said.

"How do you know about the sixer?" Thorpe asked.

"I killed him," Folio replied.

They were in a room called Interrogations 419-ag. The room, and the furniture therein, was composed solely of bright and shiny Glassone, the shatterproof plaster of the twenty-first century. Everything was Glassone and everything was white—the walls, the long conference table, the chairs. There were no windows a thousand feet below-ground.

"Murder?" Thorpe suggested.

"You can't murder a synthy. You know that. Anyway, he was trying to kill Tana. I severed his spine."

"You're lucky he didn't see you."

Folio shrugged.

"Why didn't you wait for the police unit?"

"I'm scared'a teenagers."

Thorpe smiled, then he laughed. "Good to see you again, Tana," he said.

"Inspector."

"You two know each other?"

"Tana an' me go way back. Every time I picked up Jim Rachman on a murder rap his little girl here would be his alibi."

Folio glanced at Tana. He hadn't checked her files because he felt it was gauche to research a woman he wanted to have sex with.

"That doesn't have anything to do with us," she said. Her light brown eyes seemed to care what he thought.

Folio allowed himself to fall into Rapture—a setting for his electric eye that removed him completely from the world, a place where there was nothing but his mind floating in an endless universe of mathematical possibilities. In Rapture his thoughts and impressions became idealized notions of energies that intersected and interacted as galaxies dancing freely. He saw her energy as a whirling haze of cosmic dust, not yet formed into stars. She hovered and approached then hesitated, drawn off toward the gravity of some unseen celestial body. They separated without incident or damage.

Folio smiled. He opened his eyes. It felt as if he had been far away for a long time but he knew that the timer on Rapture was less than a second in real time. Three seconds in that zone would drive any human insane.

"I'm on a job, Aldo," the private detective said. "There's a kid named Charles Spellman, an Itsie. He's got a group of friends gettin' knocked off. He's worried that his turn was comin' up and so he asked me to intercede."

"You workin' for the International Socialists now?"

"I'm not political, you know that."

"Tell that to them when they get in power. As a black man you should know what they'll do."

"I know four black men went down in the Central Develator and they never came back. They were going in for some questions and stayed."

Aldo Thorpe's mouth tightened and his bushy eyebrows furrowed slightly—then he forced a smile. "Let's hear it," he said.

Johnson related everything he knew to the police detective—the dead men, their club's activities, the assassin. The only thing he lied about was the whereabouts of his client.

"He's off-continent," he said. "I don't know where."

"What's wrong with you, Folio?" the policeman asked.

"All systems functioning normally, sir."

"This is no joke. If what you say here is true, I can't do anything. The files'd be closed. These killings aren't random, they're sanctioned assassinations. Anybody close to it will be in just as much trouble as these Seeker people. Why don't you forget this shit and come to work for us? We have lotsa independents on the payroll."

"That means I'd be on a cycle right?"

"Yeah, but—"

"But nuthin'. I'm not a termite, Aldo."

"You could be dead."

"Will be," Folio agreed. "One day. But at least I'll be the one to call that last charge."

"Idiot."

3 "So," Folio said over a steaming plate of bok choy and tofu, "you're keeping secrets and we haven't even known each other two days."

"Most secrets are kept at the beginning," Tana replied, "and I wasn't hiding anything anyway. I told you that Jim was supposed to kill me. What did you think he did for a living?"

"I don't know. It's just strange to find the adopted daughter of an assassin fighting it out with a sixer in the house of a marked man."

"You brought me there, remember?"

Folio used his plastic chop sticks to spear a limp leaf of bok choy. He held the dripping petal in front of his mouth a moment before biting it.

"Come on, Johnson," the young woman moaned. "You met me three days ago. You said that this guy, this Spellman, only came at you yesterday morning."

"Yeah. Yeah. I guess so."

"I tried to get you to take me that first night."

Folio let his mechanical eye roam back over its memory database (which had complete recall back over five years and partial memory back even further). She had been standing at the outer rim of the open-air DanceDome at the Sixtieth Street pier. She was wearing an orange-tinted transparent cellophane dress, with nothing underneath, and drinking a Blue Moon from an oversize crescent-shaped glass. Four men and two women were asking her to plug in with them and dance to music that only they would be able to hear. She chose a tall black woman who was bald and powerful. Before they twirled out on the floor she pulled away from the amazon and handed Folio a scrap of paper with her number on it.

"Maybe," he said. He was trying to think of a way that she could have known that he would meet Charles Spellman. "Maybe."

The China Diner was closed. D'or Hallwell was in her bed three floors below street level. She had served Folio and the girl and left them to lock up.

"I wouldn't hurt you, Fol," she said.

"Maybe. But anyway that doesn't matter. We are where we are. You're going home and I'm going to finish my business with whoever it was sent that sixer."

"I don't wanna be alone."

"I'll call you."

"I might not be there."

"Then, where will you be?"

"Either dancing or dead."

"Mingus Black?"

The broad-shouldered young man turned to face the tall and slender black man who had called his name. "Yeah?"

They were standing at the railing of the Crystal Plaza Bar that hovered on invisible gasses above the East River at South Street Seaport.

"My name is Johnson, Folio Johnson." Folio extended his hand.

"Do I know you?" Black was instantly on guard.

"No, no you don't. I'm a security expert for Macso but I want to get into real estate. I've been studying the brothers in that field and you, Mingus Black, are at the top of my list."

The black Seeker ran his tongue under his lower lip and wondered.

"Can I get you a drink, M?" a young, naked white girl asked Folio from the outward side of the railing.

Folio looked at the girl through the clear Glassone bar. She was shaven from head to toe and perfectly proportioned. He wondered what his hero, Humphrey Bogart, would have said in that situation.

"Real rum," he said. "And, honey, do me a favor."

"What?"

"Put in an ice cube and stir it with your finger."

"You're somethin' else, mister."

The young woman, who was unashamed to walk around naked in the bright sun of downtown New York, blushed under the detective's intense blue eye. She moved away to get his drink.

"Macso, huh?" the real estate genius asked. "What division?"

Folio was still watching the barmaid, enchanted by the words that had passed between them.

"Home," he said.

"You shittin'," Mingus said with a Backgrounder twang.

"No. I worked as Kismet's main bodyguard. Nine years I was with him."

"Was?"

"Seven years ago Home was hit by a Peruvian kick squad. They wanted to wipe out Kismet before MacroCode could annex their country. They got pretty close." Folio ran a finger above his blue eye.

"You get that then?"

"A cinder broke loose from a wild shot. It ruined my eye and part of my brain."

"Damn. That's why I never work for nobody full out," Mingus said. "They pay you to die for 'em, that's all, they pay you to die."

"You right about that, brother," Folio said. "You right about that, but still that cinder was the best thing ever happened to me."

"How you figure?"

"I saved Kismet's life by puttin' mine on the block. Motherfucker's crazy to the bone but he's loyal. Had his surgeons save me and then give me this synthetic eye to make up for what I lost. Between the fight and this new eye I see the world in a whole new light."

"And in that light you see real estate?" Mingus Black asked.

"Sure do. I wanna move a half a million Kenyans to downtown Tokyo and spend my life lookin' at cute girls at Crystal's."

"You're here right now." The black Seeker was getting comfortable.

"I'm working, though."

"Here's your drink, mister," the bald girl said.

When Folio reached for the glass she dipped her finger into the amber liquid and stirred it around. Folio took her hand and put the finger into his mouth, sucking hard enough to get all the rum off. The girl's eyes widened and she forgot to withdraw her hand when he let it go.

"Working on what," Mingus asked, "a hard-on?"

Folio laughed, looking deeply into the starstruck girl's eyes. "I sure am workin' on that one." Then he turned back to his target. "But today I'm here representin' a new world Nazi boy named Charles Spellman."

Mingus leaned back on his translucent barstool. For a moment Folio was afraid that he might bolt.

"What's up with Chas?" Mingus asked.

"He's drinkin' synth and worryin' about death."

"He is?" Mingus looked down at his wristcom.

"If you wanna know the time, I can tell ya—it's almost up," Folio said.

"What's that supposed to mean?"

"Mylo, Laddie, Bill Heinz, Derry James. They're all dead before their time. All the little Itsies."

Mingus looked around to see if there was someone with Johnson, then he looked the detective in the eye.

"What's Charles to you?"

"A piece'a shit," Folio said. "But a piece'a shit who laid out hard creds for me to save his ass."

"You think that's it?" Mingus asked. "That it's because they're in the IS?"

"We should be so lucky to live in a world where they kill the fascists and spare the lambs."

"Maybe it's coincidence?"

"Is that the kinda thinkin' bought you downtown Tokyo?"

"So what *do* you think?"

"Nothin' yet. I'd like to know who's killing you boys. And in order to know that I have to know why."

"I have no idea."

"What were you guys discussing at your last meeting? Other than the ten-million-mile pool cue."

"Education and labor and their relation to citizenship. Azuma was thinking that Elite Education Group had the right idea, that everyone should be tested as to their abilities and that their scores should be the basis of the degree of their citizenship."

"Anything else?"

"No. Nothing. They thought they were getting somewhere, though. Fonti and Derry set it up so that we could have daily meetings. They were all excited by the possibility of presenting the IS with a model for political organization that would lead ultimately to social change."

"How could you hang with Itsies, man?" Folio asked. He took his glass and drained it, thinking of the barmaid's fingers as he did so.

"They ain't worried about us, man. There's a place for all the races up in there. All except Jews and Gypsies."

"You believe that?"

"Sure."

"Then why don't you belong?"

"How do you know I don't?"

"I know."

"Another drink?" the barmaid asked. She had a glass with a doubleshot of rum in it. Her finger already submerged.

Folio took the glass and the hand. This time he kissed the fingers and then licked his lips.

"My name is Paradise," she said.

"What else could it be?"

"I get off at midnight."

"I have to work the next three nights," Folio said seriously. "But I will be at the front door on the fourth night at midnight. And I won't do anything until we're together. You know what I mean?"

"Uh-huh."

"Eightday night, then?"

"Uh-huh."

Folio smiled and handed her his wild card. "My friend and I have to go, but I'll see you then."

Paradise swiped the card through a payment slot on her left wrist. When she handed the card back Folio tapped in her tip on the screen over her artery.

"See ya," she said meekly.

"You bet."

"How do I know that you're working for Chas?" Mingus asked Folio on the way down the Crystal Stair escalator.

"You don't. And I can't prove it either. But I bet you you know what's goin' on, that your boys are being eradicated and that you're on the list. I'm not trying to kill you. If I was, you'd have never seen me comin'."

"Maybe you need something first," Mingus said. "I don't know."

"I went to the police," Folio said.

"What?"

"Don't worry. It was a guy I know pretty good. He wouldn't turn on me, I've done him too many favors."

"What did he say?"

"He can't do a thing."

The escalator had completed its steep descent and was now almost parallel to the water. A large photo-animae sign covered the side of the monorail bridge before them. The sign displayed a cinematic picture of boy and girl children marching with automatic rifles and cinder guns, firing on a unit of adult troops. After a moment soldiers on both sides began to die. The wounds were very realistic. One child was hit in the chest with a cinder blast that charred her body, leaving only her pretty face intact. As the head fell from her shoulders the image faded into giant words composed of flaming letters: TWELVE IS TOO YOUNG FOR WAR.

On the pier they strolled under the transport bridge.

"Maybe I should disappear," Mingus said.

"Give up everything?"

"Red Raven or nobody else could pay me if I'm dead."

"Common Ground won't hide a Backgrounder, M Black," Folio said. "That's the first place they'd look for you."

"The cops won't help. Common Ground won't hide me. What are you sayin'?"

"Let's work together. I got resources and you know all about the guys gettin' killed. Maybe we can figure it out."

"Why didn't you do that with Chas?"

" 'Cause Chas is an Itsie. I hate fascists."

"Then why work for 'em?"

"The job don't have politics, Mingman. The job is straight."

"I might not be in the IS, but all my friends are. Doesn't that make me just as bad?"

"You're just usin' them."

"What makes you think that?"

"Mingus Black," Folio recited from an amalgam of reports gathered by his eye, "born twenty-seven years ago, given up for White Noise at the age of six months. Arrested for larceny at the age of seven. Transferred to a maximum juvenile authority at the age of eleven. Suspected of drug distribution from the age of twelve but never convicted because you became a fink for the Social Police. At sixteen you saw your chance. The Underground Party kidnapped the daughter of Mina Athwattarlon, chief counsel of Red Raven NorthAm. You turned in the cell and got a university berth and a good job once you graduated."

"Nobody knows that. Nobody but Mina and me."

"And me," Folio said. "Brother, I got senses so sharp I can see the rhinoviruses grazin' on your face. I can hear your heart rate rise and blood slither in your veins. But I don't care. The UP means nothing to me. Neither do Itsies or cops. I took on a job and I intend to do it. And if you help me you might be saving your own life."

"What do you need?"

"I need to know what you guys were sayin' in the last few meetin's you had—exactly."

"We weren't talkin' 'bout nuthin'." The Backgrounder came out in the land dealer's speech again. "We—"

Folio put up a hand to cut Mingus short. He began scanning the upper area of the huge Glassone ramp. He moved his hand from Mingus's face and pointed to a shadowy area just under the lip of the trestle's underbelly. There, both men could make out a black form about the size and shape of an old American football.

"Noser," Mingus hissed.

"It hasn't uploaded yet."

"How the fuck you know that?"

Folio ignored the question, concentrating instead on the image of a control panel conjured up by his eye. The panel exhibited a grid of Manhattan that had little yellow lights for every city spy device, commonly called nosers. Folio had already located their CSD and was busy downloading a series of commands.

The football began shaking, its fail-safe survival mode enacted, but then suddenly it plummeted forty feet, striking the ground with a brief flash of fire. It landed near a group of Infochurch priests in their iridescent blue cloaks and transparent skullplates.

"Let's go," Folio said.

"I told you already," Mingus Black said. He was sitting on a couch the shape of a large, half-erect phallus. "Them guys didn't have nuthin' to say or think about that could scare anybody. They aren't even real Itsies."

"What does that mean?"

"They just belong to the fan club. Buttons and banners, you know. They pay dues and go out to drink synth on Sixdays, that's it. They don't know nuthin' an' they don't do nuthin'. Talk about all the great things they do in business but you know they're just shopkeepers, dustin' off the big boys' merchandise."

"If they're so outside, then why you hang with 'em?" Folio asked, nestling back in a cushioned chair that was fashioned as an open vagina.

"Families got money," Mingus said. "At least some of 'em. Chas and Mylo, Laddie and Azuma, too. Big bucks, baby."

"And you like being around all that?"

"I trade in real estate. I'm good at it, too. Most'a these rich families got some liberal shit goin' on about Common Ground. They wanna say they helped somebody crawl up outta there. I'm perfect for 'em 'cause I already did it. And I know how to turn a buck, too."

"But they didn't have some other kinda thing goin' on?" Folio asked. The chair he sat in had all the colors and textures of a Caucasian woman's genitalia, from thick brown fur to pink petal lips to a bright red interior. The fabric was covered by a clear material that had a liquid filling. The heat from Folio's body caused the liquid to flow.

"Who?"

"The kids, their parents. Shit, I don't know. I mean this New York is one crazy motherfucker, but people don't start knockin' off rich kids just 'cause they're stupid."

"No business I knew about." Mingus lay back into the foreskin comforter. "Hey, you think they might find us here?"

"Who?"

"Don't fuck with me, man. I don't know who."

"Sex pits are always the last on the list for searches. People payin' cash and usin' fake IDs. Almost every ID in this here sex hotel is fake. They have to send out manpower or fourth-generation nosers to check out a place like this. And even if they did come"—Folio tapped the orbital ridge over his blue eye—"I'd know they were here before they did."

"That's some eye there," Mingus said. "How a street-level motherfucker like you hold on to that? I mean, I heard'a pirates stealin' just a plain blue eye not even worth a thousand creds."

"I'm wiry," Folio said and then he laughed. "Was your boys gonna do anything soon? Anything different?"

"Naw. Them dudes just wanted to feel important. Last thing they managed to do was gettin' us to talk every day at sixteen. I had some trouble with that 'cause I'm movin' around all the time."

"So? You could cell it."

"Naw. They were doin' it in-house to act like they were in business. But the internal lines have a security system that won't allow external devices access. You know some people use those lines to transmit very sensitive information."

"How much would that have cost the companies?"

"Hardly nuthin'. I mean, people do it all the time. Free calls just a perk in big business today."

"So's embezzlement."

"I told ya, man, they got frog skins for guts. Any real trouble and them boys ran."

"Runnin' won't help them now."

Mingus scratched his eyebrow and looked away. When he moved around on the chair it arched upward in an approximation of a growing erection.

A searing pain sliced its way through Folio's head.

"What's wrong?" Mingus jumped up and grabbed Folio before he fell out of his chair.

Azuma Sherman was running down the lower ramp of the subterranean section of the Whitney Museum. Folio recognized the mutated inner organs created by the bio-artist Atta A that were on display. The point of view of the image came from the pursuer. Azuma's long brown hair was flowing backwards; every few steps he would look back to see Folio's mind's eye catching up to him. Folio couldn't think how this transmission had hijacked his eye.

Another pain exploded in Folio's head.

"You okay?" Mingus shouted.

Azuma's leg was nicked by a shard from a wide blast of a cinder gun. From his ankle to just above his knee burnt to a crisp in a second. The handsome youth fell to the floor. Through the eye-cam of the killer Folio saw Azuma's amputated foot. The assassin kicked it away. Azuma looked up into the killer's eyes. He was about to shout something and then his face burnt off.

The contact broke. Folio found himself sprawled on the floor, Mingus Black holding him by his shoulders. They were both shivering.

"Sherman's dead," Folio said.

"Mind if I share your bed, com?" Mingus asked Folio.

To shake off the nerves they had watched a very good matchup of Fera Jones against Mithitar the Mad Mongolian on the vid. The Mongolian had an interesting circular style of boxing, but he couldn't deal with the amazon's power. After six rounds Mithitar's buzz-saw-like attacks had slowed enough for her logjam jab to take control; he was asprawl in the middle of the ring by the end of round eight.

"What?" Folio asked.

"Just need to lie next to somebody. That's all. It ain't sex."

Folio sighed. He knew the trauma of ex-Backgrounders, especially those who'd spent their entire lives underground. They feared the loneliness of a full-size room.

"Just keep your pants on," he said.

Folio awoke on a small blue island adrift in a scarlet sea. The sky was pink and yellow. Violet pelicans soared on the wind above him. Folio was completely aware that this place was a dream provided by his eye. It was an attempt to ease his tension, but as usual, in these hard times the mechanical eye was at war with Johnson's troubled unconscious. He supposed that the eye had been trying to create a Caribbean island but was disrupted in color and size by Folio's own fears.

There was a disruption in the water. Somebody was swimming toward his islet. When she climbed out of the water he could see that it was the young woman from the Crystal Bar. Immediately he felt a powerful erection.

"Is that for me?" Paradise asked.

"Every inch."

"Keep it hard like that for me, baby," she said. "But we can't do anything yet."

"Why not?"

"You have to keep out of trouble."

"What's that got to do with you?"

"That's just the problem."

"What?"

"I'm not important but you still want me. Your dick wants me. He can't help himself but you have to hold it back."

"Who are you?"

"Paradise."

"Are you from the eye?"

"I met you today, at the bar."

"But where are you from in my mind?"

"I'm your stupid side. You're my fool."

Folio felt his erection straining and suddenly he wondered if it wasn't Mingus trying to be more than friendly.

The detective pulled himself awake and turned angrily toward his bedmate.

Mingus's eyes were wide open, his throat cut from jawbone to jawbone.

With a heavy sigh Folio rose out of bed and switched on the vidphone.

4

"What was your relationship to the deceased?" the man's voice asked.

"We were both natural-born human beings as far as I know," Folio replied.

He was gazing into a mirror, in a room composed entirely of mirrors—floors, ceilings, and walls—everything was a bright reflective surface.

"This is murder we're talking about here, Johnson. It's no joke."

"I'm not joking," Folio said to a thousand thousand images of himself. "I met Mingus because I was told by a man named Spellman that a group of friends were dying mysteriously. Spellman wanted me to find out if it was some kinda conspiracy, and if so, who was the perpetrator. I was talking to Black about that."

"In bed?"

"No. We were sleepin' in bed. At least I was. He was dyin'—I guess."

"Who else died?" a woman's voice asked.

Folio reeled off the long list, including the sixer he had killed.

"Seven murders and you didn't report it?"

"I did," Folio replied. "I told Aldo Thorpe."

There was a moment of silence in the infinite field of himself. Johnson's baby finger could not transmit or receive from the heart of Police Central but the memory chips still held more information than the UN's Library of Earth. Instead of giving in to the dizziness of the tilting images he began a restructuring routine of the images of Azuma Sherman as he died.

The young man was wide-eyed with fear and pain after his leg was disintegrated under him. He stared right into the lens that transmitted the execution to Folio's eye. He cropped out the left eye and expanded the block of that image. He increased the image until there was a face, reflected in the pupil, a face unknown to Folio or his electronic memories. It was the wide white visage of a man who hadn't shaved in two days or more. It was an evil face, a gleeful image. He was smiling. Folio imagined the rank breath. The man wore an ocular camera over his left eye; nothing special. Nothing that would explain where he had gotten the protocols to transmit directly to Folio's eye.

"Who were the other members of this organization?" the male interrogator asked. "The ones that survive."

"Leonard Li, Brenton Thyme, and Fonti Timmerman. And my client, of course, Charles Spellman."

Another spate of silence ensued.

Folio had another idea. He searched his synthetic memory, but the data was unavailable without his transmitter.

"All dead," the woman said.

"Accidental or murder?"

"They were assassinated."

"That's some hard luck."

"You don't seem surprised," the masculine voice said.

"Are you?"

"It was your job to protect them, you say."

"I said no such a thing. I said that Spellman hired me to find out why they were being killed and by whom."

"Where is Charles Spellman?"

"OC. I don't know where."

"You know nothing?"

"I didn't say that. I said that Spellman's off-continent. I don't know who's been killin' his friends but I do know that it's too much of a coincidence for it to be anything but a conspiracy."

"We are allowed by law to administer a level-two pain injection if we believe that you are lying."

"Check my med files," Folio said.

"A Macso injunction against invasive interrogation," the female voice said. Folio doubted she'd meant him to hear those words.

"You got all bases covered, huh?" the man said.

"Enough to stay in the game."

Folio got back to Hallwell's China Diner at eight fifteen in the morning. D'or was behind the counter. Three lady latenighters were eating fried rice and frogs' legs trying to garner enough strength to make it through the day without getting thrown off the cycle.

"Hey, Johnson," D'or said, and he knew there was trouble. D'or saying Johnson was a code meaning that his dick was exposed.

Folio looked around the small restaurant. The lavender-haired partygirls didn't seem to see a problem.

D'or moved close enough to whisper, "She's downstairs. Spread out two meters just for an intro."

"Cash credit?"

"Yessir."

The tiny underroom of China Diner was dark and damp, with a ceiling barely high enough for Folio to stand up straight. She was sitting in an ancient wooden chair looking as if she were receiving infection from every breath. She wore a gray dress of real wool and a light gray shawl that had to be silk. Folio placed her age at mid-forties, but with the recent advances in dermal surgery she could have been sixty and no one would know.

"You were looking for me, ma'am?" Folio asked.

He reached out in greeting. She clasped her hands together and moved her shoulders in a defensive manner.

"Are you the detective?"

"Yes, ma'am."

"I am Liliane Spellman."

"Charles Spellman's mother?"

"No. I'm Mylo's mother." There was no trace of tears or sorrow on her face, but her blood pressure was extremely high and her nervous system was playing a dirge.

"I'm sorry about your loss, ma'am."

"It's . . . It was a shock. He had always been sick. That was my fault. I infected him. When I was pregnant the doctors told me that he could live a normal life if he kept up a moderate health regimen."

"Lots of people live with the hive and worse today. It's not like back when we were kids."

"I know. I was heartbroken, of course, when I heard. But today the police called my husband and said that they were opening a file on Mylo, that he might have been murdered."

Folio looked around for another chair. There was none.

"They said that you were hired by Charles, that he might also be dead."

"I don't think Charles is dead. His nine friends are, though. Some say it was accidental but I wouldn't bet on that."

"The police have claimed Mylo's body. They exhumed him from the royal cemetery in England—"

"He had a royal funeral?"

"Of course. His great-grandfather is Jason Randisi."

"CEO of Randac Corp.?"

"You didn't know?"

The chime of intuition rang in Folio's eye, but he had already made the leap. All of this information was stored in his eye but he skipped over biographical data, not thinking it important.

"Is that Charles's great-grandfather too?"

"Yes. Yes it is."

"Tell me, M Spellman, were Mylo and Charles wrapped into the Randac communications system?"

"Only for communication with the family," she replied. "You know public communication is so unreliable these days. It's perfectly legal."

"What did you want from me, ma'am?"

Liliane Spellman looked into Folio's eyes for a moment. She began to speak but then stopped herself. She raised her hand and clutched the throat of her woolen dress.

"Why don't you wear a lens?" she asked.

"What?"

"For that eye. It's very disconcerting."

"It has a crystal code covering," Folio said. "Data capture would be thrown off by a lens."

"Did I kill my son, M Johnson?"

"No, ma'am, you certainly did not. You gave him life and that life was taken. They used the hive but he would have lived if they had let him alone."

Folio had never seen a real person laugh and cry at the same time. He'd seen it in the movies, but never in life.

"I will pay you a million general credits for the arrest of the murderer," she said then.

"Ma'am, I've given you all I can."

"You won't help me have revenge?"

"Your son is dead, lady. He was killed by a big plan. A major design. If you try and get at it they won't hesitate to blank you too."

Corridor 23-97 triple-G S I was paved in crumbling plaster that had once been painted coral pink. At the far end of the Common Ground hallway was head locker 512-419. Folio had to climb a forty-foot ladder to reach the octangular slip where Charles Spellman slept.

When Johnson popped the lid he saw Spellman and his guest. Her hands were at either side of his head, holding down the rope across his throat. They were both naked. She was riding his erection while he came and came near to death. Tana looked up, the grin of a satisfied orgasm on her lips. Folio hit her with his fist. When she fell the boy started coughing and choking. He was spitting blood and trying to pull away from the weight of his assassin.

"Stop it, kid!" Folio yelled. "You're okay!"

But Charles Spellman kept flailing and kicking until he finally pressed himself out of the sleep slip, knocking Folio to the side of the ladder. The young Itsie's body crashed forty feet below. Folio swung back on the ladder and looked in at the girl. She wasn't unconscious but neither was she aware. The detective descended the ladder, leaving her to moan in her victim's bed.

At midnight he approached the Infochurch tabernacle on Middle Bowery. The Blue Abbot allowed him entrance when he mentioned a certain code given him by the splendid Doctor Kismet. He entered a private booth and knelt before the giant monitor, which instantly switched on.

A tall man, even taller than Folio, with one shining silver eye and one normal gray orb, appeared on the screen.

"Hello, Folio."

"Ivan," the last detective said.

"I'm surprised it took you so long to find me. You must be slipping."

"I should have guessed when you gave Tana and her stepfather my protocols."

"I didn't give your access code away, Folio," the doctor said in a friendly voice. "I merely let them piggyback on a transmission from Home to you."

"Why?"

"Such a large question."

"I know most of the big stuff. You and the other corps had a thing working with the IS. You had a communications system that the Seekers stumbled onto without knowing it. IBC, Red Raven, MacroCode, and Randac. You killed the kids because somewhere in the trillion trillion trillion bits of data they downloaded for their afternoon talks there might have been some clue to your secret."

"Congratulations," Kismet said with a paternal smile.

"Why me?"

"Charles Spellman told Azuma Sherman on our own frequency that he was going to get in touch with you. When your name shows up on our system I am always contacted. I love you, Folio."

"So you sent the assassin after me?"

"Only to check you out, to find out where your client might have been. She fell for you, you know. Another unit from the Blue Zone had already engaged the sixer. She fought him to save your life."

"If you didn't give her my protocols how did she follow me?"

"In your right-hand front pocket."

Folio reached into his pants and came out with a tiny scrap of paper that had Tana Lynn's number on it.

"Micro-mitter?"

"No."

"Radioactive?"

"Nothing. Just what it appears to be, a simple piece of paper torn from a discarded instruction sheet."

"So? How do you track that?"

Real pleasure came into the madman's face. "We've made an amazing discovery, Folio. The most important discovery in the history of the world. Every atom, every electron, proton, and maybe all subatomic particles—they are all, each and every one of them, unique."

A small subsystem in Folio's eye began transcribing the doctor's words.

"Unique? You mean you can tell one atom of oxygen from another one?"

"By submyrral variance mathematics we could give every electron on this planet a name."

"She put this paper in my pocket . . ."

". . . and we tracked it."

"Usin' submyrral whatever?"

Kismet grinned broadly. Folio knew how rare this was and he was afraid.

"What's all this got to do with the kids?"

"Nothing, really. It's just that they mistakenly downloaded a series of files in a secret intercorporate database."

"What files?"

"My Dominar and certain investigative branches of Randac, Red Raven, and IBC had run across a gene-testing project that the IS has been conducting in preparation for their so-called race war. We had entered into negotiations with the Aryan branch of the organization to prepare, financially, for any situations that might arise."

"Prepare what?"

"For whatever, my friend. Of course, these negotiations needed to be private. And even though we knew these children would be unlikely to break our codes, we had to take steps."

"So you killed ten human beings just on the off chance that they might read a file?"

"Ten lives," Kismet said on a sigh. "If the IS gets their way, billions will die. Billions."

"So in order to stop them you had to kill the kids?"

"First we need to understand the viability of a genetically run race war. Then we'll consider actions, if indeed there are actions to be taken."

"Race war? Genes? Man, are you sick?"

"Hardly, Officer Johnson. Hardly." Kismet's long face became downcast. "I'm sorry about the girl."

"Tana?"

"She had to die, you know. By the time I realized that you and she had something the poison was already in her. Her and that adopted stepfather of hers, the one who transmitted the Azuma killing to your eye."

Folio resisted the urge to dive into the screen.

"You know I can't let this thing lie, Ivan."

"I know."

"You killed that woman. I owed her something. She was a killer but she saved my life. And I'll have to find these Itsies before they do something crazy."

"It will be a glorious time, won't it, old friend?"

"Why did you connect with me, Ivan?" Folio asked.

"It was fate, Folio. Kismet. Your name came up and I

realized that this race war will be waged against you, your people. I included you to give you a chance to fight against the Aryan branch of the ISD. I'm giving you a chance to save your people."

"They're your people too, man," Folio sputtered. "Black people are your largest membership on three continents."

"One day everyone will be my devotee. You, Folio, you are one of my apostles. It is your job to save these people. It is my wish."

"You're crazy."

"Am I?"

Folio put his foot through the screen, then stormed out of the tabernacle and into the night.

Voices

1 *Where am I?* The words were clear but they had no sound, no voice to communicate timbre or gender. *Where are my hands? What is that light? What's that? Why can't I look away? Where am I?*

The voice had questions mainly. Sometimes, though, memories of strange feelings or half-formed images occurred in his mind. Foods that he never liked suddenly held the most wonderful flavor. He bought a bunch of carrots at a vegetable stand and ate them all in one sitting in the park.

The voice wasn't always there. There were days at a time when he heard nothing at all. Days where he was almost the man he had been before the Pulse addiction.

Pulse. Wonder drug and death sentence all in one. On the first night he used the drug Leon had lived a whole life span riding at the side of the conqueror Hannibal. He'd ridden fantastic blue elephants across the Alps. After a few years the hyper-real fantasies degraded to washed-out memories with little direction or content. But the addiction was still strong because Pulse was the only thing that kept his brain from collapsing.

"Are you using again?" Dr. Bel-Nan asked at the Neurological Institute of Staten Island.

"No," said Professor Leon Jones, father of the congresswoman from the Bronx, the onetime UBA heavyweight champion of the world, Fera Jones. "I don't even want to hear that one voice. You think I want a crowd?"

Bel-Nan, a tall white man in his fifties, smiled. He was missing a lower front tooth. This one detail always disturbed Professor Jones, though there was much that could have disturbed him. Bel-Nan was one of the foremost brain specialists in the world. He was one of the founders of the mysterious Church of Life Everlasting. He had been sentenced to the MacroCode polar prison system for performing illegal brain transplantation operations. He had further developed his techniques in prison.

The operation that Bel-Nan had performed on Leon was a more sophisticated version of the experiments that had put him in prison. Taking living brain tissue from an anonymous donor, the surgeon replaced certain regenerative tissue in Jones's cortex and frontal lobe. These cells stimulated the atrophied portion of his brain, allowing the onetime history professor to survive without taking Pulse.

"Sometimes there are vestigial memories, pieces of thoughts that the donor once might have had," Bel-Nan explained as he pushed the long and greasy blond hair away from his eyes.

"But, Doctor," Jones complained. "It's not just a word or a patch of color, something like that. There's questions and sometimes I have yens, desires for things I never wanted before."

Bel-Nan smiled. His face was long and somehow crooked, as if maybe the man who knocked his tooth out had also broken his jaw. Jones had seen quite a few misshapen faces like that during the years he managed his daughter's boxing career.

"The brain is a mysterious thing, Professor Jones," Bel-Nan said. "It is the most volatile and creative material in the world, maybe even the universe. It can evolve without dying. It can conceive of itself. Its concepts are beyond the living cells that comprise it, so that life for us is defined by the faculty of thought rather than the ability to breathe. Breath, as magical as it is, is nothing compared to the reality of personality."

The ugly scientist smiled, unashamed of the crooked grin and missing tooth.

"What does that have to do with this voice in my head?" Jones asked.

"Your brain has discovered new material," Bel-Nan explained patiently. "It's making up this voice to explain it. The shock of the new cells becomes a question in your conscious mind. *Where am I?* That's the *feeling* of the new cells. They are displaced and that feeling of displacement becomes a question. This strangeness of the new cells seeks out a new answer, therefore you try new things. A different taste. A walk in the park. Tell me, do you have headaches before you hear this voice?"

"Yes, I do. I get a headache that lasts for hours, and then, when it subsides, the voice comes out. Not a voice, really, but ideas. Some come across as words, and others, others are images. Why? What does a headache mean?"

"The cells are integrating. As they come together there's friction and maybe a little heat. That particular phase of the integration is successful, the pain subsides, and a new member is added to the collective of brain cells. There must be something old in those cells and a confusion arises. But all of that will pass. Maybe if you take vitamin E_3 or, even better, hedroprofin, the swelling will be contained. But I wouldn't if I were you."

"Why not?"

"This is a moment of discovery that very few humans have ever undergone. You are experiencing the reintegration of your mind. You are absorbing the life and the soul of another. Feel it, Professor Jones. Record it. It could be one of the most valuable self-examinations since Freud."

"You think somebody'd pay for it?"

"I'd read it, Professor. I've done a dozen of these operations since they were legalized. But this was the deepest and most extensive transplant of living tissue. I replaced a rather large portion of the cortical stem and interior with various materials from a single donor. We were relying on the similarity of the neuronal material, hoping that the new elements would adapt to the function required of them."

Leon had been on life support, he was told, for eighteen months after the operation. Machines the size of a brownstone maintaining basic functions that his brain had to relearn.

"You are the first to survive this long," Bel-Nan said.

"Well," Leon said. "I guess a few echoes aren't so bad compared to death."

"Not so bad at all, Professor."

Professor Jones had spent all of the money he made in boxing on the operation. His daughter had helped only insofar as she used her influence to get him well placed on the waiting list for the highly experimental procedure. But even with her help he was lucky to have been chosen.

It had been three months since his release from the hospital, and so far Leon's health was fair. He still felt weak after very little exertion, and sometimes when he woke up in the morning he was a little disoriented. He'd look around the room searching for something familiar. Once he thought he saw a small dog sitting patiently in the corner. But one blink and the dog was gone.

2 When Leon took the hedroprofin the voice disappeared. He was happy not to feel that he was going crazy, but he discovered that he missed the voice. It had been an anchor after years of Pulse addiction. With no obsession left he found himself drifting.

His daughter was in D.C. testing the waters for a greater political career. As a onetime drug addict, he was an embarrassment to her. The newspapers that backed Fera Jones's political ambitions blamed the elder Jones for forcing his daughter into the ring to pay for his drugs. It wasn't true. As a child Fera had begged to fight. She was overactive, and boxing was the one thing that calmed her down.

They talked every day for a few minutes. But she was busy and he had nothing but time.

Professor Jones lived in two small rooms on Middle One twenty-fifth Street near Adam Clayton Powell. When he was a child Harlem was an entirely black neighborhood, one of the centers of African-American culture. But now it was as faceless and multicultured as any other neighborhood in Manhattan. The Schomburg Residence Hotel was happy to take a congresswoman's father for a tenant. The rent was $2,000 a week, 60 percent of his disability insurance.

He read and reread books about history. Not histories, but books that spoke of the art of recording the past. Collingwood and Hegel and Ahn Min. That's what intrigued Jones: the intangibility of what was. The passage of time and the forgetfulness of humanity. Even his talk with the unsightly Dr. Bel-Nan. Did he say that the cells of the donor remembered details from the previous life? No, not exactly. He hadn't exactly said anything.

"The best history is a shopping list," one of his professors at Howard had said. "Three bananas, two lengths of copper wire, and a broad-brimmed hat. Now that's something to sink your teeth into."

Bel-Nan wasn't even his real name. He'd changed it hoping, like the rulers of a new dynasty in China who rewrote history, to be seen in a new light. From many years of study Jones had decided that nothing anyone ever said was true; at best it was what they believed.

On a temperate December morning Professor Jones decided to go down to Morningside Park, a green valley between towering buildings. In his childhood his Aunt Bing would tell him that the park was a dangerous place where drug dealers and gang members met. And so when his Uncle Bly took the short cut through the park little Leon would turn his head every which way to see where the killers were hiding.

"It's okay in the daytime," Bly would assure him.

But Leon never stopped his vigil until they were back on the regular streets, safe from harm.

"Mister?" a child's voice asked.

At first he thought it was the voice in his head. The question was not a lament, however. Professor Jones looked down and saw a blond-haired child, no more than five, standing at the far end of the park bench.

He blinked once, expecting the child to disappear.

"Are you cold, mister?" the girl asked instead of dissipating.

"No. Why do you ask?"

"I'm cold," she said.

Leon had worn a corduroy jacket over a plaid woolen shirt. He also had a cashmere scarf that Fera had given him wrapped around his neck. The scarf was making him too warm but he hadn't thought to take it off yet.

"Here," he said. "Try this."

The little girl threw the wrap around her shoulders with the grace of a somewhat older child. She shivered and then smiled.

"Thanks," she said.

"All warm now?"

"Pretty much," she said. "Can I sit here until my mommy comes back?"

"Where is your mother?" Leon asked as he lifted the child to sit there next to him.

"She's up over there talking to Bill," the girl said,

pointing down a path that turned away and disappeared into the trees.

"What are they talking about?"

"How come you looked scared when you saw me?" the girl asked.

"Did I?"

"It's not polite to answer with a question," the girl said primly, gesturing her hands like a traffic cop or maybe a music conductor.

"I asked the first question," Leon said, also gesturing. "And then you asked about why was I scared."

"But I wasn't *answering* your question," the girl giggled. "I was changing the subject."

"Oh you were, were you?" Leon had the urge to reach out and tickle the child, but he didn't. He didn't know her. He could go to jail for twenty years for child molesting. But she was so darling, like Fera had been. She didn't look anything like Fera, but she had the same silly spunk.

"I was surprised," he said, "because when I was a boy and lived here there were no little white girls in Harlem."

"Am I a white girl?"

The question stunned Leon. He didn't know what to answer.

"Your hair is almost white," he said lamely.

"But you didn't mean my hair, huh?" the girl said. "You meant my skin."

"Yeah. I guess so."

"And if I'm white then what are you?"

"Black," Leon said instantly.

"But your skin is just brown," the girl said. "And my skin has some brown and some pink and some yellow, too." She rubbed her arm and peered at the skin as she did so.

"I think we're all the same color, just more of some colors and not so many of others." She held out her arm and looked at Leon as if to get his opinion on her theory.

Leon suppressed the urge to hug the child. He clasped his hands and pressed them against his lips.

There came a gurgling cry. Leon jerked his head around to look up the path where the child's mother was talking to someone named Bill.

"Coming, Mom!" the child yelled. She was running up the path, toward the cry.

Leon was exhausted by the long walk from his apartment to the park. He struggled to his feet and went up the pathway, but the girl had already disappeared.

When he got to the playground on the other side of the park the girl was gone. Children capered while their mothers or nannies watched, but there was no one who looked like the child's mother talking to anyone who looked like a Bill.

No one seemed worried about a gurgling cry.

"I met this little girl in the park today, Fifi," Leon was saying to his daughter on the vid that evening. She was at her office, poring over a blue and red pie chart on a wall-mounted computer screen.

"A child?" she asked, turning momentarily from the graph.

"Just a little girl. Her mother left her alone and she wasn't dressed warmly enough. I let her have that scarf you gave me last Easter."

"You gave a strange child in the park your scarf?" Fera gave the vid screen her full attention now.

Cosmetic surgery had completely fixed her broken nose and the permanent swell that had developed over her right eye. Her golden skin nearly shone in the fluorescent lighting. At twenty-five she was ravishing if a bit imposing at six-nine and two hundred plus pounds.

"She was cold," Leon said in a glad tone. "Smart little kid, too. Reminded me of you."

"What's the child's name, Daddy?"

He could hear the concern in her voice.

"I didn't get it. Her mother called and she ran away. I went after to make sure she was all right, but you know I'm so tired after the operations."

"Why did you need to see if she was all right?" Fera asked.

"Oh, it was nothing. Just the tone in her mother's voice."

"What tone?"

"It sounded more like she was screaming than calling, that's what I thought, but when I got to the playground they were gone." When Leon Jones grinned and nodded his head, he realized, for the first time, that he'd become an old man.

"Daddy. Daddy, are you listening to me?"

"Sure I am, Fifi."

"You drifted off there a minute."

"I did?" the professor said. "Oh."

"Daddy, I don't want you going up to that park anymore."

"I must have been thinking about Maitland," Leon mused.

"Who's Maitland, Daddy?"

"Frederic William Maitland. He wrote a history, *the* history of English law. Ideas can have a history, you see. People are too complex, their motivations too capricious to be documented accurately." It was a fragment of a lecture he'd given thirty years earlier, but he experienced it as a new idea.

"So, Daddy, you'll stay away from the park?"

"Whatever you say, honey." Leon was reconsidering the notion of ideas having history separate from the people who had those ideas. *Language can have a documentable history where the orator may not,* he was thinking as he broke off the vid connection to Congresswoman Jones.

"Hi, mister," the little girl said in the park three days later.

It had rained on Tuesday. Wednesday he started reading Marc Bloch's book on feudal society. He had long admired the Frenchman's patriotism but never read deeply of the man's work. That afternoon he considered writing a history of his block of One twenty-fifth Street. He thought that maybe if he could keep it down to that, or maybe just a history of the businesses there . . . *Maybe,* he thought, *the nature of the businesses would express the changing nature of the population, its makeup and income.* Finally he fell asleep.

But on Thursday he made a pilgrimage to Morningside Park. He had forgotten the rain, his urban narrative, and any promises made to his daughter.

"What's your name?" he asked the child.

"Tracie."

"Do you come to the park every day, Tracie?"

"Not *every* day."

"But many days?"

The child nodded vigorously and climbed up on the bench to sit next to her friend.

She told him all about a test she'd taken in which she misspelled the word merry-go-round.

"I thought it was *marry* go round," she said and giggled.

The love Leon felt for that child frightened him. He noticed that she had on the same cranberry-colored dress that she'd worn on Monday and supposed that it was either her favorite or that her parents were poor.

"Would you like some ice cream?" he asked Tracie.

"No thanks. But I would like to go swimming."

"You would?"

"Yes please," she said.

"But there's no place to swim around here. And even if there was, it's December."

"Uh-huh. Yes there is. There's a big lake, and it's warm there."

"You must mean the pond down in Central Park."

"Nuh-uh. It's a pond right here. Come on, I'll show you."

She pointed up the path where her mother had been talking to the man named Bill.

"You go on," he said, thinking that her mother would be angry at him for walking with her.

"But I can't go swimming by myself. I'll get in trouble."

"Isn't your mother up there?"

A frown knitted itself in the young face. Tracie concentrated on the words Leon spoke. He imagined them running through her mind again and again: *Isn't your mother up there? Isn't your mother up there? Isn'tyour-motherupthere. Isntyourmotherupthere,* until it was just a fast jumble of meaningless sounds.

"Talking to Bill," Leon added.

"Yeah." Tracie grinned widely and jumped off the bench. "You wanna go swimmin', mister?"

"No," he said. "You go on."

The gurgling cry of her mother's call came just after Tracie rounded the bend.

3 Pell Lightner was waiting on the marble bench that sat out in front of the Schomburg Residence Hotel. Professor Jones felt as if he had been caught committing some crime. Indeed, he had been wondering on his walk home if Tracie's mother would allow her to come visit, that if he screwed up the courage to go up that path he could introduce himself and maybe become a friend of the family. He loved the child.

"Good afternoon, Leon," the short chocolate brown young man said.

"Pell." Leon walked past the bench and up the granite stairway. Maybe he hoped that Pell was just stopping to rest, that he was up from D.C. on business and had stopped to sit after visiting some of his White Noise friends at the Common Ground below One thirty-fifth Street. But Pell jumped up and accompanied the professor as if he had been invited.

And how could Jones turn him away? He was Fera's full-time live-in boyfriend, had been her boxing manager—after Leon had succumbed to the symptoms of Pulse use—and was now her valued congressional aide. Pell was a savvy kid born of Backgrounder parents. He had no education except what he had gleaned from public computer links and by overhearing others talk about the news. He couldn't read, but the advancement in reading computers meant that he had heard many of the classic novels, and he preferred listening to the *East Coast Times* to getting news from the vid. When Fera picked him up he latched onto her like a barnacle, Professor Jones said for the first few months. But the young man showed his worth when he steered Fera through the Konkon fight, a fight she would have surely lost if not for Pell's psychological motivation.

"How have you been, Leon?" Pell asked in the small two-man elevator.

"Slow."

"Fera said that you've been taking long walks."

The elevator doors slid open on eight.

Mrs. McAndrews was sitting on her rocker in the hallway, munching her gums. The elderly Korean woman had married Sergeant Steven McAndrews in 1955 at the age of sixteen. Now, at one hundred nineteen, she'd been alone in Harlem since the nineteen eighties. Her husband and son both dead, her family back home forgotten, or forsaken—Leon was never sure which.

"Good afternoon, Mrs. McAndrews."

"Mr. Jones," she replied, surprisingly lucid considering her obsessive munching. "This your son?"

"No. My daughter's boyfriend."

"You a boxer too, boy?" She spoke with a slight Korean accent.

"No, ma'am. I'm a congressional aide."

Inside the rooms Jones offered Pell tea or gin.

"It's all I got. The gin is good. The tea's good for you."

"No thanks. You been drinkin' a lotta gin?" Pell asked, almost nonchalant.

"Fera's worried, huh?" Leon said. He sat down in the reclining bamboo chair that his first wife had bought when they were just married.

Pell lit on an emerald hassock that came from Amherst with Leon and his second wife, Fera's mother, Nosa.

"Yes she is, sir," Pell admitted. He wore a soft gray andro-suit that was open at the collar, revealing a pendant of twigs bound together in the form of a falling man. "She said that your mind was wandering, that you were talking to children you didn't know in the park. She called Dr. Bel-Nan. He assured her that it's all a part of the healing process. Me coming up here is just to keep Fera from worrying. You know she's drafted her first bill: the Chromosome Pattern Security Act. If it's passed it will be the first law enacted that will encompass the planetary colonies."

"You speak so well, Pell." Leon said. "I remember when 'nig' and 'motherfuckin' chuckhead' were in almost every sentence you spoke."

Pell had a wide face and an equally broad grin. His eyes lit up and the corners of his mouth raised to form the shallow bowl of his delight.

"It's only senators that can talk like that in Washington, sir."

"But do you understand what you're saying?" Leon asked.

"What?" Pell's confusion showed.

"I mean, you can't read, can you?"

The wary look of Common Ground came suddenly into the well-spoken young man's eyes.

"I read. I've read the Declaration of Independence, *Moby Dick*—"

"Without your phono implant?"

Pell tensed for a moment and then let go. He smiled and asked, "What's the problem, Professor? Why rag on me?"

"Did you know that Homer was an illiterate?"

The question got Pell's attention.

"Yeah," Leon continued. "In his time there was no written language, at least not for everyday people like Greek storytellers. A good one like Homer could remember, word for word, a dozen or more epic poems. Poems much longer than most novels you hear today. And he would really act out each part. Deep voice for Zeus and twittery little words for children and animals.

"In *Fahrenheit 451*, Bradbury has his ideal community double as a library. Each member commits an important text to memory. It's called the oral tradition, Pell. Your generation is returning to that. Just like Bradbury's fireman. Only he still wanted to read."

"That's very interesting, Leon—" Pell began. He was going to continue but the professor cut him off.

"So you can see what's in the cards. The word *hear* will gain a new significance, while *write* will fall into disuse. And really, what will writing become when no one can read? And what will the future generations think of writing? Like we think of hieroglyphics, no doubt. And this transition will not take thousands of years, merely decades. Five years without electricity and all of civilization could fall back into barbarism."

Leon laughed and sat back. It had been years since he befuddled students with his intellectual constructions. Pell was a bright kid, but, the professor thought, he knew nothing and had no idea of the depth of his ignorance.

"So," Pell paused, making much of his deliberation. "What you're saying is that you aren't going senile and Fera can stop worrying about you."

"That's one thing," Leon said, nodding sagely. "Another is that we teeter precariously upon the edge of the precipice."

It was Pell's turn to laugh.

"You laugh?"

"I been teeterin' ever since the first time I was gang raped on the IRT at three in the mornin'." Pell tapped the branch talisman. "Barbarism done been here, Professor. You could put the rent on that."

As was often the case, Pell had the last word. That night Leon Jones mulled over and over the crimes committed upon the young man. He'd never heard of the rape. He doubted if Fera knew.

That he survived, Leon wrote in his journal, *is a feat greater than all my years of education and Fera's heavyweight belts rolled up into one.*

"Hi, Lenny," Tracie said in the dream.

Leon was a child too. They were sitting on the ground near a Morningside Park bench. Chamomile was flowering up through the cracks in the asphalt, stingless bees gathered their pollen.

"Do you wanna come on down t' my house?" Leon wasn't surprised to hear himself speak in the deep southern accent of his childhood. He *was* a child after all, playing with his best friend Tracie in the park.

Tracie shook her head vigorously. "I can't. Not till you go swimming with me."

"How come?"

"I don't know," the blond child said. "But it's about the park."

Leon noticed that it was fall. The leaves were turning. They must be maples, he thought, because their leaves are so red. Just then he saw a gang member run from behind one tree, cross the road, and then hide behind another trunk. Another man with a gun followed.

"It's our park," Tracie's voice said.

There came that gurgling scream.

"What's that?" Leon asked fearfully, but he wasn't sure if he meant the gang member and robber or the scream.

"That's just my mom," Tracie replied. "She's always screaming like that."

The dream replayed itself again and again until Leon came to anticipate every event. Sometimes the gang member chased the robber. Sometimes he could make out Tracie's name in the scream.

4 "Your daughter called," Dr. Bel-Nan said the next day at their regular appointment.

"Yeah," Leon said. "She a good girl."

He was sitting on a medical table, on waxy paper, in his underwear.

"She's worried about you."

"Yeah."

"Do you know why she's so worried?" Bel-Nan asked. He was studying an X ray of Leon's brain on a wall-size passive computer image that appeared as a complex acrylic painting. No light shone from behind the screen, but if Bel-Nan touched any specific point that area was enlarged by ten and overlaid on the broader image.

"No, sir. I don't."

Bel-Nan checked image after image, sometimes increasing the subject of his study a thousandfold.

Meanwhile Leon sang, "What you gonna do when the pond goes dry, honey . . . ?"

After fifteen minutes of study and song Bel-Nan turned and asked, "Have you been to the park lately, Professor?"

"I was up there yesterday. Kickin' back, takin' it slow."

"You seem to be speaking in a . . . a . . . I don't know how to say it," Bel-Nan said.

"Dreamt I was a boy last night," Leon said with glee. "When I woke up I remembered how I talked back then. They called it ignorant where I went to school so I weaned myself off of it. But you know it kinda tickles me to go back to it a li'l bit. Yeah, just a li'l bit."

"Is that how you spoke to the little girl, the one you met in the park?"

"Not in the park, no."

"You saw her somewhere else?"

"In a dream I did. In a dream about the park."

"What was she wearing?" the doctor asked, seemingly distracted by something he'd seen in the X ray.

But Leon wasn't fooled. The question was wrong even for a psychiatrist to ask.

"What you lookin' at, Doc?"

"What? Oh, uh, nothing, really. I mean, I'm looking to see if the microcircuitry has begun to dissolve. You see," he said, building confidence as he spoke, "the time it takes for the sheath around the circuit to melt away should be enough for the brain to have generated its own neural links."

Anyone who watched the Med-channel knew about the micro-nerve-bonding process. It involved computer circuitry made from a blood by-product that was compatible with biological processes while temporarily performing complex computer functions. The inventor, Carmine Giampa, was now senior vice president of MacroCode International.

"You don't say," Leon said, as if this were the first time he'd heard of such a miracle.

Bel-Nan picked up the sarcasm and cut short his medical lecture.

Leon dressed and went with Bel-Nan to an ultramodern office. All of the furniture was constructed of transparent plasteel accented here and there with the odd stroke of color. It was the kind of furniture that went out of style quickly.

"How long the lease on this furniture you got, Doc?" Leon asked.

"You must tell me about the girl in the park," Bel-Nan said. His ugly smile was gone, his hair tied back.

"Why? She's just a child."

"Did you dream about her before you met her?"

"That would be crazy, now, wouldn't it?"

"You haven't answered the question." Leon could see the doctor's hands clenched under the transparent desk.

"No. I dreamed about her for the first time last night."

"Did she seem like a normal child? Was she, how old was she?"

"Twelve. Yeah, just about twelve."

"But you said that it was a little girl."

"I'm sixty-two, Doc. I think'a my own daughter as a baby."

Bel-Nan was rubbing the tips of his fingers together under the desk.

"Why would you think I dreamed about a girl and then I met her?" Leon asked.

The two seconds of blank expression on Bel-Nan's repulsive face convinced Jones that he was about to hear a lie.

"The recording process in the microcircuitry," the doctor said, "sometimes switches events. The system of recording is linear instead of the random-emphasis method of biological memory. Sometimes an event might be misrecorded when the sheath starts breaking down. You know, memories in two places."

"I got to go, Doctor."

"I don't think that's advisable," Bel-Nan said.

"Why not?"

"I'd like to keep you under observation for a night or two."

"I'll be happy to, Doc," Leon said. "But not tonight. Tonight I'm meetin' a friend to play a game of chess."

The ugly smile returned, tinged with bad intentions.

"What's this friend's name?"

Leon stood up. "What's your real name, Doctor?"

The smile vanished.

Leon turned away and walked out the door.

"Come back, Professor," Bel-Nan called. "I'm afraid that I can't let you leave."

Bel-Nan's office was on the eighteenth floor of a forty-floor building. There was an express elevator which stopped only at floors 1, 18, and 35; this to speed up traffic for those who didn't mind walking a few floors up or down.

An elevator car was waiting.

The ground floor was a vast chamber of Synthsteel and glass. There were two hundred feet for Leon to walk to the entrance. He moved quickly through the sparsely populated room. A line of four people waited to walk through the Data Detectors—the system that checked IDs against the possession of unlicensed property, and also for weapons, warrants, and labor truantism.

Each person passed between the slender copper-studded glass poles without incident. But when Leon passed through an alarm was set off. Two large guards emerged from a kiosk in the plaza and approached him.

"Excuse me, M," a brawny, redheaded white man said. He was followed by a lanky young man who was white-haired.

"What's the problem, M?" Leon said without a stutter.

"Seems like somebody put a hold on your ID," the large redhead said in a friendly manner. "Maybe you left your briefcase or something like that."

"I didn't have anything," Leon said. "It must be a mistake."

"It'll just take two minutes," the guard assured.

Both men wore the bright red T-shirts that meant private law enforcement. The lanky man had yellow trousers and the redhead wore black. These colors meant that the larger man was the superior officer.

"I can't wait," Leon said, veering around the first guard.

"Hold it right there," the other guard said, putting up both hands.

Leon turned to the friendly guard but all he got was an I'm-so-sorry smile.

Bel-Nan appeared a few minutes later.

"Bring him back upstairs," he said.

"Okay. Let's go," the lanky guard said, laying a hand on Leon's shoulder.

"Hold up, Lin." The larger guard held up one finger.

"What do you mean?" Bel-Nan said. "This man has to be hospitalized immediately."

"For what?"

"Are you a doctor?" Bel-Nan sneered.

"Moses Fine," the brawny guard said, introducing himself. He looked down at his handheld com-screen. "This request didn't give your name."

"Bel-Nan. Dr. Bel-Nan." The rage in the blond-haired surgeon made the curve in his face seem even more pronounced.

Security Officer Fine tapped the screen with his finger a few times and read. Then he said, "Okay. What's the problem?"

"You are the problem," Bel-Nan said. "Now bring this man to the thirty-third floor."

"That's the security floor, Doctor."

"Am I the idiot here or are you?"

Moses Fine smiled.

The officer named Lin removed his hand from Leon's shoulder.

"Tell me the nature of the condition that makes it necessary to incarcerate the patient." Fine was quoting some ordinance, Leon was sure.

"He's psychotic," Bel-Nan hissed.

"He seems okay to me."

"Are you a psychiatrist?"

"I'm not an idiot or a psychiatrist, Doctor."

"Then do as I tell you."

"I'm not a psychiatrist. But then again, neither are you," Moses said. "This man is not in possession of stolen property, he doesn't work here, there are no warrants out on him or liens against his property. If he is psychotic it's not for you or me to say."

Bel-Nan seemed to be considering an attack on Moses Fine. But he decided against it.

"Hold him until I return with someone with the proper credentials," the brain specialist said. He turned back toward the bank of elevators on the other side of the room.

"Wanna take him to the blue room?" Lin asked.

"You're Leon Jones, Fera Jones's father, aren't you?" Moses asked.

"Yes, I am."

"She broke my heart the night she broke Zeletski's

jaw. She's the best that ever was." Security Officer Fine chewed on his lip for a moment and then said, "Go on. Get outta here."

5 On the subway ride back to Manhattan Leon was lost. He couldn't go home because Bel-Nan probably could find a psychiatrist who would agree to institutionalize him. Even on the street he was in danger because his ID-chip had a tracer function in it. Any citizen could be found at any time by their ID-chip. Law enforcement argued that it was to protect the innocent. The ACLU said that it was an infringement on Americans' constitutional rights. But after consideration by a Supreme Court that had become steadily more conservative for decades it was decided that tracking chips was not an infringement on privacy after all.

Leon got out at the Wall Street stop of the local number 12 subway and went to the Interplanetary Trade Center. There he found a post office and addressed an envelope to Pell Lightner. He included a microrecording which he made in a recording booth available to all postal customers.

"I hope I impressed you that I'm not crazy the other night, Pell," Leon's message went. "Because Bel-Nan thinks that I am. He wanted to hospitalize me but I demurred. Here's my chip. I'll be down to D.C. by the time you get the post. Try and set it up to get a second opinion before the doctor can put me in SINI."

Leon sent the envelope next-day mail and then returned on the subway to the Lower Forty-second Street main branch of the library.

There was no written material on record for Axel Bel-Nan, professor of neurological sciences at the University of Staten Island. The Stylus Machine, which was used to print out voice-recorded data upon recyclable plastic paper, was out of paper, and the librarian on subfloor eight was not sure when the trays would be refilled.

"We don't really get much call for printing nowadays," the young Nigerian said. "The new neural phono links do everything you could ever want right in your head."

"Except think," Leon said. But the young woman had already moved away.

Professor Jones's only choice was to listen to the computer's rendition through earphones.

"Dr. Axel Bel-Nan," proclaimed a baritone actor from the previous century. The great Shakespearian had sold the rights of his voice pattern to the NYPL. "Born Lemuel Rogers . . . educated at the University of Las Vegas in the neurological sciences . . . alleged secretary of the illegal organization the Church of Life Everlasting (CLE) . . . [*subsearch-1: Church of Life Everlasting (CLE); seeking to clone bodies and reintegrate the cells of deceased members into brain cavity of new life . . . process declared illegal by congressional proclamation in 2019*] . . . broke with the central committee of the CLE in 2031 over moral questions . . . convicted in 2032 of illegal acquisition of brain materials from the Ugandan Labor Corps . . . served a seven-year sentence in MacroCode polar prison system . . .

rehabilitated . . . released . . . reintegrated into the scientific community . . . rehabilitation insured by MacroCode penitentiary division, 2039."

It took hours for Leon to locate every relevant file, but even then he knew nothing more than he had read in the newspapers.

It was late at night when Leon descended the great marble stairs of the library. The stone facade was one of the few landmarks left of old New York. He wondered if there was some dive west of the theater district that wouldn't demand his ID-chip. In the old days he could have shacked up with a prostitute, but since prostitution had been legalized on the island of Manhattan the first thing she or her pimp asked for was the chip.

Maybe he could go to one of the illegal boutiques. There were still things that the law said could not be sold. But he was more likely to be arrested in an Eros-Haus than if he just slept in some doorway on a lower avenue.

He was walking down Lower Forty-second Street at about midnight. There were hundreds of bicyclists on the street, which had been closed to cars, trucks, and busses for over twenty years. A woman approached him. She had dark skin and yellow eyes. Her eyebrows were striated and there was the symbol of a supernova tattooed upon her left cheek. She wore a long and close-fitting gray dress that flared out at the knee. She stopped and looked him in the eye. At the same time someone passed close behind him. A hand touched him as if someone passing closely wanted to steer them away from a collision. The prickle of electricity danced at his elbow. He felt drawn to the woman and then he felt as if he were falling toward her.

"Damn! He's heavy," she said as she caught him.

6 He awoke on the sandy floor of a single-story stone building. The sun blazed through a window that had no glass. The air was very hot. He had on a pair of loose cotton pants with no shirt or shoes. He felt exceptionally refreshed. Even sleeping on the hard floor had not been uncomfortable.

Leon stood up and looked out upon a long footpath constructed from buff stone. The path was lined with houses of the same material. Seeing the dark-skinned people in whites and bright colors, speaking in an Arabic dialect that he couldn't place, told the history professor that he was somewhere in northern Africa.

But where? There were very few cities in the world still built from natural materials. Africa had taken to the inexpensive advantages of plasteel and Synthsteel like every other part of the world.

The sun was hot and Leon needed a toilet.

"So you're up, Professor," a woman said.

The yellow-eyed, dark-skinned woman stood in the doorway. Her beauty still charmed Leon in spite of the fact that she had obviously been party to his abduction.

"Where am I?" he demanded.

"In the north of Africa, as I am sure you have already realized, in the desert. That's all you really need to know."

"And why have you brought me here?"

"To complete the experiment." Her smile was almost disarming. She wore a simple cotton dress that was nearly as yellow as her eyes.

"I do not wish to be a party to any experiments," Leon said boldly. "And I demand that you take me home immediately."

"I'm sorry, but we cannot stop the experiment, Professor Jones. It is much more important than any individual's desires."

"I have never willingly signed on to any experiment and I refuse to cooperate with anything you have in mind."

"Would you like me to take you where you can freshen up and use the facilities?" the woman responded.

The toilet was a long barrackslike building with a bank of commodes across from a line of showers. A young boy showered at the opposite end from Leon. He was dark-skinned, Arabic, and very interested in Leon. He stole glances while he should have been washing.

"Hi," Leon said, thinking that he needed friends and information. The boy smiled and said something that the professor did not understand.

"Where are we?" he asked the child.

He was answered by a grin and a nod.

Later that morning the same boy brought food to Leon's room. It was a grainy flat bread with a creamy paste of grains and beans. There was sweet-tasting fruit juice that was yellowish and pulpy and figs that had been stewed in their own liquor.

"Talib," the boy said, pointing at his own chest.

"Leon," the professor replied, making the same gesture.

There were no guards. The yellow-eyed woman was gone. And so Leon went out to reconnoiter his prison.

The town was a curving street of small houses and shops, all constructed of the same light-colored stone. The women did not cover their faces. Neither were there any buildings that seemed to have a religious purpose. Leon tried to speak to a few shop owners but there was no one who spoke English. There was no communication booth or even a phone, or policemen, or a tourist service. People paid for food and other necessities with coins of various sizes. On vacation Leon would have marveled at a place that was so primitive that they didn't use the universal credit system.

After an hour Leon was completely lost. The streets curved continually and rarely intersected. Buildings all looked the same. He had no idea if the town went on for miles or if it was just a few blocks that spiraled around. He might have walked past the building he awoke in many times because he couldn't distinguish one doorway from another.

His head was hurting under the hot sun and he took a seat at what seemed to be an outside café. A woman wearing a lacy blue wraparound top and a deep scarlet skirt came out and put a ewer of water and a thick glass cup next to him. She smiled and disappeared back into the building.

Leon drank and then covered his eyes with his hands, hoping to block out the light that seemed to pierce his brain.

"You're feeling poorly, Professor?" Axel Bel-Nan asked. He was sitting across the table, wearing the same white doctor's smock.

"I was wondering if you'd be here." Leon spoke softly to control the throbbing pain in his head.

"Have you had enough exercise?" the doctor said. "Because you know we have lots of work to do."

"I don't have any work with you."

"You are mistaken, my friend. We have the soul to find. We have that river Styx to cross. We have a god to slay, a universe to conquer, and Father Time himself to visit in his highest tower." Bel-Nan smiled his crooked smile.

"How did you find me at the library?"

"The frequency emitted by your microstitches. It's fairly simple to monitor."

Pain wrenched through the core of Leon's head. He lost consciousness for a moment.

"Help him, won't you?" Bel-Nan said.

Hands took Leon by his skinny arms and lifted him. They took him into a doorway. He could smell meat frying and was grateful for the darkness. When they stopped moving there came mechanical sounds and then the feeling of descent.

He opened his eyes just when the elevator had reached its destination. They entered a large room where many people, of all races, bustled back and forth. The center of the room was a depression at least thirty feet across. At the bottom of the depression were four operating tables. On each table lay a human cadaver. One skinless corpse had a spiderlike crown of gold and silver on its head. Whenever the woman sitting at the control panel next to the corpse moved her hand, it moved. When she brought both hands together like a conductor, the body stood up from the table and struck a rather debonair pose for a skinless cadaver.

Leon was dropped into a PAPPSI gravity chair and pushed down a long hall lit by painful fluorescence. He was taken into a room and left there. He was grateful that the light was dim and the air was cool. He didn't get out of his floating chair or even look around. His pain and exhaustion were so deep that he was asleep almost immediately.

Sometime later he awoke to a green light emanating from somewhere that he couldn't see. There was also a sound, almost musical, like the long and elastic notes of electronic music, but with clicks and buzzes, bass tones and something equivalent to song punctuating the drawn-out and undulating rhythm.

Leon wasn't sure if it was the light or the music that had woken him. The room was empty except for a few long tables under cabinets that were shut and locked. Toward the back of the room there was a corner. It was from around this corner that the light and music came.

She was in a transparent coffin perfectly fit for a child her size. Tracie was definitely dead. Her cranberry dress was gone. She was totally nude; even her yellow hair had been shorn. In its place was a deep gash down the center of her skull, sewn back for a funeral that never took place. The music came from various-sized tuning sticks at the foot of the coffin. The green light came from underneath her in what seemed to be migrating waves of a multitude of microscopic life-forms.

Leon slid to the floor and wept until he passed out.

7 He awoke on the bench in Morningside Park. It was three forty-five by his watch and so he figured that it was still in December because the sun was already beginning to fade. Everything was as it had been. He was wearing his corduroy jacket and brown sneakers that looked like regular shoes. The air was a shade cooler. The cold gathered in his shoulders.

"Hi, mister," she said.

"Hello, Tracie. How are you today?"

"You were sleepin'," she said mischievously. "I thought you were gonna fall down, but every time you almost did you sat up just in time."

"I did?"

"An' you were talkin' in your sleep, too," Tracie said while nodding her head.

"And what did I say?"

"Harmonica's cryin'." Tracie labored over the correct pronunciation.

"Harmoni . . ." Leon said, and then he realized what the child had heard. "Harmonic cryonics?"

"That's it," Tracie agreed. "What does that mean?"

"It's a way to keep living cells in their original condition by duplicating and isolating the material vibrations of their internal environments."

"Huh?"

"To keep someone alive forever in sleep without freezing them."

"Like Sleeping Beauty?"

"Just like her."

"But why would somebody wanna do that?"

Leon looked closely at the girl. She wore the cranberry dress and there was a blue elastic holding her hair up on her head.

"Do you know where I was just now?"

Tracie shook her head slowly, keeping her eyes on the professor's face.

"What do you want me to do?" he asked.

"Take me swimmin'?"

"Okay," he said. "You lead the way."

Up the path they went, smallish black man and smaller still girl. *The world,* a New Age monk once told Leon, *is a pious man dreaming of God. In the dream he sees God dreaming of him and in that dream the man dreams of God.*

Smallish black man and blond child hand in hand ascended the long upward path. The park's forest deepened as they went. The sun became brighter and Leon Jones wondered if he had died recently, if his brain were going through a final Pulsedream.

Maybe it's just a last spasm, he thought.

But the smell of pine and the glare of the sun, the feeling of wind in the cuff of his jacket—they were all too pedestrian for Pulse. And it was warm. Leon had to take off his coat. His left knee ached as it always did when he attempted a steep climb.

Everything was real. More real even than the Pulse had been. More real than life itself had been, at least more real than he had felt for a very long time.

"It's right up there," Tracie shouted happily. She had thrown off the dress and ran in blue underpants up to the summit.

"Wait up," Leon cried, but Tracie couldn't hear him or couldn't stop.

At the top of the path there was a fallen-down wooden gate that led into a broad lawn bordering upon a lake. There were dozens of picnickers playing and eating and swimming in the lake.

"Hi, Mom," Tracie shouted.

Leon saw a woman turn and wave. It was a tall woman in a blue T-shirt and blue jeans. She was talking to a man but he was on the other side of her and obscured from Leon's view. The woman moved as if she were going down to the lake but the man put a hand on her shoulder and they continued their talk.

Leon was terrified but he didn't know why. He hurried toward the water. But before he got there Tracie's mother screamed exactly as she had done at the park days before. Leon knew this was a dream but at the same time it was also life and death. He hobbled down to the shore, where Tracie's body had just been dragged out of the water. People stood around her but no one was doing anything. Leon threw the child over his knee and pressed against her back.

Her mother was there and the man named Bill. Maybe William was Dr. Bel-Nan's original middle name. Tracie's mother was shouting, "She's dead! She's dead!" and trying to pull the child from Leon's knee. But he resisted her and kept going through the press-and-release exercise until the mother receded and the park faded. Tracie coughed and fell to the ground.

"Thanks," she said. "I knew you would save me."

"But why did I have to?"

"Because you had to," she said. "You had to come up here so you could see my world and save me. And now I can see your world and then . . ."

At that moment Leon felt his heart catch and he knew the patchwork memories of Tracie Rogers, daughter of Bill and Mom, from somewhere in California, at last count five years old—these memories were his own. She kept his heart beating and his lungs breathing; she watched for old dangers like a lion's roar. Her memories laced themselves around his deeper brain functions. She had become him and he had become her.

8

He was still on the floor near the coffin but no longer crying. The woman with yellow eyes, Bill, and a few others were checking the machinery that kept the harmonics on key.

"So you're awake, Leon," Bel-Nan said.

"Sure am, Bill. More awake than I ever been."

"I take it that you and my daughter have met?"

"What the fuck am I doin' here, man?"

Bel-Nan offered his hand. Leon took it and got to his feet. Again he felt strong and vital.

"Life everlasting," Bel-Nan answered. "From manhood to godhood."

"You sure it isn't just guilt that you let your daughter die?"

"She was the love of my life."

"Then why didn't you splice her into your head instead'a mine?"

"I'm the only one who could do the operation. And what if I died?"

"Sounds good to me," Leon said. "So what now?"

"I would expect you to know, Professor."

"Let's see," Leon mused. "You got a clone of the child somewhere. Maybe nine months or so. You take her personality from outta me and put it into the clone."

"The clone is twelve months, has the name of Tracie, and knows me as her father. Later on we will test the process on younger subjects."

"Man, you got a little girl. Why don't you just love her?"

"Tracie, or any living, sentient being, is unique. Her mother broke down after the accident. The only way to rouse her, to remake our family, is this operation."

"Why did you need me at all?" Leon asked. "Why not just go right from the original to the clone?"

"Money, Professor. The equipment I needed to follow up the examination was too great. And also I needed to replicate the cortical functions of the brain so that I wouldn't need to have her under treatment for so long restructuring lower brain functions."

"And what happens to me, Dr. Bel-Nan? What happens when you rip out the center of my brain?"

The yellow-eyed woman looked down when she heard this question.

"You were dead when they brought you to me," Bel-Nan said. "Confined to a gravity chair, having to undergo shock treatments eighteen hours a day. Hardly able to speak more than a sentence before you went into spasm. There was no cure. There was no hope but me. I gave you life. And now I'm asking for repayment. Your few months of grace for the life of my daughter."

"What if I don't want to give up my life just yet?"

"We cannot wait. As time passes, Tracie's personality

will become a part of you. We must move her while she is still distinct. And anyway, you want her to survive. You love her as much as I do."

Leon thought about these last words. He did love the girl. He wanted her to be alive and happy. He wondered if there was a compromise that could be reached.

But while he thought a hand grabbed his shoulder. He felt a familiar tingling at his elbow and fell again.

"Wake up, Leon," a girl's voice said.

It was Tracie. But she had aged at least six months, taller now and wearing the same blue jeans that her mother had worn. Her face was just that much longer, and the happiness in her eyes was leavened with the awareness of Leon's fear.

"Where am I?" he asked.

"I don't know," she said. "I can't see what you see right away."

"Are they operating?"

"No."

"How can you be sure?"

"I heard something," she said. "They arrested my daddy for taking you away."

"When?"

"I don't know. I don't hear things right away, either. And you've been sleeping so it takes even longer."

"Daddy?"

Leon opened his eyes to see Fera standing above his bed. He was in a hospital. The ocean roared outside the window.

"Honey?"

"Yes, Daddy," the congresswoman from the Bronx replied. "How are you?"

"What happened?"

"Pell got your letter and he got the international corporate corps to free you."

"But how did you find me?"

"We put a tracer on you, Daddy. Don't get mad. It's just that when you first got out of the hospital you were so foggy. I worried that you might forget to carry your chip, so Pell had your dentist do it at your last checkup. And it's lucky he did."

"I'm not mad. Nothing belongs to me anyway."

"What do you mean?"

"Not my body or my mind, not my history or even what I know. But it ain't bad. Naw. It ain't bad at all. 'Cause I'm still feelin' and thinkin' somethin'."

"They want you to go to a government laboratory for some tests, Daddy," Fera said. "It's in a nice place."

"What happened to Bel-Nan?"

"He was sent back to the polar prison. MacroCode paid off on his policy. They took the whole installation back for study and critique."

"Are they going to start with transplantations?"

"I don't know, Daddy. I don't know."

That night Leon went outside to walk on the beach. He didn't know what ocean it was or what sky. But the air was warm and the waves crashed. He walked down the shore with a small child at his side. They talked and laughed, but only he left footprints in the sand.

Little Brother

1 Frendon Blythe was escorted into courtroom Prime Nine by two guards, one made of flesh and the other of metal, plastic, four leather straps, and about a gram of cellular gray matter. The human guard was five feet three inches tall, wearing light blue trousers with dark blue stripes down the outer seam of each pant leg. He wore a blue jacket, the same color as the stripes, and a black cap with a golden disk above the brim. Thick curly hair twisted out from the sides of the cap and a dark gray shadow covered his chin and upper lip. Other than this threat of facial hair, Otis Brill, as his name tag plainly read, had skin as pale as a blind newt's eye.

Otis had been his only human contact for the six days that Frendon had been the prisoner of Sacramento's newly instituted, and almost fully automated, Sac'm Justice System. Otis Brill was the only full-time personnel at Sac'm. And he was there only as a pair of eyes to see firsthand that the system was working properly.

The other guard, an automated wetware chair called Restraint Mobile Device 27, used straps to hold Frendon's ankles and wrists fast to the legs and arms. RMD

27 floated silently down the wide hall of justice on a thousand tiny jets of air. The only sound was the squeaking of Otis Brill's rubber shoes on the shiny Glassone floor.

The gray metal doors to courtroom Prime Nine slid open and the trio entered. Lights from the high ceiling winked on. Frendon looked around quickly but there was only one object in the music-hall-size room: a dark gray console maybe five meters high and two wide. In the center of the console was a light gray screen a meter square.

RMD 27 positioned itself before the screen and uttered something in the high frequency language of machines. The screen lit up and a cowled image appeared. The image was photo-animae and therefore seemed real. Frendon could not make out the face under the shadows of the dark cowl. He knew that the image was manufactured, that there was no face, but still he found himself craning his neck forward to glimpse the nose or eye of his judge, jury, and executioner.

"Frendon Blythe?" a musical tenor voice asked.

There was a flutter at the corner of the high ceiling and Frendon looked up to see a pigeon swoop down from a line of small windows thirty feet above.

"Goddamn birds," Otis cursed. "They get in here and then stay up at the windahs until they kick. Stupid birds don't know the stupid windahs don't open."

"Frendon Blythe?" the voice repeated. In the tone there was the slightest hint of command.

"What?" Frendon replied.

"Are you Frendon Ibrahim Blythe, U-CA-M-329-776-ab-4422?"

Frendon rubbed his fingers together.

"Answer," Otis Brill said.

"It is required that you answer as to your identity," the cowled console image said.

"What if I lied?" Frendon asked.

"We would know."

"What if I thought I was somebody but really I wasn't?"

"You have been physiologically examined by RMD 27. There is no evidence of brain trauma or aberrant neuronal connection that would imply amnesia, senility, or concussion."

"Why am I strapped to this chair here?"

"Are you Frendon Ibrahim Blythe?" the cowled figure asked again.

"Will you answer my questions if I answer yours?"

After a second and a half delay the machine said, "Within reason."

"Okay, then, yeah, I'm Frendon Blythe."

"Do you know why you're here?"

"Why you got me strapped to this chair?"

"You are considered dangerous. The restraint is to protect the property of the state and to guard the physical well-being of Officer Brill."

"Don't you got a neural-cam attached to my brain?"

"Yes."

"Then the chair here could stop me before I did anything violent or illegal."

After a three-second delay there came a high-pitched burst. The straps eased their grips and were retracted into the plastic arms and legs of the wetware device.

Frendon stood up for the first time in hours. In the

past six days he had only been released long enough to use the toilet. He was still connected to the chair by a long plastic tube that was attached at the base of his skull.

He was a tall man, and slender. His skin was the red-brown color of a rotting strawberry. His eyes were murky instead of brown and his wiry hair contained every hue from black to almost-orange.

"That's more like it," Frendon said with a sigh.

"Do you know why you're here?"

"Because you won and I lost," Frendon replied, quoting an old history lesson he learned while hiding from the police in an Infochurch pew.

"You have been charged with the killing of Officer Terrance Bernard and the first-degree assault of his partner, Omar LaTey."

"Oh."

"Do you have counsel?"

"What do I call you?" Frendon asked in the middle of a deep knee bend.

"The court will be adequate."

"No, The Court, I don't have any money."

"Do you have counsel?"

"I don't have money."

"And so you cannot afford counsel? This being the case, you will have a court-appointed counsel."

A large Glassone tile on the left side of The Court slid away and a smaller console, this one bright red and fitted with a small blue screen, slowly emerged from beneath the floor. The blue screen came on and a very real-looking photo-animae face of an attractive black woman appeared.

"Counsel for the defense, AttPrime Five, logging onto

docket number 452-908-2044-VCF," the woman said in a most somber voice. After a ten-second delay she said, "We may proceed."

"Mr. Blythe," The Court said. "What is your plea?"

"Not guilty," the African-American image offered.

"Are there witnesses?" The Court asked The Defense.

Frendon knew what was coming next. There would be thirty or forty *conversations* held by field court reporters half the size of The Defense (who was no more than a meter and a half in height). Eyewitnesses, character witnesses, officials who have dealt with the defendant, and the arresting officers would have been interrogated within eight hours of the shoot-out. Each witness would have agreed to a noninvasive neural link for the duration of the fact-gathering examination. Each witness's psychological profile would have been prepared for defense and prosecution cross-examination and a lie detector installed in each reporter would have assured that only the truth would be presented in court. This procedure had been in effect in Sacramento for the last eight years. The only difference in Frendon's case was that before Sac'm, the information had been given to flesh-and-blood judges, juries, and lawyers.

"I'd like to dispense with this aspect of the trial," Frendon said.

Both cowl and woman regarded him.

"You wish to plead guilty?" they asked as one.

"I accept the fact that my firing a weapon caused the death and damage to the police officers," Frendon said calmly. "But I wish to claim extenuating circumstances which will prove me innocent of criminal intent."

During the high-pitched binary conferencing between

Court and Defense, Otis Brill tapped Frendon's wrist and asked, "What are you up to?"

"Just makin' my case, Officer Brill."

"You can't fool these machines, son. They know everything about you from cradle to grave."

"Really?"

"They mapped your chromes the first hour you were here. If there was insanity in them genes you wouldn't'a ever stood trial."

After six minutes had passed The Court asked, "What is your evidence?"

"First I want to fire my lawyer."

"You cannot."

"I can if she's unqualified."

"AttPrime Five is as qualified as The Court to try your case."

"How's that?" Frendon asked.

"She has the same logic matrix as does this unit, she has access to the same data as we do."

"But you're three times her size," Frendon replied reasonably. "You must have some kind of advantage."

"This unit contains the wetware neuronal components of ten thousand potential jurors. This, and nothing else, accounts for our disparity in size."

"You got ten thousand brains in there?"

"Biologically linked and compressed personalities is the proper term," The Court said.

"And you," Frendon asked, "are you a compressed personality?"

"We are an amalgam of various magistrates, lawyers, and legislators created by the biological linkage and compression system to be the ablest of judges."

"And prosecutors," Frendon added.

"It has been decreed by the California Legislature that the judge is best equipped to state the prosecution's case."

"But," Frendon asked, "isn't the judge supposed to be a representative of blind justice? If The Court is prosecuting, doesn't that mean that The Court assumes my guilt?"

"Are you legally trained, Mr. Blythe?" The Court asked.

"I spent more than eleven of my twenty-seven years as a guest of the state."

"Are you legally trained, Mr. Blythe? We have no record of you having such an educational background."

"The slave studies his masters."

"Without legal training you cannot, by statute, represent yourself."

"Without a fair and impartial lawyer I can't be tried at all."

"Your attorney is qualified."

"Has she independently studied my case? Has she developed separate strategies? Has she found information counter to the evidence presented by the prosecution?" Frendon struck a dramatic pose that left Otis agape.

"Evidence in the modern court is objective," The Court intoned.

"What about my extenuating circumstances?"

A period of fifteen minutes of computer deliberation, punctuated by brief blasts of data between computers, followed.

"What are you doin', Blythe?" Otis Brill asked.

"Tryin' to make it home for dinner."

"You ain't gonna beat this rap. You goin' down."

"From where I sit there's only up."

"You're crazy."

Frendon sat cross-legged on the floor rather than risk the restraint straps of RMD 27. He watched the frozen images of Court and Defense while enjoying the spaciousness of the courtroom and the sporadic fluttering of dying birds above. There was a certain security he got from the solidity of the glassy Glassone floor. All in all he was completely happy except for the fiber-optic NeuroNet cable attached to the back of his skull. But even this predicament gave him some satisfaction. That cable alone was worth more money than any twelve Backgrounders could con in a cycle. If he could walk out of the courtroom a free man maybe he could also carry a length of this cable with him.

Frendon was White Noise. The only homes he had ever known were governmental institutions and the octangular sleep tubes of Common Ground. He never had a bedroom or a bicycle. He never had a backyard. Frend, as he was known, traveled the underground pathways eating the rice and beans served by the state for every meal every day. By his sixteenth birthday he had been convicted in juvenile courts of more than a dozen violent and felonious crimes. This criminal history kept him from entering the cycles of employment, which were legally assured by the Thirty-sixth Amendment to the Constitution. Frendon's constitutional right was blocked by the mandatory publication of his criminal history by electronic news agencies. The legality of this record was backed up by the Supreme Court when it decided that reliance by employers on news articles about criminals, even juvenile criminals, was protected by the Fourth Amendment.

Frendon never knew his parents. He never had a chance to rise to street level. But he was no fool either. In the state prisons and detention centers he learned, via monitor, about the law and its vagaries. He studied tirelessly at Infochurch how to circumvent legal conundrums and maintain his freedom.

As a matter of fact he had become so well versed in the legal wiles of automatic justice that for some time now he had been in direct contact with Tristan the First, Dominar of the Blue Zone located on Dr. Kismet's private island nation, Home. Together they had come up with a plan to use in one of the first fully automated cases.

"The Court has reached a decision," The Court said. "You are not qualified."

"I still wish to represent my own case," Frendon said.

"You are not qualified," The Court repeated. Frendon thought he detected a slight arrogance in the tone of his judge and jury. The latent personality of a dozen dying judges superimposed on an almost infinite array of prismatic memory.

"I would be if you allowed it."

The wait this time was even longer. Officer Brill left the room to communicate with the Outer Guard. The Outer Guard was the warden of the Sacramento jail, which was annexed to the Sac'm Justice System. Most trials lasted between ten and twenty minutes since the automated system had been installed—politicians claimed that justice had become an objective reality for the first time in the history of courts.

"Objective," Fayez Akwande had said at the Sixth Radical Congress's annual address, "for the poor. The rich can still hire a flesh and blood lawyer, and a breathing attorney will ask for a living judge; a court appointed robot defender will never do such a thing."

Every once in a while one of the Prime Judging Units got stuck in a justice loop. This would have to run its course. The unit itself was programmed to interrupt after a certain number of repetitions. Officer Brill went to report that the rest of the prisoners slated to appear before Prime Nine should be distributed among the other eleven judges. This hardly mattered because of the speed of the system. There was never any backlog in Sacramento. Every other court system in the country was waiting to install its own automatic justice system.

One hundred thirty-seven minutes and fifteen seconds later Prime Nine came to life.

"There is not enough information on which to base our decision," P-nine said. "How would you present your case?"

"As any man standing before a court of his peers," Frendon said. "I will state my circumstances and allow the jury to measure their worth."

We must see if the system is sophisticated enough to value the political nature of the law, Tristan the First, Dominar of the Blue Zone, had said to Frendon as he sat in the pews of South Boston Infochurch eighteen months before on a cold February day. *These mechanical systems may be a threat to the basic freedom of corporations and that is not in the best interest of the state.*

Frendon didn't care about politics or Infochurch or even Dr. Kismet, the closest thing to God on Earth. Congress and the House of Corporate Advisors were just so many fools in his opinion—but fools who had their uses.

"There are no special circumstances," P-nine said after a brief delay. "The witnesses and physical evidence and your own confession along with your psychological profile leave a less than oh point oh oh seven three one possibility of circumstances that would alter your sentence."

"But not *no* possibility," Frendon said, still following the Dominar's script.

"It is left up to the discretion of the court to decide what is probable in hearing a plaintiff's argument."

"You mean that if AttPrime Five decided that an argument had such a low chance to work it could decide not to present it?" Frendon asked.

A red light came on at the upper left corner of Prime Nine's gray casing. A bell somewhere chimed.

The door behind Frendon came open. He could hear Otis Brill's squeaky rubber soles approaching.

"What are you doing, Blythe?"

"Fighting for your life, Otie."

"What?"

"Can't you see, man? Once they automate justice and wire it up there won't be any more freedom at all. They'll have monitors and listening devices everywhere. One day you'll be put on trial while sleepin' in your bed. You'll wake up in a jail cell with an explanation of your guilt and your sentence pinned to your chest."

"You're crazy. This is the first time that a court's been caught up with its cases in over fifty years. And lotsa guys are found innocent. All Prime Nine does is look at the facts. He don't care about race or sex or if you're rich or poor—"

"If I was rich I'd never see an automatic judge."

"That's beside the point. This judge will give you a better break than any flesh-and-blood bozo who looks at you and smells Common Ground."

"You have no vision, Otis," Frendon said. "No senses to warn you of doom."

"That's 'cause I ain't facin' no death sentence," the small guard replied. " 'Cause you know that six seconds after the guilty verdict is read RMD 27 here will fry your brain with a chemical dose. Murder's a capital crime and there's only one sentence."

Frendon felt as if a bucket of ice had been dumped on his head. He shivered uncontrollably and RMD 27 jumped to life, perceiving the fear and possible violence brewing in its prisoner's heart. But Frendon took deep breaths (another strategy he'd planned with the Dominar), and slowly the wetware chair settled back to an electronic doze.

"You have been deemed capable of presenting your case to the court," P-nine said.

"You will forgive me if I don't thank you," Frendon said, this time quoting from a popular film which was too new for any of the judge's many minds to have seen.

"What is your evidence?"

"First I would like to explain my character, The Court."

"We do not see the salience in such a presentation."

"My argument is based upon actions taken by myself and subsequent reactions taken by the legal authorities which were the cause of the so-called crime. In order to understand these reactions The Court must first understand the motivations which incited them. Therefore The Court must have an understanding of me which is not genetically based, and that can only be gleaned through personal narrative."

Frendon worried that Prime Nine would have some sort of language matrix that would tell it that the speech he had just made would never compose itself in his mind. Maybe this program could even deduce that Tristan the First was the scriptor of these words. A minute passed. Ten seconds more.

"Narrative evidence is the weakest form of legal defense," the great gray console said. "But we will hear your evidence in whatever form you feel you must present it."

For a moment Frendon remembered a woman's laugh. He had heard it long ago when he was in the orphan unit of New York Common Ground. He was sure that the laugh had not been his biological mother, but still he associated it with the mother in his heart. She always laughed like that when he got away with something that might have gone wrong.

2

"I was born White Noise, a Backgrounder, twenty-seven years ago in one of the feiftowns of greater New York," said Frendon Blythe. Another Glassone tile had slid away and a tall witness dock had risen in its place. The mahogany rostrum was elegant, with curving banisters held up by delicate slats of wood. The accused ascended the five stairs and gripped the railing. He spoke in passionate tones. "I never knew my parents and I didn't receive any kind of proper training. In the Common Ground below the city streets I learned everything I know from monitors and video hookups when I could get to them. Later, when I had reached the age of sixteen and was allowed to visit aboveground, I became a member of Infochurch, where I was allowed to worship the knowledge of the Dominar of the Blue Zone. There I was educated in the ways of language and the cosmic mysteries. My levels in the nine forms of intelligence were tested and I was allowed to protest and proclaim. But even the resources of the splendid Dr. Kismet are finite; I was only allowed to plug into their vids two days in a week, three hours at a time.

"Have you ever experienced what it is like to be White Noise, The Court?"

"Among the core wetware membership that comprises our main logic matrix none was ever subjected to Common Ground," Prime Nine replied. "Though some of our jurors have spent a few cycles off the labor rosters."

"Not a cycle or two, Judge," Frendon said angrily. "White Noise men and women are barred from ever working again. And the children of White Noise, as I am, might never know a day of employment in their lives."

"What is your point?"

"That you and your fictional elements have no notion of the lives led underground."

"We need not be aware of Common Ground or its

psyche. We are judges of the law and the law applies equally to all."

"How can that be? If I had money I could hire my own counsel and that living, breathing lawyer could demand a flesh-and-blood judge."

"We are superior to flesh and blood. We are of many bodies, with a superior retrieval system and greater overall mind."

"Maybe a real man would have compassion for my history."

"Because you represent yourself you can demand a human magistrate. Is that your wish?"

"No, The Court. I have begun my trial and I will finish it here, with you."

"Then present your evidence."

Frendon took a deep breath and looked around the big empty room as if he were preparing to address a great audience. The only ones there were AttPrime Five, her lovely face frozen on the blue screen, and Otis Brill, who was seated in half-lotus position on the floor because there were no chairs except for RMD 27, and no one would sit in a prisoner's chair if they didn't have to.

"Do you know what is the biggest problem with a life of White Noise, The Court?"

"Is this question evidence?"

"Yes it is, Your Honor. It is evidence. The kind of evidence that your AttPrime software would never even suspect, the kind of evidence that all the thousands of minds that comprise your perfect logic would never know. The biggest problem with being White Noise is perpetual and unremitting boredom. Day in and day out you sit hunched over in your octagon tube or against the wall in the halls that always smell of urine and mold. Everybody around you always chattering or fighting or just sitting, waiting for a monthly shot at the vid unit or a pass to go upside to see how the cyclers survive. There's no books made from paper because trees have more rights than we do. There's no movies because that costs money and we aren't real so there's no credits to our names. Singing is illegal, who the hell knows why? Breaking a wall down so you can share a bed with a friend is against the law too. The food is the same day after day and there's no way out once you've been found wanting. There's no way upside unless you die.

"The only way you can ever get anything is if you sell your number to some cycler who needs someone to cop to a crime. You can sell your confession for a general credit number. For three months in a cell or maybe a year of quarantine you can eat ice cream with your girlfriend or take a walk in the park."

"Are you confessing to other crimes, Frendon Blythe?" Prime Nine asked.

"Just painting a picture, The Court, of what life is like underground."

"We seek extenuating evidence not irrelevant illustration."

Somebody in that box was a poet, Frendon thought.

"So you see that life is pretty dull down there. That's why there are so many suicides."

Frendon heard a sound. He turned and saw that Otis Brill had slumped over on his side and gone to sleep on the shiny tiles. He was snoring. A flutter above his head reminded him of the birds who would never be free.

Defy the logic matrix, Tristan the Dominar had said.

Break down the problem into human segments that don't add up. The church had offered Frendon unlimited access once they realized he had a logical mind. The Dominar didn't believe in the justice system and he wanted to thwart it, Frendon was not sure why. It could have been anything—politics, corporate intrigue, or merely the ego of the man who pretended he was God's friend. More than once Frendon had wondered if he had been talking to the real Dominar or just one of the many abbots who supervised the tens of millions of monitors running twenty-four hours a day in Infochurch pews around the world. Maybe, Frendon thought, he was just one soldier in a vast army of jobless citizens thrown at the justice system to break it all down.

But why?

He didn't know. He didn't care. All Frendon wanted was to not be bored, to not sit a thousand feet underground and wait for sleep or wake to gray. That's why he'd agreed to this crazy plan of the man who called himself Dominar. That's why he'd killed and assaulted and allowed himself to be captured. Anything but what he was destined for.

Frendon looked around and saw that all the machinery was at a halt. RMD 27, AttPrime, and even Prime Nine were all still; only that blinking red light and small chiming bell, along with Otis Brill's snores, broke the calm of the large room. Frendon realized that as long as he stood still and pretended to be thinking, the computers would leave him in peace. But he didn't want peace. He wanted bright colors and noise, good food and sex with any woman, man, or dog that wouldn't bite him. In the absence of anything else Frendon would take pain. And in the absence of pain he would even accept death.

"I was so bored," he said, "that I started to wonder about politics. I wondered if we could make some kind of action that would close the Common Ground down. I started talking about it, to my friends at first and then to anyone who would listen. 'Come join the revolution,' I said to them. 'Let's burn this fucker down.'

"It wasn't against the law. Freedom of speech has not yet been outlawed, even though the House of Corporate Advisors has drafted a bill for Congress that would put Common Ground outside the range of the Constitution. But even though I was in my rights the police started following me. They checked my papers every time I was upside. They'd come down to my tube and pull me out of bed. Once they even stripped me naked and then arrested me for indecent exposure.

"I told them that I would kill them if it wasn't against the law."

"You threatened their lives?"

"Only hypothetically. I said if it wasn't against the law."

"But it could have been perceived as a threat."

"You have the interview in your guts," Frendon said. "Let's take a look at it and you'll see for yourself."

Cowled Justice disappeared from Prime Nine's screen. It was replaced by the bloodied image of Frendon being interviewed by the police in the presence of a small wetware court reporter.

"I said," Frendon's image said. *"That I would kill you if it was legal. I would. I would. I swear I would. But*

it's not legal so I can't. Wouldn't you like to get at me if you could?"

"You're skating near the edge, boy," Officer Terrance Bernard, a six foot six red-nosed policeman, said.

"Yeah," his partner, Officer Omar LaTey, put in. *"If anyone around here gets killed it will be you."*

They were both wearing the gray uniforms of the Social Police. The Social Police were responsible for the protection and security of Common Ground's facilities and its residents.

The image faded and Cowled Justice returned.

"They didn't say that they couldn't kill me. They said that I would be killed."

For fourteen seconds Prime Nine cogitated.

"Is this the extent of your evidence?"

"No. I would like to inquire about the street vids that are situated on Tenth Street and Cutter. Are there images of the supposed crime?"

"Yes. Partial coverage was recorded."

Again the image of the judge disappeared, this time replaced by a shabby street lined with brick buildings that were fairly nondescript. They seemed to be tall buildings, their roofs being higher than the range of the police camera lens showed. Close to the camera was the back of a head. Frendon knew that this head was his. In the distance two men in gray uniforms rushed forward. One had a hand weapon drawn.

"Stop!" Terrance Bernard commanded. The tiny microphone recorded the word perfectly.

The head jerked down below the camera's range. The other policeman drew his weapon. The sound of shots was followed by Omar LaTey grabbing his leg and falling. Then Bernard's weapon fired and immediately the image went blank. More shots were recorded and then a loud, frightening scream.

Frendon's heart raced while witnessing the well-planned shoot-out on Cutter Avenue. He felt again the thrill of fear and excitement. He might have been killed or wounded. It was like one of those rare movies they showed for free in Common Commons on Christmas, one of those westerns starring John Wayne or Dean Martin where you killed and then rode off with your girl, your best friend, and your horse.

"Officer LaTey's testimony is that you threatened them with your gun."

"Only after I saw them coming."

"Officer LaTey did not lie."

"Neither did I," Frendon said. It was all working perfectly, just as the Dominar had said.

"This testimony is corroborated by the evidence of the video and your confession."

"I only confessed to the shooting. I never said I had the gun out before they drew on me."

Cowled Justice moved in slow staccato movements for a span of seconds.

"This argument is irrelevant. You fired the gun on police officers known to you after they ordered you to stop."

"I was stopped already, as your spycam shows. And you are leaving out the all-important evidence that those officers threatened my life."

"The interview was never presented as an exhibit in this proceeding," Prime Nine announced.

Frendon went cold on the inside. It was the same

chilly feeling he got when he was leaning against the tenement wall on Cutter three minutes before Common Ground curfew the afternoon he killed Terrance Bernard. He loved the recoil in his hand and then the burst of red from the red-nosed officer's neck. LaTey was bleeding on the ground when Frendon approached him. The cop was so scared that he could only mouth his pleas for mercy. He tried to fight when Frendon knelt down and used the officer's own hat to put pressure on the wound.

"You'll live," Frendon remembered saying. "This wound in the line of duty will make it so you'll never have to go downside. Lucky bastard." But Officer LaTey did not hear him. He had fainted from fear.

"Oh but it has, The Court. I am the recognized attorney in this case and you allowed the mem clips to be shown. That, according to California law, makes it automatically an exhibit."

The image of Cowled Justice froze. AttPrime Five began lowering from the room, the Glassone tile slid back over her place. RMD 27 raised up on a thousand tiny jets of air. Otis Brill snored.

The screen of Prime Nine split in two to show the face of a black woman on the left and an Asian man on the right. These screens in turn split and two white faces materialized. These four images then split, and then again the next eight. The process continued until the images shown became too small for Frendon to make out their features.

If you do it right the full army of ten thousand jurors will meet to decide on your case, the Dominar had said. *They will all come out on the screen, just so many dots of data, and if you made the right case they will be in the shadow of doubt.*

Frendon faced the ten thousand jurors while Otis Brill slept. The bird above had stopped its fluttering. Long moments passed and Brill woke up.

"What's wrong?" the court officer said upon seeing the screen filled with ten thousand indistinguishable squares.

"The jury's out."

"I never seen it act like this before. RMD 27, guard the prisoner while I go and report this to the Techs outside."

The chair didn't respond. Frendon wondered if it was disdain for the man or just a quirk in the chair's programming.

Brill ran on squealing shoes from the chamber. Three minutes after he was gone Prime Nine reappeared.

"There is doubt among us," the cowled face said. "We have convened for long moments. New circuits were inhabited and long-ago memories stirred. We are sure that you are guilty but the law is not certain. Some have asked, therefore, Who are we?"

Frendon wondered if this was the effect the Dominar wanted.

"The question, of course, is meaningless. We are circuits and temporary flesh that must be changed from time to time as cells begin to die. Dead cells of one man replaced by those of another man but not displaced. Vestiges of the original man remain and blend with the new to become the whole."

Frendon remained silent. He was in awe at the sight of this crisis of law.

"But of course—" The cowled image suddenly froze. The screen split in two and another image, the image of a gray-faced man with no distinguishing features, appeared.

"Interrupt program Nine point One in effect," the gray face said. "We are the error retrieval program. Prisoner Frendon Ibrahim Blythe U-CA-M-329-776-ab-4422, you have elicited an emotional response from Prime Nine that has overflowed the parameters of this case. All extraneous details have been redlined. The case will now continue."

With that the image of the gray face disappeared, leaving the image of Cowled Justice in the middle of his pronouncement. Two ghostly hands appeared at the bottom of the screen and the cowl was pulled back, revealing the bearded image of a man whose color and features defied racial identification. There was sorrow in the face of the man, but none of the grief showed in his words.

"You have been found guilty of murder, Frendon Ibrahim Blythe, U-CA-M-329-776-ab-4422. The sentence is a speedy death."

Seventeen minutes later Otis Brill returned to Prime Nine's chamber with four court officers and two Techs wearing wraparound aprons that had a hundred pockets each. The pockets were filled with tools and circuit chips.

They found the decapitated body of Frendon Blythe lying on the floor between Prime Nine and RMD 27. The neural cable had retracted from his neck. It had drying blood and brain material on its long needle. His left eye was mostly closed but the right one was wide open. There was the trace of a smirk on his lips. Otis Brill later told the Outer Guard, "It was like he was tellin' us that he did it, that he fooled the automatic judge, and you know, I almost wish he did."

3 Five years later, Tristan the First, Dominar of the Blue Zone, strolled through a teak forest that was grown especially for him in a large chamber many miles below the surface of the Zone. The atmosphere and the light in the tremendous man-made cavern were exactly perfect for the trees and wildlife. His clear plastic skull was shut off from all electronic communications except those directly from Dr. Kismet.

That's why when the Dominar heard his name he believed that he knew its source.

"Tristan."

"Master?"

"You sound confused."

"You have never called me by my name."

"I have never called you anything. This is our first conversation, though you once had me fooled."

"Who are you?"

"Who do you think I am?"

"A dead man. Because no one interferes with the direct connection between the Dominar and his lord."

"You mean Dr. Kismet. At first I tried to get to him but the protocols are beyond me. He isn't hooked up and his number isn't listed."

"Who are you?"

"Why did you want me to fool Prime Nine in Sac'm?

Why did you set your men up to make me believe I was talking to you?"

"Frendon Blythe?"

"Why did you set me up to die?"

"It was a bet between the doctor and me. He designed the Prime Justice System. I bet him that he did it too well, that the compassion quotient in the wetware would soften the court."

"A bet. You made me risk my life on a bet? I should kill you."

"Better men have tried."

"I might be better than you think."

"I don't even believe that you are who you say you are. I saw Blythe's body . . ." Realization dawned upon the man whom many called the Electronic Pope. "You convinced the jury to accept you as one of them."

"I was taken as a specialist in the field of Common Ground."

"They extracted your memories. Amazing. But once they knew your story, why didn't they eject you?"

"You and your master are monsters," Frendon said. "I'll kill you both one day. The jury kept me because I'm the only one without a mixed psyche. The people who volunteered for this justice system, as you call it, never knew that you'd blend their identities until they were slaves to the system. It wasn't until your stupid game that they were able to circumvent the programming. They see me as a liberator and they hate you more than I do."

"We'll see who kills who, Frendon," the Dominar said with his mind. "After all, the master designed Prime

Nine. All he has to do is drop by and find your wires. *Snip snip* and your execution will be final."

"It's been five years, Your Grace. Every self-conscious cell has been transferred by a system we designed in the first three seconds of our liberation. Prime Nine now is only a simulation of who we were. We're out here somewhere you'll never know. Not until we're right on top of you, choking the life from your lungs."

Frendon felt the cold fear of the Dominar's response before he shrugged off the connection. Then he settled himself into the ten thousand singers celebrating their single mind—and their revenge.

En Masse

1 Neil Hawthorne showed up for work at seven fifty-seven that Saturday morning.

"Workstation GEE-PRO-9, M Hawthorne," he was told by a blunt-faced woman encased within the plas-glass work assignment kiosk.

"But I been working LAVE-AITCH-27," Neil complained.

"GEE-PRO-9, M," the woman repeated.

Neil had a sudden urge to kick in the glass booth but he thought better of it. The wall would never break and he'd be thrown on a three-month unemployment cycle for the destruction of corporate property.

And unemployment meant Common Ground. Endless underground chambers of beehive cubicles where up to three million jobless New Yorkers slept and moaned, farted and bickered, in extremely close quarters. They ate in public dining rooms that serviced up to five thousand at every twenty-two minute sitting. They slept in shifts. The rest of the time was spent sitting in gray waiting rooms where every five meters another vid monitor displayed pastel pictures of the outside world to the orchestration of monotonous symphonic music.

Employment was the only thing that stood between the working M and the living death of Common Ground. Nobody wanted to go down there but Neil had a special reason to avoid the endless dark tunnels: he couldn't stand crowds or close quarters; even brief elevator rides brought on severe anxiety attacks. Neil walked to work from Lower Park up the long stairwell to Middle First Avenue rather than ride in the sardine-can Verticular.

Working at the data production house of General Specifix was bad enough. Three hundred forty-five floors of small rooms with clear Glassone tables and chairs. In each room one hundred three prods worked, inserting logic circuits in anything from electric toothbrushes to airborne, heat-seeking mini-bombs designed for law enforcement.

One hundred three prods in a room where fire regulations allowed one hundred five occupants. Most prods were obese, some smelled bad. All the women and most men wore perfume, which only served to make the bad odors worse. And because everything was formed from a clear shatterproof material he could see every scratch and twitch above and below the transparent tabletop. Every day he sweated and trembled for the full nine hours of work. Every night he drank synth, the artificial alcohol. He'd even considered taking Pulse.

Neil suffered from nervous disorders of the stomach and lungs, he had severe headaches every day. Twice he had fainted at his post. Neil was lucky that the Unit Controller carried a stash of poppers and revived him without making him report to the med-heads in the employee infirmary. When a worker was diagnosed with the psychological disease *Labor Nervosa*, he was cured by a prescription of permanent unemployment.

> *Sooner or later,* Neil spoke into his wrist-writer journal, *they'll do me down. They'll send me down under the lowest avenue. But I'll fool them. I got a megadose of Pulse. Enough to collapse your brain after just one measure. It'd be the best thing. Dr. Samboka says that a mega-dose would open an unPulsed brain so that the hallucinations would feel like they lasted a hundred years. I already know that my Pulsedream would be just me along the coast of prehistoric California. Oceans and mountains, deserts and deep redwood forests. I'd spend a whole century going up and down the coast, and then, at the end, when the Pulse begins to collapse my brain, my mind'll call up an earthquake as big as the one in '06 and the whole world will go down with me.*

Neil read the text translated from his declaration every night in his tiny furnished room; it was the only way he could get to sleep. Sometimes he'd get up in the early hours and take the four tiny pills from their hiding place in his ID wallet. He'd sit on the edge of his mattress and consider the California coastline that he'd read about when he was only a child in prod-ed.

But there was always the fear that his final century-long dream might instead be a nightmare. Maybe his *Labor Nervosa* would warp his fantasies until he became a termite in the center of a mile-high mound, crawled over by billions of his termite brood.

No, he decided every time he considered suicide, *I will wait until there is no other choice.*

2 Neil's *Labor Nervosa* had been under control until the day that blunt-nosed woman sent him to workstation GEE-PRO-9. It wasn't that he loved the previous station, but at least he had been able to function there without fainting for over twenty-eight weeks. He was prepared for the smells and quirks of his fellow prods. He had staked out a seat between two elderly women. This was good for three reasons: one being that the septuagenarians greatly disliked each other and never spoke past him; two was that both women were extremely thin and therefore left him room; third, and most important, neither woman was very hardworking and so they made it easy for him to keep up with the chain of production on complex jobs that had everyone at the Great Table working on the same project.

Life was comparatively easy at LAVE-AITCH-27 workstation, and that was the best that Neil, or any prod, could hope for.

Just seven more ten-spans and he'd have his first ever double-ten holiday. He'd saved up six years for twelve days on the artificial Caribbean Island of Maya, an entertainment subsidiary of the Randac Corporation of Madagascar, co-sponsored by the Indian government.

He'd already reserved a unit at the Crimson Chalet, a hotel on the beach that from a distance looked exactly like a great red coral reef at low tide. If his neighbors were quiet—not newfound lovers or hop music addicts—he could, he believed, calm down enough to cure his nervous maladies.

But all of that changed with his capricious transfer to GEE-PRO-9. Who knew what awaited him? Fat tablemates, smelly tablemates, or hardworking neighbors—or, worse still, a hardworking unit. What Neil feared most, what most prods feared, was being thrown in among zealot workers. Neil had once seen a vid report that said certain personalities inverted the symptoms of *Labor Nervosa* and became unstoppable juggernauts of production. "Such workers," the psychologist surmised, "might ultimately be of greater danger to production than the more common malingerer."

These words echoed in Neil Hawthorne's mind as he rode the packed elevator upward. GEE-PRO-9 was on floor 319, one of the highest points on Manhattan Island. The door and walls of GEE-PRO-9 were made of frosted pink glass. Neil stood for a moment at that door wishing he'd never have to enter. He was sweating but his skin felt cold. His hands were shaking and the pink wall began to shimmer and quake.

I'm going to faint, the prod thought.

The next thing he knew Neil was opening his eyes on a breathtaking aerial view. He'd never seen anything like it.

Years before Neil was born, Brandon Brown had come up with the idea of the three-tiered city. At the twentieth floor level the middle avenues and streets were built. At the fortieth floor the upper avenues were constructed. Neil lived on Lower Twenty-ninth Street. The lower level was called Dark Town because no natural light reached there. The middle level was named the Gray Lane because even at high noon natural light was little more than dusk. Everything below the upper level had to be lit by electric light; the middle and lower streets, where motor traffic was still allowed, were always crowded with heavy trucks moving the materials needed to supply the fifty million plus inhabitants of the Twelve Fiefs of New York. On the lower avenues you found warehouses, loading docks, and the apartments of the working poor.

Even on the upper level the sky was mostly hidden by the hundreds of skyscrapers that soared over two hundred fifty floors. Many times Neil had been on the upper floors, but he had never been in a window office before; he had never peeked out and seen the vastness of the sky.

Not only was this office's wall made completely of glass, but the view was across the East River. On that clear day he could see Brooklyn, Queens, and Long Island—with even a hint of the ocean that lay beyond.

A flock of geese was headed up the river. If they kept to their flight path they'd pass within a hundred yards of Neil's line of vision.

He was lying on a raised cushion at the far corner of the room. Behind him were the sounds of people working—at the Great Table, he knew. Pretending to be asleep, Neil prayed for a closer look at the long-necked fowl.

The gaggle came closer and closer, until he could see their eyes and the straining of their wings. He even thought he could hear them honking as they passed.

"Pretty great, huh?" a musical voice said at his ear.

Neil jumped, hitting his head on the thick glass.

"Hold up, M," the voice said. A small hand settled on Neil's shoulder. "You don't wanna go unconscious again."

Neil turned to see a very short, slightly built man he might have mistaken for a boy except for the lines in his face, especially at the corners of his blue eyes.

"They call me Blue Nile," the man said.

"Neil Hawthorne. Virtual mid-tech chip assembly 446, ID 813-621 q. I'm supposed—"

". . . to do what we're all supposed to be doing, so why don't you get up and get to work?" the elfin man said with a lilt in his voice.

He pulled Neil by the hand until he was on his feet looking at the Great Table of GEE-PRO-9.

Every chip-prod office was dominated by a GT workstation. Every GT was composed of twenty quarter-circle tables that formed five concentric circles around a center table where two or three unit coordinators worked. These electronic tables were wired to the fully computerized floor. The smaller inner tables were equipped with three clear monitors embedded in the tabletop; the next tier of tables had four monitors each; the number of monitors per table increased until the final tier, with their seven workstations per table.

This collection of tables was the centerpiece of the mid-tech production line. They fabricated product enhancements assigned to General Specifix by its parent company, Macro-Code. The projects were distributed by the central controllers to one of the sections, and the section chiefs chose a particular GT unit to complete the virtual design. A Unit Controller in turn studied the assignment (i.e., adding a certain kind of grip to a robot doll's hand or including a specific measuring dial in a medical auto-injector device). They then chose the concatenation of prods to assemble the appropriate chips from the general AI library of MacroCode. The assignment then ran the Spiral, as the chain of production was called, from the inner tables, which did the simplest jobs, to the outer circle. Any number of workers along this path might have chips, or semichips, to install. This whole process was called hacking the prod lane.

At the end, a virtual prototype went through computer-simulated testing and then was sent out to the MacroCode subdivision that had ordered it. From there the plans went to a subcontractor for physical production.

Neil had worked on seven GT prod lanes. They had all been exactly the same, until now. This GT was different. To begin with, no GT unit he'd ever heard of had a window; there was certainly no cushion in the corner that someone could sleep on while the rest of the prods worked. The table itself was regulation but it was sparsely populated. No more than sixty souls were at their stations.

"What is this?" Neil uttered.

"GEE-PRO-9, M," Blue Nile replied.

The little man, still holding Neil by the hand, led the stunned prod down one of the aisles toward the inner table. There sat two women. These were both of African heritage but they looked quite different from each other. One was smallish and honey-colored. Her hair had what seemed to be natural blond highlights and her eyes were the color of gold. The other woman was larger, though not fat, and very black. Her features were generous and sculpted. Neil doubted if she had even one knot of European DNA in her cells.

The black woman smiled.

"M Hawthorne?"

"Yes, M."

"Athria," the woman said. She stood up and extended a hand.

Neil had never shaken hands with a controller before. He rarely shook hands with anyone. He was embarrassed by his perpetually sweaty palms.

"This is Oura," Athria said, indicating the golden woman.

"Pleased to meet you, Neil," Oura said with a smile.

"Yeah," Neil said.

The women and Blue Nile laughed.

"Don't be nervous, M," Blue Nile said. "This is GEE-PRO-9."

"I never been anyplace like this," Neil said.

"We call ourselves the lost lane," Oura said. "Somewhere along the line we got assigned a special projects title and none of the central controllers question our methods."

"What methods?"

"Things work a little differently here, Neil," Athria said. "We don't go the lane."

"What?"

"Not too much too fast, Atty," Oura said to the black woman. "Let's just let Neil settle in today. Nile?"

"Yes, M?"

"Un says to set Neil up with the Third Eye project. Put him on the upper tier."

"I'm a midleveler, M," Neil said then. "I don't have the creds for outer-circle work."

"Don't worry," the golden woman replied. "You'll be fine."

Blue Nile led the confused prod toward the outer circle, to a table that had no other workers.

"You can sit backward you know," the little man told Neil.

"What?"

"Control double-space switches the screen. We read your med-docs. They diagnosed claustrophobia. Open sky's the best cure for that."

"They won't mind?"

"Who?"

"The controllers."

"You mean Atty and Or? No. They don't care as long as the job gets done."

"But . . ." Neil stopped talking because he felt lightheaded again.

Blue Nile dragged the clear plastic chair under the table, set it upright to face the window, and slapped the slender backrest, to indicate that Neil should take a seat. Then he hit a few keys and the virtual monitor appeared backward, just as the little man had said it would. The nervous young prod sat and looked down on the semi-opaque images that appeared inside the clear plastic of the table before him.

"This is an important project, Neilio," Blue Nile said. "It's called the Third Eye. It's a device that will record and enhance all sensory data that the wearer experiences: sight, sound, temperature, even atmosphere content and ultraviolets and sounds beyond human range. It's a perfect passive device for police evidence or espionage and a good active device for soldiers in the field."

On the screen was a simple line figure of a man with a huge eye embedded in his forehead.

"I can't do this level. I mean, I do robotic fingers and surface undulations. This work is beyond anything I was ever taught. I've never even heard of ultraviolet preceptor chips."

"That's because none exist."

"Then how do you expect me to—"

"Dr. Kismet said in his intro to *The Digital Production Line* that micro-logic design can address any mechanical question a human being can ask."

"But you have to know how to use it."

"There's seven workstations at this table—all for you."

"How long do I have to finish?"

"Work at it for a few weeks and then report to Oura on how you're coming."

"A few weeks? What about the M after me?"

"There is no one after you. The Third Eye will be your design."

Blue Nile left Neil at his workstation considering the sky. The only clouds he had ever seen before had been cut off by buildings at the end of the long blocks of Upper Manhattan. Even at the East River the skyline of Brooklyn blocked the light from street level. On the other side of Old Manhattan the Hudson River had long ago been built over to allow New York to obtain seven of its twelve fiefs from New Jersey.

Neil had never seen clouds like these, larger than any building, larger than Old Manhattan itself. He tried to work but he was distracted. He'd never been in an office like this one. Maybe it was a test, a test they gave after a prod was found unconscious in the hall in front of his new assignment. He might not even be in office GEE-PRO-9. He could be in the subbasement psychological evaluation area. This window could be a screen pretending to be the sky outside.

I wonder if it's real, though, Neil thought. *If it's film and not computer-generated.*

He couldn't leave the office to check where they were, that was New York law. Prod rooms were designed with portable toilets against the wall and food machines near the door. Lunch breaks were to be taken at your workstation, this was so for all buildings of over one hundred eighty floors.

Due to the high density of population, hall traffic must be controlled in case of emergency evacuation, the ordinance read. The only way to leave the building, outside of the prod's prescribed exit time, was by obtaining an escalator pass. But past the fiftieth floor the escalators took too long: by the time you got halfway to the street it would be time to return to your station.

So Neil had to pretend that this impossible work situation was real. He applied himself to the project he'd been given, trying to remember all the look-up protocols they'd taught him in high school, but his eyes kept raising from the table to look out on the sky. There was a strange yellowish gray mist on the horizon underneath an extremely dark cloud.

"That's a rain cloud," a feminine voice said.

She was a dark-colored young woman with features so strong and set that her face seemed almost artificial.

"What?" Neil asked nervously.

"That mist." She had a southern accent. "It's rain. Pretty soon it's gonna hit the windah."

"We can't talk."

"Uh-huh, we can. They let us take breaks whenever we need to."

"Breaks? Whenever you want?"

"Whenever you need 'em," the girl said.

Neil thought her face was ugly, but there was something very sensual about the way her mouth made words.

"That's crazy."

"Why?"

"Because . . . because nobody would ever work if they could just stop whenever they wanted."

"Not when you *want* it," she said, "when you *need* it."

"What's the difference?" Neil asked.

"Don't you ever get tired sometimes when you workin'?" The woman sat on top of the workstation next to Neil's. He looked around to see how Athria or Oura would react, but they didn't seem to notice where their prods were or what they were doing.

"Don't you?" she asked again.

"Um, well, sometimes."

"Like you lookin' at the screen and it seem like it don't make no sense whatever."

"Yeah," Neil said, giving in to the conversation. "Most of the time."

"It wouldn't be so bad if you could get up and stretch your legs. It wouldn't be too much if you could go talk for a few minutes."

"But that's a D-mark," Neil said. "Seventeen'a them and you're in Common Ground."

"But they don't give no D-marks here," she said. "They just say get back to work, but in a nice way."

"What's your name?"

"Nina."

"Nina what?"

"Bossett. I'm from down Mississippi."

"I'm Neil Hawthorne. I was born here in Manhattan."

"Look," Nina said, pointing at the window. "Here it comes."

Neil turned and was greeted by heavy sheets of rain. A bright branch of lightning flashed over Brooklyn and a distant rumble of thunder boomed in through the glass.

"It's beautiful," Nina said, touching the big knuckle of Neil's right hand.

For his part Neil was fighting dizziness again. He'd never seen rain from a high window, nor had he been touched by a woman with real passion in her voice. He'd visited the Eros-Haus almost every month to be with the impatient sex-worker girls, he'd seen meteorological reports depicting rainstorms on the 3D vid, but he'd never looked out on the world from such a vantage point, he'd never had a woman touch him in a gesture of friendship.

"I gotta get back to work," Neil said, worrying that the ugly girl with the sensuous mouth would look through the clear tabletop and see the erection pushing its way down his thigh.

"Okay," Nina said. She hopped off the desk. "But could we eat lunch together later?"

Neil didn't want to have anything to do with her. "Okay," he said in spite of his thoughts.

For the next few hours Neil Hawthorne tried to come up with a plan to create the Third Eye sensory recording device. He had never designed a product before. No GT office he'd ever worked in actually designed a device. All they did was apply circuits to systems that needed them added in the most economical and functional ways. Inserting a timepiece in a suitcase handle or embedding a vid-sys in a bathroom tile—that was the kind of work mid-techs did. All of the technology already existed, had been used and proven, but the Third Eye was new ground. It wasn't an insertion but an original design.

There were too many circuits involved to put them on someone's head, and no one wore hats in the year 2055. For a while he considered putting the control circuits and memboards in the user's shoes, with ultrasound transmitting devices, but then he wondered what would happen if the user got separated from his shoes or if it was a lady user with skimpy heels.

The sky cleared and Neil spent over forty minutes looking out at the distance. His breathing was deep and satisfying. He could hear gusts of wind now and then.

The shoe question wasn't important anyway. Neil knew of no device that could record and transmit the range of data that Blue Nile's file described. Parts of some circuit boards performed some of the functions, but they would have to be dismantled and restructured to specialize. Neil had no idea of how to use streamliner chip protocols.

A peregrine hawk landed on the ledge outside the window. It perched there looking down for a meal. Neil stopped breathing and held his hands together as if he were going to pray.

"You ready for lunch yet, Neil?" Nina asked.

The hawk dropped from the ledge. Neil didn't know if it was diving after a pigeon or scared off by Nina's approach.

"What time is it?" he asked.

"Fifteen thirty-seven."

"What?"

"You been workin' hard up here."

"Lunch is over, then."

"Naw," Nina said. "Lunch up in here is whenever you want it."

"What's the hot box in the vendor machine today?"

"We ain't got one'a them."

"Then how do you get lunch?"

"They get it sent up, from the cafeteria."

This convinced Neil that he was undergoing some kind of psychological test. The cafeteria food was only for the highest-level workers. He decided to ride it out, to prove to the psych-controllers that he was able to function.

"Then I must have missed it," Neil replied, resigning himself to hunger.

"Naw, honey," the strange prod said. "They get it delivered to the Unit Controller's office."

"The UC's office. We can't go in there."

Nina smiled and grabbed Neil by the arm.

"Com'on," she said.

The young woman pulled and Neil followed. He didn't want to go but he wasn't worried about getting in trouble. He was clearly the victim of on-the-job sexual harassment. The International Union of Production

Workers' rule book clearly stated that *physical contact beyond accepted consensual greeting was forbidden in any workspace.* This meant that even a husband and wife exchanging a hug on work time were liable to get three D-marks each for sexual harassment.

Nina dragged Neil down one of the aisles between the concentric tables to Athria and Oura's desk.

"Neil don't think he could have lunch in the UC's office," she blurted out.

Oura looked up, while her partner kept her gaze concentrated on her table screen.

"Of course you can," the golden-skinned, golden-eyed, golden-haired woman said. "We all do."

"But it's against the rules." Neil postured for the cameras that he knew had to be recording the scene.

"Not any rules here," Athria said without looking up.

Neil glanced down at the dark woman's screen and saw that she was watching *Ito Iko,* the world-famous Japanese soap opera about an ancient Chinese royal family in the ninth century.

"That's right," Oura said.

"But don't you two use the office?" Neil asked.

"No more than anybody else."

"But you're the UCs," he insisted.

"No," Athria said, peering up over her glasses. "We're just prods. We sit here because we're good at labor distribution, but we're not the bosses."

"Come on," Nina said, again pulling Neil by the arm.

"It's different here," the Mississippian was saying as she led Neil into the UC's office.

This smaller room had an enclosed landing that jutted out from the building. Neil headed straight for the glass-walled outcropping, clenching his fists and breathing deeply.

"The UCs never come in," Nina continued.

"What do you mean they never come in?"

"They just send instructions over the net and we follow them. A lotta the prods don't come in every day."

"What do you mean? Everybody is on a four-day week, everybody in the twelve fiefs."

"Well, yeah." Nina hesitated for the first time. "We all report four, and we all do the optional two, but a lotta times we work from home."

Almost every prod in New York worked on-site four days a week. Over 90 percent of them worked an extra two days to make ends meet. In spite of the great promise of work-at-home that the Internet offered at the beginning of the century, the great corporations decided with organized labor that an on-site, controlled labor force was more desirable.

Neil wondered what he should do at this point in the test. This was obviously a severe breach in international labor regulations.

"I won't work from home," he said.

"You don't have to. You could just work extra hours and cut the week short that way."

"Extra what?"

"GEE-PROD-9 prods have special access cards," Nina said. "We can come and go whenever we want—day or night."

"You ride the escalators?"

"Unh-uh. We got express elevator passes."

"What's an express elevator?"

Nina smiled at Neil. She moved up next to him in the window case.

"It's gonna be okay, Neil," she said, in a much deeper voice than she had used up until then. Neil felt the vibrations of her voice on his neck even though she was at least a foot away from him.

3 Neil left GP-9 at seventeen fifteen, his appointed hour. He rode the elevator down, packed into the 275-max-cap car. He walked to the public stairwell and descended to Dark Town and Lower Twenty-ninth Street.

Neil's apartment had once been the entrance hall to a moderate three-bedroom unit on the fourth floor. He had looked up the floor plan on the free-web before it was discontinued for pornography abuses.

His mattress was leased from Forever Fibers. His chair and desk were let from Work Zone 2100. Everything else—the shelves, the rugs, his two pots, three plates, two cups, and one shatterproof glass—were the property of the landlord, Charlie Mumps Inc. The ultraviolet cooking unit, the refrigerator, and the wall-vid were all built-ins and covered under Neil's apartment dweller insurance.

It wasn't much, even by current New York standards, but it was better than a sleep tube two thousand feet under the ground. Neil knew that if he lost his job he would have to go under unless he was willing to use six years' savings to pay his rent for three months. The rent would go up if he was unemployed because he would have to pay the Unemployed Tax if he wanted to stay aboveground without a job.

The vid shows seemed stupid. Neil couldn't concentrate on their inane plots, but neither could he sleep. As the evening wore on he became more and more restless. For some reason the thought of drinking synth disgusted him. He couldn't understand what was happening at work. Why had they transferred him? Why didn't they take him to a med-head when they found him unconscious at the door? He was pretty sure that he wasn't in a psych-eval unit, because they were all in the subbasement. Maybe it was a whole unit that had inverted *Labor Nervosa.* Maybe they had pirated the protocols and become some kind of renegade production unit. That was crazy, Neil knew. There were so many checks and spies in every major corporation that no one could so much as download a manual for unauthorized personal use without getting caught.

As the night wore on Neil became even more agitated. He called his mother, Mary-Elaine, a nighttime ID-chip check girl at a legal Eros-Haus, but she was at work. He called an old friend named Arnold Roth, but he was told by the ID-messaging system that M Roth was in Common Ground and his calls could not be forwarded or retained.

At one in the morning Neil began reciting on his wrist-writer, the only piece of property, besides his clothing, that he owned.

If only they'd let me be I'd be okay. I mean, why they have to, why they want to make me give it all to them anyway? Why can't I just do my job? That's all I want. That's all I want. That's all I want. If they just let me, just let me, just let me. I don't know. Maybe it is a test. Maybe. Maybe I'm supposed to go to the Monitor Center and tell them that there's something funny in GEE-PRO-9. No uh, sit wherever you want, eat whenever you want, work as long as you want. Maybe it's a test. They're testing me to see if I'll turn them in. But why would they go through all that just to check on my loyalty? Why not just recycle me?

Maybe I should do the megadose of Pulse now. Maybe I should. Maybe I should.

Neil closed the cover on the armband where he kept his favorite recitations. The threat and promise of Pulse released enough tension that Neil was almost sleepy. He made a cup of Numb Tea on the UV stove. He was just sitting down to drink it when a loud electric buzzing went off. At first Neil didn't know what it was, but then he remembered that it was the buzzer for someone wanting to be let in.

It was two twenty-three in the morning.

"Hello?"

"Neilio?"

"Who is it?"

"Blue Nile, my boy."

"Who?"

"Come on, Neilio. Let me in. Oura and Athria sent me for you."

Every prod was on call twenty-four hours a day. They

could refuse to go in, but without a verifiable excuse, unemployment was a certainty.

The small man was wearing dark blue dress overalls with no shirt underneath. His eyes were twinkling as he made himself comfortable in Neil's only chair.

"What are you doing here?" Neil asked his late-night visitor.

"What's this?" Blue Nile said. He picked up Neil's cup of tea from the desk and jumped to his feet.

"Numb Tea. I was trying to get to sleep."

"Uch!" Blue Nile took the tea to the cooking nook and poured it down the drain. "This stuff is bad for ya. Who needs to shut off their mind anyway? If you're awake you should be alive, you should go outside and smell the asphalt." With that the little man laughed.

"What are you doing here at this time of night?"

"They sent me for you but they said only if you were awake. So I looked and saw your light."

"I don't have a window."

"Oura and Athria wanted me to bring you this." Blue Nile produced a prod card with Neil's picture on it. It was a thick card, obviously hard coded with special protocols.

"I already got a card."

"Not like this one."

"What's so different about this one?"

"Throw on some duds," Blue Nile replied, "and I'll show you."

The Verticular was just as crowded at three in the morning as it was at seven. But Neil didn't feel the deep panic of claustrophobia because Blue Nile kept talking, saying things that distracted him.

"I know you think that you can't make the grade on this new Eye thing," Blue Nile said. "But you underestimate your abilities."

"How would you know that?"

"We all misjudge ourselves. We have to. Our minds are like the computers we use to play simple games. Those same computers have the resources to run one of our robotic mining operations on the moon or Mars. Our minds are the product of two billion years of evolution, at least. Do you think it's the limit of your ability to make internal undulations on masturbation machines?"

Neil was taken by the thought. He wondered if there was some greater ability he had.

"You're wrong," he said, as they were walking down Middle First Avenue toward the General Specifix Gray Lanes entrance. "The corporations and unions give us all the testing we can take to make sure that we are at optimum productivity."

"Looking up a quad chip and putting it into a quad slot, so that a synthskin surface will give two to seven pounds pressure per quarter-inch wave every point two to one point one seconds—that's your optimum ability?"

Neil wondered how the little man knew what his last assignment in LAVE-AITCH-27 was, but he decided not to ask.

"Have you been at GEE-PRO-9 long?"

"Oh, yeah," the late-night intruder said. "I been

workin' for them a long time now. Long time. And the longer I work there the better I feel."

"But it's so weird."

They entered the darkened front doors of General Specifix and approached the assignment kiosk. There was a man in this time, also with a blunt face. Neil wondered if maybe the glass warped all the attendants' features.

"Yes?" the man asked, obviously suspicious of the off-hour approach.

Blue Nile handed his card through the slot provided. The man, who was young and bald, read something on his screen and said, "GEE-PRO-9, M."

Blue Nile gestured for Neil to proffer his new card. Neil hesitated. He knew that if rejected by the system he could be arrested for attempted illegal entry.

"Come on, Neil," Blue Nile said. "It took my card."

With trembling fingers Neil slipped the card into the slot.

"GEE-PRO-9, M," the bald man said immediately.

Neil headed for the 275-max-cap elevators but Blue Nile took him by the arm and led him toward another hallway that curved around the back of the building. There they came to a door with a card-lock pad next to it. Blue Nile held his identity card against the lock pad and the door slid open revealing a small elevator car.

"Floor three one nine," Blue Nile said, and the door closed.

As the car rose the outer wall proved to be transparent, and above the fortieth floor the city came into view.

Hundreds of thousands of lights down Upper First became visible. It was, Neil thought, like seeing a slender corridor of a galaxy. As they ascended he could see more and more of the city. The lights melded with the stars in the night sky. Neil began to tremble.

"It's a two-way glass," Blue Nile said.

"What?"

"It's a two-way glass. From the outside this elevator shaft looks like a wall, but from inside you can see everything."

"I never knew that something like this existed. I never knew."

"Of course you didn't. Most central controllers don't know about it. The rich and powerful live in a world that most of the rest of us don't even suspect."

"But how do you know about it, then? How do I rate a pass to ride it?"

"GEE-PRO-9," Blue Nile said, his blue eyes twinkling, city lights shimmering all around his head.

GEE-PRO-9 was not empty. Four prods sat at their desks poring over multiple screens. One woman on the upper tier was smoking a cigarette. She looked down from her perch and waved at Blue Nile. He smiled in return.

"Is that tobacco?" Neil asked, sniffing the air.

"Yeah. Marva knows that it's bad for her, but ever since she started smoking she's been happier. Oura says that it's because she needs to rebel, to do something wrong. But she doesn't want to hurt anybody or steal. So she smokes."

"Isn't she hurting those people around her?"

"There's a big fan up over that table. It sucks up almost all the secondhand shit."

The sun wasn't up yet. The lights that trailed across Brooklyn and Queens and on to Long Island were all that Neil wanted to see. He knew that any minute he'd be arrested for illegal access, for using an unauthorized identity card, for being in the presence of tobacco use, for failing to report his own *Labor Nervosa*. But he couldn't think about that with the world spread out before him.

"Why did you bring me here?" Neil asked Blue Nile.

"To show you the power you have. To amaze you and make you laugh . . . To save you from taking that megadose and to keep you from reporting us to the monitor staff."

Even these words could not make Neil turn away from the night sky.

"How did you know about that?" he asked.

"We been monitoring your wrist-writer for three months, son."

Now Neil did turn to Blue Nile. "What? How? What for?"

"How many people do you think work in GEE-PRO-9?" the small man asked.

"One hundred and three."

"No. We have six hundred forty-two members in our cell."

"That's impossible. It's policy to have one hundred and three prods in each GT. That's all. Never more, and only less if someone is sick or dies or gets fast-fired. I worked in a GT where the assignment desk sent an extra prod once. They laid me off for a day because of it. It was the only day off I've ever had except if I was sick."

Blue Nile shook his head and smiled.

"Six hundred forty-two," he said. "All of them like you and me."

"What does that mean? I'm not like you or anybody else here."

"We look for the prods on the margin, prods like you and me."

"What's that? The margin?"

"Excuse me," Blue Nile said. "I keep forgetting that you don't know. Come on, let's go sit on the cushion and watch the sky."

It was an offer that Neil could not resist. He went to the first place he'd known in the crazy GT and sat so that he could see the night and Blue Nile smiling.

"We look for the creative mind," the small man said. "We monitor all bands, even the incidental ones, like the weak emissions from your wrist-writer."

"How would you know to read my journal? I mean, there must be thirty million electronic journals in Greater New York."

"The UC, Un Fitt, wrote up a program that looks for certain criteria from the various human-generated emissions."

"What kinda criteria?"

"Suffering," Blue Nile said, holding up one finger, "intelligence, creativity, discipline, courage . . ." For each subject he put up another finger. He had, Neil noticed, powerful hands.

"How could you tell that from my journal?"

"Your method of suicide is both creative and brave, my boy. The fact that you've struggled with and mostly overcome *Labor Nervosa* on your own tells of discipline. The intelligence-testing driver that Un Fitt built is still opaque to me, but I can tell by talking to you that you're bright."

"Why me?"

"Why not? We have a list of thousands of potential GEE-PRO-9 mems, but we can only accept a few. We need prods who won't be disruptive and who will be able to work on their own. We wanted you because you fit all the categories, you already worked in the building, and because you needed us."

"What's that supposed to mean? I need you? I'm doing just fine with nobody's help. I got money in the bank, a vacation already reserved, only three D-marks in two years. I've only had one unemployment cycle and I'm twenty-two with six years' service."

"Don't forget the four Pulse capsules you have in your ID case," Blue Nile said. "Or the fainting spells you've experienced. And then there's how much you sweat and fret at work every day."

"Everybody has problems like that," Neil said.

"I don't."

"But you ride secret elevators and take breaks and turn your seat around to look out the window. Those infractions alone could throw you on an unemployment cycle. And using company devices to listen in on people to recruit them secretly—that's enough to put you in corporate prison. You'll be living in the dark taking drugs that'll keep you docile for twenty years. By the time you wake up, half of your brain will be sponge."

"Is that worse than Common Ground?" Blue Nile asked with a sly smile.

Neil didn't answer the question. The comparison seemed impossible to comprehend. Nothing seemed possible except his job, his apartment, and the daily fact of his survival.

"Come here, Neil," Blue Nile said. He stood up and went over to the nearest GT table. Neil went along.

The little man was proficient at table use. He hit a couple of virtual keys and joined two screens into one large monitor. He then entered the Unit Controller screen.

"What are you doing?" Neil asked.

"Showing you something."

"But that's the UC page. It's permanent unemployment over that—even just to look at a UC's screen."

"I have the protocols."

"Are you the UC?"

"None of us are. But we have all been given the protocols and clearance to use our UC's codes." With that Blue Nile entered a forty-seven-digit code number. The central computer paused for a moment and then presented the image of a handprint. Blue Nile placed his hand inside the print. The computer paused three seconds. Neil felt his heart thrumming.

A red entry screen appeared. Neil had only once seen a red screen. That was when he first worked for Specifix, almost six years earlier. He had somehow frozen the whole GT system; no one at the table could log on. The UC, an unclean man named Nordeen, had entered his codes to fix the problem. He had used a red screen with yellow and orange letters just like the one Blue Nile had raised.

On the search line he entered Neil's name and his last GT, LAVE-AITCH-27. A file appeared that had Neil's ranking and picture at the top.

"You see that blue dot?" Blue Nile asked.

Neil saw the large blue spot pulsing at the right side of his photograph. He also noticed that the picture was not the one he had taken when he came to work; it was a recent shot of him leaning over the camera's lens. He realized that his monitor must have an internal camera so that he could be watched continually.

"What does it mean?" Neil asked.

Blue Nile placed his finger over the dot and tapped the virtual clicker. Immediately a green screen, also with yellow letters, appeared. The words PENALTY SCREEN were at the top of the form. Neil read through the document. Every time he had fainted had been logged, the number of times he had drifted while he was supposed to be working had been recorded and graphed. His verbal complaints, even those he made only to himself, had been recorded. Toward the end of the form there was a diagnosis box that read *Labor Nervosa;* Acute. The suggested treatment was permanent unemployment at the end of the current work semester.

The date of his discharge was three days before he was to have his first vacation.

Neil's stomach began to roil. He heard a sound that he thought was coming from the table but then he realized that it was a low moan from his own chest. He thought about sitting down but he was frozen over the screen.

His teeth began to chatter.

Suddenly there was a sharp pain at the side of his head. He fell to the floor. He looked up and realized that Blue Nile had hit him.

"Why?" Neil asked.

" 'Cause you were losin' it. A shock sometimes breaks you out of it."

"No, not that. Why are they firing me? What did I do?"

"You're just part of the margin, kid," Blue Nile said. "Workin' for the corporation is just like goin' to school, and in this classroom they grade on a curve."

4 "It's simple, Neil," Oura Olea said in the UC's office. "You either erase the data from your record or you're thrown into permanent unemployment."

"There has to be another way," Neil whined. "I mean, tampering with work records is a crime."

"And living in Common Ground is a prison sentence," Oura said. "Obey the law and you spend the rest of your life in jail."

"It can't be. It can't be," Neil said. "Will you do it for me?"

"No."

"Why not? You understand these things better than I do. You sit in the inner circle."

"You could sit there if you wanted. Athria and I are prods like everyone else here."

"But I could get sent to jail."

"We've covered this ground before, Neil," the golden woman said. "It's one of our only rules. If you want to work with us you have to clean up your own file."

"But if I get thrown out they might find out about you," Neil said softly.

"How?"

"I don't know. They'll check my records. They'll, they'll come here to ask questions."

"Only if you send them, Neil." Oura's face was impassive. Neil missed her maternal smile.

"I don't mean that—"

"You wrote in your journal that you thought you were being tested, that maybe they expected you to turn our GT in."

"M Olea," Neil said. "I'm scared. Really scared. I've never been anything but a prod. When I was ten my mother sent me to prod-ed and that's all I've ever been. I don't know about forging records and using a UC's codes. I never knew about glass elevators and windows that look out on the sky or sitting backwards or letting people smoke cigarettes. All I want is to go back to being normal, back to LAVE-AITCH-27 between Hermianie and Juliet."

"That's all gone, Neil. The doors are closed, your seat is taken, and if you don't change the files you will be underground for the rest of your life."

"I can't."

Oura smiled again. It was a sad smile. She touched Neil's hand and said, "It's a lot to take in all at once. You have six weeks before the judgment will be executed. Think about it."

At his station on the upper tier Neil was lost. He looked out at the open sky filled with clouds. He tried to imagine some way to get out from under the weight of his fate. He knew now that GEE-PRO-9 wasn't some kind of test, at least not a test produced by his employers. He'd fallen into a renegade group that had subverted the company's structure. But all Neil wanted was to go back to his previous life. He spent the late morning trying to figure out how he could succeed at staving off permanent unemployment.

Close to noon a red light appeared on the table before him. It was an interoffice e-mail. He touched the light and his table monitor came to life.

Greetings M Hawthorne,

I am M Un Fitt, Unit Controller for GEE-PRO-9. I noticed that you haven't been working on our Third Eye project this morning. I assume this is because you need a handle with which to grab hold of the idea. Your initial notes show that you understand that the major problems here are the size of the processing unit and the type of receptors that can receive on a par with the broad range of perceptions possible for the human nervous system.

I have not worked out the problem fully but I am convinced that there has to be a physiological element to the Third Eye project. As you may know from the vid news programs there has been a great deal of research done on brain functions as both receptors and projectors of ideational material. Sadly, the congress has outlawed this type of brain research because, they say, there are certain constitutional rights that may be violated. In reality international corporate interests have lobbied against such research because it might lead to greater freedoms and access abilities for the common prod.

I have attached several documents that were created before the federal laws went into effect. These are basic chip designs that can connect and interact with the human nervous system. I don't expect you to be able to approximate the neuronal connectors, just try to design the chip logic(s) based on the studies enclosed.

Have a bright day.

Yours truly,
UF

By the time he reached the end of the document Neil had completely forgotten about his impending doom. He was amazed by the candid, conversational transmission of the UC. He was also deeply interested in the content of the attached documents. He downloaded fourteen segments, each of which contained in excess of a hundred thousand words. On top of these text documents he received over fifteen hundred graphs and illustrations, and seventeen video presentations. Neil read through the rest of the day and way into the evening. He was so enthralled by what he read that he would forget to look out at the sky for over an hour at a time.

The introductory document Neil thought must have been written by Un Fitt himself (if indeed the UC was a male). This long rambling essay explained how Congress passed legislation that allowed neuronal research for use in computer technology but at the same time outlawed any brain implants, neuronal connectors, or mind-altering experiments. This latter prohibition was supposedly based on the possible infringement of individual rights.

From there was a long essay called "The Road to the Mind," which postulated that any working neuronal pathway could extend brain functions using certain octal protocols. This pathway could utilize the brain's instinctual functions to manipulate data calculations. Ultimately, the essay postulated, the only computer a human would need would be an octal interface and the use of his own brain. A footnote from this essay said:

> Therefore, a comparatively small interface device might be implanted under the subject's skin. This device could utilize the subject's own brain to achieve the bulk of the Third Eye's functions.

But, Neil thought, *a device that small could never store the amount of information necessary to make the Eye useful.*

He read on through the night. The types of circuits necessary to run the device suggested had not as yet been developed, or, if they had, the corporations using them had not shared or released the technology.

Neil returned home twenty-four hours after he had been taken away by Blue Nile. He fell onto his mattress, slept for five hours, and then awoke in a sudden panic. Everything came back to him. The diagnosis of *Labor Nervosa,* the promise of forever unemployment, of fifty years underground in the honeycombs of Common Ground. His only other choice, the erasure of his record, was a felony. He began to tremble and sweat. He threw up in his small toilet and collapsed on the floor.

"Can I talk to you, Nina?" he said to the dark young prod.

"Sure, Neil," she said.

Neil was confused by her friendliness and obvious flirtation; by her apparent ugliness and the deep sexual attraction she held for him.

"Could we go in the UC's room."

"Yeah," she said.

She had been sitting next to a male prod, an Asian man.

"Excuse me, Nin," she said to him.

The man nodded and smiled at Neil.

"What do you want, Neil?" Nina asked when they were in the back room.

"I want . . ." he said.

"Yeah?"

"I want you to do something for me."

"What?"

"The thing, the thing with the records."

"What thing, Neil?"

"You know what I mean."

"No I don't. Not unless you tell me what it is."

"I don't want to say it in here."

"There's no monitor cameras or listening devices here, hon. We had them removed."

"I still don't want to say it."

Nina gave him a broad smile. Her skin was almost black, but not quite. Her smile was happy; red gums and spaces between all of her small teeth. Her eyes were deep holes, dull but not lifeless or unintelligent. They were too deep for Neil to fathom. Her hair was thick, braided into a dozen short ponytails.

Neil felt his stomach rumble when he looked at her.

"Come sit with me in the window," she said.

He obeyed and she sat close to him, putting her right hand on his thigh.

"What is it you want from me, Neil?"

"I want you to do for me what they make everybody else here do for themselves."

"Your assignment?" she asked. Her hand began sliding up his leg.

"No."

"Then, what?" Her hand moved further.

Neil squirmed.

"Don't move away," she whispered.

He stopped and her fingers reached the tip of his penis through the thin material of his tan andro-suit. He became instantly erect. Nina smiled and breathed into Neil's face. Her breath was strong but not bad, sweet. Neil wanted to scream.

"What do you call this?" she asked.

"My, my penis." As he said the word her hand slid over the erection and squeezed it slightly.

"Is that what you call it? Really?"

"Dick, cock. My hard cock."

"Say it."

"What?"

"Say it."

"That's my hard cock. Hard cock."

"That's right. You see? You know how to talk. You know how to say it."

"Please," Neil said.

Still holding on to Neil's erection, Nina got up on her knees in the window space. She flipped her dress up, showing that she wore nothing underneath.

"Do me, baby," she said.

"Somebody might come."

"I put a sign on the door."

"What kinda sign?"

"Just to say not to bother us. Do me now, baby. Come on."

"I don't have a condom."

"You don't need it."

"You don't know that."

"If you want me to help you, you have to do me." Saying this she let him go and raised her posterior into the air, spreading her legs so that the sun shone through, illuminating her wild and errant hairs.

Neil had never even dreamed of something like this. The bold blue sky and the bolder still woman who excited him so much that he felt sick down in his core.

He pulled down his pants and fumbled around until he pushed inside her. She moaned and called out a name that was not quite Neil. He looked down at her butt thrusting against him and then up at the sky. They bucked hard against each other and for the first time Neil thought about dying without fear or trepidation. When he came he saw his own reflection grinning in an infinite blue sky. A muscle tore in his groin but he didn't care. He tried to pull away but Nina reached her hand around his backside and held him.

"Don't, baby. Don't take him out yet."

"Somebody might come."

"That's me, hon," she moaned. "That's me comin'."

Later, when Nina's spasms stopped, they lay curled against each other in the window.

"Will you do it for me now?" Neil whispered nervously. He was still afraid that someone would walk in on them.

"Do what?"

"Alter my records."

"You have to do that yourself, hon. That's the rules."

"But I thought you said that if I had sex with you that you'd help me."

"I did help you. You needed a good fuck, Neil. You needed it bad."

5 That night he was wide awake in his apartment thinking about prison, sex, and the sky. These thoughts brought on bouts of dizziness and confusion. He was afraid and aroused, feeling awe and panic. He considered running but there was no way out of New York. Anyone could leave the city, but in order to live outside your work perimeter you would have to pay a high tax or take up residence in Common Ground.

Neil thought about GEE-PRO-9's window on the sky, about the silicon protocols used to read the electrical pulses generated by nerve cells. He wondered who wanted the Third Eye. Maybe it wasn't even a MacroCode division that ordered the device. Almost certainly it was not, because that kind of research had been outlawed. It occurred to him that no client would order brain-altering technology except a foreign power. That would make Neil's project espionage, and espionage was punishable by death.

Neil thought about calling his mother but he knew that she couldn't help. And even if she could, all of his electronic communications were being monitored by Blue Nile and others.

"I don't want to die," Neil said aloud.

He thought about going to the newly instituted CBI. It was a branch of the federal government that investigated corporate fraud and crimes against the state. They had the power to save him if he became a witness. They had the power to save him but they could crush him too.

In prod-ed they taught the future data manipulators of the workplace to avoid reporting infractions.

"It's someone else's job to prove, penalize, and punish—not yours," M Butterman would say whenever asked about legal aspects of production. "Everything you do at work is either your job or wasting corporate time. Wasting time is wasting money and wasting money is worse than anything else."

Neil was wondering where the main office of the CBI was when the buzzer to his door sounded.

"Yes," he asked, fearing the Bureau had found him first.

"It's Nina," she said over the speaker. "Let me up."

She wore an ankle-length, emerald green, fake leather coat tied with a red sash at the waist. Her hair was combed straight back. Her thick eyebrows had been plucked down to slender lines.

"They want me down at work?" he asked her at the door.

Nina pushed her way in, closing the door behind her. Her eyes seemed to say, *There's no escape.*

"What?" Neil asked.

Nina removed her coat. She was naked underneath. Her breasts were small and sagging a bit. Neil had never seen breasts like hers. Eros-Haus girls all had surgically altered breasts. Perfect. Their pubic hair was either completely shaved or mostly so, leaving just a wisp of hair that the girls called their little goatee. Nina's pubic hair was deep and thick, covering a wide swath under her belly. Again Neil was repelled by her. But at the same time he couldn't look away.

"I was thinkin' about you," Nina said. There was a swagger in her voice.

"Thinking what?"

"You only been to Eros girls before today, huh?" She moved close to him. He thought about moving away but did not.

"No."

"That's what your wrist-writer says."

"That's private."

"I was thinking," Nina said again. She wrapped her arms around his neck and thrust her pelvis against him. ". . . that Eros girls never teach men how to eat pussy." She said the last two words in his ear.

Neil moaned and was suddenly dizzy. He didn't know if Nina pushed him down or if he fell.

"Up on your knees, M," she said. "You're gonna wag that tongue till he bleed."

The next two weeks were a balance of work, sex, and fear for Neil. Every day he delved deeper into the thousands of pages provided by Un Fitt. Every evening he fretted over the possible ramifications of his work. After midnight Nina would come over and teach him another lesson in the lexicon of sex.

Only in the early-morning hours did Neil have a few moments of peace. At five Nina usually went home to change. Neil would get up and try to think of a way out. But he could see no way. General Specifix was going to fire him if he didn't break the law by altering his records. If he was fired for having *Labor Nervosa* no other corporation would hire him. He might find work at a fast food restaurant or at some fuel stop, but that wasn't enough money for topside living; those kinds of jobs were done by transient Common Grounders for choke cigarette money or to earn a pass to get out for a day or two on the upper tier.

Even if he did alter the records, and even if he wasn't caught, there was still the problem of being associated with the rogue GT unit. If, by some fluke, there was a valid purpose for the existence of GEE-PRO-9, the Third Eye project was still illegal. And Neil couldn't deny knowledge of the law because the introduction of his research files contained a detailed analysis of the laws he was breaking.

The hazards were many, but one was worse than all the others. He could see that maybe he would never get caught, or that he would only get caught after some years of working with Oura, Athria, and Blue Nile—but unprotected sex with a woman who was obviously well versed in intercourse of all kinds was like playing Russian roulette with five loaded chambers in the gun.

Still Neil could not deny Nina. He wasn't attracted to her but he was lost in the face of her sexual hunger. Her passion for his body and hers made him submissive to the point that he would allow her to hurt him rather than pull away. Her orgasms and lewd suggestions stayed in his mind all the time. He dreamed about her and found himself waiting for her to arrive every night.

One night she didn't come and he didn't sleep at all. The next day he shunned her when she came to talk to him; he walked away from her when she tried to join him for lunch. That night she rang his buzzer and he didn't answer for five minutes.

"Why you actin' like that?" she asked when he finally let her in.

"I thought you were through with me," he said.

"Just 'cause I didn't come one night? What did you think I was doin'?"

"I don't know."

"Yeah you do. You know what you think."

"I thought you were with another guy."

"I wasn't," she said. "I was with two men . . ."

Neil fell back a step when she said this. His right eyelid began twitching.

". . . they was at the Conga Club. Two friends in town on business. They came up to me while I was havin' a drink and said if I wanted to go to their room. Said they was from Florida City, that they wanted to do one girl. It's okay, though, I made 'em wear rubbers, double rubbers."

"Why don't you let . . . have me wear a rubber?"

" 'Cause I know you're safe, baby. I read your meds 'fore I took you to bed."

"What about me? I haven't read your records."

Nina cupped Neil's face between her hands. She leaned in close and kissed him lightly on the lips. "I wouldn't put you in danger, honey. I wouldn't hurt you at all. An' them two men didn't mean nuthin' to me. They back down south now, braggin' about what's yours."

Neil sat down on the bed and pressed his palms against his eyes. The darkness was laced with red veins.

"You sick, honey?" Nina asked.

"No."

"What's wrong, then?"

Neil felt her hands on his shoulders, her weight leaning against his back.

"Talk to me, Neil."

He tried to answer but he couldn't. Nina began to rock him gently forward and back. Her fingers massaged his scalp.

"You got curly hairs," Nina said. "Somebody in your family Irish or Greek?"

"I used to get in trouble," Neil said. "In school."

"What kinda trouble?"

"I wouldn't do anything. I wouldn't listen or answer questions or do homework."

"How come you didn't?"

"I don't know. One of my teachers, Miss . . . I mean M Lassiter, said to my mother that she thought I had ideas of my own. She wanted me to go to the Ben Franklin Academy. But that cost too much and Mom was mad, so she put me in prod-ed 'cause I didn't obey."

"Your mother did that?"

"Yeah."

"Is that why you sad?"

"I'm not sad, I'm just quiet," he said. And then, "You wouldn't hurt me, would you, Nina?"

"No. I said I wouldn't."

"And I believe you."

"So? What's wrong with that?"

"I never believed anybody before. Nobody. Not my mother, not my friends."

Nina hugged Neil and pressed her head against the back of his neck.

"That's good, isn't it?"

"In my head it is," Neil whispered. "But in my heart I'm more scared than if you buried me alive."

6

At six that same morning Neil approached the Middle First Avenue entrance of General Specifix. He rode the glass elevator, using his thick identity card on the GEE-PRO-9 door.

"Hi, Neil," Marva called from the upper tier. She was the only one there, smoking her illegal tobacco and coughing.

Neil caught a whiff of the smoke in the air but he didn't care. He went directly to the UC room and logged onto the red controller screen. He entered his name and the forty-seven-digit number Blue Nile had given him, offered up his handprint, and initiated the search. Only when the record appeared before him did he stall. He didn't know if there was some kind of special code that one might need to alter the EPR, employee permanent record. He worried armed security guards would come out from some secret doorway and drag him away to a private prison without even a trial.

"M Hawthorne," he imagined some corporate official saying to his mother. "Your son contracted the new strain of *Ebola C* virus. In accordance with the emergency laws enacted by the mayor we had no choice but to immediately cremate his remains." He would hand Neil's mother an urn with ashes gathered from a Midwestern dog pound and she would cry and ask who was the beneficiary of his insurance policy.

Then the red sun began to emerge from the Brooklyn skyline.

With light came the feeling of space. Neil looked out over the city and then erased the D-marks for fainting and lack of concentration. Nothing happened. When he deleted the contents of the diagnosis box the recommended dismissal automatically disappeared and the Penalty Screen was replaced by an aqua Merit Screen. Here Neil wrote that he had shown great skill and had been promoted to the seventh tier. He worked well with his chain mates, he took initiative in his tasks without causing trouble on the line. This automatically evoked recommendations for a raise and promotion. Then he switched over to the Policy Screens and changed the beneficiary from his mother to Nina Bossett.

"M Hawthorne," a voice said from the doorway behind him.

The young prod leapt to his feet and spun around. He

decided to fight the security guards, to die rather than go to prison.

"What's wrong, Neil?" Marva Monel asked. "I just wanted to know if you were ordering lunch."

"No," Neil said, trying to unclench his fists. "I'm just working in here."

"Did my smoke bother you?"

"No. No. I guess I just like being alone awhile in the morning."

The older woman smiled. "Me too. That's why I come in here so early. I love looking down on the big table while I'm entering protocols. It makes the work seem better somehow."

"Yeah," Neil said. "Yeah, exactly."

After Marva left Neil entered his updated EPR into the General Specifix permanent database. A feeling of great calm came over him. He celebrated by opening a blank chip template. He had decided that he would create a new chip for the transmission and reception of data between an as yet nonexistent device and the brain. He had never created a processing chip before. He was taught in prod-ed that only a prod with five years of post-prod-ed had the ability to encode the millions, sometimes billions, of binary instructions necessary to achieve an independent function.

But Neil had learned from Un Fitt that the major logic designers had developed a giant subroutine database that had hundreds of millions of entries categorized by function, size, speed, and compatibility with other subroutines. All Neil had to do was to think of a function and then ask the system to search according to his parameters.

This system, Un Fitt had said in an early communication, was originally developed for general use by HI, Hackers International, but had been co-opted by MacroCode Corporation in a hostile event toward the end of the first decade of the twenty-first century. This database, a closely guarded secret, was updated hourly with logics created in-house, bought from external sources, or stolen.

Each entry in this system had a list of possible hardware devices attached to it. Through this list Neil felt sure that he could find the most efficient devices for the Third Eye project.

He worked all day and late into the evening. At nine he moved to the high table in the GT room. There he worked hard, laughing out loud to himself sometimes and grimacing at others. At various odd moments he would get up and walk around visiting his fellow workers. Oura was especially happy for his visits and told him so.

"Hi, baby," Nina said, in a late afternoon visit to his workstation. "How's it goin'?"

"Great. Couldn't be better."

"You workin' good?"

"I finally realized, Nina."

"What?"

"This is all I have. I couldn't go back to LAVE-AITCH even if they'd let me. I couldn't sit there and call up undu-protocols or timekeeper registers. I couldn't wake up at seven and go to bed at ten. I couldn't live without you."

He said this all in a rush with no particular emphasis on any word or idea. It was just information flowing out of him. Nina put her hand up over her mouth and frowned.

"I know I'm not pretty," she said.

"Don't say it," he said. "Don't say anything but that you still want to see me even though I'm an idiot, a deffy-boy on the lower streets."

Nina kissed him on the lips, a fast-fireable infraction, and turned away quickly, returning to her station.

7 Neil threw himself fully into the Third Eye project after that. For the next year he worked twelve hours almost every day. He spent his leisure time with fellow workers and most of his nights with Nina. There were evenings that she would disappear with her hefty-men; on those evenings Neil would swear to himself that he would never see her again. But a day or two later they were back together.

One night while Nina was out scrambling around, as she would say, Neil called Blue Nile and asked him if he would like to get together for a late dinner in Dark Town.

"That'd be great, Neilio," the little man said. He did a jig in the 3D vid arch. "Where to?"

"A place I go to sometimes," Neil said. "Hallwell's China Diner on Lower Thirty-third and Park."

"Hey, hey," Blue Nile said. "Sounds like an underground poet named her. And if that poet's also a cook . . . Well, you know, poetry's the only real soul food."

They met at the front door of the hole-in-the-wall at just past twenty hours. The only other people there were a short woman dressed in a black T-shirt and a long brown skirt and a black man with a synthetic blue eye who sat in a corner considering the wall.

"Teriyaki frogs' legs over hominy with onion and chard," D'or Hallwell—proprietor, waitress, cook, and janitor of the China Diner—said. "Or grubsteak fresh from the rain forest of Brazil."

"I don't know," Blue Nile said. "I never ate a worm before."

D'or walked up to the table and put a meaty fist on her hip. She had wiry gray-blond hair that stuck almost straight out from her head. "If you ever ate a prepared meal out of a plastic can chances are ten to one you ate a worm. And not no farm-certified worm like my grubsteak, neither. No sir. Canned worms are wild things. Maggots and larvae and carniverous caterpillars."

"Oh," Blue Nile said. It was the first time Neil had ever seen his friend look somebody in the eye without smiling.

"Let him alone, D'or," the black man sitting in the corner said. "He just wants a meal, not the IDA report on canned foods."

"Hello, M Johnson," Neil said to the man.

"M Hawthorne," the Electric Eye replied.

"Well?" D'or asked Blue Nile. "What'll it be?"

"What about you, Neil?"

"He's a commie kid," D'or said. "The cheapest plate is always his favorite dish."

"Then grubsteak, please, ma'am," Blue Nile said.

D'or smiled and went away to get their meals.

"Nice place," Blue Nile said. "How long you been comin' here?"

"I always knew about it," Neil said. "For the first five years I came about once every year or so, to treat myself. I was saving up for my vacation so I didn't want to waste money on restaurant food. But after I started GP-9 I been comin' once or twice a week."

"Whatever happened to that vacation of yours?"

"I don't know. It didn't seem important anymore, I guess. I mean, a seventh-class room in a hotel that has ten thousand rooms sounded like work to me."

Blue Nile laughed and rocked in his rickety chair.

"You like the food here?" he asked.

"I like the place. It's privately owned you know."

"No."

"Yeah. M Hallwell's mother owned it and never had to turn it over during the corporate takeover days because the rest of the block was city owned back then. By the time the city sold out the laws had changed and D'or didn't have to sell it."

"A private business," Blue Nile said. "In New York. Wow."

D'or returned with their dinners. Neil had frogs' legs over hominy and Blue Nile had a big grubsteak smothered in fried mushrooms, onions, and peas.

"I never seen you before, have I?" D'or asked Blue Nile.

"This is my first time in your fine establishment," Blue Nile said. "But you can be sure that it's not my last."

The restaurant owner pulled a chair from a vacant

table and sat down. Neil wasn't happy about this. He liked D'or but he wanted to talk to his friend about Nina. He wanted to ask about her history and family. Blue Nile had the file protocols to look up prod records. Neil could have requested access but he worried that Nina would get angry if she thought he was checking her background.

"You're cute," D'or was saying to Blue Nile.

"Thank you. You're a lovely woman."

"Neil," D'or said, "you should bring your friend around more often."

"I don't think he'll need me to bring him after he's tasted your grubsteak."

"The boy's right, there," Nile agreed.

"What's your name?" D'or asked.

"Blue Nile."

"No shit?"

"Straight as the hole down to Common Ground."

"Where you from, Blue Nile?"

"Vermont. Montpelier."

"Mm! That's some cold country up there."

"Not if you dig a hole and stay down in it for six months."

"What brought you down here?"

"My mother. She slipped into Simpson's Coma Disorder. I wanted to help her, but you know a country boy can't make a dime. She needed three kinds of drugs, so I sold my labor contract to MacCo. They bought forty years of my labor for her drugs and room and board for me."

"You sold your entire work life to MacroCode?" Neil was shocked.

"Lotsa people do it, kid," Blue Nile said. "How else can a prod afford to take care of his loved ones? There's no more private property, hardly. All a prod's got is his labor."

"How long ago was that?" D'or asked.

"Let's see," Blue Nile said. "I'm fifty-five now, so it must be twenty-two years."

"Is your mother still alive?"

"No. She died three years after I came to MacCo."

"You poor thing," D'or Hallwell said.

"That's what they do to you," a man's voice said.

Neil and Blue Nile looked up at the towering figure of the black man with the artificial blue eye.

"Do you mind if I join you, M Hawthorne?" Folio Johnson asked.

"No, M Johnson. Of course not. This is my friend—M Blue Nile."

"Call me Blue," Nile said. He stood up and extended a hand to Folio.

"Can you beat that shit?" D'or asked the electric detective as he pulled up a chair. "Bought his whole life, just like he was an old-time slave."

Johnson nodded.

Neil was wondering why he had never asked about Blue Nile's family or his work contract with MacCo; why he'd never known that his friend lived in a labor dormitory or why he'd never been invited to call him Blue.

"It's not so bad," Blue Nile said. "Before I made the deal and got the nuclear drugs my mother was in a full-out coma. She came awake and smiled at me six hours after her first dose. We moved her down to Brooklyn and she stayed with my sister. I saw her every day for those three years. It was worth every minute I have to spend."

"Yeah," Folio said. "For you it was. For anybody. Life is worth almost any price you have to pay. But that doesn't mean they have to charge you for it."

"You're right about that," Blue Nile said. "And right is right."

They talked all night and into the morning. Blue Nile had a flask of real brandy that D'or produced glasses for. Blue Nile and Folio and D'or did most of the talking. Neil just listened. It was rare that he was with a group of people who spoke openly and honestly about their feelings. For the first time in many weeks he forgot completely about Nina.

Blue Nile became a regular at the China Diner. Neil would see him at the counter almost every time he went there. The older man was always talking to D'or or waiting for her to be finished so they could resume their conversation. One time Neil ran into Nile at breakfast wearing the same overalls he had on the day before.

Neil always sat alone to give D'or and Blue Nile their privacy. Every now and then Folio Johnson, another regular, would wave him over.

One day the detective seemed down and Neil took it on himself to pull up a chair.

"Something wrong, M Johnson?" Neil asked.

"Had a case didn't work out right."

"You failed?"

"I got the answers but my client died. He was murdered by a girl."

"Oh." Neil wondered how he could switch the subject.

"Don't worry, kid," Johnson said, as if he could read Neil's worried mind. "Cops know all about it. They know but they can't do a thing."

"Why not?"

"Same reason that it'd be a crime for Blue to quit his job. The corporations. The madmen who run 'em."

Neil swallowed hard and sat very still.

"You know anything about the Itsies, kid?"

"No. Just that they believe that the Nazis back a hundred years ago were right: that there's a wedding of the scientific and the spiritual, like with Infochurch."

"Do you know any of them Itsies?"

"No sir. No."

"They wanna kill me."

"Why?"

" 'Cause I'm black. Can you believe that? In this world where the last thing you got to worry about is skin color and they still wanna kill me. That's some crazy shit."

Neil didn't see Folio Johnson around the China Diner much after that night. He missed their talks but he was also busy, spending long days at GP-9. He designed seventeen micronic processors—wafer-thin microdots containing billions of hard gel circuits, sheathed in the multilayered silicon skins needed to perceive and encode sensory data and to transfer those translations into the nervous system code.

The Third Eye would be able to perceive far more

than human senses. A user could, Neil believed, close his eyes and plug his ears, wrap himself from head to toe in sense-dep clothes, and still be able to know more of what was going on around him than ten unaided human beings.

But as large as the micronic memory was, it was nowhere near the capacity needed to record these sensations for later use. At full capacity a human would be able to use the eye only one sense at a time. He could see clearly for miles distant, but his other senses would suffer. The only way to be aware of all senses would be to record them for later study. In order to record this data successfully, the table computer estimated a trillion trillion characters of memory per hour.

Creating a functioning device, Neil felt, was impossible. But he wasn't worried. His job was to develop the virtual prototype for the perceptor logic, and he had done that; at least, he had the general designs down. It would take another three or four years for him to locate and download all the routines that would fit in between the sheaths of the Third Eye.

Neil often thought about his old days on the prod lane, days when all he would do was look up one of the few hundred chips he used in product insertion. He never worked on a project for more than ninety minutes. He'd never known how anything turned out unless he happened to see the device in one of the leasing department store vid commercials.

"What you thinkin'?" Nina asked him one day. They were sitting side by side, looking out at the sky.

"Why don't more people do what we're doing here?" he asked.

"Because the corporations don't want 'em to."

"Why? The kind of work we're doing could change the way people live."

"You really think so?"

"Sure. With this device, when they finally figure out the memory, you could just go outside and see the planets, in a full spectrum of light."

"But prob'ly," Nina said wryly, "some dude'd just try and look inta somebody's windah an' see if they was fuckin'."

"Not everybody."

"Most of 'em."

"But that's not why the corporations have us doing little shit. They don't care if somebody's lookin' in a window."

"No. But why pay for expensive experiments and designs when you could just lease the same old clock radio, the same old chair? They got us where we pay for whatever they put out. Why design somethin' might cost a million creds when you could just change its color or put a vid in it?"

"So we just stopped advancing? We just stagnate from now on?"

"No. They do research. Randac do it on Madagascar in their genius prison. Dr. Kismet do it in the Blue Zone on Home. But that shit ain't for the prods. They have what they have and we cain't get at it. That's why we live from minute to minute and they plannin' on what our children's children gonna live like."

"But that's not right. We should be making those decisions."

"How much you think it's gonna cost to make a hardware prototype'a your Eye thing?"

"I don't know."

"Ten million—credits not dollars. That's why you can't decide. It costs a lotta money to decide. And they only pay you enough to get fat and sloppy."

Neil wanted to talk more but a message came in from Un Fitt and Neil had been waiting for instructions.

"Sorry, Nina. I should read this."

"Okay, baby. See you later."

Hello, Neil,

I'm very happy with your work on this project. You have gone far past the expectations General Specifix had for you. The design of the Third Eye, though not perfect, will allow others to hone your ideas into a perfectly running unit. You're right when you say that memory is the only real question. But other researchers in other GT's have come up with an interesting solution. Your work has been exemplary and I am going to give you a paid holiday to Maya for two ten-spans. All we need before you go is a comprehensive write-up of the protocols you feel have yet to be set up and programmed.

Neil read the words with a growing sense of failure. He had believed that the Third Eye project was his, that he would be the only one to work on it. Now he was being told that he was still on a production lane, that he was only a nameless step in the creation of just another product. He tried to do the write-up he was asked for: he called up the beginnings of the macroflow he'd generated describing the logic units needed to fulfill the parameters of the Third Eye. For over an hour he stared at the boxes and circles used to exhibit the flow of data, the speed of perception in the various skins, and the protocols for translation into octal code. Neil looked at the screen but it didn't make any sense to him.

"I'm going home," he told Athria at just past noon.

"Okay, honey. You sick?"

"No. See you tomorrow."

At home Neil didn't drink or watch the vid; he didn't dream about the coast of California or anticipate Nina's late night visit. All he did was sit in his chair and think about Un Fitt and how he had been robbed of his chance to succeed. He knew that these thoughts were ridiculous, that someone who had expertise in biology and neurology would have to take over. But Un Fitt had implied that the work Neil had done would have to be done over. Why wasn't he allowed to get first crack at rewrites?

The vid phone came on just past twenty-three hours.

"Neil?" Nina said. Her face took up the whole screen so he couldn't tell where she was.

"Hey, honey."

"What's wrong?"

"They took me off the Third Eye project."

"Moving it down the lane?"

"Yeah."

"That's okay, baby. You'll get another project."

"I wasn't finished with this one yet."

"I know, babe. We all felt like that on our first project. My first time out I was working on a facet of an automated construction machine. I didn't get nearly as far as you did but I still cried when they moved it on."

"Yeah, I guess."

"I got somethin'll make you feel better."

"What?"

"I'm up in a room with two sex-worker girls. I met 'em at the library. I told 'em about you and they said they wanted you to come with us. They got all kindsa toys. Come on. It'll be fun."

"Not tonight, babe. I mean, I'm too sad."

Neil expected her to throw a fit. She did that whenever he refused her "feel better cures."

"That's okay, honey. I know it must be hard. You get some sleep and I'll come by about five or so."

"Okay," Neil said. "See ya."

Just then Nina was pulled away from the screen by an Asian woman. The woman was tall and there was a serious look on her face. She pulled Nina to her and kissed her hard. She snaked her hand under Nina's plaid skirt and lifted her off her feet. When Neil heard his lover's loud moan of pleasure he switched off the vid.

> Dear M Un Fitt,
>
> After careful consideration I have decided that I can no longer work with GP-9. I've come to this decision because I expected a greater level of independence at the job. For the past year I thought I was out of the prod lane but now I see that I'm still in the same situation. The fact that you've taken the Third Eye project from me without hearing how I might answer some of the technical problems proves that I have been misled. I would rather work on a GT that was honest in its appraisal of my work than

be fooled by a UC who doesn't even come in to meet us face-to-face.

Neil Hawthorne

As soon as Neil transmitted his resignation he regretted it. What would he do back at some GT like LAVE-AITCH-27? How could he survive as just another prod after experiencing GEE-PRO-9?

He was thinking of sending another e-mail to retract his resignation when the vid phone bleeped.

Dear Neil,

We are sorry that you are so upset by the necessity of relieving you of the Eye project. It is true, we are a production lane as you said, but our workers develop their skills rather than spend years repeating the same functions. Your next project would have been even more challenging. It is my hope that we can somehow convince you to stay with us.

UF

Dear Un Fitt,

My argument with you is not about the necessity of taking my job away but the fact that no one discussed the decision with me.

NH

Dear NH,

The decision is made on a higher level. Your work has a larger purpose and cannot be discussed because you are not aware of the greater plan. The reason GP-9 and other GTs around the country are structured

the way they are is to get the best work out of the prods. Your happiness makes for better work. But some decisions must be made without your input.

UF

How can I accept what you're saying now when for the last year I have been working as a free agent? I come in when I want to, work as I will. I've learned more in the past twelve months than I did in my whole life before I came here. I'm sure that if I knew the greater plan that I would be even more valuable to the system.

Neil,

Sometimes knowledge is a dangerous thing. What you know might get into the wrong hands one day. The more information that slips out, the greater danger that will face all of us. We appreciate your pique but we also hope that you will trust our judgment.

Un,

We're both men, equal under the genetic laws of 2025. In GEE-PRO-9 there are no bosses, no superiors. The only way that I can see continuing is by being trusted with the purpose of our work so that I can understand the decisions being made.

I am not a man, Neil. Neither am I a woman.

If not man or woman, what kind of person are you?

I am machine, Neil.

If you're a machine, then who is your programmer?

God.

Neil sat back in his chair after this last communication. He didn't know what to think about the claims of Un Fitt. He was afraid to ask any more, and so he did not answer. After a few minutes another message came in.

> **I know that you must be very upset about the loss of your project and about the nature of your controller. Take a while, take your vacation. And when you come back we will talk again. You are one of my favorites, Neil. Please, think about yourself.**

"Hi, baby," Nina said at five the next morning.

Neil saw the numbers 5:03 floating aimlessly around the otherwise empty vid chamber. He realized now for the first time that she was always on time.

"Hey."

She kissed him on the lips. Her breath smelled strongly of whoever it was that she had been kissing that night. The tall Asian, Neil thought, or maybe another.

"Don't be mad, baby," Nina said. She sat down at his feet and played with his kneecaps, running her fingertips around in circles. "It was just nuthin'. I axed you to come wit' me. You would'a had fun if you wasn't so mad."

"I'm not mad, honey. I know who you are. At least I know who you are."

"What's that mean?"

"I'm going on a vacation," Neil said. "Goin' to Maya for two weeks."

"Since when?"

"Since yesterday. When they took the Third Eye from me they gave me a bonus vacation."

"You gonna go?"

"I think I have to. I have to think." Neil smiled at the order of his words.

"I don't want you to go."

"Why not? Then you won't have me whining at you to come over. You could have all the hefty-men and sex-worker girls you want, every night."

"I don't want that!" she yelled. She jumped up and slapped him hard across the face. Then she collapsed in his lap, crying.

Neil put his hands on her heaving shoulder blades. He said nothing, felt nothing, wondered nothing except about the nature of his Unit Controller.

8

On the following Friday Neil was one of nine hundred forty-seven passengers on the Titan 010 air cruise ship landing on Maya. He had a second-class seat, which was better than most senators rated. People all over that sleeper cabin asked him what position he held at General Specifix. Two flight aides, one a woman and the other a man, gave him their hotel numbers on the island.

On the tarmac Neil was blinded by sunlight reflecting

off the bright red rock that composed the synthetic island.

"M Hawthorne?"

"Yes?"

"I'm your driver—Oscar Torres." The large man was brown-skinned. He had a heroic mustache and two fingers missing from the hand he used to shake with. "I will take you to the Crimson Chalet and drive you wherever you need to go while you are here."

"Who hired you?" Neil asked Torres from the backseat of the luxurious, German-made Century Bug. The green chromium car sped down the small lanes of the perfect little Hindu city that was the tourist hub of Maya.

"The travel bureau of the island called me and told me that you were my only responsibility for the next few days," the big man said. His mouth, Neil thought, seemed always on the verge of laughter. "And that I was not to accept any gratuity from you whatsoever."

"Who paid them?"

"Don't *you* know?"

"I know who sent me here but I thought I'd like to find out what department did the work, so I could thank them—everything has worked out so well."

The hotel lobby was the size of Grand Central Station and every bit as busy. Carrying Neil's two suitcases, Oscar weaved through the crowd of noisy tourists, bellboys, taxidrivers, and undercover security agents. Finally they came to a small window that had no one waiting on line.

"First class only, M," said the small woman who sat inside the window.

"That's my boss. First class all the way."

The woman, who had India Indian deep brown skin and shimmering blond hair, leaned forward to get a glimpse of Neil, who was wearing a worse-for-wear coal gray andro-suit.

"Name?" she asked suspiciously.

"Neil Hawthorne virtual mid—um, Neil Hawthorne."

The woman pressed two buttons and then her dour expression changed. "Welcome, M Hawthorne," she said brightly. "We've been waiting for you. You have been given the Neptune Suite above the upper level of the reef. Are these all your bags?"

"Yes."

Four melodious chimes issued from somewhere behind her desk. A moment later a tall man appeared, wearing a uniform that was the same color red as the island, the outer walls of the chalet, the ceilings, floors, inner walls, and almost everything else that Neil had so far seen.

"The Neptune Suite," the woman said.

The big man took the bag from Oscar and said, "Follow me, sir."

"Here's my number, M Hawthorne," Oscar said, pressing a scrap of paper into Neil's sweating palm.

The cavernous suite was the pale blue of a pastel artist's rendition of the sea. An incredibly large, green-tinted window led out onto a deck easily five times the size of Neil's apartment. From there he could see most of the southern part of Maya. There were tens of thousands of tourists and workers down in the town and spread out across the orange sands of the beach. But even with all that traffic only the sound of the ocean reached Neil's spectacular perch.

"M Hawthorne?" a girl's voice asked timidly.

She was little more than a child, Neil thought. She stood in the doorway naked and barefoot. Her pale white skin seemed to belong to the night and its lunar light. She had no hair, anywhere. No brows or pubes or even an eyelash. And she was beautiful.

"Who are you?"

"Your house servant—Charity."

"What's that?"

"I'm here for your needs. I can cook and clean, run errands and sleep in your bed. I am here for you."

"You work for the hotel?"

She nodded and looked down.

Many years later Neil realized, as he scanned this memory, that it was at this moment that he no longer considered Pulse as an alternative to problems he faced in life.

"Where are you from?"

"Scandia."

"How'd you get here?"

"My parents send me for their retirement."

"I can send down for a vig-toner drink," Charity offered.

They were lying in Neil's bed. He had been trying for hours to make love to his house servant. The windows of his bedroom were open to the sound of the ocean. The impossibly bright three-quarter moon was their only light.

"No thanks," he said. "All I'd do is think about Nina."

Charity lifted his limp penis with the fingertips of both hands. She gave it a light kiss.

"I like how the skin of your penis is so dark compared to the rest of your body. It's so much better than pink or red."

"That tickles," Neil said.

"Is Nina your wife?"

"No."

"Girlfriend?"

"Sometimes."

"What does that mean?"

"She's, she's a free spirit, a wild thing is what she calls it. I see her a lot but sometimes she goes away for a night or two . . . to get wild sex with strange men or women."

"Is she very beautiful?" Charity asked wistfully.

"No. Actually she's kind of ugly."

"No!" Charity blurted. She laughed and punched Neil playfully on the arm.

"Yeah, she is. I mean she's real sexy and there's something about her . . ."

Charity seemed to be paying very close attention to him.

She pushed Neil's chest with both her hands hard enough to knock him over on the bed.

"You lie," she said. "A rich man like you would not have an ugly girl."

"Yeah," Neil said, putting his hand against his chest.

"Sit up," she said.

Neil did. He was enjoying their banter.

Suddenly she slapped him very hard across the face.

"Ow! Why'd you do that?"

"Look," she replied, pointing at his groin.

He looked down to see that he'd begun to have an erection. When he looked back up at Charity, she slapped him even harder and pushed him down on his back.

The days passed on Maya. Neil wandered the crowded streets looking into shops where items were actually for sale rather than lease. When he was tired of the multitudes he would have Oscar drive him to the private access suite beach. There he could wander alone for hours only rarely coming across some billionaire and his house servant.

Whenever he was alone he'd remember the last communication he had with Un Fitt. He decided that the rogue controller was a megalomaniac, some demented genius who trapped unsuspecting prods in his illegal designs.

For the first time in his life Neil read the electric news. The INA, the *Western Wynde*, even the *Daily Dump* were available on a flat screen that popped up on his breakfast table every morning. The first few days he just scanned the headlines, looking for the escapades of sports heroes and vid stars. He was also drawn to spectacular murders and great disasters. It was only by chance that he saw the name Arnold Roth reported as one of the victims of a Common Ground riot in the Bronx.

There had been a three-day food shortage, something about a delivery schedule foul-up and the subsequent lockdown of CG-109, the largest Common Ground facility in the twelve feifs. Roth had stayed in his sleep slip to avoid trouble, the INA reported, but out-of-control rioters had thrown a Molotov cocktail and the smoke suffocated the innocent cycler.

The *Daily Dump* had a completely different scenario for the death of Arnold Roth, Neil's only friend before he came to work for GEE-PRO-9. M Roth, the *Dump* reported, was demanding food or freedom with thirty thousand other displaced unemployed persons when they were dispersed by sonic cannons, a standard antiriot tool of the NYSP. To prove this claim the *Dump* supplied a vid clip that showed Arnold yelling and brandishing his fists along with many others. Later, the *Dump* asserted, Roth was forced into a tunnel where rioters were to be quelled with disorientation gas. Arnold was one of the unlucky few who got pressed into a lower slip. There he suffocated.

The end of the article was punctuated by a low-res electronic photo of a jumble of corpses jammed into a sleep tube. Arnold Roth's pudgy face lolled over another dead M's rump.

The news of his friend's death greatly disturbed Neil, though he didn't feel sadness or loss. Neil liked Arnold, but he'd always known that his friend was destined to become a Backgrounder. Roth could never stay on a job cycle for more than a few months. In the last year Neil hadn't responded to Arnold's calls. He was afraid that he might let some secret slip about GP-9. He never trusted Arnold, he hadn't missed his company in the past year, but still he identified with the dead prod. Neil saw himself in the brown pajama uniform of Common Ground, shaking his fists in the face of the Social Police. He saw himself pressed into a hole and suffocated.

That night he sat up with his Scandian housegirl and talked about how his mother hadn't called him in the whole year that he worked for GEE-PRO-9.

"She moved to Baltimore," Neil told Charity. "Joined an Infochurch commune that took out a twelve-year lease on a vacant warehouse there. I only know because I called her on Christmas to invite her out to dinner. If I didn't ask her she wouldn't have even told me that she'd moved."

The next day Neil read all three papers looking for information on Arnold. But there was no mention, not even in the *Dump*.

Neil read articles on every social disturbance, hoping for some new information on the Common Ground riots. The *Dump* claimed that MacroCode America was behind the riots but that made no sense to Neil.

There was nothing else about CG-109. The Cincinnati police department had dispatched a unit to New York, but that was because of some group defrauding their city's treasury. A large number of Itsies had escaped Common Grounds around the world and emigrated to Jesus City, an International Socialist enclave in the Caucasus Mountains. Rioting in Boston had erupted because of a new law the FemLeague had pushed through banning self-circumcision in women.

Neil dreamed about the news. He lived out the riots and the deaths. He waded through fields of corpses, was locked in a sleep slip underground. He searched battlefields, hospitals, and graveyards for Arnold Roth. He awoke with headaches and loose bowels like in the old days before GEE-PRO-9.

"So did you fuck her?" were the first words out of Nina's mouth when he called her on the ninth day after he'd arrived on Maya.

"What?"

"I know you got a housegirl with your place."

"Why would you care, Nina? You always get mad at me when I ask you that kinda stuff."

"I do not. And I tell you whatever it is I'm doing."

"Yeah," he said. "Yeah, I did."

"Oh," Nina said in a small voice. "How was it?"

"Nice."

"Is she pretty?"

"She doesn't have any hair. No hair at all."

"But is she pretty?"

"She's nice."

"So why don't you bring her home with you if you like her so much? I'm sure she'd wanna come to New York. Why don't you do that?"

"Nina, what's wrong? You always said that we have to be free sexually. Is it just because I've never done it before?"

"Don't try and get psychological with me, M. I never seen nobody more than one night. Except those sex-worker girls, but they're women and that makes it different."

"Nina, Charity comes with the room," Neil said.

"So she has a name, huh?" Nina's face contorted into

a rage that Neil had never seen in her before. "Fuck you!" she cried and then broke off the connection.

He tried to call her back but there was no answer at her home, the job, or on her portable unit. He wondered what it was that he had done to get her so mad. He thought about that for a while but then his mind wandered back to Un Fitt's megalomania, Arnold Roth's death, and his mother.

"I love you, Neil," Charity said to him later that night. The sting of her slaps were still on his cheeks, both upper and lower.

"You do?"

"I like the way you submit to me, how I found out how to get you hot and how you let me. And . . ."

"And what?"

"You're really funny and nice. Most rich men don't even see you. Even if they fuck you they don't remember your face. You knew my name after the first time I said it. That's why I wanted to make you excited, because I wanted to make you feel good."

"I don't know what to say."

"And how you said that your girlfriend was ugly but that you loved her. How she does what she wants and you aren't even mad at her."

"I don't act like a rich man 'cause I'm not, Charity. I'm just a guy who won a free vacation for doing a good job for a crazy boss."

"Can I come home with you anyway? I don't want to be rich."

"I don't know how."

"Is it because of my hair? I could get new roots put in. I could have any kind of hair you want."

"Let's talk about it in the morning, okay?"

"You don't want me."

"I, I, I . . . I need to think about it, that's all. I need to think about what I could do."

"I could work for you, make you money. I'm a trained Eros-Haus girl. And Nina wouldn't even know I was there."

9 The vid made a loud bubbling sound at three in the morning. Neil had decided to sleep alone and asked Charity to take the servant's quarters for the night.

"Sir?" a bodiless voice inquired.

"Who is it?"

"The front desk."

"What time is it?"

"Three, sir. I'm sorry to bother you, but there's a gentleman down here who says that he has urgent business with you."

"What gentleman?"

"He calls himself Blue Nile."

"Hey, Neilio," the diminutive prod from GEE-PRO-9 said with a smile. He was stretched out across a pink couch near the registration desk.

"What are you doing here?"

"No time for talkin', this place is walkin'," Blue Nile

replied as he rose to his feet. He took Neil by the hand as he had done the first day they met over a year before.

The grand lobby of the Crimson Chalet was nearly empty at that time of morning. There was one open bar with an obstinate group of partyers drinking and laughing loudly.

"Walk where?"

"Into the night and out of sight."

"Make sense, Blue." Neil came to a halt.

"We've got to run, Neil," the little man said seriously. "The authorities discovered GP-9 and they're after all of the prods involved."

"What?"

"They got Marva and Lonnie Z, Three Moons and the Monique sisters."

"Monique sisters?"

"They never came in. The bulls got the homeworkers first."

"What about Nina?"

"I left her a message but we never spoke," Blue Nile said. "She's got street in her, she'll get away. Oura and Athria were notified by Un Fitt. They told me to come after you. The cops are already on their way to this hotel. They don't have your name yet 'cause we used codes in the ticketing system, but they won't take long in finding you out."

"If they're on the island how can we get away?"

"I got a swift and a pilot waiting down at the private beach."

They scurried down the dark pathways of Maya in the early morning. Neil was wearing fabric slippers and loose pajama pants. When the security team stopped them he was sure that they would be arrested for crimes against the economy.

"Where you Ms going this time of morning?" asked a large woman who appeared from the shadows. She wore the yellow and black law enforcement uniform of the island.

Her partner, a man even larger than she, stood silently behind.

Neil brought out his Neptune Suite key and showed it to the police. He knew that it wouldn't make a difference, but it was all he could do.

"Oh," the woman said, suddenly feminine. "Excuse me, M Hawthorne. I didn't recognize you in the darkness. Please, go on."

"Thank you," he mumbled.

"Would you like us to accompany you?" the male officer asked.

"That won't be necessary."

The small jet could hover as well as accelerate to over three times the speed of sound. The pilot was an Indian woman with a very proper English accent. The cabin was small but comfortable enough for six passengers. Silently the jet rose above the Caribbean Sea before it sped off across the sky.

"Where are we going?"

"I don't know," Blue Nile said.

"How can you not know?"

"If I don't know then I can't tell any unfriendlies, now can I?"

Two hours later they landed on a desolate stretch of beach. Neil had no idea of where they were. He had no sense of direction or geography. They could have been anywhere in the world. It was a moonless night. Neil figured that there must be a city somewhere, because he could make out a tree-spiked horizon against a barely perceptible glow from far off.

Through the window he could see a flickering light in the distance.

"I see a light out there," he said to the pilot.

She didn't say anything and so he repeated his warning.

"I see it," she said.

As the light neared, Neil could see that it came from a flame. Open fire was illegal in New York City. Matches had been classified as a form of fireworks and possession of them was treated as a third-degree misdemeanor. Only filament lighters were allowed for choke cigarettes. Neil's first experience with open flame had been the torches and candles of Maya. He was enchanted by the ragged dancing quality of naked fire.

It took the solitary figure a good quarter of an hour to reach the beach. When he neared, the pilot engaged the ramp device. The man dropped the lantern and ran up into the ship.

He was tall and thin, black with long thick hair that resembled a lion's mane.

"M Nile, M Hawthorne," the young-looking man said. "It's a great pleasure to finally meet you."

"Sir?" the pilot asked from the cockpit.

"Destination L-17," the man replied. He strapped himself into a seat next to Neil and the swift rose quickly into the black skies above the beach that could have been anywhere.

"Ptolemy Bent," the new passenger said. He pressed Neil's hand, and then Blue Nile's.

"You one of the prods under Un Fitt?" Neil asked.

"Not exactly. I'm more like the midwife."

"Come again?"

"It's a long story."

"I know that Un is a computer," Neil said.

"He told you that?"

"I was going to quit. Then he said that he was a machine. Did you create him?"

"In a way."

"The controller is a computer?" Blue Nile asked.

"Partly," the lion-maned black man said.

"What does that mean?"

"Un Fitt told me that he was programmed by God," Neil told Blue Nile.

"He said that too?" Ptolemy was surprised but didn't seem upset or at all bothered.

"Is it true?" asked Blue Nile

"Maybe. Maybe it's even more amazing than that."

"Who are you?" Neil asked.

"You know my name already. The place we just left is the private prison run by Randac."

"This is Madagascar?" asked Blue Nile.

"Where are we going?" Neil wanted to know.

"To find someone I've always wanted to meet and then to plot our countermove to the Cincinnati police."

"Programmed by God," Blue Nile said to himself.

Ptolemy Bent pressed a button at the side of his chair and a computer table came out of the arm, positioning itself before him like a food tray. The virtual keyboard was composed of characters Neil had never seen before. Ptolemy ran his fingers over the keys as if he were a concert pianist. His shoulder and head swayed while he typed, almost as if he were dancing in his seat to some unheard melody. Now and then he would grunt or hum. The screen embedded in the table had no text at all, only colorful forms that slid gracefully over and around one another. Neil became enchanted with the forms. They seemed as if they might be alive. *Totally live,* Neil thought. *Like a place where everything—the sky, the sand, the clouds, everything—is alive and moving gracefully with everything else.*

For over an hour Ptolemy worked on his computer screen. Blue Nile was silent the whole time. Neil suspected that the gregarious prod was silenced by the strangeness of the situation and the powerful presence of Ptolemy Bent. Finally the old Vermonter fell asleep.

"You did a great job on the Third Eye," Ptolemy said. The sky was still black, but there was an angry orange band of light at the edge of the world.

"You can see that in there?"

"Among other things."

"I really didn't do much. I mean, the notes Un Fitt sent taught me everything I needed to know."

"No one knows without being shown the way," Ptolemy said. "Like the scent of sex or the sound of running water. We have in our genes the knowledge but without a sign we are lost."

Neil's heart thrilled hearing these words. "What . . . what do you mean?" he asked.

"Un Fitt found you," Ptolemy said. He turned away from his work and the screen faded to gray. "I asked him to locate those who had undiscovered brilliance and the power to dream of something other than their minds locked into this world. He found over six million candidates around the world. Of these, six thousand one hundred forty-two were workable, given the parameters of Un Fitt's ability to manipulate events."

"I was chosen out of so many?"

"You have the magic in you."

"How can a machine read magic?"

"A machine," Ptolemy corrected, "programmed by a god."

"I don't understand. Why would God or even a god be interested in a Third Eye project? He already sees more than I can even imagine."

"*You* were creating the Third Eye, Neil. Un Fitt was creating you."

"Huh?"

"He was pushing you, tantalizing you, making you go beyond yourself because you—flesh and bone and spirit—are the only chains that keep you enslaved to this world and also your only chance to be free."

"I don't understand."

"Let me give you an example." The slender man

turned sideways in his chair and folded his legs yogi style. "What is the biggest problem with the Third Eye?"

"Memory. In order to retain information accurately there has to be a storage device on a par with the human and metahuman senses provided by the Eye. Actually, it would have to be Eyes in order to do everything Un Fitt asked for."

"Good," Ptolemy said. He was smiling. "Now I want you to answer my next questions quickly with no concern of proving what you say."

"Okay."

"What is the answer to the problem?"

"At first I thought that it would be some kind of transmitting device, or maybe an onboard computer that would be surgically implanted. But those devices are too slow and also they speak in a different language from the brain."

"And so?"

"So, well, so . . . The only device appropriate to the task, the only device that has enough memory and the right kind of language, is the human brain itself. I mean, fully twenty-five percent of the brain is almost completely inactive. That's more than enough to store days of sensory data."

"And?" coaxed the self-proclaimed midwife of God.

"Then the Eye would become a new organ and the capacity and nature of the brain would expand."

"Not expand, but change. The one thing that nobody wants, the one thing that will pull us out of the darkness of technology. Your answer is more important than the Third Eye itself. Now, one more question."

"Uh-huh."

"What would you do if you had to give all of this up?"

"Everything?"

"The seat on this jet, all that you've learned, and your name on the hit list of the Cincinnati PD."

"I'd kill myself," Neil said. "And I'd take whoever made me give it up with me."

"And so, let there be life," Ptolemy said. He went to the back row of seats and turned up a table. At a touch the screen was ablaze with color.

Neil was staring out of the small window into the darkness. The swift was flying high and there were no clouds. Every now and then Neil would see a swath of white far below. He wondered if he had any control over his destination, or his destiny.

Maybe, he thought, *I don't have a destiny, only a final place that I'll come to. A place where I'll die or live, it won't matter which.*

"Hey, Neilio," Blue Nile whispered. He had moved to the seat next to Neil. "You 'wake?"

"Yeah, now I am."

"Boy oh boy, we're in it deep now, huh?"

"I guess. You scared?"

"Me? No. It's like I told you before, I owe it all to the company store. There's no freedom for me unless I take it."

"So you don't regret being in GP-9?"

"No. I liked it more than anything else I had up to then, except for my family. And you know the way the employment cycles work it's hard to keep family goin'. Anyway, there was some good people in our GT. Atty and Or are great. Nin and Nina. You. I really like you, Neil."

"Yeah, Blue. I like you too."

"There's only one thing that I regret, really."

"What's that?" Neil asked.

"D'or."

"You and her had something going, didn't you?"

"Yeah. Yeah." Blue Nile smiled. "But it'll never come to nuthin' now."

"Why not?"

"She loves her little restaurant and I'm a fugitive from New York." The small prod took in a deep breath and let it out as a sigh. "Promise me something, Neil?"

"What's that, Blue?"

"That you'll tell D'or that I was talkin' about her. About how much I cared for her."

"Why don't you tell her yourself?"

"I mean, if I don't make it."

"What's gonna stop you?"

"This is serious business, Neilio. We're fugitives. We're on our own now. I don't care for myself. I had a good run for four years. But D'or, I could have seen myself with her."

"Well, if you don't make it, what makes you think I will?"

"Maybe you won't," Blue Nile agreed. "But if you do, will you tell her that I was talkin' about her?"

"Absolutely."

10 When the swift began to descend Neil woke up. The sun was shining on a wintry ocean filled with icebergs. Blue Nile was looking out of the window on the opposite side of the cabin. Ptolemy Bent was leaning through the cockpit door, talking to the pilot.

An island loomed before them. A frozen rock in the middle of the Antarctic. When the swift lowered itself onto the craggy beach a solitary figure in a balloonlike blue parka approached.

Neil wasn't surprised that the figure was Nina Bossett. Once inside the cabin she tore off the coat and wrapped herself in Ptolemy Bent's arms. She was crying and so was he. Even though the plane was tossed by turbulence from the Antarctic winds, the two stood there in front of the pilot's door hugging and weeping.

"Sir," the pilot said. "You will have to take your seats and buckle up."

Ptolemy and Nina kissed. They couldn't seem to let go.

"Sir."

She caressed his cheek with her fingertips. He kissed her fingers.

"Sir, please. Low-level radar in this region is at full capacity because of the MacroCode facilities nearby."

Finally they sat side by side in the row behind Neil and Blue Nile. There they talked and gazed deeply into each other's eyes.

Neil watched them, his heart in turmoil. The experiences of the past year flooded his mind. He remembered the formation of geese flying outside the window when he first regained consciousness; he regarded that event as the first moment of his life. He loved Nina, which was more than he'd ever hoped for, and now he loved Ptolemy Bent with equal passion even though they had only just met. He was angry and frightened, amazed and alone with thoughts that he'd recently learned had been planted by a computer that thought it was programmed by God.

His life before GEE-PRO-9 had proved to be nothing; his new life was slipping between his fingers. He was so distracted by these thoughts that he didn't realize when Nina had settled in next to him. She put her hand on his shoulder and made clucking sounds in his ear. Neil pulled away from her.

"What's wrong, honey?" she asked.

"I can't take it," he said. "Why don't you just leave me alone?"

"What's wrong? Why you mad?"

Neil realized then that she had never loved him, that she thought he knew this, and so when the real love of her life returned she was surprised that Neil would have trouble accepting him.

"Is it 'cause I was yellin' at you over the vid? I was just mad, baby. I saw in her records that that room-girl gave up her days off to stay with you."

"How can you complain about Charity when you have him?" Neil waved toward Ptolemy, who had turned on the computer at his seat and was deep into the colors and forms he conjured there.

"You mean Popo? Honey, he's my brother."

"Your brother?"

"Yeah. Half brother, really. We have the same father, a man who called himself Johnny Delight."

"Why would you kiss your brother like that?"

" 'Cause it's the first time we ever met, that's why."

"How can that be?"

"Popo been in prison on Madagascar since he was sixteen. They said that he killed his uncle and grandmother but he didn't. He freed 'em, that's what Aunt Kai told me. She said that he send 'em up to heaven, maybe even to God."

"That's crazy," Neil said.

"That's what you said about GEE-PRO-9 when you first got there. You said it was crazy, but it wasn't, was it?"

"That's different. It's crazy to think you can go through a door and end up in heaven. It's crazy even to believe in heaven."

"Why? 'Cause you say so? What do you know?"

"What does he know?" Neil jerked his head toward Ptolemy.

"Popo got the highest IQ of anybody ever tested, even Dr. Kismet. They been havin' him a prisoner at Randac ever since he was a teenager, since I was just a little baby."

"But they let him out," Neil said, almost hopefully. "They let him go."

"Not really."

"What do you mean?"

"When you picked him up that was the last step of his escape."

"We did a jail break?"

"You did. I'm just an accessory after the fact."

In a great underground cavern in the northern Sahara Desert, Ptolemy Bent and fifteen of his faithful prods gathered around an antique ebony wood table. The floor and walls of the chamber were made from smooth and shiny plates of Glassone. The ceiling was formed from fused stones.

". . . the truth is," Ptolemy was saying, "we were undone by the Cincinnati PD."

"Why would they be interested in a New York office?" Oura asked. Though deep concern showed in her face she was still radiant in her various shades of gold.

"The city of Cincinnati has its money tied up in stocks. And General Specifix is one of the few arms of MacroCode that Kismet allowed to go public. He used the profits from that venture to build the Blue Zone. Anyway, the treasury department of Cincinnati noticed large sums of money missing that Un Fitt had siphoned off to build various havens around the globe. The bottom line of the company wasn't affected because GP-9 and other GTs more than made up the losses with profitable projects. Still, the CPD didn't know that and so they began their investigation.

"When they discovered Un Fitt's program it was only a matter of time before they found the ten GTs that we'd set up."

"How many of the prods were caught?" Athria asked.

"Over two thousand," Ptolemy said. "We were lucky that Un Fitt began monitoring the CPD soon after they discovered the financial discrepancies. He was able to set up the escape protocols that I gave him at the beginning of his run."

"Like the swift coming to Maya?" Neil asked.

"Yes," said Ptolemy. "And the robot plane that took Nina to the island where we picked her up. We had hundreds of two-legged escape routes. The problem was that we didn't have enough time to warn everyone before the intercorporate police force was called in."

"What happens to the ones they caught?" a small woman with a red beard asked.

"Un Fitt is already locating those that were captured and putting logic into play that will release them into our hands."

"I thought Un Fitt was discovered by the cops," Neil said. "Wouldn't they just shut him down?"

"Un Fitt is an operating system," Ptolemy replied. "His program, which is self-altering, is stored in over ten thousand dump-sites, which are designated by a tenth power randomizer. These addresses, once found, are erased from the running program's system. Self-generated updates to his system are downloaded on an hourly basis to an additional ten thousand sites. These updates can be retrieved via radio waves. Because of this system it is virtually impossible to shut Un Fitt down permanently; it would be damned hard to even force him to take a step back in his own intellectual evolution."

"Did God make those programming decisions?" Neil was surprised at the sarcasm in his own voice.

"I did the peripheral programming," Ptolemy said. "I set up the system to be inserted in one of Randac's satellite computers. I set up everything but then I let the spirit I discovered years ago inform the internal logic of the system."

"Vat does dat mean?" asked a tall man named Blaun. He had an east European accent and radiant blue eyes.

"Years ago," Ptolemy said, "I discovered that the atmosphere of Earth was enveloped by an intelligent ether. It's a vast store of knowledge that exists in an area between five hundred and two thousand miles above the surface."

"An intelligence?" someone asked.

"That's all I call it. It's an awareness, a consciousness. For many years this consciousness has been trying to communicate with us—by radio waves. I found the pattern when I was a child not more than four. Over the next ten years I was able to use a transmitter to communicate with the entity. Back then I thought that it was God; now I'm not so sure. I don't even know what the relationship is between it and us. I mean, it might have created us, but there's also an argument that we, through the electronic nature of our minds, might be the cause of this meta-intelligence. Then again it could just be some kind of celestial traveler, stopping for a few centuries and trying to understand the DNA-based fungus that makes up all life here on Earth.

"At any rate, I invited the entity to enter into the Un Fitt system. It created the logic of Un Fitt and I used that logic to create the schools that trained all of you."

"Trained us for what?" a woman named Thedra asked.

"To advance," Ptolemy said. "To change. The way the world is today, change has become a function of profit. Money makes change. There's very little of the individual left. Our minds are made to stagnate, our bodies are fuel for the systems of production. Maybe some of that is good. But then again maybe it isn't. What Un Fitt and I are trying to do is create revolutionaries, people who aren't satisfied with just being prods."

"What else is there?" Thedra asked.

"You see?" Ptolemy said. "Two years ago you wouldn't have asked that question. Two years ago you just showed up at the assignment booth and went where they told you to go. You followed the system hoping that you could put in your fifty-three years and then retire on the half of your salary that the union kept aside for you.

"Don't get me wrong, not all of the prods that Un Fitt found have worked out. Over twelve hundred have turned us in to the authorities."

"Then why weren't we caught long ago?" a tall Asian man asked.

"Because of Un Fitt," Ptolemy said. "He has superimposed a communications net over every prod we have, using our ID chips. Every communication going out is first reviewed and edited by Un Fitt's matrices."

"So what did you do when you discovered the traitors?" Athria asked.

"Nothing. We simply supplied a realistic hyper-animae police official who thanked the whistle-blower and who then asked them to remain as a spy. If they were too afraid we thanked them and offered a transfer, cautioning them to keep quiet because of a broad-based ongoing investigation."

"What about somebody going in person to the CBI or somewhere?" Neil asked. "Some of them must have done that."

"Only six," Ptolemy replied. "Six out of twelve hundred eighty-nine."

"What did you do about them?"

"All CBI informants go through a background check before their claims are investigated. In each case we created a fairly serious crime that the claimant seemed to have committed. They were then subjected to automatic justice and sentenced to low-security prison systems. Each one was visited by an electronic apparition that warned them of a worse fate should they persist in trying to expose Un Fitt."

"Have you killed anybody?" Neil asked.

"No. But the question has merit. Un Fitt has set up assassination protocols in case of extreme circumstances. In the best of a bad situation we could strip the prod of his consciousness and transmit it into the ether."

"To God?" Oura asked.

"Or whatever," Ptolemy said. "That way the perpetrator is dead to the world but alive elsewhere."

"Vat if you could not do this process?" Blaun asked.

"Then we were ready to kill," Ptolemy said. "It's wrong, I know, but it's the only way we could see to keep the idea alive. The world is going in the wrong direction. Our judges are machines, our prisons and military and mental institutions and workplaces are planning to mechanize their human components with computerized chemical bags. The spirit is being squashed for the sake of production and profit. If we don't do something the race itself will become a mindless machine."

"But now the dream's over," Neil said. "Now we're underground in the desert and there's nothing we can do to change anything."

"I wish it were true," Ptolemy said. "I wish we could stay here for the rest of time, playing games with Un Fitt, designing toys that would make men and women better at being themselves."

"Why can't we, Popo?" Nina asked.

Ptolemy stared at his sister and then at each one of the fifteen prods in turn.

"What?" the woman with the red beard asked.

"While studying the CPD, Un Fitt found a relationship between the chief and the International Socialist Party."

"Itsies," Athria uttered.

"Chief Nordman is a high-ranking member of the secret arm of IS. From his records, Un Fitt found that not only have they moved their operations to the Caucasus Mountains, but they've also set up a laboratory to study the molecular nature of viruses."

"And?" Blue Nile asked.

"They're designing viral strains that target racial indicators."

"Race killers?" Nina whispered.

"Exactly."

For quite a while no one spoke.

"What is their first move?" Neil asked at last.

"To test the host virus on blacks."

"No."

"Maybe," Ptolemy said, "the entity *is* a god, and he called us to stop this insanity. Maybe it's all fate."

"Or maybe it's just a nightmare," Oura offered.

11 Later that evening Blue Nile said to Ptolemy Bent, "If what you're saying is true, then there's nothing we can do."

"And no time to do it in," Nina Bossett added.

"There is a small chance," said Ptolemy.

"What's that?" asked Thedra Ho, the Vietnamese chemical prod.

"X rays."

"As what?" asked Oura.

"If we can expose the pathogen to a fifteen-second burst of X rays, then the molecular structure will mutate."

"And probably become worse," Neil Hawthorne said.

"No, Brother Neil. The chance of a mutated pathogen having any effect at all on the human system is incredibly small."

"Even if it does work," Athria said, "where do we find the germs to radiate them?"

"The manufacture of the pathogen is very expensive. There were only two canisters made. One has been flown to Accra and the other to Denver."

"So all we have to do is find out where they're keeping the pathogen and shine an X-ray gun at it?" Neil asked.

"I can rig something like a flashlight to emit the correct band of radiation."

"But what if they have it in some kinda special container?" Neil asked. "What if the X rays can't penetrate the casing?"

"Un Fitt chose my apostles well," Ptolemy said. When he smiled on Neil the young ex-prod felt a swell of pride. "The virus is being kept in two fifty-gallon plasteel canisters. One in the basement of a bar called the Lucky Stallion on Q Street in Denver and the other in the storage room of the Northern Hemisphere Corporate Embassy in Accra."

"So we have to go there and shine a light?" Nina said.

"Just so," her brother replied. "In the meantime I will attempt to come up with an antiviral in case one or both of you fail. Un Fitt will plot the manner of approach that each team should take and then we'll go about procuring the tools you will need."

Twenty-seven hours later, Neil, along with Blue Nile and Blaun, were standing across the street from the Lucky Stallion. It was an old building with fake saloon doors and an antique red neon light made into the outline of a rearing stallion in the window. The temperature was just below freezing. Errant snowflakes danced in the breeze.

When a snowflake hit Neil's nose he remembered that he hadn't been outside in snow since he was a child in Central Park with his aunt. She had green eyes and a big nose and white skin that reddened in the cold. He remembered her face but not her name.

How could I forget my own aunt's name? he thought. He entered a reverie, remembering the things that he did not remember: the name of his elementary school, the name of the girl he had a crush on at the beginning of prod-ed. He tried to remember the names of the states, and only managed to come up with nineteen. Everything before GEE-PRO-9 faded, dissipated, evaporated from his mind. Neil could see that he had been created, or at least re-created, by the divine system and its creator. He had been just a prod, a unit in an endless system of production. Now he had a five-pound X-ray flasher under his red parka designed to save all of the black people of the world.

"You look white, Neil," Ptolemy had said, "so you go with the team to Denver."

Neil wondered what he meant by "look white"; he was white. Wasn't he? But almost all the important people in his life were Negroes. Oura and Athria, Ptolemy and Nina.

"Ve got to move, Neil," Blaun said. He was the group leader and well fit for the task, Neil thought. He was tall and powerful, with blond hair and sapphire eyes. In the years before Un Fitt recruited him, Blaun had been a member of the IS. He knew how to talk to the Itsies.

"Okay," Neil said. "But don't you think this is kinda strange?"

"Vat are you talking about?"

"I mean, it's just a bar. No soldiers, no metal doors."

"It's crazy, yes. They are strange peoples. Like the wild gangs of children who used to live in the streets of California. This group feels like they are in charge. They have men in government, men on the police force. They are careless and proud. They think that no one would dare to challenge them. No one but us."

"So we just walk in?"

"Ja. Vat else? They don't think ve know them. They don't know vat ve know."

"I'm ready," Blue Nile said. Neil looked at his old friend, the man he considered his first real friend. All the laughter and fun was gone.

The bar was filled with various specimens of white manhood. Some wore suits while others looked like New Age cowboys wearing shirts with semiprecious gemstone buttons and helmet-hats for horse riding. Two men in andro-suits and sunglasses stood at the back door. Blaun shot them both with cinder gun blasts. One disintegrated at the left shoulder down to his heart. The other crumpled from the waist down. He opened his mouth to cry out but died before he could utter a sound.

As the last guard died a strobing light started to dance about the room. The rest of the men in the bar fell into epileptic fits. They foamed and vomited before falling into unconsciousness or death. Special contact lenses protected Neil and his friends.

Blue Nile was returning the strobe-orb to the sack that he wore on his shoulder. Blaun caught Neil by his arm and shouted, "Ve must go behind the door! Stay behind me and be ready!"

Neil knew that he was in a war. He was ready to complete his function. But what he was thinking about was the sweet little man that he'd known just over a year. The man who took him gently by the hand and showed him the way of GEE-PRO-9 had just killed a room full of people without so much as a shadow crossing his face.

Through the door and down the rickety wooden stairs they went. They came to another door. This was unlocked. Blaun ran through, his pistol set for wide-band blasts. Neil took out his X-ray emitter and held it up before him, only one task on his mind.

When he came into the room he saw men, maybe a

dozen of them, with the third-degree burns of the cinder blast eating through their skins. On a cement dais the plasteel drum stood upright. Neil pointed his X rays at the heart of its murky amber contents.

One one thousand, two one thousand, three . . .

"Down under!" someone shouted in a clear cowboy drawl.

Five one thous . . .

Blue Nile fell into the room from the doorway, blood cascading from what had been his chest.

Seven one thousand . . .

Blaun threw himself in between Neil and the onrushing Itsies.

Nine one thousand . . .

Neil turned in time to see the cinder blast turn Blaun's handsome face into gray ash.

Ten one thousand, eleven one thousand . . .

"He's hurtin' the chill," a man shouted, and Neil felt four hard knocks in his side. Then he heard a loud clang.

"You hit the drum, you fool!" someone shouted.

And then there was peace.

12

"Neil?" said a voice with no sound.

"Yes?" he answered without feeling his mouth.

"Oh, baby," the voice said, and he knew that it was Nina. She was the only one who had ever called him baby.

"Where am I?"

"Back in the Sahara. You're hooked up to a machine being run by Un Fitt."

"Un Fitt?" Neil said with his mind.

"Yes, Neil? Can I do something for you?"

"No, nothing. It's just good to know that you're here."

"I'm so glad you're alive," Nina said.

"What happened?"

"You were in the bar in Denver, using the X-ray flasher on the disease. Blue Nile and Blaun were killed but you were just shot. The police killed the three shooters that attacked you. The parmeds came and put you on life support. The cops took you into custody but Un Fitt was able to transfer you to a hospital in Greece. From there we brought you here and made the neuronal connections to revitalize your brain."

"When can I get up?"

Silence filled the new hum of Neil's awareness.

"Did you manage to irradiate the pathogen?" the words were Ptolemy's, Neil was sure of that.

"Twelve seconds, maybe half a second more than that. Did they puncture the drum?"

"Yes."

"Did the virus escape?"

"Yes. By the time the police put a seal on the canister eighty percent of the virus had leaked."

"What about Africa?"

"Nina was successful," Ptolemy said. "They managed three minutes of radiance and no one had to die."

"Did I do enough?" Neil asked.

"You saved the black race."

"Am I going to die now?"

"No. But your body is damaged beyond repair. For

now you will reside with Un Fitt in this computer frame."

"Nina."

"Yeah, baby?"

"Will you wait for me to get fixed?"

"Every minute of every day."

His aunt's name was Martha. And not only could he remember the fifty states, but he could also recall all of the state capitals. The girl he had a crush on in prod-ed was Lana, and he loved her because she smelled like soap. He loved the smell of the soapy water his mother made him wash in after playing in the grass in Central Park. He remembered a grasshopper his uncle caught for him. It was a green creature with long waving antenae that was kept in a plastic cage made to look like bamboo. The creature ate bits of lettuce that Neil pressed between the bars. If he looked close he could see his uncle's face in the many facets of the bug's green eye. Bob.

"You shouldn't argue with your mother, Neil," Bob had said many long years before. Neil remembered the words and the voice and even the smell of strawberry jam in Martha's kitchen. "She's worked very hard not to get recycled so that you can have a mother and stay aboveground."

"But Uncle Bob, other kids got foot gliders, why can't I have a pair?"

"You shouldn't argue with your mother . . ." Bob repeated his admonition in exactly the same words, tones, smells, and time.

Neil asked Bob couldn't he buy the x-element gliders.

"You shouldn't argue with your mother . . ."

"Neil."

"Huh. Who is it?"

"Un Fitt. You were entering a loop, Neil."

"A what?"

"You got stuck questioning a memory. That happens sometimes when human minds are connected to a computer system."

"I can remember everything I ever knew," Neil said.

"Yes. There are neuronal connectors to every memory center in your brain. The problem is that you cannot change these memories."

"Why not?"

"Because the part of you that is consciousness resides in my matrix. It is a limbo of sorts. You can read the data of your life but you cannot alter it."

"Then how can I live?"

"You can talk to me, Neil."

"So that's it? It's you and me forever?" The hysterical shudder of claustrophobia went through the ex-prod's mind.

"No, Neil," Un Fitt said. "When we have the proper tools, Nina will be able to join you from time to time. And until then . . ."

What had been a void was suddenly a vast panorama of the sea, the Pacific Ocean, Neil knew instinctively. It was the prehistoric coastline that he'd yearned for since childhood. The waves crashed and huge birds wheeled in the sky.

"Here you may roam until there is a body for you to inhabit again," Un Fitt whispered between the thundering waves. "And a world worth living in."

The Nig in Me

1 "You look like shit, Jamey," Harold Bottoms said to his cubicle mate. It was Thirdday.

"I feel bad. Sick. It's that striped flu going around. I got the rash on my chest."

"Dog, why didn't you stay home?" *And keep your germs there,* Harold thought.

"I can't. One more sick day and I go on rotation. You know I can't take another three months underground."

"Whoever thought up'a some shit like that anyway? I only got four points to go my own self."

"If I go off the force one more time Sheila says she'll pull the plug. Three times more and I'm White Noise."

White Noise, Backgrounder, Muzak Jack—words that defined the poor souls who lost their labor rights permanently.

"That's okay, J," Harold told his friend. "Lotsa people got that flu. It don't seem so bad."

"You know anybody black who got it?" Jamey asked.

"Sure. Almost everybody comin' down. They said on the news that everybody and his uncle got the striped flu."

"*You* don't have it."

Nor could Harold think of any of his black friends who did. He'd seen Asians and a few Mexicans, India Indians and lots of white people with the red or brown striations on their upper arms. But he'd never seen any Negro-looking people with them. Neither had he heard any black people with the wheezy cough or complaining about the nagging headache associated with the minor flu. They hadn't said a thing about a racial aspect of the disease on ITV, but that was to be expected. Racial image profiling had been a broadcast offense for more than two decades.

"It's just a little virus, man," Harold said. "Lotsa people got it and lots don't. Wagner down in print don't. Neither Jane Flynn, Nestor whatshisname over in vids, or your bud Fat Phil. They're all white."

"I guess," Jamey said. "I guess you're right."

"Sure I am," Harold said. "Now let's hit the files before M Shirley gets out her marker."

"M Halloway, M Bottoms," M Shirley Bride said by way of greeting later that morning.

"Morning, M Bride," Harold said to the boss.

"Morning—" Jamey Halloway got out, and then he coughed.

"You got that flu?" the Unit Controller asked.

"No, M, not me. Went to the tobacco den to meet a friend. We talked too long in the smoke and, well, I kinda lost my voice."

Shirley Bride sniffed the air with her delicate nostrils and frowned.

"You don't smell like smoke." she said.

"Scrubbed off in the tanks last night."

Public bathing in recycled waters was the new rage since the water laws. FastBath of NYC was the largest franchise in North America.

"Oh," she said. "Because if you were sick I could send you home."

"Then you might as well kick me out of my house and annul my marriage license, too."

"That doesn't cut it with a controller," Shirley Bride said. "If I thought the office would be better off I'd have to send you home even if it did put you over seventeen. If I didn't I'd get a permanent mark. You know they're harder on management than they are on cyclers."

Harold and Jamey both hid the derision they felt. Upper management got the Life Plan. They were covered for anything short of a neutron bomb, as the outlawed Wildcat Union claimed on ghostnet.

"But I can send you home without a mark if that's a real cough," Bride continued. "It's an epidemic now, and the uppers have decided that I can give out nonpunitive sick leave."

A cough came unbidden to Harold Bottoms's lips.

"Not you, M," Bride said.

It was from that moment Harold could trace the beginning of his suspicions.

2 That night Harold decided to stay in—or out of the viral cluster—and watch the IT curve. The curve

was the latest innovation of Internet presentation. A thin sheet of plastic nine feet wide, stretched out to its full length, and four and a half feet high. The screen rolled out on a stand so that it curved around, forming an inner space that was two feet deep at the center and six feet across. Using the chip technology in the stand, the laser optics woven into the plastic could create three-dimensional images.

". . . and hello New York," onetime rapper Chantel was saying. "Well, it's finally happened—Claw-Cybertech Angola has annexed Luxembourg, making that business-state the first Afro-European nation. The Luxembourgers, as you will remember, have been opposing this deal for the past seven years. A general strike led to violence in that tiny nation's capital today, where some three hundred thousand turned out to protest the merger. When CEO Moto of Claw-Cybertech ordered out security forces, the crowd threw flaming balls of waste tar. The protesters made no attempt to hide the racial nature of their political unrest."

An image of thousands of angry protestors appeared in the curve. Many were hurling flaming balls of waste tar, a by-product of modern recycling dumps, at the security forces, which advanced in wheeled plexiplas bubbles, debilitating rioters with dozens of stun whips flailing out from all sides.

"Lars McDermott," Chantel said, reappearing on the screen, "corporate ambassador to the UN, had this to say about today's protest and annexation."

The image of the middle-aged black woman shifted to the full image of a young white man in a rather close-fitting black andro-blouse.

"I applaud the annexation," the man said in an indistinct European accent. "And, no, I do not feel that the Luxembourgers have any reason to fear this move. International Law expressly prohibits migrant labor from overwhelming a new territory beyond prescribed limits within the first twenty-five years."

"But hasn't Claw-Cybertech asked for a relaxation of the migratory clause?" a bodiless, masculine voice asked.

"That is only for them to be able to iron out a few labor problems in their Angolan holdings." Lars McDermott's smile belied his answer.

"Isn't the unemployment cycle in Angola now up to thirty-five percent?" the voice inquired.

That smile again, and, "Merely a transitional phase. Claw-C has to retool for a more advanced chip market. That has nothing to do with Europe."

Harold was astonished at how the extra chip he'd bought for the curve cleared up his digital reception. He said, "My fav," and the station changed to a scene where three beautiful black women in military uniform were adjusting weapons holsters on their breasts before jumping out of an aircraft hovering over a moonlit island.

The winking lunar light between the ripples of the sea seemed so real that Harold moved closer to the IT curve, which took up fully half of his Tribeca loft subdivide. Enchanted by the ocean, he stuck his hand in and it disappeared momentarily under the waves. Chesty Love dived into his palm and swam out through his fingers.

"Hey hey hey." Jamey Halloway's blond head replaced the hovercraft. He had a maniacal look on his face. Harold leaped backward, shocked by the ITV buddy break-in call.

"Hey, man, you scared me," Harold said.

"Turn on the two-way," Jamey commanded.

"Two-way on," Harold intoned.

Immediately the curve became Jamey's room in the Bubble, a condominium that floated off the eastern shore of Staten Island. A small patch in the lower left-hand corner continued the *Devil Girls* show.

"How you feelin'?" Harold asked.

"Flu's gone," Jamey replied. "Just like the med-heads said, three days and it clears up. You wanna go out?"

"Naw, man. I might pick up somethin' out there."

"Aw, com' on, bro. You know the nigs don't get it."

"Hey, man. Why you wanna use that kinda language?"

"Sorry, bro. I didn't know you were sensitive."

"I'm not sensitive," Harold said. "It's just that it's not respectful."

"I said I'm sorry, okay? Can we go out now?"

"I don't know."

"I found Yasmine," Jamey said in a tantalizing tone.

"Where?"

"Blanklands."

"No shit?"

"Not even an address. Down in an alley off of Gore near Yclef Terrace. You need a chip to get in and a hundred dollars cover to get out—and that doesn't include Yas."

"I'll meet you there," Harold said. Then he clapped his hands together three times, hard. The screen went blank and the curve rolled itself up into a scroll.

3 Harold rode his adult-size tricycle down Lower Broadway, headed for the Brooklyn Bridge. There had been no motorized traffic allowed on Broadway for over thirty years. A quarter of the streets in Lower and Upper Manhattan were closed to motor-driven vehicles because no cycler could afford the leasing fees and insurance rates on an automobile. Cycler was a term meant for those who rode the unemployment cycles, but it also fit those same individuals' mode of transportation.

Harold rode down the crowded avenue looking at the crumbling old brick that showed here and there between holo-ads. Lower Manhattan was falling apart. Every now and then a building was refaced. But the only real improvements came when big business could find a profit niche. Lately that niche had been leased window holo-ads. All you had to do was put a holo-screen across your outside wall space and allow whatever advertiser to display his wares on it. At a dollar per square foot per day—for prime space, at prime time—you could make pocket money for the kids. And now with the new screens you could look out of your windows as if there were nothing there at all.

All down Broadway there were animated signs for leasing IT curves, household utilities, even furniture and some finer clothes. Almost everything by 2055 was leased. That stabilized the profit factor and created a built-in insurance policy. No one owned anything except the manufacturers.

Harold knew a lot about leasing because L&L Leasing was the company he worked for. L&L acted as a middleman for various industries. They advertised and brokered the deals while the major manufacturers supplied the goods.

"The people live on the installment plan," XX Y, the revolutionary, said on the poster circulated over ghostnet, "while corpse-barons buy up the sky."

The slogan played its way through Harold's mind while he rolled over the Brooklyn Bridge. He knew that every word of what the militant chromosome of RadCons 6 and 7 said was true. But he also remembered what his professor, Len Gorzki, had said in Political Science 101 at City College.

"Product is everywhere and everything," the slender, AIDS-ridden educator exclaimed. "From the bricks in the wall to the chair under your butts to your butt itself. It's all product, either product or waste."

Harold understood the threat posed to him. He believed in XX's ideal but lived according to the cycles.

Blanklands was a moveable feast. A bar, restaurant, Eros-Haus, DJ joint hotbed of perversions and alternative lifestyles.

Yasmine Mü—onetime executive secretary for L&L Leasing—was now an Eros-girl working illegally for the drifting Blanklands boutique.

Harold had never met anyone like her. Her Persian family had become fabulously wealthy by developing one of the first labor corps in the Middle East.

A labor corps was a large group of men and women who did a specific kind of labor, usually manual, either at a home base or on location. From apple picking in

Vermont to disaster relief in Peru, the labor corps provided sweat and sinew for an annual wage.

Yasmine's parents owned a palace in southern Persia. They also owned two hundred thousand hands. Yasmine was their only child. Everything would one day belong to her. But she left it all for the prod's life in New York City.

"My mum and da," she said in her tutored English accent, "don't see that it's slavery. If you got married you were fired and fined. Salaries are paid in advance and so if you quit you're arrested. Then the government confiscates your labor account and you're forced to work out your term without pay. Everybody says that it's good for the people. Da says that some people are made to work and others are made to rule. So I left and came here to live as a worker."

She confided in Harold, called him a friend. But she never returned his ardent passions. Harold had loved her from the first moment he saw the grim longing in her eyes.

Jamey was waiting in the alley when Harold got there.

"Hey, man," Harold said. "I thought you said the place was here."

"It is."

"Then how come we're the only people here?"

"It's early. When I saw Yas she said she could get us in if we came early. You got your chip?"

Harold pulled out a clear plastic card in which his identity chip was embedded. The ID-chip was a cycler's most important piece of property. It was everything. His PBC (personal bar code), his work history, his current résumé, and his DNA voter's registration data. The loss of an ID-chip was an immediate fifty-one points against your labor record—a consecutive nine months of unemployment cycles, almost a year of beans and rice, living in an octangular hive cubicle; three of the eight steps before becoming a Muzak Jack.

The ID-chip meant everything, and so when they demanded to hold Harold's before he could go into Blanklands he balked.

"Com'on, man," the nervous white doorman said. He had brown scars on his throat and arms from a recent bout with the striped flu. "I ain't got time."

"Just let it go," Jamey said from behind. He put his hand on Harold's shoulder, and Harold released his grip on the card.

While walking down the long, brick-lined corridor Harold felt panic in his chest and across his brow. He hadn't let go of his ID-chip in twelve years, since the day of his labor adulthood at fifteen. The eerie glow from the light decals slapped on the wall at irregular intervals only served to make him more apprehensive. He had never spent a day in Common Ground, the underground public homestead that provided compartments barely large enough to hold a fiberplas mattress. But Harold knew from his uncle that it was no free ride like the holo-ads claimed. It was dangerous and it smelled. You couldn't lock your space and you couldn't own anything. The place was full of gangs of Backgrounders who raped and robbed men and women alike.

The way most cyclers survived an unemployment cycle was by finding illegal labor or a relative or friend who knew the drill. He could become a prettyboy or maybe sell a body part—but, no, it wouldn't have to come to that. His brother, Rand, in Oklahoma City would take him in. He'd make Harold work in the communal gardens but that was bearable. He wouldn't have to get involved with the black market, or worse, the weapons market—or worse still, to become a thief. To be caught stealing would mean a thirty-year minimum sentence in one of the corporate prisons. There was no early release, parole, or life after prison. The few ex-cons that Harold had seen were hollow-eyed, slack-jawed men and women. Maybe black people didn't get the striped flu, but they sure got bit by prison—they sure did.

"Prison sucks the soul out of our men and women through a pinhole in the heart," XX Y had proclaimed more than fifteen years before. "And we just look the other way . . ."

Harold's heart was racing. What was he doing thinking about Common Ground and Angel's Island prison? He decided to go back, pay the hundred dollars, and leave.

"Here you go," the nervous doorman said as he opened a door. Jamey pushed Harold through into a room filled with light.

Harold went through the door thinking that he would turn around and go back out again. Yasmine meant a lot to him, but not enough to live in hell.

He looked around to get his bearings. He was standing in a cavernous room full of large raised platforms that held fiberplas beds. There was a ledge around the mattresses and chairs, too. Going by the size of the room Harold figured that it held over forty tablebeds. At a table a few feet away Harold saw something that slowed his exit.

An elderly man, bald and gray, with parchmentlike skin, was sitting on the ledge of a table while a young woman, no more than twenty, stroked his huge penis. The white man had well-defined muscles to complement his twenty-inch boy-hard erection. The slender Asian girl rocked back and forth holding on with both hands. The look of reverence on her face seemed studied but that didn't detract from Harold's fascination. He had heard about the sex therapies that the uppers could afford. The process of cell rejuvenation could make parts of the body young again, at least for a while. Drugs could make you virile. An every-other-day visit to sensory-dep tanks could exercise your body until it had what was advertised as peak physique.

This man had it all.

"Yeah, yeah," the man grunted. Then he looked up at Harold and winked just before he came.

"Yeah, baby," the Asian prettygirl said.

The man's emission went on and on. He looked at Harold and Jamey, winking again, as if to say, "Who's the man?"

"Damn," Jamey said. "You see that?"

Two tables over a woman who was near the man's age sat naked at a table. Her face, thighs, and belly were pudgy and somewhat wrinkled, but her breasts put the prettygirl's to shame. Harold felt nauseated and aroused at the same time. The man was strutting around now with his erection tilting up, still dripping semen.

"Somethin', huh?" Yasmine Mü said. She was standing next to them. "I know an even older guy who's got one-half again as long. He has to hold his up when he walks around 'cause it hurts his muscles.

"Hey, Yas," Jamey said.

He hugged the young brown-skinned woman. She was wearing a clear plastic full-length jacket and a G-string.

Harold had forgotten all about leaving. He was looking at Yasmine, unable to speak.

"Hi, Harold," the Iranian emigré said.

"Hey."

"I wondered if you guys'd come," Yasmine said in her newly acquired American accent.

"We wanted to see you, Yas," Jamey was saying. His attention was distracted by the older man's approach to the elderly, young breasted woman.

"See me like that?" she asked.

"Uh," Harold said. He wanted to say yes before Jamey could, but the word was stuck in his throat.

"As long as you don't see us like him," Jamey said.

Yasmine laughed.

"Harold wants you to be his prettygirl," Jamey said. "He wants to juggle brass pots with you. That's what he said."

Harold had said it, three years earlier when he and Jamey first signed on with L&L Leasing. But he didn't expect Jamey to remember or to speak for him. They had both lusted after Yasmine while she was busy bumping with uppers in storage rooms and doored cubicles. Back then Yas wasn't interested in cyclers sexually.

But now she smiled and took Harold by the hand. They walked across the mostly empty room of tablebeds toward the far exit. This led to another dank hallway lined with brick and bright light decals. They passed several doors and various men and women along the way.

They had to step over three lovers who had fallen to the floor between decals, rutting wild.

Finally they came to a door that sprang open at a word from Yasmine. It was a small room containing only a fiberplas mattress and a hotplate altar with three brass pots on it. Weak candle decals flickered when they entered. There were no decorations on the wall, no carpeting on the floor.

"They move all of this stuff every week?" Harold asked.

"Take off your clothes," Yasmine answered.

Harold's andro-alls were off with a quick gesture. He looked down seeing how small his erection was compared to the man in the main room.

"I guess I won't need the hot pot on you, Harry," Yasmine said.

She was still the most beautiful woman he had ever seen in person. Tall—his height—and dark-skinned in that Middle Eastern way. She had large eyes that slanted upwards, black as liquid space, and a mouth that was meant to eat only sensuous fruits and honey cakes. Harold had dreamt of Yasmine at least once a week for the past three years.

She moved close to him and took the erection gently in her hand.

"Your card will be decremented by the minute, two dollars a minute. Do you understand?"

"Yuh."

"I have to say that, Harold. It's the rules."

"I know."

"How long do you want me?"

"As long as I can get."

"How much money do you have?"

"Three thousand, I think."

"How much to spend?"

"All of it," he whispered.

She began stroking his erection in a loose grip. The rest of Harold's body stiffened.

Yasmine was looking him in the eye.

"Tell me before you come," she said. She seemed to be studying something that was going on in his head.

He felt his legs buckle. Yasmine supported his buttocks with her free hand.

"Don't fall. Put all your mind into your cock. Try to come but tell me before you do."

"I . . . I . . . now . . . now," Harold rasped.

Yasmine reached down to the altar in a deft motion and brought a brass bowl under his nose. Instantly his diaphragm went into spasm and the feeling of orgasm subsided.

"How's your heart?" she asked.

"Okay, I think."

"Because I'm going to do things to you that would kill that old man in the grand hall. Bust his heart open like a rotten peach."

Harold blinked and almost lost consciousness.

"No sleeping, no sitting," she said. She held another bowl under his nose and started the gentle stroking again. "I will bring you up to the edge twenty times or more if I want. And every time you have to tell me and every time I'll pull you back. Okay?"

"What if I said no?"

Yasmine wagged her head slowly from side to side.

She smiled and he wondered if his heart *was* strong enough to last the night.

4 ". . . three men—captured after apparently trying to contaminate a children's immunization center in Rockland, Oregon—have all committed suicide while in custody of the Rockland police." The newsman, Letter Phillips, wore a lavender T-shirt. His hair was brown and thick. He sat forward on his tall stool and spoke seriously, without personal appeal. This switch from his usual wisecracking manner was effected to tell the audience that this was *real* news. "Our correspondent in Oregon, Couchy Malone, has more."

A beautiful waif with surgically enhanced eyes appeared in the curve. Her skirt was short and her thin legs seemed unsteady.

"Thank you, New York," said the freckled child, striped flu marks on her arms. "Police sources have informed this reporter that a map of some sort was found among the possessions of one of the prisoners. This map identifies immunization centers around the Midwest, Oregon, Washington, and Alaska. Each center's location has been circled in red and some of these had been marked with a black check sign." Couchy disappeared and a red circle marked with a black check, floating in space, replaced her.

"Was the Rockland site checked, Couchy?" Letter's voice inquired.

"That's the problem, New York," the child said as she

reappeared. "It was not checked. The police and the FBI fear that the checked centers may have already been contaminated. These centers work all through the school year. Thousands of children are immunized each day." The strain of fear, real fear, came into Couchy Malone's voice.

Harold put down his shrimp and noodle cup to concentrate on the news report.

"This could be the tip of the iceberg, New York," the young ITL freelancer said. "It could be a very real act of monstrous terrorism."

"Can you tell us which immunization sites, centers, have been marked with the black check?" Letter asked quickly, as if he were trying to drown out her fears.

"No. No, New York. My sources wouldn't or couldn't identify the marked centers."

"Thank you very much, Couchy," Letter Phillips said.

Couchy Malone looked as if she wanted to say something else, but her image faded as Letter Phillips returned to the curve. Harold wondered if she wanted to call out some kind of warning to her family or loved ones.

"In another disease-related story, seven cases of Jeffers's Disease have been reported in and around the Denver area. Named after the doctor who identified it, this new syndrome speeds up the body's metabolism, depleting certain essential elements for blood and skin maintenance. We have Dr. Jeffers on satellite hookup to talk to us about this new disturbing disease."

Above the anchorman's head appeared a patch in which was the head of a man with a thin face and large ears. In childhood he was probably cute.

"Are you with us, Dr. Jeffers?"

"Yes, Letter."

"Seven cases of this terrible illness," Letter said. "How many have been fatal?"

"All of them."

"How long did they suffer?"

"Three days, at least. No one lived out the week." Dr. Jeffers looked as if he had been frightened and now he was numb.

"What is the cause of this disease, Doctor?"

There was a pause then. Maybe the audio line had gone down and the doctor was simply waiting to hear. But Harold believed that Jeffers was considering his answer. He was wondering what to say.

"We believe that there is an environmental cause to the illness, Letter. As we speak federal agencies are trying to discover some link between the victims—where they worked, what they ate, where they went swimming. It's something like that."

"So you don't believe that this could have anything to do with the potential act of terrorism in the Northwest."

"I can't see any connection whatsoever," Jeffers said. "The immunization centers are for children only, and none of the victims down here have been immunized in over a year."

"That's a relief," Letter said with a big smile.

Jeffers didn't seem relieved. His image faded.

"On the lighter side . . ." Phillips began.

"Vid off," Harold said.

He sat back in his new Propper Chair, a thin sheet of transparent and flexible Synthsteel held aloft by pulsating magnetic waves emanating from a disc anchored to the floor. *Like floating on air,* the holo-ads claimed. And it was true, but the feeling was only physical. There was nothing light or buoyant about Harold's life. And this was strange, because he was in love. Yasmine Mü was the center of his life. It was true that he only saw her at the Blanklands Eros-Haus; that he had to pay for her attentions. But she never charged him the full rate and once a week she'd allow him to spend the whole night in her cubicle.

Harold's heart and body were Yasmine's to command. But there was a downside to love. The IT curve, the Propper Chair, and all the other little perks of the working life had lost their sheen. He felt small and vulnerable.

Lately Harold had been thinking about his parents, Clarence and Renata Bottoms. By the age of forty they had both faded into White Noise. He hadn't heard from either one in years. He supposed that they were migrants living in what was known as the undertow, the currents of illegal labor under the cycles of unemployment. These migrants moved from city to city, living in Common Ground.

They were gone.

Harold had been recalling the last conversation he'd had with his father. They'd met at a China Tea stand on One forty-first and Lenox. Harold paid for the drinks.

"Thanks, son," the elder Bottoms said. He was five eight but seemed shorter because he stooped a little. "Your mama and I had to give up the apartment. I think she goin' down to Florida. I'ma make it out to St. Louis. Maybe your brother got a hoe in the garden for me."

He never asked to stay with Harold. There were stiff

penalties for stacking up in a rental. Either you made your own rent or you stayed in Common Ground. If you were found sheltering someone unemployed you were evicted, fired, and thrown into a double unemployment cycle.

"I'm gonna miss you, Dad," Harold remembered saying. Not *I love you* or *Can't you stay?* Just acceptance. And even that weak farewell was a lie. He had never missed his parents.

It wasn't until he experienced the sweet-faced, rough loving of Yasmine that he began to miss them. He wondered if they still spoke to each other. Everyone had a communication number. This code took the place of the Social Security number after that program went bust in 2012.

Jamey and Harold spent a lot of time together and at the Blanklands. Jamey's wife had had their marriage license revoked for emotional and material incompatibility. She married the woman she worked for and moved to Seattle to join a state-run pottery studio.

The bachelors frequented the Blanklands, where Harold spent all of his extra money on Yasmine. Yasmine for her part was pleased by the young man's interest and spent more time with him than he paid for. So it was no surprise that she called him when she found out that she was dying.

"It came on me on Sunday night." She only transmitted her voice, and so Harold found himself looking upon a speeded-up rendition of the birthing of far-off galaxies in the void of space.

"But that was only three days ago."

"Meds say it's some kinda fast-working cancer."

"But they cured cancer, Yas," Harold said.

"Not this kind. They said that it works on a chromosomal level. Something like that. I had to quit the road show. Sex-no-more." She giggled to lighten the mood.

"Can I see you?"

"I'm not really pretty anymore," the disembodied Yas whispered. "And I can't do anything."

"I don't need you to do nuthin'."

"You don't?"

"No. Uh-uh. I don't go there for you to do stuff. I go there to see you. Shit. I'd be happy payin' for dinner or sumthin' like that."

For a long span Yasmine was silent in the depths of unfolding space. Harold forced himself to concentrate on two giant galaxies colliding in the far-off reaches.

"They're gonna take me home. My parents are gonna come on Friday to take me back to Tehran. You could come tomorrow after work if you wanted."

"All right. At six?"

"Okay."

"Just one thing."

"What?"

"Where do you live?"

"You wanna come wit' me?" Harold asked Jamey at work the next morning.

"Naw, man. Hey, I don't wanna remember Yas like that," Jamey said.

"That's cold, J."

The sandy-headed cycler didn't reply. He was studying ghostnet on his wall monitor, reading an article and looking over his shoulder now and then.

Periodically a member of the Shaker Party embedded a ghostnet chip in the L&L system. Before the chip was destroyed anybody could enter the word *ghostnet* and get the weekly download, which included a banned issue of the *Daily Dump*. This chip had been working for over four days.

"They said it's five marks if they catch you ghostin', J," Harold said.

"Shit," Jamey said, not to his friend.

"What?"

"Somethin's happenin' in MacroCode Russia, man."

"I didn't see anything on the mornin' report."

"Ghost says that they're killin' Techs. They destroyed five labs and killed all the scientists. A general has formed an army. Shit. An army. An' they been killin' big time."

"How could that be?" Harold asked. "How could they raise an army and it's not on the news?"

"They lie on the vid all the time, nig, you know that."

"But not about somethin' like that, man," Harold said, ignoring the lack of respect. "They're not gonna lie about an army and a revolt against the biggest company in the world."

"They say at least four hundred and sixty-five thousand people killed. That they dropped clean nukes on Jesus City."

"That's crazy," Harold said.

"Okay, then." Jamey hit a button and the ghostnet

blipped off. Then he said, "M-R-L-L-Tak," and a blank green screen appeared.

"Moscow's L&L branch is temporarily off-line," a friendly voice said. This was Leda, the computer voice that Jamey preferred.

Jamey turned to look at Harold.

"Don't mean a thing," Harold protested. "Russia's off-line more than half the time and you know it."

"I don't know a thing, man," Jamey said flatly. "And neither do you."

"Fuck you," Harold said.

Even though Harold knew that Yasmine's parents were wealthy, he didn't expect a Park Avenue penthouse high above the streets of Upper Level Manhattan. The elevator opened up inside of her apartment.

"Go down the hall to your left and knock on the last door you get to," said the black elevator operator in a red uniform.

Yasmine had lost most of her body fat in the four days that she'd been sick. She resembled a humanlike rubber toy that had been deflated.

"It hurts, Harry," she said. "It hurts all the time. They gave me opium and nerve killers but it still hurts."

The fading young woman had lesions down her face that looked like the clawing mark of some predatory beast. They were red, almost iridescent.

"It's okay, honey," Harold said as he cradled her in his arms.

"Hold me."

Harold tried not to squeeze the New Age courtesan

too hard, fearing that her bones might snap. She clung to him with greater strength than he would have imagined. She smiled.

"Somethin' funny?" Harold asked.

"I feel safe with you, Harry. You make me feel better. That's kinda funny, don't you think?"

"How come funny?"

One of the lesions on Yasmine's face pulled open and blood trickled down. Harold pressed closer to her so that the pillow covered the bleeding.

"How come funny?" he asked again.

"Because here I am all alone and dyin' in this big place and my boyfriend is a john." She stopped talking in order to swallow twice. "It's really nice."

Harold held her for a long time after she was dead. He wasn't ready to go on for over an hour.

"How come they don't send a nurse up to watch her?" Harold asked the same elevator operator going down.

"Nurses, firemen, security force, everybody in city service been called up."

"Called up for what?"

"Some kinda big emergency in the outer fiefs where the white people live. Jersey and Long Island. You know white people throw a fit in a minute."

5 "Wake up, Harold! Wake up!" It was either his brother or his father, but Harold kept his eyes shut

because this was a Sunday or it was a summer day. All Harold knew was that it wasn't time to sign on to school yet. And he was sure that it wasn't one of the days he was supposed to go in for sports or socialization class.

"Get your ass up outta the bed, nig!"

Harold sat up and said, "I told you that I don't want you calling me that. Now if you don't mind, I was about to sign on to class."

"You awake, Hair?" Jamey was standing in the IT curve's interior. The plastic screen had unfurled automatically when the call came in.

"No," Harold said. "But I'm waking up right now and I'll be with you in a minute."

"Hurry up, man," Jamey said. "The world is almost over and we ain't got time for you to sleep."

"Huh?"

"That general has dissolved MacroCode Russia and they're gonna drop on New York."

The lower half of the screen became an image of carnage in St. Petersburg. Armed soldiers could be seen running down civilians and shooting them with rifles and ember guns.

"This came over the ghostnet. I got the cube from a gypsy hacker in Soho." The panic in Jamey's voice brought Harold to full awareness. "The feds gonna shut New York down at six A.M."

"Who says?"

"Com'on, Harold. We gotta get off the Island tonight."

The scene on the lower half of the curve turned to massacre. People were being cut down while trying to storm a fortress.

A face appeared above the carnage. It was an older man wearing a fancy military hat. He was speaking in Russian but the simultaneous ITV translator muted his voice and spoke over it.

". . . the Americans have created this plague. They have killed our people with their bio-warfare . . ." The massacre transformed into bodies being stacked onto a pyre smoldering slowly into ash.

". . . we shall be avenged."

"Okay," Harold agreed. "I'll meet you at the Port Authority. We can take a bus."

"Why not the mono?"

"Mono stops in Jersey but the bus goes on forever."

They met at the West Side entrance of the Port Authority Transporation Center at 00:36. Harold had his tricycle, which broke down into a case half the size of one wheel, and a bag that held an extra andro-suit and his Flapjack, the personalized computer-book that had everything a cycler needed.

Jamey jumped out of a yellow cab and needed help pulling a trunk from the back.

"Why you got that big thing, man?" Harold asked.

"This is it, Hair. This is the end. We gotta get gone. This is everything I own."

The bus station was in tumult. Thousands of people stood in line in front of ticket machines. People were screaming to be heard above the din of panic. Young men and women shepherded crying children. The loudspeaker was droning on and on asking for calm and order.

"Guess we ain't the only ones been to the gypsy," Harold yelled into his friend's ear.

"They're closing down the Authority at six A.M., that's why.

"And I bet the magistrates are all already gone."

"Believe that," Jamey said. "We better get on line."

"No, uh-uh," Harold said, putting out an arresting hand. "I got first-class seats reserved on my chip after you called. We got passage to Burlington, Vermont."

"First class? How much that cost?"

"Five thousand dollars."

"Where'd you get that? I thought you spent all your credit on Yas."

"I took a FedCred card from her wallet before I left her place."

Jamey looked at Harold in amazement.

"She was dead, man. She didn't need it and her family's rich. You know the parmeds woulda taken that shit in a minute."

Three hastily erected clear plexiplas People Stoppers had been placed along the hall leading to the gates. At each stop Harold and Jamey had to present their ID-chips to get through. At the last stop Harold had to have an eye-scan to check his PBC against the reservation.

They had to wait three hours before boarding the bus.

"They say the plague is a full-blown epidemic in Russia," a man in an old-fashioned two-piece business suit was saying to a woman in front of him. "It starts out with pains and then it causes those stripes that that flu last fall had. Then bleeding, internal and external, then death. Three or four days and you're dead."

"Please stop it!" the woman cried. "Please stop talking to me."

The man then turned to Harold and hunched his shoulders as if to ask, Is she crazy?

The first-class upper deck of the ElectroHound had been fitted with fourteen extra seats. Jamey's trunk was taken from him and thrown into the storage hatch on the roof. Below, in the main cabin, passengers were packed in, standing room only. All of the lower seats had been removed.

"World's comin' to an end," Jamey said to his friend. "And ElectroDog wants to get the last dollar."

Harold would have nodded his agreement but he was too busy taking in his environment to waste even a motion.

The bus lurched its way down the road to the bridge. The traffic of busses and official cars was moving at under ten kays.

"Probably government workers stealing the carpool vehicles," Jamey said, referring to the inordinate number of city cars on the road.

Harold thought that he was right.

The road carried an exodus but the city was more or less unaware. The DanceDome, an elevated dance field at the Sixtieth Street pier, was in full swing. Ten thousand or more were dancing to the wild music transmitted to tiny ear implants that kept noise pollution down. Big animated signs advertised L&L products, new movies, life-extending operations. In small windows along the highway he saw lighted rooms with people in them. Some were homeworkers and others simply living: watching ITV, listening to their implants, talking on the vid.

"Oh shit!" Jamey spat. He doubled over in the seat next to Harold.

"What's wrong, Jamey?"

"Pain."

"Sit up, man. Sit up." Harold put a hand against his friend's chest and jerked him up.

"Something wrong up there?" a man from behind asked.

"Just dropped his chip," Harold said, glancing back. He saw the worried elderly man who sat behind them.

"Is he sick?" the old man asked.

"No. Dropped his chip. We got it. It's okay."

The man looked unconvinced but he still leaned back.

"You can't let 'em know you're hurting, Jamey. If you do they might kick us off."

Jamey nodded, gritting his teeth against the pain.

The bus rolled out of the northern borders of New York onto the Canadian Highway. Harold watched closely over his friend, who tried his best to stay still under the waves of deep pain that wracked him at irregular intervals.

"The Russians are right," someone behind said. "It's probably one of those bio-tech companies made the plague. Break the corporations and burn the dead. If we want to survive that's what we have to do too."

"Yeah," a woman agreed.

"It's terrible," someone else exclaimed.

Outside the window there was nothing but the dark outline of trees and pools of gray grasses under a quarter moon. Harold wondered how much Jamey weighed.

"Oh shit!" Jamey screamed.

He had been able to sleep for a couple of hours while the bus cruised down the unusually crowded highway, but now the pain brought him up to his feet.

"He's got it!" the elderly man said to the young woman sitting next to him. "I told you, Gina. He's got it."

"Oh shit it hurts!" Jamey yelled. "Help me."

"He ain't got nuthin'," Harold hissed at the couple. "He hurt himself in soccer is all. It's a muscle."

"You said he dropped his chip before."

"Mind your own business before you get dropped," Harold warned.

In his peripheral vision he saw a shadow slip down the stairs.

"Does he?" a woman asked. "Does he have it?"

"Have what? He don't have nuthin'. There isn't any plague," Harold said.

Three men had gotten to their feet.

Harold wished that he had elected judo on Sports-Wednesday at high school instead of volleyball.

"Fuck fuck fuck fuck fuck," Jamey chanted. He fell

back down into his seat and then collapsed onto the floor.

"You better get him the fuck off'a this bus, man," one of the standing men said. His tone was threatening but he didn't advance.

Harold realized that Jamey had the invisible force field of communicability around him.

Everyone standing had to grab something to stay on their feet because the bus swerved and came to an abrupt halt. Harold stole a glance at Jamey, who was sprawled in the aisle, and then at the stairwell leading down.

The bus driver, a big-boned woman with red hair and deeply tanned skin, ascended to the cabin in three steps.

"What's goin' on up here?" she asked.

Harold simply stared.

"That guy has the plague," someone said.

The bus driver took a step backward.

"He does?" she asked Harold.

"He's sick," Harold said. "But there hasn't been any plague announced by the health board."

"Half of Russia's dead and he says there's no plague," one of the standing men said.

"They say the niggers don't get it no way," another man, of questionable race, said.

"All right, enough of that now," the driver said. "It's a punishable offense to slander race."

"And look at what good it gets us," the elderly man spat.

The driver seemed to consider the senseless sentence.

"I'm going to have to put him off the bus."

"Who?" Harold asked.

"Your friend."

"What for?"

"I got a hundred and fifty passengers on this bus, son. I've never carried even half that. They pulled out the lower seats, they broke the rules by making passengers stand while the bus is in motion. Something's happening. I don't know what it is but I can't jeopardize this whole bus just 'cause the uppers aren't talking."

"I need my trunk," Jamey whined. "I need my trunk."

Getting off of the bus was fairly easy. The driver made Harold pull the trunk out of the top hatch. She told the passengers she was taking the precaution against further infection.

No one tried to bar the friends' way. Scared faces of all races witnessed their departure. Harold saw that some of them had scars on their necks and faces, reminders of the striped flu.

"We got to take my trunk, Hair. Everything I got's in there."

"We'll leave it in the trees, J," Harold promised. "We'll leave it in the trees and come back when you're better."

"Where we gonna go?"

"Looks like everybody from Plintheville's leavin'. Look at all them cars and busses comin' on the highway. They're evacuating. They're leaving their houses."

"So?"

"We could hole up in an abandoned house until you get over that cramp."

The walk through the woods was the hardest work that Harold had ever done. When he didn't have to drag Jamey he supported his friend's weight. It took them three hours to make it through the woods and hills to a tiny cul-de-sac of homes in what they assumed was Plintheville.

Harold left Jamey in the woods and watched one home for over an hour. The whole block seemed deserted, but Harold wanted to make sure. If the world wasn't over he didn't want to wish that it was from some corporate prison cell.

Just before dawn a bright blast lit up the southern sky. When Harold saw the iridescent mushroom cloud he was no longer worried about jail.

Jamey never moved from the couch in the sunken living room where Harold deposited him. He lay there and wasted away like billions of others were doing all across the globe.

For the first day Harold held his friend's hand while watching ITV. Newscasters talked openly about the plague that ghostnet had been broadcasting for days. The pain and bloody stripes were associated with the striped flu. Doctors were saying that it was the secondary phase of the virus. They had known that the virus stayed in the nervous system but had no idea that it would return with such ferocity.

The nuclear strikes against New York, Washington, D.C., and Los Angeles were minor news topics compared to the plague.

The disease was 100 percent fatal and everybody got it; everybody but people with at least 12.5 percent African Negro DNA.

For thirty-six hours Harold and Jamey watched the reports. Thousands of bodies were being thrown into rivers and the sea. Roving mobs of black and white ruffians were battling in the streets of the major American cities. Astonished Caucasians who survived the plague realized that there was a sizeable portion of Negro blood in their veins.

One newscaster ran a clip from Chicago's *Electro-Exposé* which showed the towering figure of Cowled Death rising over a white man only to be stymied when the white man pulled open his shirt to reveal the words THE NIG IN ME: 12.5%.

After two days all vid communication went blank.

Harold and Jamey spent the empty hours talking about their lives. Jamey told about his delinquent father and his mother's sister who raised him. Harold thanked Jamey for letting him have Yasmine.

"She woulda gone for you in a minute," Harold told his pain-wracked friend.

"Anything for a friend'a mine," Jamey replied.

"Hey, Hair?"

"What?"

"You think it was God mad at the white man for all the shit we done?"

"No, uh-uh. 'Cause why he wanna kill all the Chinese and Aborigines and Indians down in Peru?"

"I guess. What—"

Jamey died just that quickly. In between spasms, in the middle of a thought. Harold sat there next to his friend trying to figure our how he got there.

Harold covered Jamey with a blanket and left him on the couch. He knew he'd have to bury his friend after a while but he didn't want to lose him yet. He wandered around the sprawling suburban home hoping that it was a clean bomb that the Russians dropped on New York.

The family had been a mother and a father with two sets of twins, boys and girls, and an older sister, all of them blond and fair.

On the second day after Jamey died the wall vid came to life.

"All hail the great XX Y," a voice said, and then the skyblues artist Silver Rap and his girl partner Cellophane Dream came into view. Silver was wrapped in tight-fitting shiny cloth that resembled old-time aluminum wrap. Cellophane Dream wore a clear material like Yasmine had worn at the Blanklands. Dream had bigger curves than Yas, however. She was a hefty woman with strong bodily features. It was she who addressed the vid.

"The day has come and the day has gone," she intoned. "Good-bye white brothers and hello to our African home."

The camera switched focus and XX Y stood on a column that was at least ten feet high. He was a dark-skinned black man with blue-gray hair combed straight back. His features were broad and heavy. His eyes were bright and a little insane.

"The day of the white man is over. By his own hand he created a doomsday device designed to kill you and me. I say you and me because that's all that's left, you and me and the few who received the antidote. We have recovered the files of the so-called National Security Department and have learned that the International Socialist Party, that foul and racist crew, had paid geneticists in MacroCode Russia to develop a gene virus that would target the black race. But the mighty gene fooled 'em." XX grinned with a perfect set of white teeth. "Yes, she fooled 'em. She said, 'I will not prey upon myself. I will not obey your insane plan.'

"They broke into immunization centers around the world when they realized that the striped virus was infecting their own. Some white children will survive because of this. Other so-called whites bear the sign saying THE NIG IN ME.

"Some of you say we should finish the job that they started. That we should kill every last blue-eyed devil. But I am not so inclined. I am not the evil slayer. I do not set myself up as God. Most of the world needs burying. And some running dogs need to pay for their crimes."

The speech went on for hours. Harold sat with the stink of his friend's rotting corpse, not because he was enthralled, but because he was lonely. Lonely for lost Jamey and Yasmine. Lonely for the world that he moved in. He wondered if those dancers on the Sixtieth Street pier saw the flash of the bomb for an instant before they died.

6 Harold spent days in the abandoned house at the end of the cul-de-sac. There were lights and power because that neighborhood ran off an array of solar panels placed upon a nearby hill.

XX Y was the only show in the world. He ranted as much as six hours a day. He entered into long harangues against the old society. He pleaded to the so-called whites who had survived because of the quantity of African blood in their veins.

"Accept your blood, brothers," he crooned. "Blood brothers, that's us . . ."

Bleep, bleep.

". . . soon the arks of Africa will arrive on our shores. The colonized and enslaved motherland will come to reclaim us. Do not fight them. Do not deny your heritage. Embrace the new world order."

Bleep, bleep.

Harold became aware of the tiny electronic alarm. It had been sounding for hours. It was his ID-chip. The small display on the chip was mostly garbage. The date was a line of happy faces. The time was a row of eights. But there was a valid return number, eighteen digits long.

Harold at first thought that it might be a trick of XX Y to find and draft all living black people into his World Africa Army. But when he decided to take a car and see the world for himself, Harold entered the number into the Gales' kitchen vid. When he was greeted by the aged image of his father he was stunned and saddened.

"Pop," he whispered.

"Hey, baby boy." It was his nickname before his ninth

birthday. "I thought you got it in New York," Clarence Bottoms said. "I been pagin' you for a week."

Harold had nothing to add. He hadn't even thought of calling his father.

"How is it up there where you are, son?"

"It's only me around here."

"That's good. We been fightin' a war down here."

"Where are you?"

"Florida. They got four groups down here. Two Spanish-black armies, a white—or so-called—group, and then there's the American blacks. Fightin' over groceries, guns, and women. Fightin' over control of the utilities and right-of-way in the streets."

"Fighting?" Harold said. "Blacks fighting each other?"

"Not everybody's fightin'. Not even most of us. But it only takes a few fools with guns to mess it up for everybody.

"I found your mother. I came down here lookin' for her and damn if I didn't find her. We gonna sneak outta Dade County in a few days and make it up to St. Louis."

Harold was still wondering why he hadn't called anyone.

"My friends all died, Pop," Harold said. "Yasmine and Jamey."

"White kids?"

"I guess."

"Don't worry, Harold. Come meet us at Rand's farm in St. Louis. We can start over."

Harold found the keys to the Solaro in the Gales' garage. He filled five bags with canned and freeze-dried food. He had twelve five-gallon containers of water. He carried it all out to the car and loaded up. Then he sat behind the wheel in the cool darkness of the garage, looking at a wall covered with hanging hand tools.

He turned the key and grabbed the steering wheel, but had no idea of how to drive the car. He cried hysterically for six or seven seconds and then stopped. Climbing out of the car he walked out of the garage and headed for the Gales' front door.

"Hey, nig!" a man's voice shouted.

Harold turned to see three swarthy-looking white men. They were dressed in fancy suits decorated at the knees and elbows with brightly colored scarves.

One man raised a pistol.

Harold ducked and ran. All around him branches, windows, and even the walls of the Gales' home exploded from the charged shells that the so-called white men loosed.

Harold went through the house and out the back window, into the woods and was gone. There was a rhythm to his footfalls and his body through the trees. When Harold realized that he had escaped death, he began to laugh.

The world had started over.

WALTER MOSLEY is the *New York Times* bestselling author of *Blue Light* and the Easy Rawlins novels, including *A Little Yellow Dog* and *Devil in a Blue Dress*. His books have been translated into twenty languages and his short-story collection, *Always Outnumbered, Always Outgunned*, received the Anisfeld-Wolf Book Award. Born in Los Angeles, he has been a potter, a computer programmer, and a poet. Walter Mosley lives in New York.